I Got You

STACY WILLIAMS

ISBN: 979-8-9890449-0-0 (ebook)
979-8-9890449-1-7 (paperback)

For the unloved.

It's not true.
Say it. Say it again…out loud.

Now it's time to hunt. Hunt for it. Don't ever stop. Search in every nook and cranny. It may not be easy. It might be really hard. But when you eventually find it, whether it's right in front of you or it takes you years to find, hold on tight and don't ever let go.

Love…it's what we're made for. That includes you.

Chapter 1

MAGGIE

"Biscuits!"

The back of my hand hits the corner of my nightstand. Shooting pain ricochets up my arm to my shoulder. I clench my jaw, holding my breath as my fourth alarm blares some kind of country-rap crap from one of the local stations. I bring my hand to my chest, fisting and flexing, keeping the curse between my lips. I need five more minutes, but I'm out of alarms. Reality is, five more minutes isn't going to help a damn thing. I need a year to hibernate and recover, but there's no time for that.

I flip over on my back, stretch my arms overhead, and point and flex my toes. Moaning, I swing my feet off the side, forcing myself upright. My body slumps with the temptation to tip right back over. I need a good shove to piss me off and get me moving.

Knowing I can't give in to temptation, I haul myself to the shower in total darkness, bypassing the giant pile of dirty clothes in the middle of the floor. My room is a mess, but consistency is key.

I shower and tug on a pair of black leggings and a plain white t-shirt before dragging my butt to the kitchen, where my favorite appliance is percolating fuel.

I pull four bowls and boxes of cereal from the cabinet, hearing the toilet flush upstairs, followed by the sound of the sink, and I know the boys are up. *One less battle I'll have to fight this morning.*

As I pack lunches, Hank slugs into the kitchen, grabbing a bowl and the box of peanut butter Captain Crunch. He takes a seat at the table in his usual silent manner. The two of us loathe morning chit-chat, but unfortunately, life invades.

"Do you need to be picked up after practice?" I break the morning peace.

He grunts what sounds like a "No."

"So you'll be home right after?" I clarify, given his current need to test boundaries.

Over my shoulder, his eyes meet mine with a look of complete boredom and a twist of the suckage that is teenage life.

"Yes."

Garrett and Teddy enter the kitchen, grabbing bowls and their preferred cereal boxes.

If cereal preferences could predict personalities, these boys could be the subject of a psychological study. Garrett is Raisin Bran, and Teddy, Trix.

As the kitchen fills with the sounds of clinking spoons and slurps, I take my first amazing sip of steaming hot coffee. *Shit!* I push my tongue to the top of my mouth, wondering if it's possible it's gone.

Letting the black liquid cool and my tongue resuscitate itself, I move on from packing lunches to throwing dinner into a little magic machine. Dinner may have the same mushy consistency every night of the week, but it's healthy and homemade.

"What are you making for dinner?" Garrett's mouth is crammed full, and I wonder if he could wedge one more raisin in there.

"BBQ chicken and potatoes."

The boys groan, and I turn to stab them with a glare. "The minute you guys want to plan meals and get your butts down here early enough to whip dinner together, be my guest. I'd love a chance to grumble about what you make."

I can feel their eyes roll like they've pulled them out and smacked me in the back, but I choose to ignore it.

Rinsing my hands in the sink, Liv appears in the doorway, rubbing her sleepy eyes with her bunny clutched to her chest.

"Well, good morning, Beauty." I lean over to scoop her up, realizing soon she'll be too big for this, so I snuggle her a little closer. "You're up awfully early."

"Teddy threw that snake at me again. I don't like that thing."

Liv rests her head on my shoulder as I give Teddy, who's wiggling in his seat as he eats, the eye. The little wild child is oblivious, as usual. I remind myself that the jokester keeps things light when everything else feels heavy.

"Are you ready for some breakfast?"

Liv nods, rubbing her eyes, and I set her down next to Garrett to warm up her oatmeal.

"Boys, finish up and brush your teeth before the bus pulls up. And don't make me smell your breath. Nobody's got time for extra dentist visits, Teddy."

They bring their bowls to the sink and charge back up the stairs. While Liv eats, I grab a banana with peanut butter and pull a smoothie out of the freezer. A horn blares from the driveway, and Hank is the first out the door.

"Make good choices today", I holler as the door closes, and Garrett and Teddy return for their lunches and backpacks. "Gwen will be here when you get home, but I should be earlier today. Please try to get your homework done. We don't need any more late nights." I shoot Teddy another look he ignores.

I squeeze them both before they head out to wait for the bus. "You two look out for each other today and be kind." Garrett hugs me while Teddy struggles to get away.

Just before I hear the click of the door closing, a Nerf dart hit me in the butt cheek. That little sneaky rotten turd could win a sharpshooter competition. It's on when he gets home, and he'll have no idea what hit him.

Liv climbs down from her chair, bringing me her bowl.

"Let's get you dressed. Gwen should be here any minute."

Gwen has worked for our family for years and is the thick rubber band that holds us together. My dad hired her after Hank was born, and she's been a part of our family ever since. Thank goodness she's stuck with us because I don't know what I'd do without her.

As I brush Liv's hair, Cole's ringtone comes from my phone tucked into the waist of my leggings.

"I'm impressed you're up this early. What do you want from me?"

He laughs. "What crawled into your coffee this morning? You're awfully chipper."

I roll my eyes, biting the tip of my tongue to see if I've regained feeling. "Haha. You know I don't have a choice but to be Little Miss Sunshine these days. Believe me, Hank and I could survive on grunts until noon in another life." His laugh makes me smile. "Seriously, why are you calling me?"

I love my oldest brother, the full-blooded one who's only a couple of years younger, but I know with one hundred percent certainty there's no way he's calling me this early to chat. I wait.

"I need you to check out some of the guys at practice today. They aren't cutting it and need to be in your class ASAP."

Cole is the starting quarterback for Colorado State, and he's good. Really good.

He lives, eats, and breathes the game. He always has. I can't remember a time when he wasn't throwing a football.

He's slated to be high in the draft picks after graduation this year, but he takes on a responsibility to live up to the expectations set by others. Those expectations stem from the fact that he's Tim 'The Rocket' Matthews's son. It's a legacy he wears on his shoulders, and he wears it well, but sometimes, I wonder if the load ever gets too heavy. He accepts only excellence from himself, but also from his teammates. When he sees someone lacking, he'll do what's necessary to get them leveled up.

Do I play football? No. Do I know a bit about the game? Yes. I grew up watching my dad play, but I didn't just watch.

I spent hours sitting in his lap, dissecting games and strategies. I listened to him and his teammates discuss the ins and outs, x's and o's, plays, and bad calls. I absorbed the intricate details of the game. My dad's game.

My childhood was spent standing on the sidelines and sitting in the stands, watching, listening, and taking it all in. What I bring to the table is getting guys to hop off the line and maneuver the field like their bodies are one of those slimy, stretchy lizards.

Last year, Cole convinced a few of the guys who were stiff, tight, and unable to react to take my barre class. Shortly after, Coach Cavanaugh filled my studio with giant, egotistical football players. These big dudes didn't know what hit them but were moving more fluidly, with fewer injuries. Their price, having to don ballet shoes and face the pain of realizing just how inflexible and weak they really were.

"Does Coach know you are asking for my help?" CC would be just as likely to seek me out, but I'm careful not to step on the man's toes.

"I told him I was going to have you take a look. I didn't say anything to the new defensive coach or Coach Almas, but what can they say if CC's on board? These guys can't touch their toes or move their hips, let alone run and twist to catch a ball. You know two games in, they'll be out with sprains and pulled muscles. The whole team needs to go into the season without pain."

"Jumping into my class won't help that. They should've been taking Yoga or Pilates all summer."

There's a long sigh, and I know he's running his long, skinny fingers over his face.

"Yeah, but I also know getting them in there now will only help them heal faster when they get hurt. It's better than nothing. Please. Once you see them, you'll immediately know where to start."

"Cole, maybe you should stick them with one of the sports therapists?" It's not that I don't believe in my ability to help. I do, but these guys need fast results, which is one more thing I don't have time for.

I twist the hair tie around the end of Liv's braid a few times and let out a huff when he doesn't say anything.

"But I know what you can do. I trust you."

The little shit knows just how to bait me. "So what do I get out of this?"

"How about I take the kids to a movie after church on Sunday? You can have the whole afternoon to yourself before the season starts."

And there's the hook. I'm no dummy. A few minutes of my time scoring an afternoon to myself is a no-brainer.

"Deal. I'll be there this afternoon, unless I get caught up with a student after class. I can't stay long. I told the boys I'd be home early today."

"Ok. Perfect. Thanks, Mags."

"Oh, don't worry. I'm going to enjoy every minute of my time on Sunday. It really is my pleasure."

He laughs. "I've got to get to class. See you later."

Liv and I go back downstairs to find Gwen cleaning up the kitchen. "Good morning," I sing.

"Good morning. I would've fixed something for dinner so you didn't have to take time to get it going." Gwen hugs me, and it never ceases to feel warm and grandmotherly.

"I know, but you already do so much. I can at least throw a mess into the crockpot and turn the knob."

"Gwenni, can we play princesses today? We have to wash Ariel. Teddy stuck her in the mud last night and got her all dirty."

"I was hoping we could play princesses. I also thought we'd wash the sheets. If you help me gather them, we'll make a sheet mountain Elsa can climb."

"Yay!" Liv claps her hands.

"Ok. Lovely ladies, I'll leave you to your princesses and mountain climbing. I have dancers to make." I grab my coffee and thawing smoothie as Gwen side-hugs me on my way out the door.

On my drive to campus, I sort through my mental to-do list: Schedule Garrett's allergist check-up and Liv's eye doctor appointment. Sign Teddy up for soccer. Order groceries. Email the other dance instructors about working with the dance team.

The list goes on and on, and hopefully, I can fit in a few phone calls during lunch.

I pull into my designated spot outside the gym and swing my bag over my shoulder. The sun is high, and the mountain air is clear and refreshing. It never gets old after spending so many years in the city.

I greet the students at the front desk on my way to the dance studio. I unlock the door and flip the switch. Natural light floods the space from the floor-to-ceiling windows at the far end. The large mirrors and windows make this the best office in the entire world.

I turn on the sound system and pull up my playlist, realizing I have ten minutes to spare before my first class. I settle on the floor to put on my ballet shoes and give myself five minutes to scroll my phone. It's my reward for making it through another morning.

Two girls enter, dropping their bags and digging for their shoes.

"Morning, ladies."

These girls are on the dance team and will be fun to work with this semester. I love to see how they incorporate what they've learned into their routines. What happens on the field is nothing close to ballet, but the fluidity of their movement changes as the semester progresses. It's like my small contribution to the world of dance.

It's not the big stage and bright lights I'd imagined, but I love it all the same. I take a sip of my now-cold coffee as more students filter in, ready to get moving to the sounds of the classical music that feeds my soul.

Chapter 2

SHANE

The weight bar clangs against the rack. I sit up and wipe the sweat off my face with the bottom of my shirt. Working out over the past few weeks has been harder than it should be. It's been a month, and I think I'm finally getting used to the thinner air.

Music blares in my ears, and I grab my phone to check my messages. None. I switch to the email account assigned to me as the new Colorado State defensive coordinator. The Colorado Moose. It seems like it should be Mooses, but it's Moose. What the hell kind of mascot is a freaking Moose?

I haven't had a chance to go hiking and probably won't until the season is over, if my knee can handle it, but I've heard that crossing a moose on the trail can be unforgiving. So maybe not such a sissy mascot after all.

I turn off the music, punch the button to close the garage door, and head into my rental for the next few months until I decide if this might be a place I want to stay. For now, it's temporary.

I've spent the past nine months trying to figure out what I'm supposed to do now that my professional career is over. I've tried to pretend that somehow my injury will heal and I can go back to doing the only thing I love, but here I am, and it's still over.

I'd spent my days in physical therapy and my nights with a bottle. I was pissing away years of hard work, or that's what my agent said I was doing. I felt like I was doing just fine, trying to come to grips with the fact that I'll never set foot on the field in pads and a helmet again. The game that's kept me moving and breathing and out of trouble since I was fifteen.

Now, when I still had years left to play and a Super Bowl ring to earn, I'm helping a bunch of kids play the greatest sport on earth. The shitty thing is, I want to be the one running onto the field and making the tackles.

I set my phone on the counter and looked in the refrigerator. It's empty except for sports drinks, some beer, milk, and eggs. I pull out the carton of eggs and start scrambling a few in the one pan I own. Until I know if this is a place I want to be and coaching is how I want to spend my time, my belongings will remain in storage, and I'll live off the bare essentials.

My phone rings, and I already know it's my agent. He's the one who pushed me into accepting this position when I would've been content to continue living like a hermit and drinking my days away. Well, that's not entirely true, but I'll never tell him that.

Rob dragged my sorry ass to the airport, put me on a flight for the interview, and accepted the position on my behalf. Every part of me knows that if I want to stay in the sport, this is an opportunity I can't pass up, and I need to give it my all.

Colorado State's team was on fire last year. They've got golden boy Cole Matthews. Tim 'The Rocket' Matthews's son and a solid offensive line that works like a well-oiled machine. From the tape I've seen, the defense needs work, but has a lot going for it this season.

I'd have been crazy to turn it down unless I wanted to go into commentating, and that was a hell no. I hate dealing with reporters and interviews. Being on camera was my least favorite part of playing in the NFL, much to my agent's dismay. If there was a way to avoid it, I did. So I owe Rob, my relentlessly stubborn and most annoying agent, for all but kicking my ass to Colorado.

"Hey, Rob." My voice sounds like it hasn't been used in days. It hasn't, except for cursing.

"Has the wolf left the cave recently?"

Rob thinks he's funny. I don't remind him he's not.

"So, are you ready for another week, coach? I bet those kids didn't know what hit them last week. The great Shane Carter, gracing their field."

"Rob, I made my expectations clear, and they got to work. We didn't sit around having story time and snacks."

He ignores my clipped response. "How's working with Cavanaugh?"

Rob is referring to the head coach, who's known for molding teams and carrying them to the top. The man speaks at only one volume, loud, but looks out for his players as if they were his own. I've already seen this, as he works with these kids and in his invitations for me to join him and his wife for dinner.

"He's fine, although I'll need a hearing aid by the end of the season."

There's a sigh of annoyance, and I have no doubt Rob's rocking back in his chair.

"That's seriously all you're going to give me? No, 'thank you' for saving your butt from becoming permanently ingrained in the couch or getting you a job where you can still flex your endless array of knowledge, skill, and talent?"

"No."

"How about tickets? I'll fly out and take you to dinner to ensure you're at least conversing with someone outside of work hours once this quarter."

"I'll see what I can do about tickets. Not sure about dinner. I may have plans."

He laughs, and even though he can't see it, I might've smiled—a little.

"All right, I'll look forward to it." He's unusually quiet for a minute. "You're doing the right thing. It may not feel like it now, but you can make a difference in these kids' lives. You still have so much to offer the game."

I don't respond, and he says goodbye. If only I felt that way. Maybe I will. Right now, it still feels like I don't have anything left to offer anyone, or maybe that I want to offer . . . even myself.

Even after two weeks, I walk into the practice facility, unsure of what to expect. A few players are working out between classes, and I try to come up with their names. As the defense coordinator, I'm focused on the defensive line, but I need to get to know the team.

I have no idea what this coaching job will turn into, but since my conversation with Rob this morning, I've been thinking a lot about what he said and his confidence in my ability to help these kids become great. My coaches, along with my drive, are what allowed me to achieve my dream.

I tip my head to the players as I pass on my way to my tiny shoebox of an office. I step inside and feel like a gorilla stuck in a cage. The small space makes me jittery. Besides a desk and computer, the office is empty, and I intend to keep it that way. The less stuff, the more breathing room.

I sign onto the computer and get to work. I'm still trying to get down to the nitty-gritty of what I want to focus on and where the individual players need work. If I have a chance to help this team, I need to evaluate each player's strengths and weaknesses.

After spending a couple of hours on the computer and making notes, I hear the guys filing down the hallway toward the locker room for practice.

Coach Cavanaugh sticks his head around the door frame.

His one-volume-only, loud and gravelly voice could shake the foundation. "I have a meeting, but I'll be on the field as soon as it wraps. Get the boys warmed up, then we'll split."

"Sure."

I shake the ringing from my ears, knowing I need to talk with him about my plans, but I'm giving myself another day or two to see these boys in action before I kick things into high gear.

So far, the team appears to be a tight-knit group, led by Cole Matthews as team captain. I have to earn their trust and demonstrate my ability to make them better, stronger. That all starts by gaining their confidence and respect on the field.

They are all familiar with my stats and accomplishments as a player, but I have to show them I can incorporate that into making them better players and a better team. To do that, I have to quit moping around and get my ass back to playing football, even if I'm not the one running onto the field.

With my clipboard in hand and a whistle around my neck—*I wear a whistle for shit's sake*—I stride out of my office toward the field. I glance around, not seeing Matthews. That doesn't sit well with me. He's the team captain. He should be the first one on the field and the last to leave. I don't care how good of a player he is or that he's The Rocket's son. He should be here.

The team gathers around, waiting for instructions.

"Where's Matthews?"

They shuffle closer, not answering. I survey the field, spotting a girl sitting in the bleachers a few rows up.

Great. Just what we need. Girlfriends or jersey chasers staking out practice, causing distraction or worse.

"Finish stretching if you need to, then we'll start drills. Coach is wrapping up a meeting. We'll split when he's ready."

They spread out, getting to work. If we're going to make things happen this season, we can't have girlfriends hanging out during practice.

"Whose girlfriend is holding down the cheering section?" They continue to move about, but I hear some snickering. "We don't allow guests at practice, so I suggest one of you go tell her to find something better to do with her time."

They get back to business, no one moving to tell this poor girl that they have better things to do than make googly eyes during practice. I give it a minute, but when no one heads in her direction, I do.

I climb the steps into the stands, and when the woman's piercing blue eyes hit mine, I see what looks like just a hint of a smile. She otherwise doesn't move a muscle, apparently waiting for me to speak.

"Sorry. Practices are closed. Whichever one is your boyfriend out there, I gave him an opportunity to tell you himself. Apparently, he didn't want to disappoint."

She tips her head to the side, still staring at me. "Boyfriend?"

That slight smile creeps just a little higher as if something I said is amusing.

I don't have time for this. "Sorry, but you need to pack up and head out. They don't need distractions."

"Annnndddd I'm a distraction?"

I'd really like her to quit responding with questions. I settle my hands on my hips. This isn't helping me get down to business.

She rests her elbows on the row behind her like she's settling in and making herself comfortable. "You don't need to be all grizz. CC hasn't had an issue with it in the past."

It's my turn for questions. "Grizz? And who the hell is CC?"

"Coach Cavanaugh. For all you know, he could have asked me to check the team out. And you don't need to act like a big grizzly bear whose cave was disturbed. I was just going to watch for a few minutes."

A fire ignites in those blue eyes. I rub my hand over my face, exasperated with this exchange. Seriously, why? I'm just here to do a job, coach, not chase away smart-mouthed . . . Wait, did she say who she is?

"Coach Cavanaugh asked *you* to check out the team?"

Her response is to continue to stare me down, her eyes narrowing. Her former ease has turned into irritation, and I can see it beginning to boil the more I question her.

After a second of looking me over with a glare of contempt, she grabs her phone and keys and starts making her way down. She stops on the bleacher right in front of me, so we're basically eye to eye.

Her oversized white t-shirt falls off her shoulder, revealing a purple bra strap. She's pretty. No, she's strikingly beautiful but has an attitude that sets me on edge. Strands of her light brown hair fall around her face from her short ponytail, and I can understand why one of the players would want to keep her close, but right now, she's way too close to me.

Her mouth moves to something that looks like a smirk, and it pushes every single one of my buttons. "Because there's no way I could possibly know what it takes to be an elite athlete or have anything of value to contribute here, right?"

She tips her head to the side again, searching my eyes like she knows me. I scratch my neck, which burns with discomfort.

I'm struck dumb. When was the last time anyone made me feel uncomfortable? My skin literally feels two sizes too small. My irritation now matches hers. *What. The. Hell?*

When I don't respond, she hops down and makes her way to the field confident and unbothered, which pisses me off.

As I turn to follow her, it's apparent that most of the team has spent this time watching our exchange instead of warming up. I see extra sprints in their future.

I trail behind her down the sidelines, hearing a couple of the players say something to her, and she gives a slight wave in return. Up ahead, Matthews jogs out from the locker room with Coach Cavanaugh following behind.

She slows as they approach.

Matthews extends his arms out to the side. "Mags, what's up?"

She tosses a look at me over her shoulder. "Evidently, practices are closed. You so owe me," she tells him, her irritation crystal clear.

Cole glances at me, then back at her, remaining silent.

"Sorry, quality time with your girlfriend should happen on your own time."

Mags crosses her arms over her chest, glaring at Cole.

Cole's eyes grow wide and focus on me. "Girlfriend?"

Coach strides up, joining our little party. "Maggie, my girl." He throws an arm around her shoulders and hugs her, his voice booming.

Now, I'm seriously confused by what's happening, and all the players are standing around doing anything but running drills.

"I'm glad you're here. Cole and I were just talking about getting a few of these guys in your class."

Class? What class?

Maggie nods. "Sure. I might have some openings. If not, we can set something up through the gym. I can stay for about five more minutes, but then I have to go."

"Good. Matthews, get 'em lined up," Coach orders, releasing her, ready to get down to business, but I'm left standing in the dark.

Maggie moves with him to the fifty-yard line. I follow like a lost puppy trying to get someone to throw me a bone and fill me in on what in the hell is going on here.

"Maggie, this is Coach Carter." He gestures towards me over his shoulder. "Although, I'm sure you already know that."

Her head tips up, and there's that smirk again riding across her mouth like a wave that tells me she knows something, but I have no freaking clue what that something is.

"Sure do. It's been a real pleasure."

"You are?" I want to know exactly who she is and why she's here.

Not responding, she studies the players on the field as they set up. "Maggie."

So freaking helpful. "And what kind of classes do these players need to attend, Maggie?" I try really hard not to sound condescending, but I'm a shit liar.

Her eyes stay straight ahead, focused on the players in motion. "Ballet."

I'm not sure my ears heard correctly because it sounded like she said ballet, as in tutus and tights.

"Bal-let." It comes out slowly like I'm some nitwit trying out the word for the first time.

"Yes. I've been watching twenty-eight and forty-three. Their bodies are all locked up. They can't twist at the hips or jump to save their life. You'll get nothing from them. Their mobility is completely restricted. There's no way they can catch a rogue ball or dodge defense. And look at thirty-two." She holds out her hand, waiting for the ball to be snapped. "See right there." She points, leaning closer to me.

I catch a whiff of something in the air that's feminine and sweet. I'm tempted to plug my nose holes because smelling this chick seems far too intimate for my distaste for her.

"He's all muscle, but he's dead weight. If he gets loosened up, he'll be so much swifter. Right now, he couldn't ditch a sloth. Good luck if you need him to run. He's already in pain, by the looks of it. He'll be the first one out on the bench, and you're going to need him."

She looks at her watch, and I think about what she just said.

"Actually, they should all be in my class, but what would I know, right?" Her chin tips up like she's expecting an argument.

Damn her and her cocky ass. My brain is still trying to process what she laid out.

She walks over to Coach and hugs him, likely relaying what she told me about those three players.

"They'll be in your class this week," I hear Coach say from thirty feet away. "You come over to dinner soon, darlin'."

"Will do, CC." Maggie waves as she strolls away, passing by me. "Good luck this season." She throws it out like a challenge she doesn't think I can win.

I have no idea what just happened these last fifteen minutes, but I feel like I just got schooled. I still have no clue who this chick is or what she was doing here, but I have a feeling I'm going to find out.

Sitting in my office after practice, I try to complete my notes about who needs to work on what, and I can't help but reflect on what Maggie said. I watched the three players she singled out, and I'll be damned. She's right. I feel like an asshole, and I'm not even sure I understand why, what went down, or even what that whole thing was about.

A knock on my door has me peering up, and Cole Matthews stands in my doorway.

"Hey, coach. Do you have a minute?"

I nod for him to come in, although there isn't anywhere for him to go beyond the doorway.

"I wanted to say I'm sorry for inviting Maggie to the field without asking you and the other coaches first. I've talked to Coach Cavanaugh about it in the past, and he's had her come out before. I didn't think it would be a problem."

I pull my glasses off and set them on my desk. I don't know this kid, but he has a great arm and mind for the game. He seems to have a real knack for leadership, and the team respects him, which tells me a lot. But I'm waiting to see if he's earned it or riding his dad's coattails.

"I'm not exactly sure I understand what she was doing here. At first, I thought she was someone's girlfriend. I'm sure you can see why we can't have a bunch of fangirling at practice."

Cole's head falls forward, and he rubs his face as if what I just said is bad. "She's not anyone's girlfriend. She's my sister."

Well, shit, that hits differently. I had no idea The Rocket had a daughter. "Your sister?"

"Yeah, she teaches dance here."

Tim "The Rocket" Matthews' daughter. I wasn't expecting that, but things might be starting to make sense. Maybe.

"And you asked her to check out the team?"

Cole's shoulders drop, and he gives me a look similar to the one his sister gave me earlier, like I'm dense. "Do I have permission to speak freely?"

His cautiousness piques my interest, so I rest back in my chair, crossing my arms. "This isn't the military."

"All the same, sir, you are in a position of authority, and I take my role on this team extremely seriously."

"Ok."

"I asked my sister to come today because she has a really good eye for spotting deficiencies. She came out last year, pulled a couple of guys into her class, and before we could even blink, they were performing better, faster, and with fewer injuries."

"And by class, you mean ballet?"

Cole's shoulders roll back, stiffening like he might've taken offense to my question.

"She teaches dance, but her expertise is in ballet. The guys tend to show up at her barre classes in the gym, though. It may seem silly to you, but it works. They're stronger, and they can move." He pauses, and I see him reel in his frustration. "She's good. She knows what she's doing, and she knows football."

"Do you take her class?" I raise an eyebrow, wanting to know if he's too good to take his own advice.

"Man, I've been in ballet shoes and tutus since she could dress me up. She's had me working on third position and pirouettes for years. I don't take her class, but believe me, if she thought I needed to be there beyond the Yoga and Pilates I do on my own, she'd be the first to tell me, and I'd be the first one in her class."

Despite his attempt at humor, I can tell he takes this seriously and believes in his sister's ability. "Ok. We'll see what she can do."

He nods and turns to leave, but stops. "Am I still allowed to speak freely?"

I want to groan. This kid. I give him the go-ahead, my arms still crossed.

"I'm not exactly sure what was said between you, but I saw my sister's face. I know that look. You said something offensive. I'm going to guess that since you thought she was *fangirling,* it was something demeaning, even if it was meant to be harmless." He lets out a breath and looks me in the eye. "She's my sister, and I don't like it when some guy, any guy, says something that makes her feel inferior. I'm sure you'd feel the same about your sister."

He has balls. I like that. "You'd be right." I'll give him that.

"Mine is the best. She didn't have to come today, except I asked her to. She did when she already has a load so full that she had every reason to flip both of us off." He doesn't drop his gaze. "It'd be really nice if you could apologize because…she deserves it. Also, once you see what she does with these guys, you'll want her on your side."

He gives a quick nod and leaves the doorway. I'm not sure what to think about his little rant, but despite what most people think of me, I wouldn't stand for someone offending my sister if I had one.

And even though I'm a man of few words, I probably have a couple I could say to Maggie Matthews. Maybe.

Chapter 3

MAGGIE

"Shhhhhh," I tell Liv as we crouch outside the bathroom door. The shower just shut off, and our unsuspecting brother is about to open it.

From behind us, I hear a whisper.

"What are you doing?" Garrett crouches down opposite us on the other side of the door.

I point to the pie plate filled with shaving cream. It's a simple prank, but Teddy will love it even though he'll have to shower again. He'll hate that part, and that makes it sooooo much better.

We had a quiet evening after I got home. The boys had most of their homework done except for practicing spelling words. Teddy had to read out loud to me while I cleaned up dinner and figured out what to make with the leftovers. Then, the kids played outside while I packed lunches.

But now, it's game time, and I'm about to get the little sucker back for hitting me in the butt with a dart this morning.

I hear Teddy humming, and joy rolls through my body with anticipation. I grin at Garrett, knowing he's going to open the door any moment.

Wham! He stands perfectly still as the aluminum pie plate clatters to the floor. A mound of shaving cream drips off his face, forming a dollop on his chest. Liv starts to giggle, and Teddy reaches up to wipe his eyes and mouth. Slowly, a massive grin grows around the foam.

Before I can react, he takes the extra cream and smears it over my head. We all scramble in the hallway, laughing as he tries to get us.

"You look like the Marshmallow Man," Garrett says through laughter.

Teddy growls and walks stiffly toward him. "Who wants marshmallows?"

Liv and I duck back, still laughing, as he gets closer. "I got you, you little punk. Now, get your butt back in the shower and wash for real this time."

The big marshmallow head turns in my direction. "If shaving cream is allowed now, the possibilities are endless." He waggles his creamed eyebrows at me.

I laugh. "This was a one-time exception and for me only."

"No fair." He scrunches his face, and we all start laughing again as he heads back into the bathroom.

These moments. This silliness with these kids helps us all. They don't often show it, but the weight of absent parents is hard on them. Even though they're young enough to not quite understand, they're old enough to know our dad is ill and he's not going to get better. It pulls us all down and doesn't take into account that they were too much for their mom, who ran off and hasn't looked back.

So, I'll give these kids as many silly and messy moments as possible. They do us all good, and the laughter makes everything better, at least for the moment.

"All right, let's get you two in bed."

Liv and Garrett whine as I push them toward their rooms.

"But Hank isn't even home yet," Garrett argues.

"I know, but he's working on a project with Sadie."

Sadie lives next door, and I'm pretty sure she has an epic-level crush on Hank, which he is completely ignorant of. Right now, she's helping him not flunk his English test, which would result in him getting kicked off the soccer team before the season starts.

"You can read one of your medical mystery books for a while, and I'll check on you once I get Liv in bed." I pass the room he shares with Teddy, carrying Liv.

Liv climbs up into her fully pinked-out bed.

"Ok, Beauty. What's it going to be tonight?"

Her room is the smallest but the most loved, with twinkle lights and every imaginable girly thing anyone could possibly think of. Dolls. Unicorns. Hair bows. Princess dresses. Rainbows. Stuff is everywhere like a girly funhouse exploded all over the place, but cleaning this mess up is not something I have time for. So it's the way Liv's room remains, and something about all of her things surrounding her seems to bring her comfort.

"I want to read the one about the baby bird again." She pulls the covers around her tightly, just how she likes them.

We've read *Are You My Mother?* every night for weeks. Liv is the only one who asks about their mom. How do you tell an almost five-year-old their mom doesn't have space in her newly invented life for her? So many questions, and none of which I have answers to other than these kids are here with me. I'm doing my best to provide them the love and security I promised my dad I would.

"Do you think my mama is looking for me, Maggie?" Liv asks as we finish the story for the second time.

I pull oxygen in through my nose to give myself time to sort through responses, hoping to find the right one or at least one that's satisfactory and shoulders some of the heartache.

"I think for right now, you're supposed to be here with me, and I wouldn't want you to be anywhere else."

She snuggles closer to me.

"Do you think we could go visit Daddy sometime soon?"

A jolt of heartache moves swiftly through my chest but settles in the center. Taking the kids to see Dad is so hard. He's nothing of the man he was, even a few months ago. Hank and maybe Garrett are the ones who really have any memory of him in dad form. Working to help them maintain a relationship with a man who's basically non-existent doesn't seem to serve anyone positively.

"We'll see, ok? For now, I think it's best if we have some sweet dreams. Gwen said she'd take you to the park tomorrow, and I bet you'll need lots of energy to keep up with the other kids."

"Ok." She smiles, and I kiss her forehead before turning out the light.

I check on the boys next door, tucking them in. I lean down to give Teddy a hug. "You smell like a man."

"Maybe you should smash shaving cream into my face every night." He grins his toothless grin.

"Maybe I should. Then, at least, you'll smell clean." I tickle him, and he squirms. "You're the best, you know that." I squeeze his foot and cross the small space to Garrett's side. "What gross thing did you learn about tonight?"

"Did you know that the largest pimple in the world is called a carbuncle? It means coal." Garrett removes his glasses and sets them on top of his book on the nightstand.

I wrinkle my nose. "I don't think I want to know anymore." The little Doogie Howser smiles. "I don't know how you don't have nightmares about giant pimples."

"I do. The little fart across the room gives me nightmares every night." The boys giggle, and I can't help it either.

"You two get some sleep. I have to find Hank and see if I can pry three words out of him."

"We should get him with shaving cream next time," I hear Teddy whisper.

"Yeah, only if you have a death wish," Garrett whispers back.

My smile remains as I find Hank scrounging around in the refrigerator. "How was studying?"

He shrugs his lean shoulders.

"How's Sadie?" I try to sound casual, but one of these days, he's going to get a clue about how sweet, cute, and smart she is. So far, he's only noticing the shallow cheerleader types. The ones who don't seem to mind that he doesn't talk and only really care that he's a freshman on the varsity soccer team.

"Fine."

Exhausted with trying to make conversation with his grumpy ass, I cut to the chase. "Are you going to pass your test tomorrow?"

"Yeah. I think so."

"Well, don't stay up too late. I want to see you start in that game in a few weeks. I'm warming up my jersey and expecting you to kick some balls."

At that, he gives me a smug smile and nods. "Ok."

I pass through the living room, ignoring the mess, and head down the hall to my room. After a quick shower and washing the shaving cream out of my hair, I also smell like a man. I inhale, not minding the smell, although I'd prefer it to belong to a real man who could wrap his arms around me and tell me that everything is going to be all right.

Ugh, like I have any time for a man.

After throwing on a tank top and shorts, I climb up on my bed, that's extra high thanks to the blissful pillow top. It's like a cloud hovering off the floor. My king-size bed is massive compared to my five foot three, hundred and twenty-pound self. It's the one thing I splurged on when we moved into the house, knowing if I was going to survive, I'd need the best possible sleep when I was afforded it.

I grab the remote and turn on *SportsCenter*. The chatter of the latest sports news is a massage for my tired and weary soul. It's calming and familiar, and tonight, I want to zone out while I scroll my phone for a few minutes, but instead, I find myself googling Shane Carter.

When the man approached me, I knew exactly who he was. He was one of the best defensive ends in the NFL and had been for the past six or seven years. He played most of his career with the Carolina Breeze, but last season, he shattered his right knee, ending his career.

I'd seen Shane play on screen so many times. He was good. Crazy good. What I had not expected was the bear that came at me. Mr. Unsocial and Uptight. Mr. Too-Handsome-For-All-That-Arrogant-Grumpiness.

The screen on my phone fills with pictures of his dark hair, hazel eyes, and strong, scruffy jaw. He's handsome. And yes, standing in front of me today with that broody scowl, he was a little too good-looking . . . until his mouth opened. Then he was just a jerk.

As I scroll, most pictures are of him on the field, helmet at his side. Some press conference pictures, where I have no doubt he hardly said a word, looking good as ever. *Damn him.*

There were just a few pictures of him in a suit, all cleaned up on the red carpet with a model hanging off his arm. He doesn't look overly affectionate standing next to her, but in his position, he likely didn't need to. I'm certain he has women hanging on his every furrowed brow.

Why am I even looking at this?

I toss my phone on the bed, not spending another second thinking about Shane Carter and how he assumed I was just some girl waiting for one of the players to notice me. *Gross.* Just some girl who couldn't possibly know anything about football or, hell, anything worthwhile at all. *Big dumb butthead.*

My phone rings. Cole.

I swipe. "I don't even want to hear it."

"Mags, come on. I had no idea Coach Carter would give you a hard time."

I don't say anything because I want him to feel bad for a little longer.

"I'm really sorry. What did he say to you anyway?"

"Nothing. I think he takes that whole wearing a whistle thing a little too seriously."

His laugh gets me like it always does. "I know he said something to piss you off. I'm sorry I was late. Coach pulled me into a meeting about this year's benefit."

"It's fine. Coach Crabby Pants is the least of my worries. Did you talk to Amy today? I tried to catch her on my way home, but she was already gone."

Amy is our dad's primary nurse at the long-term care facility where he's stayed for the past few years.

"I talked to her around lunchtime. She said Dad was having a good day."

A good day for our dad is barely eating and maybe a smile if you're lucky.

"Liv asked me if she could visit him soon. That was after she asked me if I thought her mom was looking for her."

Cole lets out a breath. "That sucks. What do you think about taking the kids to see Dad? Probably on some level, he'd enjoy it."

Just the thought that he doesn't know when we visit or talk to him makes me sick to my stomach. "I don't know." I push out a breath. "I think it's harder on the boys to see him like that. It took them days to readjust after the last time. I think Liv is trying to make sense of a lot of things right now. I'm not sure seeing him would help."

"I'll go with you if you decide you want to take them." Cole would do anything to make things better if he could. It's just who he is.

"Ok. How did practice go after I left? You guys are looking good from the little bit I saw."

"Yeah. I'm anxious to see how Coach Carter beefs up our defense. He's been lying back, but I think he's about to let loose. He's going to be good."

"I hope he can look a little less constipated for opening day."

Cole snorts. "I'll make that suggestion."

"Please do. Let him know that's my expert opinion."

"Love you, Mags."

"Love you too."

We hang up, and I lay listening to commentators talk about the upcoming season and who's on fire. I remember the days when I'd hear them talk about my dad, and soon it'll be Cole who's lighting up a field somewhere.

I think about all the years my dad spent playing football, only to end up like this. It was his life, but not so much that he didn't make Cole and me his first priority after Mom died.

When he wasn't away playing, he was there for every one of Cole's games and every single recital or show, holding flowers and hugging me like he was the proudest man alive. I miss him every day and still want to make him proud.

It takes me a while to fall asleep, but before I do, the last thing that rolls through my mind on this particular night is the look on Shane Carter's face when he realized I might know just a little something about his game.

Chapter 4

SHANE

I swing open the door to the gym, and students are everywhere.

Don't morning classes exist anymore?

There's a certain level of dread I've recently become comfortable with, but today, the little ticker is pushing past the tolerable line.

This isn't what I want to be doing right now. I'd really rather be doing just about anything, apart from getting my eyes jabbed out with a hot poker, and for two days, I've tried to avoid it. I've tried to ignore my conscience and move on with my life, but despite my best efforts, here I am.

What Cole said in my office stuck with me like an annoying PR person after a night of debauchery. That twenty-two year old kid laid into me when it came to his sister. Now I'm hunting her down like a dog with its tail tucked between its legs and hating every freaking second of it.

I look around the main area filled with equipment. I used to spend my days in a state-of-the-art training facility, but since my injury and all of the physical therapy after, I prefer to work out in the privacy of my garage. Alone.

I approach the front desk, where a girl looks up at me from her open textbook and smiles. After a second, she starts twirling her hair and tells me she'll scan my card. It's not that I'm not used to women flirting with me, but these college girls really need to cast their net somewhere else.

I clear my throat. "I'm looking for Maggie Matthews's office. I was told this is where she teaches."

The girl's eyes widen. "Um, Miss Maggie doesn't have an office, but I think she's teaching in Studio A. If you go around the corner, it's at the end of the first hallway. I can show you if you want." Her smile grows wide as she pushes up to stand.

"No, that's ok. I can find it." I turn in that direction, and she stops me.

"Um, sir." She's standing now and leaning over the raised counter, one hesitant cheek scrunched. "Um, if you don't have a member card, you really can't go back there un…supervised."

And what is she going to do, stop me?

I let out a low grumble with a curse word mixed in that I keep to myself. "I have a faculty ID. Will that work?"

"Oh, yeah. Ok. Can I see it?" I pull my campus ID out of my wallet and hand it over. She looks at it and then looks at me. "Ok. Sorry. It's my job. Had to make sure that you weren't some crazy stalker hunting Maggie down."

I bristle at the thought, and it makes me want to ask if that's been an issue in the past. The shock of even thinking it and the protective instincts it sets off are annoying as hell. I keep my mouth shut.

I turn back around, passing the free weights, where a few players stand off to the side, talking to girls rather than working out. I tip my head and keep moving, not feeling in the mood to chat. I'll see them later on the field. I just want to get this over with.

I make my way down a hallway, passing studios until I get to A. From inside, I hear classical music and the rhythmic counting by someone I assume is Maggie. As I get closer, I can see her through the picture window. She's standing in front, watching the students take turns moving across the room.

Her sweatpants are rolled down at the waist and pulled up on her shins over some kind of skin-tight black leotard thing. The mirror reflects the straps that cross down her bare back.

No wonder the players don't complain about attending her class.

"Good, good!" she hollers over the music to one of the students.

The next second, she hits a button to stop the music as she demonstrates something. I watch her move effortlessly, doing precisely what the others should look like.

"Ok. Great class, guys. Practice, practice. I want to see improvement next time."

The students mill around the room, changing shoes and collecting their things, so I wait as they take their sweet ass time getting out. Of course, one student has to stay behind and ask questions. I want to groan, but I don't.

When the student finally leaves, I enter, ready to get this over with so I can get on with my life. Maggie peeks up at me from where she's digging through her bag. Her surprise is apparent, but quickly turns to the same fierce determination I recognize from the other day in the stands.

I've seen this kind of blatant fierceness pointed at me before on the field, but I've never met a woman who has the ability. It makes me want to identify and push every big red button she has.

Her chin tips up a little further. "Sorry, I require ballet shoes and tights in my class."

I'm not delusional in thinking she'd be happy to see me, but the glare I'm receiving seems a little overkill. "The kid just in here didn't have tights on."

"Well, he's one of my advanced students. You'd definitely need to be in the beginners class, and tights are required."

"Huh." I scratch my unshaven chin. "I've spent years in football pants, which aren't much different. I'm not worried, but that's not why I'm here."

She stands and crosses her arms over her chest, her head barely meeting my shoulder. Her blue eyes stare into me as she rolls her lips, waiting. I see the hint of a dimple on one cheek as a piece of her brownish hair comes free from her short ponytail and slides down the side of her face. She just lets it hang there like it doesn't bother her. That severe stubbornness makes my skin prickle, but I ignore it.

There have been few times in my life where I've just wanted to see how far I can push things, and for some reason, she makes me want to find every loose string she has and give them all a good, hard tug. I have no idea what it is about Maggie Matthews, but this just tells me it's time to get on with it and get out.

"I came to–"

Her phone starts ringing, and she holds up her finger, gesturing for me to wait. I huff. She clearly thinks I have all the time in the world.

She reaches into her bag and pulls out her phone. "Hey, Amy. Everything ok?"

I watch as she listens, all color draining from her face like a tank with a leak. Her shaking hand moves to cover her mouth, but she's not saying a word, just listening. One tear slips out of the corner of her eye and down her cheek.

"How long?" is all she says, closing her eyes. And then, "Ok."

She hangs up, looking back up at me before dropping to the floor with her head in her hands.

I squat in front of her, not knowing what to do as she sits shaking, trying to take deep breaths.

"Hey. Are you ok?" I've suddenly gone from increasingly annoyed to concerned.

As if my voice snaps her out of it, she's immediately up and moving. "I have to go." She grabs her bag and frantically starts digging through it.

"Hey."

She doesn't acknowledge me or slow down her panicked search.

"How about I drive you wherever you need to go?" There's no chance she should drive herself anywhere in this state.

She looks at me, the blood drained from her face and nods.

"My truck is out front."

She takes off running, and I follow, trying to keep up. We hop in my truck, and she identifies the hospital she needs me to take her to. Her body vibrates in the passenger seat, so I don't attempt to ask questions.

"Cole," she blurts out, her eyes wide. "I have to find Cole."

"I can call him as soon as we get there." She only nods.

Twenty minutes later, we pull into the visitor parking lot, and she jumps out of the truck. The only thing I know to do is follow her.

At the front desk, Maggie asks for directions to the ICU. An older gentleman gives us brief directions, and we're off again. She moves so fast that I have no idea if she knows I'm following, but I'm going with my inexperienced gut, which tells me I shouldn't leave her like this.

Minutes later, we enter a room where a much smaller and almost unrecognizable version of 'The Rocket' lies hooked up to every imaginable machine. The sterile smell, fluorescent lights, and quiet hum of the machines hit my senses with a jolt.

My sensory overload is interrupted by the gut-wrenching sound that pours out of Maggie. It's a cross between a gasp and a sob. She carefully goes to him and rests her head on his chest, gently rubbing his hand.

"Hey, Daddy. I'm here. Hang on, please." Her sniffly pleading is painful to hear. "Don't go. Just a little longer, Daddy. I know you're tired." After another second, I hear her whisper. "I love you."

A belt cinches around my gut as tears stream down her cheeks and soak into his gown. I know I'm intruding on a very personal moment, but I'm unsure whether I should stay or leave. Leaving her seems impossible, even though I'm the last person who should be here or knows how to handle anything like this. I quietly move to the corner to give her as much privacy as possible.

I stare at the shell of a man lying in bed, who was an American hero. My hero. An icon. He's no longer the man I remember standing on the field tossing me the ball. The man who encouraged me to follow my dreams. The man who gave my brothers and me an opportunity that changed the course of our lives.

I not only watched him play every game growing up and dreamed of being just like him, but his organization for disadvantaged youth also allowed us to attend his camp. It's where I gained the foundation for everything I know about the game. But not only that, it was my first glimpse of life beyond my circumstances.

The strong, invincible man now lies frail and looking lifeless. There's no resemblance to the man who once filled my screen and represented one of the only positive male role models my brothers and I had.

Maggie rests her head next to his, murmuring softly. I know, along with all the other fans, I didn't even understand the best parts of him. His greatness had nothing to do with football, something the kid in me, as well as the man, might need to understand. There's more to life than the game. However, I've never lived that way.

Maggie blinks, wiping her tears away. "I need you to find Cole. I don't think we have a lot of time."

I step toward her, holding out my hand. "Give me your phone. I'll keep calling until he answers."

She hands me her phone and lays her head back down, holding her father tightly.

It takes me five tries before Cole answers. Thirty minutes later, he rushes into the room, looking just as pale and scared as Maggie. They embrace, and Cole brushes a hand over his father's head.

"What happened?" he asks, looking more like a scared kid than the young man in charge of a team.

"Amy told me it was a stroke. You know he has a DNR. They're checking for brain activity." She pauses as more tears fall. "They don't think . . ." She trails off as if she can't say it.

I stand in the corner quietly with no clue what I should be doing.

Do I go? Should I stay?

I'm the last person who should be here and absolutely no good in any type of emotional situation.

"Cole, what are we going to do? What about the kids?" Maggie sounds panicked, and I definitely feel like I should step out.

"I don't know." He rubs his face. "We have to tell them. They should have a chance to say goodbye."

"You know what this means. I thought I had more time." Tears drip down her cheeks, leaving wet streaks behind. "What am I going to do? They'll be like vultures the minute they hear about this."

Cole puts his arm around his sister and pulls her close. "Shhh. You can't think about that right now. We'll figure something out."

Cole eyes me in shock, as if he doesn't remember I was the one who called him. His brows come together. "Coach, why are you here?"

"He was with me when I got the call." Maggie sniffs, wiping her nose on the back of her hand. "I couldn't drive, so he brought me."

"I'm going to go." I move toward the door, ready to escape and give them privacy. "Is there anything I can do?"

The alarmed look on Maggie's face stops me.

Another tear trails down her cheek, and she pushes it away. "I should go get the kids. Can you stay and see what you can get out of the doctor? You can't let them do anything until I get back." Her voice cracks, and it's like a punch in the throat.

Cole swallows hard. "Yeah. I'll wait here."

Maggie finds a tissue, trying to gather herself before turning to me. "Can you take me back to my car?"

"Ok."

Leaving Cole here alone doesn't seem like a good idea, but I sense the urgency.

We move towards the door, but Cole stops me. "Coach, I . . . I won't be at practice today."

I put my hand on his shoulder in an unnatural gesture of comfort. "Sure. Don't worry about it. I'll let Coach Cavanaugh know."

"Actually, can you tell Coach C what's going on? Just Coach. He…he's my dad's best friend." I hear the struggle in Cole's voice, and I wish I could do more.

"Absolutely. I'll let him know as soon as I can."

Maggie gives her brother a long hug. "Don't let them do anything until I get back." It's a command, and Cole nods.

A second later, we're walking quickly and silently back out to my truck. I still have no idea what to say or even think about the unexpected events of this day.

We climb into the cab, and as I reach to push the start button, Maggie's hand grabs my arm.

"Can we just sit here a minute? Please?"

The gentleness of her plea catches me off guard. "Sure."

Her head falls into her hands. The only sound that fills the space inside my truck is her sobs.

I move my hand to place it on her back to let her know I'm here, but that doesn't feel comfortable or appropriate. I sit quietly, giving her time, and eventually, she digs through her bag for a tissue.

"Is there anything I can do?" I ask, wishing for her to be specific and something tangible because I have no freaking idea how to help with any of this.

She spits out a self-deprecating laugh through her sniffles. "You?" She side-eyes me. "Tell me how to explain to four kids that it's time to say goodbye to the father they hardly know." She blows her nose. "Or do you know someone looking for an instant family because the minute my dad's brother finds out that he's gone, he and his wife are coming for them."

I'm speechless. I had no idea Tim Matthews had young kids.

"You're taking care of four kids?" I try to process this, but come up empty.

She looks at me, tears threatening in her eyes. "Yes."

"How long?" My voice is a bit high, and I can't hide my amazement at this revelation.

Her gaze turns to the window and away from me. "Two years. Shortly after my dad started to really deteriorate mentally, their mom took off with his doctor. Apparently, Dad was suddenly too old, failing, and she wanted to start over. Without kids. She left, got a nice divorce settlement, and hasn't looked back."

I remain quiet, and she continues to talk like she knows this is shocking.

"The kids have the most amazing nanny, and my dad did the best he could for a while, but it wasn't long before he couldn't handle them. They were so young, so I came home."

"What's the deal with your . . . uncle?" This is none of my business, and I'm definitely invading her privacy, but this is unbelievable. The fact that she's caring for four kids. I don't know how old she is, but she can't be much older than Cole.

"Tale as old as time. Jealousy. Bad blood. He's younger and hates my dad for his talent, fame, and everything he became, including being a father. What better revenge than stealing his children, especially when you have none. They couldn't do anything while he was alive, despite their efforts. I've been their temporary guardian, but now, if he's . . . "

She doesn't finish, but I know.

"His will appoints me as their legal guardian, but their high society asses will take me to court. I'm just a stumbling block in their eyes."

"Damn. Can they do that?"

"They can contest the will and his mental stability when it was last revised. They've attempted to prove I'm not equipped to care for them, arguing the kids would be better off in a two-parent household, but they didn't have grounds while . . . "

"And if you're married, that helps?" *Shit.* This is unbelievable. I can't seem to stop asking questions. Everything I thought I knew about Tim Matthews, and I had no idea. What I just saw. What Maggie is telling me. My mind is racing.

She shrugs, and it's pathetic, which has my temperature rising. "It shows stability and an established family unit. They have money and status, which I can match to an extent, but I'm only me, trying to raise four kids. Cole's gone after this year. I knew this was coming, and I didn't do anything."

She takes a deep breath and pushes it out. "I can't let anything happen to them. I promised my dad I'd care for them and look out for them." Her voice quivers. "They'd use them and . . . How could I live with myself if anything happens to them?"

She sniffs, running her finger underneath each eye with force like it's punishment before her lips turn up into what I suspect is an uncharacteristically defeated smile. "Like I have time to swipe right every Friday night in hopes of finding prince charming." She shakes her head. "Sorry, I'm ready now. I need to get them back here quickly."

I start the truck, thinking about everything she just said and how much I judged her, especially after finding out she's Tim's daughter. A nagging feeling in the back of my brain has me gripping the steering wheel a little too tightly and almost breaking my turn signal.

As I drive back to campus, it's like there's a tapeworm gnawing away at something sacred, and I need it to stop.

Maggie directs me, and I pull my truck up next to her Suburban. Grabbing her bag, she climbs out of my truck, and I follow, feeling unsure of how to handle the situation but knowing I should say or do something.

She stops at her door, her face tipping up to mine. "Thank you . . . for everything. I'm sorry you had to be a part of all of this." Her eyes drop to the asphalt. "I hope you understand this is all very private."

"Of course. Are you going to be ok?"

She takes a deep breath and then moves into me. I have no idea what she's doing, so I stand perfectly still while she wraps her arms around my middle and rests her head against my chest. Neither of us speaks.

I'm not a touchy-feely guy, and honestly, I can't remember the last time I was hugged. Actually, I'm not sure I've ever been hugged like this. I push my discomfort and inexperience aside, holding on to the hope that maybe this is me helping in some way.

When she takes another deep breath, I go to release her, but she hangs on.

"No, not yet."

Ok then. I let my arms linger around her a little longer.

She sniffs. "I know we don't know each other, but thanks for helping me. Maybe you aren't so grizzly."

"You probably shouldn't jump to conclusions under extreme circumstances," I say, wanting to lighten things up for her, if only for a moment.

She looks up at me with a glared smirk, but oh man, those blue eyes are so full of heartbreak and fear. That little worm chomps away at what I know is my conscience.

She finally releases me and climbs into her car.

"Let me know if I can do anything and make sure Cole knows he doesn't need to worry about practice."

She leaves me with glossy eyes, and I stand in the parking lot for only a second before heading to find Coach Cavanaugh to send him on his way.

My uneasiness continues to grow, building through practice and into the evening as I head home. I have a hard time reconciling the man who was my hero, the football player I wanted to be, and the man who lies dying in a bed surrounded by his kids. The love, a kind I've not known, more than evident. My thoughts are consumed with Maggie and four kids and some words I haven't thought about in a very long time.

Chapter 5

MAGGIE

"Ugh. I want to take a searing hot bubble bath, fall into my bed, and not come out for a year." I rest my head on top of my arms. "Who's taking over? I'm tapping out."

Simone's meticulously manicured nails tap the tabletop. She's my hairstylist turned best friend that looks like a freaking supermodel. She's tall, with naturally dark, bronze skin, long, curly black hair, and a no-BS attitude.

Our friend Carmen designated one night a month as girls' night, and here we sit. Because my ability to go out is minimal, we usually meet here, eat takeout, and sometimes Simone cuts our hair.

"Missy, I know this all totally sucks. You're exhausted, completely heartbroken, and nothing seems like it will be ok, but we've got to focus. The kids need you, and you need a man."

I lift my head. "Is that seriously the best you've got?"

Two days ago, I stood at the graveside as they lowered my dad into the ground. Cole and the boys stood next to me as I held Liv, watching. I quickly wiped my tears, and the boys tried hard not to let anyone see theirs. It was silent except for the squeak of the crank. A sound I can still hear.

Coach Cavanaugh and his wife, Clara, stood by, hands clasped and gazes down, releasing years of emotions as they watched his body fail. CC and Dad played college ball together and remained best friends to the end.

Until these last few years, my dad spent the better part of his life in the public eye, achieving every major height a professional athlete could dream of. But it was just our small group standing over him as we sent him onward.

It's how he wanted it. No fanfare. No spectacle or publicity that would follow the kids to school or our home, and I need to keep Cliff and Joan at bay as long as possible.

He wanted the kids to have a quiet life. A life they could define on their own terms and not based on who he was. He wanted to go and be remembered the way that he was before. Not as the man confined to a debilitating diagnosis that took his dignity and pride.

He was known not just for his physical ability but strategizing and seeing beyond the limits of the field. Ultimately, he lost both his ability and his mind until there was nothing left of the man the world once knew.

But he was so much more than that. He was my dad. I miss him so terribly that sometimes I can't breathe, but that started years ago. I'd said goodbye to the man who raised me. The man who cheered me on through life, held me when I fell, and showed me how to dust myself off and get back up to try again. The man who'd be sitting next to me right now with his hand on my back telling me it was time to get my butt off the bench and my head in the game.

So, no matter how badly I want to curl into a ball and hide, to let myself cry and crumble into a million pieces, I won't. I can't. I have four kids, depending on me. They rely on me to be ok, to keep going, to be the one who keeps things steady and them safe.

"Carmen, please tell me you have something for me."

Carmen is the blond, curvy, sweet, and tender-hearted one of us. She's engaged to the kindest, burliest man and is getting married in only a few months.

"Honey, maybe there's another way, or maybe we should just pray your aunt and uncle have moved on from their vendetta."

I roll my head to the side just enough to peek at her with one eye. One side of her face is scrunched like she knows it's wishful thinking.

"However," she adds, twisting her water bottle between her fingers. "We could get you signed up online. I could write a program to help identify the real possibilities."

The laugh that bubbles out of me is like a breath of fresh air. It's light and freeing.

"Come on, there has to be something other than getting married," Simone says. "Like, can't you just prove they're worthless pieces of shit who are manipulative and sick in the head? I mean, they tried to turn you into some southern debutante, and his wife is just as messed up as he is."

"I wish it were that easy. It should be that easy. Unfortunately, everything they can offer looks dependable and more capable than I am. The lawyer said my best chance of keeping the kids with me is if I'm married. I need to demonstrate a stable family unit." I slouch in my chair, resting my head against the back. "It's only a matter of time until they find out Dad is gone, and they attack."

There's more, but I don't want to talk about it. I could testify about my own experience with them, but I can't. It's embarrassing and shameful, causing the minimal contents of my stomach to catch a ride upward just thinking about it. It's my word against theirs during one of the darkest times of my life. A time I have no desire to revisit. Ever.

Simone sets her chin on her fist like she's trying to solve a puzzle. Her perfect brows narrowed. "But doesn't his will declare you as guardian?"

"Yes, but you have to think like lowlifes. They'll argue he wasn't mentally sound when he decided that. The last time it was updated was years ago when Monica left. They'll pull every string, including whatever they can dig up, to prove I'm unfit."

"What about Monica?" Carmen refers to the kids' neglectful, unattached, self-centered, sorry excuse of a mother. "Have you heard from her?"

A laugh of hysteria spills out of my mouth. "She calls occasionally like she's checking in with a long-lost friend. She asks about the kids and sends them a card or a birthday gift, but she has no attachment to them. She's living her best life."

"Why did he ever marry her?"

Simone asks the question I've asked myself a million times. Each time, I toss it down immediately because if my dad hadn't married Monica, I wouldn't have the boys and Liv. So it doesn't matter why he married her. What matters is what I'm going to do to protect them.

I push my undrunk beer away. "Let's talk about something else. I need a distraction from my life."

"We should go out," Simone suggests. "A legit girls' night. Laughter and dancing. Maybe you'll meet Mr. Love-at-First-Sight, or we could invite the new coach." She waggles her eyebrows.

I'd told the girls about my run-in with Shane on the football field and that he drove me to the hospital. I did not tell them how I'd spilled my guts or the embarrassing fact that I'd hugged him in the gym parking lot and wouldn't let go.

I'm chalking it up to emotional overdrive and a momentary mental breakdown. They'd never know how much I needed that hug and how much he likely detested it. That hug is the most action I've seen since I broke up with my ex before moving back from New York, and it was a nice hug, even if Shane hated every second of my holding on to him. It's been a really long time since I've felt safe and not alone, and surprisingly, for that brief moment, that's exactly how I felt wrapped in his massive arms.

"I can call John and have him invite some friends." Carmen offers sweetly like that might help my desperate situation.

"I can't. Cole will be bringing the kids back anytime. He has to study since he missed so many classes this week. And I won't be inviting Shane Carter to hang out. He's Cole's football coach, and I'm pretty sure he's got a permanent frown."

Simone snorts. "Grumpy or not, he's hot. All those muscles, that strong jaw, and those intense eyes."

Carmen pipes in, ignoring Simone. "Won't Shane be at Coach Cavanaugh and Clara's party?"

The back of my head hits the top of the chair. These girls are stuck on Shane. *Seriously.*

I don't want to think about Shane. If I had to admit it, I'd agree. He's gorgeous, but that's it. He helped me when I needed it. I still have no idea why he was even there that day, but regardless, he's one of Cole's coaches.

Will he be at the party? Most likely, but I don't care.

CC and Clara throw a party for the team each year before the season starts. A time for team bonding and all that. CC is a no-nonsense coach. The game is strictly business, but his players are his for the season, and he takes that just as seriously.

After the burial, he and Clara asked if the kids and I would come to quietly honor my dad, which he would've enjoyed. Those he loved, celebrating the game he loved. He didn't want a funeral or a large gathering, but he'd be okay with this.

"I assume he'll be there, but the party is for the team and the start of the season. Only Cole, the kids, and I know we're remembering my dad. I need to focus on ensuring I'm being a good example and providing a stable environment, not chasing after guys like some desperate woman."

I peel the label on my warm beer. "I just want this all to go away," I whisper, feeling the weight of every single thing.

I haven't cried since the day my dad was buried, but the lump in my throat is swelling larger by the minute and will explode with the slightest additional pressure.

"We know." Carmen rubs my shoulder. "Maybe we should go so you can take a hot bath before the kids get home."

We say goodnight, and I run a bath and sink into it, trying to clear my mind. I've done my best to keep things positive and light for the kids, and they seem to be doing all right. They also said goodbye to their father, but they remember a man they've only experienced on a screen.

It's what makes me the saddest. I have years of memories of the man who showed me what it is to be loved. The kids have Cole and me, but soon, it'll only be me. It's my job to keep them safe and show them what it means to be loved, and I'm scared to death I'll screw it all up.

I left New York when Dad could no longer care for himself. I promised him I'd look after them and show them the love he would've if he'd been able. Doing this alone is the most difficult and terrifyingly lonely thing I've ever done.

I'm twenty-five, and instead of going out, dating, and planning adventures, I'm praying that I'm not making a mess of four awesome kids.

Hearing my friends talk about their relationships makes me wish for a partner. Someone who could help carry the load, whisper my fears to, and hold my hand when things get really tough. I'm tired and sad, and I don't want to do this by myself.

My throat grows tight, and I feel the swell of a full-on breakdown, but I can't let myself. It won't help anything. I have to keep doing my best to show the kids I'm here and not going anywhere. I want them to know they're safe and loved. Hopefully, if I can do that, show they're happy and thriving, it'll somehow be enough.

Chapter 6

SHANE

I shut down my computer and rub my eyes, grabbing my keys. It's late, and I've looked at so many spreadsheets that the gridlines might be permanently etched in my vision. I lock my office door and hear a voice that sounds like it's coming from the locker room. I frown, thinking all the players would have left by now after a long practice and extra drills.

As I get closer, the voice becomes louder and more tense, sounding a bit panicked.

"No, you can't do that. That's dangerous." Pause. "I don't care. I'll quit, move back in, and we'll figure it out." Pause.

I step around the corner and see Cole resting his head against his locker with his phone to his ear.

"No, Maggie. This isn't all on you. I promised him, too. They won't get their hands on them. I don't care what we have to do. They're sick, and what they did to you . . . " He pauses, listening, taking deep breaths. "I know." His tone is soft. "Ok. I love you too."

He hangs up, drops his head, and slams his locker shut so hard that the door bounces back open as it vibrates. He sits down on the bench, his head in his hands.

I give him a second to cool down. "You all right?"

His head snaps up in surprise. "Sorry, coach." He stands. "I . . . " He doesn't finish, but the kid looks like he's about to fall apart.

I'm not good with emotions, but I've seen my fair share of locker slams. I know that when my brothers have issues, letting them fester only makes it worse, so we get to the bottom of it, even if we have to beat it out of each other. This kid just lost his father, and based on what Maggie told me and his side of the phone conversation, the grief and pressure of their situation are alive and screaming.

"I heard you when I was locking up. I didn't mean to eavesdrop." I step toward him, shoving my hands in my pockets. "Want to talk about it?" *Please say no.*

His head drops again with a strangled laugh. "Where do I even start?"

He falls onto the bench, hunched over his arms on his knees. "This game is all I have left of him." He takes a deep breath. "But, my brothers and sister . . . I promised him I'd watch out for them. I told him I'd help Maggie do whatever is necessary to take care of them and keep them safe. First, their mom takes off. I mean, who does that?"

A familiar spear slices through my chest as he breathes.

"Now, my dad's brother . . . Saying they were enemies is putting it mildly." Cole shakes his head. "They will do nothing but use these kids for revenge or leverage or whatever they can get out of them. And Maggie . . . It will destroy her."

He runs a hand over his face. "She's given up everything to take care of them, so I can keep playing. Now, her friends have signed her up on one of those dating websites and are introducing her to guys. Can you even imagine the men who will prey on her when they find out who my dad is?" He sounds pained as his eyes meet mine, and I can't say he's wrong to be concerned. "She keeps saying she'll figure it out, and I can't quit, but how can I not? I can't let anything happen to them. Any of them."

Tears form in his eyes, and I look away, giving him space from my presence.

"I love playing football. It means everything to carry the name on the back of my jersey when I step out on the field. I want nothing more than to make my dad proud, but I can't do that and let any of them lose each other. *I* can't lose them."

I sit beside him, letting everything he just said ruminate. I can't relate to any of it except I'd go down swinging for my brothers, but they are grown men, not children. What Cole laid out was a lot, and based on his state, the fear is real, and it stirs that nagging feeling inside me I've been ignoring since the day Maggie climbed out of my truck.

I push out a breath, having no idea what to say to this kid, but I try. "Football was all I had. I loved every minute, even when I puked, was in pain, or felt like I'd never make it. Some days, it was what kept my head above water rather than drowning in a world that was just waiting to suck me under." I match his posture, placing my arms on my knees. "We don't just give it up and walk away."

"What am I supposed to do?" His voice rises in irritation, and I know it's not directed at me. "I made a promise, and they're more important. My dad taught me that as much as he taught me how to throw a perfect spiral."

"I'm just saying, don't make a rash decision. Responding to panic won't get you anywhere. Maybe talk with Maggie and see what other options there are."

"There aren't any. She's met with lawyers, and the longer I sit here. . . We're running out of time."

This kid and I come from two worlds that couldn't be further apart, but the fear in his voice and the worry for these kids raises the hair on the back of my neck.

As a kid, I lived every day in fear, and Cole's is not for himself but for four kids who don't have a say in any of this. The place in my chest where a heart once was aches for them, and my conscience comes calling. I want to tell it to shut the hell up.

Those damn words I want to mean nothing skirt through my mind, and I try to chase them away.

I fist my hands and release them, needing to go back to not empathizing or feeling . . . things.

"Just give it some time," I say, knowing time won't likely help.

He nods gently, straightening and gathering himself. It's as if I can see him slide a shield around himself.

"Sorry about unloading. These are my issues. They'll stay out of the locker room from now on."

I haven't been around this kid long, but it's clear he strives for perfection. I don't know much, but I know we aren't perfect.

"Give yourself a break. We can't be on every moment. You're facing a lot. Just take it one day at a time." *Where the hell did that come from?*

I stand, my skin feeling tight and itchy. Too much about this brings about thoughts and memories I never want to revisit.

"Hang in there," I say, needing to escape.

"Sure." He stands gathering his things.

I turn, but his voice stops me.

"Hey, coach. Thanks." I see the sincerity in his eyes, and it only makes me run for the doors.

I sit on the edge of my bed, my fingers unfolding the creased-lined notebook paper. It's been days since my time with Maggie at the hospital, and I'd safely pushed away the gnawing feeling threatening to disrupt my carefully constructed, quiet, simple state. Cole's untimely emotional locker room dump kicked that little tapeworm back into action, and it's eating away at my well-guarded conscience.

So here I sit, unable to ignore the beckoning of these words any longer. The last time I held this letter was the day I was drafted into the NFL. It's the only thing I have of my mother.

The day she left me standing with the envelope in my hand was the last day I ever saw her. The distinct smell of her flowery perfume lingered around me as her thin arms held me tight for one last hug. I can still feel the press of her warm lips against my cheek and see the glistening tears in her brown eyes as she walked away.

I've wondered my whole life if there would ever come a time when the words in this letter would find me. Would there be a day when I could believe any part of what she left me with?

I want to hear every single word and know she meant them, but I've spent my life trying to ignore each one because it's easier than accepting they can't possibly be true.

It was that day, sitting in my truck with Maggie, when the memory of these words I've never been sure I'll understand gripped me, and they haven't let go.

> *Maybe one day, there will come a time when you are faced with a circumstance or an opportunity, and you will know that sacrifice is the only right thing. Doing something for the sake of another because there isn't another choice.*

I've spent my life alone. Unwanted and tossed into the system that raised me. I learned at an early age to take care of myself and let go of the dream of ever having a home surrounded by people who love me.

When I started playing football, my team became a distant family, but letting anyone in meant they could and would walk away. So I kept my head down, stayed focused, and worked hard playing the game that saved me from myself.

I never want to get married. Anyone who knows my past only looks at me with pity and a rescue plan. That pity churns my stomach, and I don't need to be saved. I've only ever wanted someone to see me as I am, what I've never had, and not try to fix any of it. Even if I met someone, I'm not sure I'd allow myself to believe it could actually last, that they wouldn't wake up one day and decide I wasn't worth it, or that there was someone better in the world for them than me.

The closest I've ever come to a relationship like that is with my two foster brothers, whom I've known since I was twelve. We're the same. We come from the same world. They've seen the good and the bad, kicked my ass when I needed it, and have stood by me no matter the stakes.

But now, these words swarm around me, attacking my thoughts and making me question their legitimacy once again. A relatable pain roared deep in my soul when Maggie and Cole told me about the kids and their mom leaving them for a different life. Then again, when I saw the overwhelming fear in Cole's eyes. It was at that moment that my mother's words resurfaced. They've taken flight, and I can't get them to settle back down.

I carefully fold the letter and place it back in my dresser. I yank my keys from my pocket, needing this team party to give me a reprieve from thoughts of Maggie, the kids, and a life decision I'm not sure I'm willing to make.

"Come on, coach. You've got to tell us what it was like playing for the Breeze. Standing in the middle of the stadium, hearing all those fans."

The team has peppered me with questions since I arrived. They're clearly feeling more comfortable here than on the field, and I can't deny that it's nice seeing them relax and observing their personalities. It'll be beneficial in working to fine-tune our defense strategy.

I never thought I'd be coaching, at least at this stage in my life, but here I am, and I have a lot to learn. Knowing what I was capable of on the field is one thing. Trying to figure out what this group of guys can do and then pulling it out of them at game time is a new challenge.

When I arrived today, most of the team and staff had already gathered. I spent a few minutes talking with the other coaches, but I want to get to know these kids better. The camaraderie I've seen on the field is only more evident when they aren't in their jerseys. They laugh and joke and play with each other. I'm not the most social guy, but seeing these boys in this element makes me miss my team.

I scratch my chin. "It was the absolute best feeling in the world. The first time I walked on that field, it was my dream come true."

"That's going to be me someday," one kid announces, bumping his chest, and his teammates snicker at his cockiness.

The team and a few girlfriends are spread throughout Coach Cavanaugh's backyard. One particular girl, a redhead, has sidled up beside me, giving me the eye. I need her to move on. *Not happening, sweetheart.*

The large yard is surrounded by evergreens, and in the middle, a bonfire roars for cooking hot dogs and s'mores. Tables filled with food and coolers with drinks are set up near the house where Clara, Coach's wife, is stationed. She hugged and welcomed me to the family while also scolding me for not coming by for dinner sooner.

Like a mother hen, she's been doting on these players and ensuring everyone has everything they need. Coach has been marching around, making sure to talk to each player, and it's clear this is so much more than a game to him. I've had great coaches in my career, but I'm learning a lot from this man about what it means to be a leader.

"Miss Maggie!" one of the players bellows as others hoot and holler.

I turn to see her coming around the corner of the house. Three boys are in tow beside her, and a little girl in pigtails is holding her hand.

Damn. I wasn't expecting to see her here and with the kids. It's the absolute last thing I need.

The oldest boy, who I'd guess to be around fifteen, looks like a younger version of Cole. He has the same dark hair and strong facial features. The unimpressed look on his face tells me it wasn't his idea to come.

The two younger boys appear close in age. One in glasses smiles and returns Clara's hug, while the shorter one takes off running towards Cole. Cole throws him over his shoulder while he carries on, and I can only guess he's a wild one.

My gaze returns to Maggie and the little girl who clings to her leg while she talks to Clara.

"Man, I wish all our teachers were that smokin'," one of the players whispers, and I hit him with a glare.

"Be respectful."

None of these asswipes should be looking at her that way. I can't blame them, though. She looks pretty freaking amazing in a button-down sunflower yellow dress that shows off her petite frame and spectacular legs. *What the hell am I doing?* I avert my eyes immediately.

All three boys join Cole and the team, but my gaze draws back to Maggie. She looks tired and like she's putting on a brave face. I almost texted her a few times to give her my condolences, but I've been a chicken shit.

Coach's voice breaks through the chatter and calls us toward the house. "I'd like to say a few words and a blessing. Then we'll dig in."

We gather around the food tables, and I make sure to steer clear of the redhead who hasn't left my side. Maggie ends up across the table from me, holding the girl's hand. Her eyes meet mine, and I nod before she looks away.

Coach clears his rough voice. "Before we get back to kicking off what I hope is another exceptional season, I want to tell you I'm honored to be coaching such an outstanding group of young men again this year. I'm an old man, and I've been doing this a long time, but you all are what makes this a team. Win or lose, we're going to jog out together, and we're going to play like it's the last game each time."

The guys holler and cheer as he continues.

"I promise to do my part the best I know how, and I need each of you to bring your very best, whether on the field or off. I expect you to conduct yourselves as if your mother stands beside you. We are a team. We hold each other up and demand excellence from one another."

There's a pause as he puts his arm around his wife. "I lost my best friend recently. Best football player there may have ever been or will be. A legend. A man who knew the game inside and out, treating each game as if he were approaching war. He lifted his team up and played with a one-for-all and all-for-one mentality. But I can tell you, it was when he walked off the field . . . "

I hear a sniff and see Clara slide an arm around Maggie.

"When he walked off the field, the man underneath the helmet was one of the finest men and fathers I've ever known. It's the truest measure of a man, and you would all be wise to remember that."

My eyes drift to the sons of the man who was just described. Their heads are forward, their hands still, and the look in each of their blue eyes tells me exactly what I need to do. A jolt runs through me like I've been struck by lightning. My skin feels singed, the tips of my fingers tingle, and a breath is caught in my chest.

After Coach prays, everyone starts filling plates. I move back, making room, needing space to figure out what the hell is happening to me. I find a bench around the fire and sit down, bracing my arms on my legs. I take a sip of water to coat my dry throat. I push out a shaky breath and hear a small voice.

"Can you help me?"

My eyes dart to a little girl with a large plate wobbling in one hand, the other clutching a stuffed bunny close to her chest.

I frantically search the surrounding area, thinking she can't possibly be talking to me, but there's no one. Literally, freaking no one. I set my water bottle on the ground, taking in air, needing my lungs to function properly again.

I grip her plate a little too forcefully, bending it almost in half, but slide my other hand underneath just in time to keep her food from spilling to the ground. I set the plate on the bench, and she climbs up and sits right next to me, as if this is the most natural thing in the world.

"Maggie needs to make sure that Garrett doesn't get anything with peas in it. He's allergic." She wiggles a little closer, even though there's no room between us. "I'm Alivia Reign Matthews. Do you play football?"

I peer down at her, still holding the bunny tight. I've not only been hit by some kind of severe subconscious force, but I've also been struck dumb. I have no idea what to say to this child. She asked a simple question, and I can't formulate an answer.

She stares up at me expectantly, and I will myself to get my shit together. "I . . . I'm Shane." I sound like a freaking eight-year-old on the playground. Shit. "I used to play football, but now I'm a coach."

"Are you Cole's coach? He's my brother. Sometimes when he takes me places, people think he's my dad, but my dad died. He's in heaven now." She adds the last part quietly.

I barely catch the curse before it shoots out. I don't know much about hanging out with kids, but I know that would be inappropriate. I have no idea what to do with children, let alone talk about things such as death.

I breathe, wiping my sweating palms on my shorts. "I'm really sorry about your dad." I leave it at that, needing someone to rescue me.

I search the surrounding area, wishing I had a flare gun. Everyone is taking their sweet ass time getting their plates, and I don't see Maggie or Cole. I'm totally screwed.

"Can you help me cook my hot dog? Maggie told me I'm not allowed close to the fire by myself."

I look down at her plate filled with an uncooked hot dog, a bun, chips, and mac and cheese. "Sure."

I want to run for my life. This child and her ability to chat scare me, but I man up, grabbing a roasting fork to stab her hot dog and place it over the flames.

"Can I help?" She hops off the bench and stands next to my leg.

A few players join us, but they're no help.

"My daddy was a really good football player. Did you know him when you played?"

Wanting to be careful with my words, I opt for simplicity. "I watched him play on TV. He was an outstanding player."

She places her little hands just above mine on the fork, helping me cook her hot dog. "I don't have a mommy either. I asked Maggie if she thinks my mom is looking for me like the bird looks for its mama, but Maggie said she's happy that I get to stay with her."

The level of nerves this little girl is setting off inside me is disturbing, and in about two point two, I'm going to freak the hell out. "I think you're really lucky to have someone who loves you and wants to take care of you." *There, that was a good answer. Calm the hell down.*

"Do you have a mommy?"

Shit. Of course, she would ask. I clear my throat to give myself a second to think about how Mr. Rogers would answer this question. "I . . . My mom wasn't able to take care of me either."

Her sweet, innocent face tips up to mine, her smile lighting up her blue eyes. "We're the same."

My racing heart stutters at the power of her simple words. This little girl and I, we are the same.

"We should be friends. Can you come over and play princesses with me sometime? My favorite is Belle. Which princess is your favorite?"

"Liv, you were supposed to sit and wait for me, but I see you found someone to help you."

My head snaps up so fast I might suffer whiplash. I've never been so happy to see another adult in my life. Having it be Maggie is even better. My entire body relaxes, and I've suddenly morphed into Gumby.

"This is Shaney. He's going to come over and play princesses sometime. He used to watch Daddy on TV." Liv's tone saddens. "He doesn't have a mommy either."

"Really." Maggie's eyes meet mine over Liv's head. "Sounds like you two had quite the conversation. I never pictured you as a princess kind of guy."

I shrug, trying to play it so damn cool and hoping I didn't say anything I shouldn't have. "You should never judge a book by its cover." That earns me the softest smile.

"Maggie reads to me every night," Liv says. "What's your favorite book? Garrett reads books about yucky doctor stuff. I'm not old enough for those, but I don't think I'd like them anyway." Her little nose scrunches.

"*Treasure Island* is my favorite."

Maggie raises an eyebrow as if she's surprised I can read, and I feel like I'm back on solid ground.

"I don't have that book. Maybe you could read it to me. Is it a book for kids?"

Maggie finally jumps in and saves me from the little interrogator. "Liv, it looks like your hot dog is done. Why don't you leave Bun Bun here with me so you don't spill your food? Your drink is at the table, and Cole is helping Teddy and Garrett, so they'll be there in a minute."

"Ok, but only if Teddy doesn't put hot sauce on my food."

I help her put her hot dog on her bun, and she picks up her plate.

"Will you come to sit next to me?" She looks up at me with those big blue eyes that match her sister's, and I wonder if she ever gets told no.

Maggie grabs the stuffed bunny and points Liv toward the picnic table. "Teddy doesn't have access to hot sauce, so I think you'll be ok."

Liv sets off with her plate, and Maggie's gaze returns to me.

"Teddy mixed hot sauce with the ketchup last night, and I'm pretty sure no one will ever trust it at our house again." She takes a seat and crosses her legs. "So, Shaney," she smiles. "Thanks for helping her. I'm sure she told you more about all the things you never wanted to know."

"Well, at least now I have a friend I can call when I want to play princesses."

She laughs. "I'd like to see that."

I study her for just a second, but pull my eyes away before it gets awkward. "How are you? I should've texted you. I'm sorry."

She frowns. "I never gave you my number."

I rub my chin, remembering that I didn't tell her. "I put my number in your phone when you gave it to me at the hospital, just in case you or Cole needed something, then called mine. I forgot to tell you."

"Well, aren't you slick?" She tips her head to the side and then focuses on the bunny in her hands. "I should apologize for laying all of my problems out on your dashboard. Not to mention acting like a crazy woman and the completely unprofessional parking lot hug."

"It's ok. Happens all the time." I deadpan.

She snorts. "I'm sure you have no lack of unwanted hugs." She pauses, searching my face this time like she's trying to figure me out. "Anyway, thank you for helping me that day and tolerating my meltdown."

"How are the kids?"

"They're doing ok. They never had what Cole and I had with him, so . . . I have difficulty reconciling whether that's good or bad. At least their world hasn't turned upside down . . . yet."

I hear the worry in her tone and try to find the courage to say it, but there's a Grand Canyon-sized pit in my stomach. A sheen of sweat breaks out over my entire body, and I can't look at her, so I train my eyes on the fire. I bite the inside of my cheek, hoping to force my mouth open.

"What if I could help you out with that?" In my peripheral vision, I see her head snap in my direction.

"Uh . . . what now?" Her shock and hesitancy are written all over her face.

I sit back, trying to appear way more confident than I am, while my singed skin starts to itch with irritation. "What if I said I'd help you make sure that the kids stayed with you?"

Maggie stares at me, her mouth open and at a loss for words. "I'm. . . not sure I understand. What are you saying? Are you saying you'll marry me? Why would you do that?"

I can't answer that. I'm not sure I could explain it even if I tried.

Still gaping at me, she stutters around like she's trying to comprehend what I just said. "We don't even know each other. How do you know I'm not some psychopath? Or what if you actually never smile? Like you aren't capable of doing it. Plus, you're Cole's coach. You're really interested in taking on four kids? This won't be for just a couple of months, and they've had enough people disappear on them." She inhales, trying to slow herself. "I'm sorry. You can't be serious. Are you?"

"Yes. I'm serious." My stomach punches my esophagus in retaliation.

Her eyes return to the blazing fire, and I realize that even though there are people around, no one seems to notice our intense conversation, which is only mildly comforting.

She turns her body towards me, the shock still in force. "I need a minute to process this."

"Ok." I'm on the edge of a panic attack myself, but I try to look cool. *Cool. Just be cool. Shit. Dammit. What did I just do?*

"Miss Maggie." We both turn to one of the players standing beside Cole. "What is this about you and Cole and a *Staying Alive* routine? We've got to see this."

"No way, man." Cole shakes his head and takes a step back from his teammates. "I was in junior high."

She tries to smile and shake loose from our conversation.

"Come on. We want to see our star quarterback strut around like John Travolta. Besides, Miss Maggie, you never told us you could dance any other way than in those fancy ballet shoes."

"Her ex-boyfriend is a notorious hip-hop dancer," Cole instigates. "Don't let her fool you."

A surprising curiosity spikes at the mention of an ex-boyfriend, but I push it down along with all of my nerves. "I don't think you're going to get out of this."

"Get up here, Miss Maggie. You and Cole have been holding out on us. I've got the song loaded up."

She looks at me again, searching my face like she's trying to make sense of the curveball I just threw at her. "We need to finish this conversation."

"We will," I assure her.

The players start chanting her name as she slowly stands and walks toward the tables. Cole moves to take his place beside her, shaking his head. Maggie slips off her shoes as the music starts to play, and she and Cole slap each other's hands, breaking into a remarkably smooth and what looks like a professional rendition of "Staying Alive."

I can't help the smile that creeps over my face as they laugh and dance together. The team surrounds them, cheering them on, and Maggie clearly has more up her sleeve than ballet. It only takes another minute before her brothers and Alivia join in, moving as if they, too, have had some instruction. They dance and laugh with smiles so bright I can't hide my own, all my previous discomfort fading with the sun.

The picture is clear to me. Maggie isn't a psychopath. She's created a family for these kids, and I'd guess she's doing an excellent job. It may sound absolutely insane, but I'm confident I want to help her and these kids.

Standing here watching them smile and laugh, I see the love that radiates between them. How could I let that be taken away?

As scary as it is to admit, even if it's only to myself, I might not mind being a part of what they have.

Chapter 7

MAGGIE

SHANE: We didn't get a chance to finish our conversation.

ME: Are you serious? I'm questioning your sanity.

SHANE: I already answered that question.

ME: We don't even know each other.

SHANE: Have a better offer?

ME: How do I know you aren't a lunatic?

SHANE: You don't.

ME: Why? Why would you do this? Marry me. In case you forgot what you were suggesting. Are you insane?

SHANE: We need to talk. Can you have dinner?

ME: Are you serious about this?

SHANE: Stop asking me that.

ME: Grizz, you're scaring me. Like, you really want to talk about GETTING MARRIED?

SHANE: Dinner?

ME: I'm not sure I can breathe. Aren't you having a panic attack?
ME: Do you smile? Laugh? Ever in your life have fun?
ME: Do you like people?

SHANE: Some. Sometimes. Rarely. Dinner?

ME: Oh my gosh!
ME: I can't believe I'm even considering this. I think I need to hire a PI to find my mind.

SHANE: DINNER?

ME: Fine. I agree to dinner ONLY.

SHANE: Ok.

"Where is my list?"

"Oh boy. You have a list? Are you trying to scare away the one man willing to marry you? Maggie, he's totally gorgeous. All that scowl and muscle. You could do way worse than the brooding Shane Carter. I wouldn't mind snuggling up to him at night."

"Simone, you're not helping. This isn't about looks or sleeping or anything else normal people consider when marrying someone. I'm desperate, and that's never a good place to make decisions."

She laughs through my car speaker as I shift through the never-ending piles of food wrappers, cups, and school papers littered throughout my car. And even though I'll never admit it to her, Shane wouldn't be a bad sight to wake up to.

When I saw him at the team party, he was striking. He stood across from me, tall, strong, and broad like a brick wall in a gray T-shirt pulled taut around his massive biceps and chest. It was my first time seeing him without a hat pulled low on his head. His close-cut, dark brown hair, unshaven face, and hazel-green eyes would make any woman suddenly inhale when they found his eyes on her.

"Ah ha! I found it under an empty Happy Meal box. I should've known." The elation I feel at this recovery tells of how pathetic and mundane my life really is. "Ok. He's going to be here any minute, and I need to calm myself before I bounce in there high on nerves." I settle myself back in my seat, needing just a second. "Please tell me I'm not totally and completely insane for even entertaining this."

"You're not insane. Maggie, you said he would've had a background check before they gave him the coaching job, so at least you know that he doesn't have a record."

"Right, no criminal record. We're setting the bar high."

"You've read every article you can find about him. You know he doesn't have women making scary claims. It doesn't even sound like he dated that much. Reality check, chicky. You've been taking care of the kids for two years. Even if you didn't have to worry about your freak of an aunt and uncle coming after them, wouldn't it be nice to have someone else carry just a bit of the load? Someone to talk to. Someone to, I don't know, yell at when you feel like you can't take another minute."

I rest my forehead on the steering wheel. The weight of it all is exhausting and suffocating.

"How in the world could this ever work? He's a complete stranger. What if he's terrible with the kids or a bad influence? What if we can't get along, or we end up hating each other and can't make it work? Then what? Divorce in this situation isn't an option. At least until I can be assured the kids won't be taken away." I'm scared out of my mind with the endless possibilities of everything that could go wrong, but I'm even more scared of losing the kids.

"Just have dinner with him. It's like a first date. If it goes well, you can think about marrying him. If it's horrible and he's an arrogant, egotistical creep, you aren't any worse off than you are right now. It's just dinner, and you can knee him in the balls on the way out."

"Ok. It's just dinner and a list. Like an interview. I can do this," I say, giving myself a little boost of encouragement.

There's a tap on my window, and I jump. Shane stands there staring at me through the glass, his face emotionless as usual. I smile softly, hoping I can disguise my big ball of nerves.

"Simone, I gotta go."

"Don't scare him off with the list," she rushes. "And Maggie, don't forget, even if there's lots of fighting, the making-up part is really great."

A wave of heat crawls up my neck and floods my face, and I quickly end the call. I climb out of my car, joining the man who may become my husband, really hoping he didn't just hear that.

"Table for two," Shane orders as we enter the machine shed-turned-upscale brewery.

The hostess gawks at Shane, taking a long perusal before checking the seating map.

He surveys the open space, ignoring her obvious ogling. "Can we have one of the tables toward the back?" It comes out as more of a demand than a request.

"Sure." She bats her fake eyelashes, and if they move any faster, she might take flight.

After marking the chart and grabbing menus, she leads us to our table with a bit of a chassé in her step. I look up at Shane, rolling my eyes, and he pretends to not understand the gesture. I laugh, not failing to notice the whispers as we make our way to the back.

I hadn't thought about people recognizing Shane. Growing up, my dad would autograph shirts and stop for pictures everywhere we went, but it's been so long since that happened that I've almost forgotten what it's like. Although it's a little different when it's a giant, attractive man towering behind me.

We arrive at our table, and Shane's large hand lightly brushes the small of my back, waiting for me to sit. Part of me wants to press into it to see what his strong hand feels like, but I resist the urge. That's not what we are here for.

Our hostess continues to work to get his attention, chomping her gum a little more obscenely. I just hope she doesn't lose it on our menus.

Shane clears his throat in annoyance, and she scurries away like she was caught red-handed.

We are left alone, and I sit on my hands, needing comfort. *What in the world am I doing? I think the kids have actually driven me to insanity.*

I suck in a breath and hold it while Shane acts like a perfectly normal human and surveys the menu.

I study him while he holds the menu in his large hands. He's so freaking big. My dad and Cole aren't small, so you'd think I'd be used to it, but Shane is huge. In jeans and a short-sleeve button-down shirt, he looks like a regular guy, except Hulkish. His cut muscles bulge, and veins pop all the way down his arms.

"Are you all right?"

My eyes pop up to his at his low concerned tone. *Why does he have to look so calm?* I haven't eaten, but I'm pretty sure my stomach is volunteering to make an appearance.

I shove it down with sarcasm. "I was worried your girlfriend would choke on her gum or throw an eyelash trying to get your attention." He ignores my comment just like he ignored spider lashes. I'm not ready to talk about why we're here, so I deflect. "Does it ever get old? The attention?" I'm genuinely curious how he feels about it because he hasn't struck me as the cocky-chatty type.

He weighs his head from side to side. "I wanted to play football, and my goal was to be the best, so it came with the territory. I would've been fine if it hadn't. Being the center of any kind of attention is not my thing."

"You don't say."

"How old are you?" he asks bluntly.

Ready or not, here we go. "You're never supposed to ask a lady how old she is?"

"Given why we're here, it's entirely appropriate."

Our waitress drops off glasses of water and takes our drink order.

"I'm twenty-five," I say once the waitress leaves.

"You're young to be teaching at the college level. Is this where you went to school?"

I shake my head, wiping at the condensation on my glass with my finger, glad he's keeping it light for now. It's weird. It does kind of feel like a date, although I've never been on one that's felt this intense before. Shane is all business.

"No, Juilliard."

He pauses with his beer halfway to his lips. "Really?"

"You want the long or short version?"

"Long."

He says it in his soooo serious tone, and I wonder if he ever cracks a joke or if there's a sense of humor lying desolate in that big body. I'm a smart-ass, so this could be *really* interesting.

"I danced before I could walk. My mom was a ballerina and then opened her own dance studio. Ballet stole my heart. When she died, I think it's where I felt closest to her."

Shane's eyes are set on me, acute but not hard. He's attentive and interested.

I rub the corner of my napkin between my fingers. "When I was fifteen, I set my sights on Juilliard. I wanted to be the best. It kind of runs in the family." One side of my mouth tugs upward, releasing some nerves. "Every second I wasn't in school was spent in the studio. At sixteen, my dad flew with me to New York. I auditioned, and by some miracle, I got in."

"I took every dance class I could fit into my schedule, mostly ballet, but some others. Dad came to visit, but by then, he'd married Monica and had Hank. When I graduated, I appeared in a few Broadway productions, no ballets, but at that point, it didn't matter. It was Broadway, and I was being paid to do what I love."

He nods like he gets it.

"The last time my dad came to see me, I knew something was wrong. Monica had left, and he didn't look well. He told me he was diagnosed with CTE."

Almost every football player understands the risk of repeated head trauma.

"I think he'd been having symptoms for a long time, but I was so far away. I'd been cast in my dream role as the lead ballerina, but before rehearsals even began, I broke my ankle, so I was out. Instead of sitting around feeling sorry for myself, I came home to help my dad with the kids. It ended up this is where I needed to be."

"I'm sorry you never got to fulfill your dream." There's understanding in his tone, and I know he gets it.

"It's ok. Really. I had a little time with my dad before he moved to a facility, and the kids needed me. Their mom had disappeared, and my dad was fading away mentally."

"I'm sorry about your dad. It's a terrible disease."

"He was meant to be on a field, not a prisoner in his own body. He's free now." I inhale, ready to keep pushing us forward, and my grief tucked away. "I want to know about you. All the things I can't find on the internet."

One dark eyebrow raises just a fraction of an inch.

"You seriously think I didn't internet stalk you coming into this dinner? If we're going to talk about the big 'M' word, then I need to know who you are. Not the made-up guy the articles knit together."

He twists his beer between his fingers. "I'm certain you've already gathered my age and stats. You know I shattered my knee toward the end of last season, ending my professional career. My agent called me about this open coaching position, and I took it."

I don't know what my face shows, but my insides say, *'Oh, hell no.'* "Shane, come on. You aren't giving me anything I don't already know. What about your family? Do you have a girlfriend or any floaters I need to know about? What happens when this season is over? I can go on."

Shane stiffens and tries to settle back in his chair when we're interrupted by the waitress. I can tell I've set him a little bit on edge, so when the waitress leaves, I wait.

When he doesn't speak, I lean forward. "Listen, I know enough about you from what I've found online to know that you're a private person, but these four kids are my responsibility, and right now, they're my life, so I'm going to be straight up with you. I don't know why you'd do this or what's in it for you, but I'm not interested in discussing this further unless you understand a few things."

This man just flipped my 'on' switch, and I'm not messing around. We're talking about marrying each other, for crying out loud. Why would he suggest this if he won't open up even the tiniest bit?

"I'm not sure if you think we can just get married on paper, and I'll be good, but that won't work. We're talking about having to live together. Doing life together. My phone will be blowing up any day when people find out about my dad. One call, in particular, is why we're even here. Ideally, we have something in place before lawyers get involved."

I pause, hoping he's getting the message that this is more than paperwork.

"Shane, I have to prove that we're sustaining a well-functioning family environment in which the kids are thriving to have a chance at keeping them with me. You'll have to be a part of that. I'm not interested in letting you into their lives when I don't know anything about you or whether you actually plan to be there."

His gaze drifts like he's taking in everything I said. Eventually, his eyes make their way back to me. "What do you want to know?"

"Uh, everything? Shane, why would you do this?"

Chapter 8

SHANE

Maggie's brilliant blue eyes, which I know came from her father, hold mine from across the table. I see that uninhibited tenacity again, and if I weren't cold and dead inside, I might think it's the sexiest thing I've ever seen. She's fearless when it comes to protecting these kids, which tells me a lot. It tells me so much about who she is and settles some of my nerves about what I might be getting into.

I don't like talking about myself, especially my past or where I come from, and even though I know I should just tell her that I've changed my mind, I can't. I should be able to explain why I'm willing to do this, but I only know that it's something I *can* do.

It's like when I first knew I was supposed to play football. It came naturally to me, and I was good at it. I'm certain that helping Maggie will be anything but natural, but I can help her make sure these kids are safe and cared for in a way I never was.

I scratch my jaw, needing out of the hot seat. "I'm not sure I can explain why I'll do this. There's nothing in it for me. It's just that after you told me about your situation, I . . . felt like I needed to help."

She sits back and crosses her arms over her chest like my response isn't good enough. *Shit.*

I push out a breath, trying again. "I grew up in the system. Foster care. I don't have anyone except for my two foster brothers, who I consider my family. I don't have a girlfriend or *floaters,* as you call them. I didn't intend to marry, so this line of thinking is new."

Maggie's stiff posture softens slightly, but there isn't an ounce of pity or sorrow in her focused eyes. That look I hate, like I'm broken and in need of fixing. I'm not. I'm a whole person who's spent his life alone.

"I don't know anything about kids or what it takes to care for them, but I know what it's like to not have anyone. My contract is for this season, and I'm not sure what will happen when it ends. I don't know where my career is going, but I can help you, and I can help these kids stay where they belong."

"So you're willing to commit yourself to me and the kids for the foreseeable future, and you don't want anything in return?" Her skepticism is in full view.

"I don't need or expect anything. I live a simple life. Right now, I'm taking it one day at a time."

I take a sip of my beer while Maggie picks at her napkin, determining what to do with my response. I didn't expect this to be easy or for her not to question my motives, but I need her to settle back down so we can figure out if this will work.

"Tell me about the kids."

I watch her chest rise as she inhales deeply. I have no doubt this is the determining moment for her. Is she going to let her guard down and her protective instincts to crack the door to allow me a peek into her world with four kids?

While she's deciding, our food arrives. I give her the space she needs and take a bite of my burger. She picks at her plate, then turns her attention to me, revealing vulnerability for the first time tonight.

"Hank's fourteen. He's quiet and moody. Actually, you two would probably get along swimmingly." One of those brown eyebrows arches, and I force myself to remain neutral. "He's a giant body of hormones that I have absolutely no idea what to do with. He starts on the varsity soccer team. He's really good and should be captain, but no one asked me. He's a good kid, softer on the inside than he'll ever let anyone see."

Maggie's head falls to the side, studying me like she figures that might be another thing Hank and I have in common, but I give her nothing.

"Garrett's eleven. He's my guy who wears his heart on his sleeve. He's a brainiac and obsessed with all things science. I've no doubt he'll skip sports and be a doctor or a rocket scientist. He has a severe allergy to peas, and we have to make sure he's not exposed, especially with all of the new health foods containing pea protein."

"Teddy's eight and my wild child. He's a lover but a maverick. He's all about danger and pranks. You have to watch your back with him, but he keeps things light and messy and has probably shortened my life by years already."

Her soft pink lips turn upward, and I think we might finally get somewhere.

"And you already know Liv. She told our nanny, Gwen, all about you and that you're coming over to play princesses. She's smitten, so you better not break her heart."

I see the seriousness in her eyes and have to clear my throat, trying not to choke. An image comes forth of that little girl looking at me with those big blue eyes and telling me that she and I are the same. It's the reason I'm here.

"Sounds like you have your hands full."

She laughs. "I never thought at twenty-five I'd be making cupcakes for the team, planning birthday parties, or scheduling playdays. But even on the hardest days, I wouldn't trade it for anything. They're amazing kids."

Just like when I watched the six of them dancing together at the party, as Maggie describes each of the kids, I can see the enormity of love she has for her siblings. I can't help but think about what it would've been like to have that. How different I'd be.

"I want to help you," I say confidently as my knee bounces under the table.

She holds one slim finger up. "You might hold that thought for a second. I made a list of things we'll have to do. My friend, Simone, is afraid it'll scare you off."

"That so? I can't wait."

She rolls her eyes, and it's the first time tonight I feel like I'm seeing the real Maggie.

"I'm sure you have some expectations too."

Actually, I don't. I haven't thought that far ahead, but I'll keep that shit to myself. "Just so you know, I'm not signing anything."

She pulls a crumpled piece of paper out of her purse, which I can see is filled with handwritten notes. This may require another beer, but also, for some reason, I want to smile.

"So," Maggie starts. "We have to seem like a family unit, and you'll have to live with us. The kids need to get to know you, and we'll have to spend time together. I know your schedule will be crazy with games, but when you're home, you'll live with us."

"Fine." I figured I'd have to move in with them, so this isn't surprising.

"Sundays are our family day. We go to church in the morning and then spend the afternoon eating and watching football. Cole comes with us when he can."

"I've never been to church." I put it out there, but I don't mention that I'm not interested in starting. "I'm good with eating and watching football. Have you said anything to Cole about this?"

She scrunches her nose, her lips moving to one side. "I have no idea how he's going to react, and I wasn't saying anything until we talked."

"What else? I'm not joining any committees or sewing circles."

"Fine, no PTA for you. The moms will be highly disappointed. Speaking of." Her finger extends in my direction, and I have a feeling if there weren't a table between us, it'd be poking my chest. "No dating or being involved with other people. If we get married, I'll be committed to you, and I expect the same until we know there's no longer a risk of me losing the kids and we dissolve the marriage."

"Ok."

She has no idea what a nonissue this is for me. I've never been all that good at dating, and most of the women I find myself surrounded by are only interested in me for my name.

She starts fidgeting with the paper and peeks at me from under her long, dark eyelashes. "We'll sleep in the same bed."

I can only look at her. I hadn't thought about this, and sleeping next to her brings about a whole bunch of thoughts and ideas.

She holds up her hand, stopping my mind in its tracks.

"I'm not going to tell the kids we're getting married to prevent them from being taken from me. They don't know much about Cliff and Joan. I won't lie to them, but I also don't want them to worry about something that hasn't happened yet. Plus, we can get married, and they could win anyway."

I tug on the collar of my shirt. It's suddenly stuffy in here as she marches on like this will be no big deal.

"My lawyer says that being married and having additional support will be highly beneficial in my case, but there are no guarantees. I don't want the kids' first example of marriage to be some weird fake arrangement where you sleep in the basement, and the whole you or I sleep on the floor thing is just not happening. We're both adults, and I love my bed."

"What if my bed is bigger and better?" I'm not a small guy, and I already know any amount of touching could be a real issue.

Her face does this thing that tells me my question couldn't be more ridiculous. "My bed is my sanctuary and the most comfortable bed in the entire universe. It's a California king because I like to sleep in the middle and feel like I'm in a giant cloud. This is non-negotiable. I will move over to give you room, but it's my bed or nothing. Sorry."

"You seriously have that big of a bed? Do you get lost in it?"

"I wish," she sighs.

"Do you snore?" I need to get a grip and not let her see me sweat over the idea of sleeping together. She's insanely beautiful, funny, and a fighter. There isn't a man who would have an issue sharing a bed with her.

"No, I don't snore, but I've been told I talk in my sleep."

"Great," I grumble.

"And." She jumps back in. "Before you even think it, there will be no sex. Just because we're married doesn't mean we're married like that." I choke on my beer, and she grins. "I'm sure you haven't heard the word no often, but I don't do friends or whatever we'll be with benefits."

She seems so convinced this will be no big deal. I can't help but want to tug her down to my level of uneasiness.

"How can you be confident you won't change your mind?" I watch her cheeks flush as her phone starts ringing.

She grabs her purse. "Sorry, I need to make sure it's not the kids." She pulls out her phone. "It's my friend Carmen. She and her fiancé are watching them."

She answers, and I see her shoulders slump. I sit quietly, listening to her side of the conversation.

"Ok. He hasn't messaged? Yeah. I know. Thanks." After hanging up, she sends a text, curses, and then looks at me. "I'm sorry, but I have to go. Hank was supposed to be home an hour ago and hasn't responded to Carmen's unconvincing threats. He knows he can push the boundaries."

She stands, but I stop her. "Wait. Let me get the check, and I'll go with you."

Her eyebrows raise. "You don't have anything better to do?"

I flag the waitress. "Actually, I don't. Besides, trial by fire, right? If we're going to do this, then I guess I'll get a taste of what it's like."

We've been in my truck for fifteen minutes, and Maggie has a death grip on her phone. She's texted a couple of moms, and no one seems to know where Hank might be.

"Ugh. I'm going to kill him! I think he has a new girlfriend, who, according to my sources, is a junior. I suspect he's with her."

"Did you check social media?"

The look she shoots in my direction informs me that I'm slow and clearly the novice here.

"He's not very active, but I watch him like a full-time stalker." She checks her phone again. "Is it unfair of me to call our neighbor, who has a massive crush on him, to see if she knows where he might be?"

"If she's anything like some of the crazy fans I've been around, she probably knows something."

She starts tapping away on her phone. "She's not crazy, just completely smitten with his moody butt. She's really too much of a sweetheart for him. Although I'd much rather him be with her than Miss Boobs, which is probably exactly what he's all up in right now."

I don't comment, but I'd venture that's a good guess. Maggie messages the neighbor girl, who fills her in on the details of a party she heard about, which is where we're headed.

We pull up to a house with cars lining the streets. All the lights are on inside, and some kids are lingering in the front yard. Before I've even put the truck in park, Maggie pushes the passenger door open and marches toward the front door. Ignoring the stiffness in my knee, I jog after her.

I'm sure this house is filled with kids, but I'm glad she isn't barging in there alone.

She opens the door to a group of teenagers standing around with red cups in hand and pushes forward like a lion looking for its prey. I follow behind as the kids are stunned still. I'm not sure if it's my size, the fact that they recognize me, or if they're scared shitless of the little lady in front of me who looks like she just entered a battlefield prepared for war.

We walk through the kitchen and family room, where a group sits around a large screen playing video games.

She stops in the middle of the open space, surveys again, and then turns to me. "So help me if I find him in one of the bedrooms—"

"Let's try out back first," I offer, really hoping we don't have to search rooms.

We step out onto the deck, and the scent of weed fills the air. It's dark, but the lights from inside help us make out faces. Some are scattered around in chairs, while others stand along the edge. Maggie does a sweep and stops abruptly in front of me.

Looking over her head and across the deck, I see Hank in a chair with a girl on his lap, laughing at something someone said.

Maggie takes a moment and then moves forward like she's more in control now that she knows he's ok. I stay put, noticing some of the kids from inside have followed us out, whispering in the corner behind me.

I hear a, "Dude, I told you. It's Shane Carter."

The last thing we need is someone to capture this.

"Don't even think of taking a picture." I give him a fair warning before following Maggie, like somehow I can help in this situation.

The moment Hank sees her, his eyes grow wide. It takes the girl on his lap a second to realize something is up before she finally climbs off.

"Is your phone broken?" Maggie's tone is way calmer than I'd expected, and if I were Hank, I'd be terrified.

The look on his face tells me he's no dummy.

He pulls it out of his pocket. "Sorry, it's dead."

A laugh that's filled with sarcasm bubbles out of her. "Oh, well, that's a relief. You want to stay, or do you want to go?"

He looks dumbfounded by her question, and then he notices me.

"Why's he here?"

It's a tone that's way too ballsy for where he is right now.

"Hmmm. Let me see." Her hands move to rest on her hips. "Maybe because I was with him when I got the APB, you didn't come home when you were supposed to. Then, when I expected you to text me so that I knew you weren't lying on the side of the road, kidnapped, or being used for your good looks, he offered to come with me to search all of the greater Denver areas to find your way-too-smug-for-tight-pants-ass."

She takes a breath, and so much of me wants to laugh because this little lady should be the coach.

"Now, you have a choice to make. You can get your tail out to his truck right now, or you can stay here. I suggest the former, but if you think you're responsible enough to drink and smoke and *not* make sure your phone is charged, you better find whoever owns this house and let them know you're moving in."

She grabs my hand, pulling me back out the way we came. When we hit the front yard, she drops it and takes a deep breath.

"I seriously think I might kill him. Do you have an issue with hiding a body?" She paces. "And if Miss Boobs remained his lap one second longer—"

"Hey, take another breath." I watch her pace like a caged tiger. "He's fine, just testing the boundaries."

"Well, I'm glad you can be so calm."

"Uh. You were scary calm in there. Don't think I didn't want to pull the little punk out of that chair the way he was talking to you."

Maggie's head tips back with a laugh, and I'm not sure if she thinks I'm joking.

In the next second, Hank walks down the lawn toward us and says nothing as he climbs into the back of my truck. Maggie and I join him, and the silence as I push the start button is deafening.

I can't help but be curious to see how Maggie handles this. My brothers and I would've taken to the front yard and knocked some sense into each other.

Maggie turns in her seat to face Hank. "Were you drinking? And don't even think about lying to me because we'll head straight to the clink, where I'm sure they'd be happy to administer a breathalyzer."

"No," he huffs, keeping his eyes down. "Why were you with him? Are you dating him?"

Maggie makes some kind of snorting noise. "I'll be asking the questions right now, but you should thank him. If I'd been home and you'd been five minutes late, I would've had time to plan a scene so extravagant, you'd go down in high school glory."

"Because it was so much better to have you stomping your way through there with him."

I want to pull the truck over and let this little boy know he'll be seeing a lot more of me. I never handled the smart-mouth rookies with gentleness.

Maggie twists in her seat a little further. "Are you high because I think you've lost your ever-loving mind?"

From the rearview, I see him cross his arms over his chest and stare out the window.

Maggie looks at me. "Would you pull over when you can?"

I do as she asks, and we find ourselves in a shopping center parking lot.

Maggie unbuckles and turns around in her seat. "First of all, you aren't going to do the man of few words routine. I want to know what you were thinking. I'm not your mother, but don't think for one second that every time you set foot outside the house, I don't worry about you and all the things that could happen. You could've told me you wanted to go to a party."

"Yeah, like you would have said ok."

"You're right, at least not *that* party, but not because I don't trust you. Despite what you showed me tonight, I know you aren't dumb enough to drink, get in a car with someone who has, or do anything else that would jeopardize your spot on the team. But you sitting there not doing those things might not be as innocent as you think."

She holds her hand out and gestures toward me. "Would you like to ask Shane, or we can call Cole and have a nice chat about what would happen if your handsome face showed up online at a party thrown by some high schooler where alcohol and pot and whatever else is flowing freely. You think anybody will give two shits when you say you weren't partaking?"

She gives him a second. "Hank, you know better than that, and half of the team and their parents would like nothing better than to see your butt on the bench. You work too hard and have too much to lose to not be using the brain I know you have."

I wish I would've had a Maggie in my corner fifteen years ago. The dynamic of their relationship is certainly something I've never experienced. Each moment I spend with her, I find myself curious about who this woman is, and I already know she's something.

Hank finally looks at her and speaks softly. "I'm sorry. I just wanted to hang out with my friends. For one night, I didn't live up to the Matthews level of perfection."

He throws it out like a jab, and it's then that I turn in my seat. I have a small amount of patience, but none for disrespect. Maggie puts her hand on my arm and leaves it there. It's warm and calming and . . . new.

"Seriously, Hank. Let's be real. We both know living up to Dad and Cole is impossible. They suck, and I've never wanted their boring, uncomplicated, suffocatingly mundane way of doing things. You know me better than that. I'm pretty sure I'm screwing up every second of every day, and the four of you will have therapy bills so excessive they'll bankrupt you by the time you're thirty."

Hank tips his head to the side unamused, but Maggie doesn't skip a beat.

"I'm so far from perfect, and I don't want to be. When I was your age, living in New York, don't think for one second I didn't make some really stupid decisions. Things that Dad and Cole would've called my ass to carpet for, and they would've been right."

Maggie takes a deep breath, letting that sink in. "Hank, I don't expect you to not make mistakes or want to have fun with your friends or have your head up your ass sometimes. Just be smart about how and when you're choosing to do it. And I expect you to tell me where you're going and what you'll be doing. I won't lie to you, so don't lie to me."

"Fine."

Maggie turns around in her seat, buckles, and I put the truck back in drive. Then she turns and looks over her shoulder at him. "And that chick with the big rack who had the balls to stay draped all over you, you better be careful. She's too old for you and not with you for your brains. Nothing good will come from that. And if you want to talk about imperfection, I'll tell you how I know."

I'm up for story time because I'd like to know what she's talking about, but she didn't ask me. I see a hint of a smile in the rearview and then a mumble.

"Isn't referring to it as a rack a little sexist?"

Maggie's head rolls. "She's seventeen or whatever, and she has way bigger boobs than I'll ever experience. I can call them whatever I want."

Hank's hand goes to his face, and I don't even try to stifle my laugh.

Maggie's head snaps in my direction. "Oh. My. Goodness. Did you just laugh . . . at my lack of boobage?"

Hank groans.

"Boobage?" I ask.

"Please let me out," Hank demands. "I'd rather walk than hear anything more about your . . . chest."

"Hey." I surprise Hank as he meets my eyes in the mirror. "If you're going to hang out with girls like that, you better be man enough to talk about a lot more than breasts."

Maggie looks at me and grins.

We ride the last few minutes in silence, and I pull back into the restaurant parking lot next to her car. Hank immediately hops out and climbs into the passenger seat of her Suburban.

Maggie gets out and comes around to my side as I step out.

"I'm sorry about all of that." She pulls her eyes away from the car and tips her chin up to look at me. "Are you sure you don't want to keep living your simple life?"

"You handled that like an expert. I would've just kicked his little ass."

She laughs. "Shane, I don't have any idea what I'm doing."

"It doesn't look like that to me."

"I'm going to hug you now, whether you like it or not." She moves into me. "Thank you for going with me."

Her arms come around my middle, and I tentatively wrap my arms around her. This hugging thing is strange, but also not completely terrible.

"I think we have a thing about parking lots." Her face presses against my chest. "I really hope he's watching and getting all riled up about this."

I can tell she's smiling at the idea of torturing the little shit.

She releases me and steps back. "I'll give you a bit to think this over. Even someone in love with me would have every right to question marrying me after tonight."

"I don't need time, Maggie. I told you I'm in."

Her eyes meet mine, wide and shocked. "I still don't understand why you're willing to do this, but just to be sure, why don't you come over Sunday and eat and watch movies with us. To be fair, you should experience the whole lot of us before you make your final decision."

I nod. "Ok."

I'll go, but I'm not changing my mind. If tonight showed me anything, I can't *not* do this. I know what I'm giving up. My privacy. My solitude. My freedom. All the things that bring me comfort and that I've earned by surviving life in the system.

Maybe the woman I never got to know was right. Sometimes there isn't another choice because it's obvious to me that these kids need to stay with Maggie.

Chapter 9

MAGGIE

"Coach Carter? You've been talking to Coach Carter? And he said he'll marry you?" Cole whispers as we push through the church doors and toward our cars.

I spent the last hour all but on my knees praying for direction. Taking on the responsibility of four kids didn't happen overnight. It was gradual, but marrying Shane is a split decision, and saying 'I do' terrifies me. The only thing I know with certainty is that losing the kids scares me so much more.

So I'll do it, even if it means giving up a chance to find real love and a family of my own, at least any time soon.

"What choice do I have? It's not like I have any other options. You've heard what my lawyer said. It's my best chance. I can't let Cliff and Joan have even the slightest advantage."

"But Carter? The man is stoic and growls. He wasn't known for his sweet and tender side on the field, and off the field, he's blunt and unsociable. Do you think he'll be good with the kids? Plus, you said you'd never date a football player."

"Well, things change. He was actually pretty good at helping me with Hank the other night. I think there's more than meets the eye with him. He's a foster kid, and I'm sure he didn't have it easy." I don't know if I'm trying to convince Cole or myself that this will all be fine. "I think we could be friends."

Friends. That's my new relationship goal.

I tug on Cole's arm, and he stops next to me as my heart starts hammering in my chest.

"I'm running out of time. Ed's been calling."

Ed has been my dad's agent from the beginning. Besides their business relationship, they were also good friends. Since my dad started to decline, he's been looking out for us to ensure things remain private.

"Reporters are asking questions. He thinks someone from the living facility is talking. They want a statement." It's always been a risk, but now that Dad is gone, there's less loyalty, and private information sells.

Cole rubs his temples with his thumb and middle finger. "It's just going to be so weird having him there today. He'll be my brother-in-law. What are you going to tell the kids?"

"I'm going to tell them I'm getting married. Are you worried about the team getting weird when they find out?"

Cole puts his arm around me as the kids climb in the car. "Nah. If they do, they can deal with it. It's not like I don't pull my weight and carry some of theirs." Cole winks at me. "You know I'll support you no matter what, right?"

I nod, sucking back my emotions.

"They're so lucky they've got you." He hugs me. "Plus, those crazies don't stand a chance against us Matthews. And, well, I guess Carters."

Cole smiles, and I hug him tight again before climbing in the car, wondering if I'm making a huge mistake. But like I told Hank, I'm not one to play it safe. I got that from my mom, and I made a promise to my dad that I intend to keep.

"Ok, guys," I say, as the kids are gathered around the kitchen, helping make food for the rest of the day.

Cole is in the corner smashing the burgers. Hank is slicing tomatoes, onions, carrots, and broccoli. Garrett is washing the fruit. Teddy is dumping different types of chips in a bowl and mixing them because that's how we Matthews do it, and Liv sits next to me on the counter, stirring the brownies.

"Do you guys remember Coach Carter from the party last week?"

Liv sticks her finger in her mouth with a glob of brownie on the end. "Yeah! Shaney. He's my friend."

"Right. Shane. Well, he's coming over to hang out this afternoon."

The boys, excluding Cole, freeze.

"Why? Is he your *boyfriend*?" Teddy makes kissing noises.

Garrett looks at me across the island with a hesitant smile.

I inhale, willing my voice to stay confident and peppy. "Actually, I was thinking maybe he could come to live with us and be a part of our family."

Hank groans, his head tipping up to the ceiling as Cole shoots him a look.

Garrett pushes his glasses up his nose. "Are you saying you're going to get married?"

"He and I are talking about it. I wanted you guys to meet him and for us to spend the day together. Then we can talk about it. I know this is kind of sudden, but . . . " I don't know what else to say as Hank gives me a look, and I know I need to talk with him separately. "Anyway, how does that sound?"

"Can I be your flower girl?" Liv asks. "I want Shaney to live with us. He doesn't have a mommy either, so you should take care of him too."

"I bet he would love that." I laugh, scooping the batter into a pan and sticking it in the oven.

There's a knock at the front door, and Teddy dashes from the kitchen. I have no doubt he's been quietly planning. I smile, wondering how Shane will handle it.

Liv climbs down from the counter and runs to the door, swinging it open. "Shaney, you're going to come live with us!" She grins up at him.

"That so?" Shane looks like Gulliver towering over her in shorts, a T-shirt, and a backward hat. He sets his brown-green eyes on me, and they dip to my stomach for a split second before popping back up.

I glance down at my loose jeans and cropped T-shirt, expecting a smear of brownie, but . . . nothing. *Huh.* "Can you tell Cole to start the grill?" I push Liv back toward the kitchen.

"Yep. Can you sit by me at lunch? Then I can show you all my princesses." Liv skips off before Shane can answer.

I hold on to the door like a security blanket while my heart suddenly decides it's time for a jog. This is all just so weird.

I push my fingers into the loose hairs at the back of my neck. "Sorry, I should have talked to you before I said anything to the kids, but I have no idea what I'm doing. I told them you were coming over and might live with us." I press a hand to my forehead. "I don't know how to do this."

"It's fine. I told you I wasn't going to change my mind. They might as well know."

"I also talked to Cole, and he's surprisingly ok with it."

"Really?" He sounds doubtful.

"Come in. For some reason, this is more nerve-racking than it would've been introducing you to my dad." Shane steps in, not looking the least bit on edge. "Seriously, you aren't nervous?"

"How do you know I'm not nervous?" That stiff brow furrows under the clasp of his hat.

I wave my hand and close the door. I'm not telling him that before games, when the camera landed on his face, I could see he was already in play in his head. But also, like he might puke.

"Oh, wait." I grab his arm but immediately release it. His skin is hot, and I can't help but think of what it will be like sleeping next to him. My own personal furnace. I stop that train of thought right in its tracks. "Watch out for Teddy. He's our little prankster, and I have no doubt he has you in his crosshairs."

"Got it."

Ok, then. I need a little of his confidence and certainty to wash over me.

I lead Shane from the entryway, past our family room, and into the kitchen. He sets his keys and phone on the counter, and the simple gesture makes my stomach clench. What will it be like to have him come home and put his keys and phone next to mine each day? Someone else here with me being a part of our everyday chaos.

Garrett sits at the island reading. I lean down and wrap my arms around his shoulders, comforting both of us. "Garrett, this is Shane." I know this kid has some anxiety rolling around inside him.

"Hi," he says quietly.

"Hey." Shane leans over, placing his forearms on the counter. "I heard your little brother's probably got big plans for me. You want to find out what he's up to, and we'll join forces to reroute his plans?"

Garrett smiles. "Yeah. Give me a few minutes." He takes off upstairs.

"He gets anxious with change, so thanks for distracting him."

"I'm not being taken down by an eight year old," Shane grumbles.

"We'll see about that. Let's go outside until the food is done."

We step out on the patio that opens to our big yard, bordered by Aspen and Pine trees, where Cole is manning the grill while Hank shows Liv something on his phone.

"Hey, coach." Cole and Shane do some hand-slapping thing.

"Let's just go with Shane here."

"Ok. I'll try," Cole responds. "I hope you like burgers."

"Sounds good," Shane says, taking in his surroundings.

I wonder what he's thinking. This whole thing feels so awkward, and I have no idea how I'm supposed to act. It's like I've suddenly become socially inept.

"Hank, grab the football, and let's see what this old man's got," Cole orders, and I want to hug him.

"Watch it, kid, or you'll see just how old I am." Shane shoots back as Cole smirks.

Hank grabs the ball as Teddy and Garrett come running out of the house. "We want to play!"

"Garrett, you're with me," Shane says, claiming him.

Liv bounces up and down. "I want to be on your team, Shaney."

"Teddy, you're with Hank and me," Cole hollers, and Teddy throws his hands in the air like he's already scored.

"You playing?" Shane asks me like it's a dare.

I tug up my loose jeans, joining Shane, Garrett, and Liv on one side of the yard. "Somehow, I feel like I'm back in grade school and the last one standing."

Shane looks at me, his face emotionless. "Something tells me you weren't picked last."

I stare at him as he surveys the yard. I have no idea what to make of this quiet, impassive man. I know there's so much hiding inside that large, muscular body. Layers upon layers, and there's an archaeologist inside me who wants to gather all my tools and start picking away.

Shane shifts into coach mode, pulling us into a huddle. "Garrett, I need the 411 on Teddy."

"He's going with a whoopee cushion. Simple but effective. I switched it to his chair when he wasn't looking."

"That's it?" Shane is wise to be skeptical.

Garrett raises and lowers one shoulder. "As far as I know. You better watch your back."

He and Garrett pound fists as Cole yells at us to get it together.

"Maggie, you snap the ball to me and Liv. Garrett, I'll fake it to you, then you hang right and back. I'll wait for the opening."

I scoff. "I can do more than snap the ball, big guy."

"I've no doubt." He says it under his breath, and I'd like to know what the hell is going on here. *Is he flirting? I. Cannot. Tell.* Quiet Shane: Ok. This other version that's emerging: I have no idea. *Poop.*

I toss the ball to Liv and Shane, taking off, and in seconds, Garrett scores. Shane tosses Liv in the air and gives us each a high five. Hank takes the ball, and I know his competitive ass will aim for Cole, so I rush him and get in his face as Shane runs at Cole and Teddy. Shane scoops Teddy up under one arm on his way to Cole and blocks the pass.

The game continues, and the laughter and talking smack flow, which feels normal. When Cole announces the burgers are done, we head into the house, and I can tell by the way Shane is walking that his knee is sore.

I bump his shoulder. "You want some ice?"

"Nah. It's ok. It's just a little tender still."

I side-eye him. "Liar."

He grumbles, and I laugh.

We assemble our plates and take seats at the table, where I set out napkins, silverware, and bottles of water. One by one, we sit, and as expected, a loud farting sound erupts when Teddy hops up into his chair.

"Aw, man. Who found me out?" Teddy demands.

"You know what they say about snitches." I try not to laugh. "Besides, it's not nice to prank a newbie."

"It was just a little fart joke."

I roll my eyes. "Yeah, well, it's not like there isn't enough of that with you boys already."

We take our places around the table, and Liv pulls her chair closer to Shane. I smile at him as he helps her with her plate.

"Who wants to start by telling us what's up this week?" I ask.

Each Sunday, we talk about what's happening at school, which helps me understand what the schedule will look like for the week. Despite trying to stay in tune with all the school events among the kids, I can't keep up.

Garrett starts. "Science club begins this week. Wednesdays after school until 4:30."

"Ok. I got that." I make a mental note. "I'll pick you up on my way home."

"Scott's birthday party is next weekend at the ice rink," Teddy adds with a mouthful. "We're playing hockey. He's on the team, and I want you to sign me up."

"We'll see. I need to know how rough eight year olds are, but remind me to get a gift."

"How many days until my birthday?" Liv bounces in her seat.

"About a month, sweetie."

"How many days is that? Can I have a Belle party, and can Molly and Celia come? Carmen and John are, and I hope Simone is. She looks like a real princess."

One more thing to add to my never-ending list. "We'll get to work on your party soon. Ok?"

"Shaney, you have to come to my party. It's going to be so fun." Liv scoots even closer to him, invading his space.

I'm pretty sure if it were anyone else, he'd sneer.

Shane grabs his water bottle, twisting the cap to take a drink as water spews out of holes like a sprinkler. I can't help but laugh as the boys giggle. Shane glares as moisture drips down the front of him.

"Teddy, go get a towel, you little punk," I say, but like the stealth operative I am, as he turns for the kitchen, I pull a Nerf gun from under the table and nail him twice in the back.

Being Teddy, he freezes and dramatically falls to the ground like he's been shot. The whole table erupts again, and as I catch Shane's eye, I wink in an 'I got your back' kind of way.

Oh my goodness, I just winked at him, and the intensity in his eyes makes my knees go just a little bit weak.

What. Is. Going. On and what in the world am I getting myself into?

The football coach at the end of the table and I seemed to have just formed some kind of unspoken alliance.

I'm not sure I understand exactly what this alliance will entail, but my growing curiosity is eager to find out.

Chapter 10

SHANE

I sit on the large sectional in Maggie's living room with a bag of frozen corn on my knee. The Matthews work like a well-oiled machine, clearing the table and cleaning the kitchen while Liv introduces me to each of her princesses.

Every single thing about this is foreign to me. All the way from this two-story suburban home in a neighborhood lined with minivans and playhouses to the inside jokes and laughter that fill this house.

I didn't know what to expect when I pulled up, but it wasn't the understated brick home that looked like it belonged to an ordinary American family. It's not that it isn't a beautiful home. It's just that I expected Tim Matthews' children to live in something more like a fortified mansion on a hill, complete with a gate and security guard.

Stepping inside, it felt warm and inviting. The stuff scattered about. The pictures. The constant noise. It feels like a home. When you grow up without one, you notice all the little things others take for granted.

I didn't grow up with any kind of stable structure or routine. I lived each day hoping to stay under the radar and make it to the next unscathed. In the group home, that was easy. I followed the rules and did what was expected of me.

During my brief stays in foster homes, I never knew what was coming, so I tried to blend in. The more I could go unnoticed, the better. That was something I benefited from on the field. Even though I was big, I could make myself small, unnoticeable until I wasn't.

Being here, I find myself reverting to old habits, shrinking, and trying to blend in with this family. So far, maybe I'm not doing such a bad job.

I don't know anything about playing princesses, but Liv doesn't care. These boys seem to be ok with my presence, except Hank, but I think Maggie might be right when she said he and I are a lot alike. Cole seems cool. For now. I have no doubt I'll get an earful if Maggie and I go through with this.

Maggie turns on *SportsCenter's* preseason highlights and settles back into the corner of the couch, stretching her bare feet towards me. Watching her with these kids has me in awe. I have no idea how she does this. Today is only a tiny glimpse into her world, but she doesn't have a clue how extraordinary this all is.

As a young boy, my days were full of anxiety and nerves. I sometimes wonder how I survived. But upon turning eighteen and obtaining freedom, I vowed to never let myself be at the mercy of others. I won't let fear and anxiety rule my days. Although I've been in uncomfortable situations, I've always had an easy exit.

I've had gorgeous women throw themselves at me, lie down at my feet, willing to give up anything I demanded. For me, it was never hard to walk away. My heart had lost all feeling years ago. It's permanently broken. I didn't need to fill the void with anything or anyone that would only leave me emptier.

But this little spitfire has me standing on a ledge I haven't faced before. I'm finding I never know what to expect from her. She surprises me at every turn, and I'm not exactly sure what to think about that.

Teddy nestles in beside her to read out loud. I can hear his struggle and her patient reassurance as the commentators drone on about the upcoming season.

"Look at that, Mags," Cole says from a recliner on the other end of the couch that fills this large living room. "Sandberg's arm is looking smooth as butter."

My eyes focus on the large screen above the stone fireplace flanked by bookshelves filled with family pictures. Mark Sandberg is my brother, but not in conventional terms. Only a handful of people know we spent our teenage years in a group home together and played on the same high school football team. We beat the odds, and now he's a starting quarterback for one of the best teams in the NFL.

Teddy pauses his reading while Maggie studies the screen. She watches his pass to a receiver and then the replay.

"Ahh. He's fisting and flexing his hand. I don't know. That tells me there's still something going on. He'll be out this season. You can put your money on that." The camera zooms back in on Mark. "Watch. Right there," Maggie says as he throws another pass, but it's the after-effect we're all waiting for.

"Damn," Cole says.

"Cole said a bad word," Liv chimes from the floor, surrounded by crayons and markers.

Teddy grins. "You owe us a dollar, bruh."

"Sorry," Cole apologizes.

I study the screen again, and I'll be damned, I see what she's saying. *How does she do that?*

It's the most minuscule stutter, like he's either in pain or hasn't forgotten the pain that was once there. Mark hasn't mentioned his shoulder still hurting, but that's probably because I kept telling him to ease up last season before he forced himself into surgery.

Hank enters the living room dressed in workout clothes with a soccer ball tucked under his arm. "I'm going to meet some guys at the field. I'll be back before dark."

"Is your homework done?" Maggie asks.

"Yes."

"Is your phone charged?" Cole laughs.

Hank rolls his eyes.

"Is Miss Boobs going to be there?" Teddy bursts out laughing and almost falls off the couch.

I want to laugh too, but I hold it in.

"Teddy," Maggie half-heartedly scolds, but waits for Hank to answer.

"Seriously." Hank's head falls to the side, then succumbs to pressure. "No. Shelby won't be there. Just the guys."

"Ok. Home before dark," Maggie orders.

"And don't get injured before your big game this week," Cole hollers. "We're all wearing jerseys just to make him crazy, right?"

Maggie scoffs. "Uh, yeah. And I'm bringing the cowbell for the snotty parents. Plus, it'll embarrass him even more."

I interrupt their conversation. "What position does he play?"

"Forward," Maggie answers. "He plays in a travel league during the summer. He wants to head to Europe after graduation."

"When is his game?"

Maggie stares at me for a second before answering. "Next Saturday afternoon. You should come if you're free. You can give the dads something to talk about besides how Hank is only playing varsity because of his name."

"If Hank sucked, they might have a case," Garrett adds from the floor, holding some kind of circuit board that lights up and makes noise as he moves things around. "He's the only reason they have a shot at winning."

And so the afternoon goes. Cole leaves to study as the snacks on the table disappear. Liv sits next to me, playing with her dolls, while the boys pretend to blow up army men. Maggie switches and folds laundry, and I try to absorb what it'll be like to be part of this.

"Hit the showers, boys," Maggie says, returning after carrying the empty snack bowls into the kitchen. "And Teddy, if you don't scrub, you're sleeping outside with the other animals."

Teddy groans as he and Garrett head upstairs.

Maggie stops me as I start to get up. "Can you hang out for a bit?"

"Yeah, then you can read me a story." Liv pops up on her knees beside me.

Maggie smiles. "We'll see. Shane might need some space. First, you need a bath. Head into my bathroom, and I'll be there in a minute."

"Do you have time to stay until I get them in bed? If not, it's ok." Maggie's hair spills out of her short ponytail as she picks up a few toys.

"Sure." I'm surprised to find I really don't mind.

I flip channels, imagining what it'll be like to live here. After lunch, Maggie showed me the house, skipping her bedroom, which will soon be our bedroom. The thought makes my skin grow warm and tight.

The kids' rooms are on the second floor, and the furnished basement holds another TV, workout equipment, and Hank's bedroom. As I walked through the house, there were messes everywhere. A constant littering of toys, school papers, books, shoes, and socks. Every inch of this space is utilized, and it's . . . nice.

I lived in some unpleasant conditions, and now organization and structure bring me comfort. But there's something about the mess that feels warm and safe. You know life is being lived, and memories are being made.

In a matter of minutes, Liv skips back into the room, grabs my hand, and tugs me up to her room to read her a story. No matter how far out of my comfort zone it might be, I find myself sitting on a little pink bed beside a tiny girl reading about a baby bird who's looking for its mom.

"See, Shaney, the momma bird is waiting for her baby. I wonder if my momma is waiting for me. Maggie says I can't look for her. I need to stay here."

I hear the sadness in her voice, and I instantly want to protect her from everything bad in the world.

"You have a really nice family, and you're safe and surrounded by people who love you. You should definitely stay here where you're loved and protected."

She rests her head on my shoulder, and something inside my chest warms.

"Will you come live with us? I like it when you're here."

How is it that I'd do pretty much anything for this tiny child?

"I need to talk to Maggie about that, but if I do, you'll be the first to know."

"Really?" She squeezes my arm with both hands.

"Yes. Now, is it time for you to go to sleep?" And like she knew I'd need help, Maggie appears in the doorway.

"Ok, missy. Time for bed." Maggie leans over and brushes Liv's hair out of her face to kiss her cheek. "Only the good dreams. Tell the bad ones that princesses kick serious butt." Liv giggles, and Maggie turns off her light.

"Fifteen minutes, boys. Then lights out," Maggie commands as we pass by their room.

They holler goodnight, and we head back downstairs. In the living room, I rest back on the couch.

"You want a beer?" Maggie asks before taking a seat.

"Only if you're having one." She raises an eyebrow as if that were a ridiculous statement.

She brings back two bottles and settles on the couch beside me. "Are you ready to run for the hills?" She sits facing me, her leg bent and arm on the back of the couch.

"You look tired. I don't know how you manage to do all this by yourself. I'm tired, and I didn't do anything but eat and watch TV."

"I'm used to it, I guess. But yes, I'm exhausted." She picks at the couch cushion, and I can see she wants to say something.

"What's wrong?"

"I just want to be sure you know what you're agreeing to. Today was smooth, but many days it's not, and by the time I reach this point in the day, I have nothing left. I take a long shower and crawl in bed only to do it all again the next day."

She uses her free hand to tug the hem of her shirt down. "Shane, you have a choice. You told me you like your simple life, and I can tell you we're anything but that. You're single and well-known, and incredibly talented. You can do anything, have anyone. I guess . . . " She starts, then pauses. "I'm worried a month into this, you'll find yourself wishing you could go back or, worse, resent me as if I wasn't honest about what this is really like."

Maggie looks defeated, like she has nothing left but to hope I'll tell her something to convince her I'm in for the long haul. I honestly don't know how anyone wouldn't want to help her.

I'm not an idiot, and I'm not naive. I have no freaking clue what to do with a wife and kids or how it will be. But I think about Liv and what she said about her mom and wanting me here. Teddy's uncontrollable laughter as water ran down the front of me. Garrett's anxiety, and his slight smile as he bumped my fist. Now, Maggie, admitting she has nothing left at the end of the day.

I've seen how much they care for each other, and the love and bonds are so evident. What kind of man would I be if I didn't help ensure these kids remain with her?

My mom couldn't keep me. She couldn't care for me and thought she was giving me a better chance at life than I would've had with her. Given what I know, that's probably true.

From what Maggie has told me, the kids' mom is gone for good, and letting anyone take them from her isn't something I can let happen. Giving up my freedom to come and go as I please and leaving my solitude behind seems like a small sacrifice to make sure four kids have the best chance in this world. A chance to be loved and a family. I can give them something I never had.

"Maggie, I have no idea what this will be like. It'll all be completely new to me, but I'm not backing out. You all need to stay together. That's clear to me."

She rests her head on the couch. "This will be so weird. You do realize we'll be husband and wife. Legally bound together."

I take a sip of my beer. "Yeah, about that. I haven't said anything to anyone about this. I'll have to tell my agent, and he'll want to publicize it before it's leaked. Good press so to speak."

"Great. I guess we'll make the news along with my dad's passing. His agent called me. Rumors are circulating, but nothing has been confirmed yet." She pauses and pushes out a breath. "So, in public, we'll have to seem like newlyweds?"

"Yeah, especially if we want everyone, including your aunt and uncle, to think this is real. Actually, the press might help in that case. When do you want to do this?" If we're going to do it, I'd rather not wait. "The season starts in a few weeks. We should do it before then, so I can move my stuff. Plus, I have no doubt my agent will have reporters at the first game, and they'll be asking questions."

"Ok. The sooner, the better. When news breaks about my dad, it will seem like we've had this planned for a while. Hopefully, Cliff and Joan will think the same. Maybe we can go to the courthouse this week. I want the kids to be there, so I'll see if I can pull them out of school for a bit." She rubs her face. "Is this totally insane?"

I take a sip of my beer. "Yeah."

She hits my arm. "You're supposed to make me feel better. Tell me this is all going to be ok."

"Will that be one of my responsibilities? Lie to make you feel better." I meet her eyes.

She pulls a Nerf gun off the floor, and I try to block her shot. "Actually, yes, *husband.* That's going to be part of your role. When my day sucks, and everything falls apart, and I'm scared out of my mind, you're going to try to make me feel better."

"That so." Like I have a clue how to make someone feel better. *Shit. I'm going to need a manual.*

"Well, I guess we'll see. You'll likely be terrible at that. It's hard to make someone feel better with all that scowl and grumbling, you big grizzly bear." She laughs, and I let my head fall to the back of the couch.

"As long as I get to make my own list of responsibilities, wife." That is a word I never thought I'd use in relation to myself.

Shit. Yet, looking at Maggie and seeing just a hint of a blush, maybe it won't be so bad. Good thing I'm an empty man, heartless, because if not, it's quite possible I could find myself in trouble with this woman.

"Hold on. Wait. Wait, just a fucking second? Did you say you're getting married? To. The Rocket's. Daughter?" Mark asks the last part with distinct clarity, as if it were a detonating code.

"Dude. Did I even know he had a daughter?" Sean wonders out loud.

I've been dreading this call to my brothers from abandoning mothers. Not because these morons wouldn't be the first guys I'd tell, it's just I know I'll never hear the end of it.

They know I've had no intention of getting married. Ever. So calling to break the news after living in Colorado for a month is sure to blow their minds.

"I'd like to hear how the conversation went when you told The Rocket you'll be shacking up with his daughter." Mark's cocky ass thinks he's funny.

I pull into the driveway of the house I just moved into and will be moving out of in a matter of days.

Before I left Maggie's tonight, I told her I needed to call these two idiots about us getting married. She said I could tell them about her dad as long as I trusted them. As ridiculous as they are, I trust them with my life.

When I told her that one of them was Mark Sandberg, the stereotypical NFL playboy, she looked at me blankly for about five seconds, then smacked my arm for not saying anything when she and Cole were talking about him. She then made me promise to keep quiet about her unqualified observation.

"I won't be discussing this with Tim." I pause. "He died a few weeks ago." Silence takes over the line. "And there are young kids involved, so you two need to keep your mouths shut even when this hits the feed."

"Damn," Sean says, like his mind is blown. "The Rocket. He was a legend. He's the reason we all made it."

The three of us spent Sundays watching Tim call plays and make passes we could only dream of attempting to emulate one day. By some miracle and despite our circumstances, the three of us were able to attend his camp.

We spent the summer learning from the man we watched replay after replay of and tried to mimic. He worked with us and encouraged us. He made us believe we could actually make it if we gave it everything we had, and we did. His confidence gave three young men with no hope or real possibility a chance in a world that told us we'd never amount to anything.

From that point on, we worked day and night. Football was everything, and somehow we made the high school team, which led to us playing college ball.

"Is that what this is about? Are you doing her some kind of legal favor?" Mark's skepticism is evident.

"I'm not discussing that. It's between Maggie and me."

"The kids," Sean states, and it's as if I can hear a light bulb go on. "Is this about the letter?"

They are the only two people besides my social worker when I was five, who know about the letter. Given that we have no parents or family, I let them read the letter one summer when I was trying for the millionth time to understand. We haven't talked about it since. Part of me is surprised Sean even remembers, but he's definitely the most perceptive of us.

"I'm not talking about that either," I say, closing the subject.

The line is silent as I close the garage door and enter my empty house.

"At least tell us she's hot?"

I don't respond, knowing Mark's only half joking.

"Wait. Wait. Wait. Oh man, she's a smoke show."

My body temperature rises, wondering what in the hell he's talking about.

"Sean, Google her, dude." He pauses, and I know he's scrolling now.

It hadn't occurred to me to internet stalk her in return. I put them on speaker so I can see what they're seeing.

"She's a dancer? Come on." Mark might be drooling, and I want to smack him.

I assume that's a rhetorical question, as I start scrolling through old pictures of her and Cole with their dad. Then I land on some of her in New York in costume.

Sean laughs. "No way. It looks like she dated Danny Zebo."

"Who's that?" I snap without thinking about my tone.

Sean clearly finds all this amusing. "Man, you seriously live under a rock. He's one of the best hip-hop dancers out there. He's all over social media. I've seen him at some event. I bet there are pics of them together. I have to see this."

"Well, whether this thing is legit or not, you definitely could have done worse. I'd be a happy man sleeping in her bed at night."

"Mark," I warn, and he laughs.

"You sure this is strictly business? You sound a little territorial." He's laughing, and I wish I could reach through the phone and poke his eyes out.

"You know I wouldn't be getting married otherwise. I can help, and these kids need it." It suddenly feels like it's a thousand degrees in here, and I peel my shirt off, rolling my neck, to try to relieve the building tension.

"Look, I just want you to be happy. You've had a rough year. I can't wait to come out and meet her, so make room. Bye week is all yours this year, buddy," Mark says.

"Count me in," Sean agrees.

"Great," I grumble.

"Come on. We have to see you in husband mode if this is our only chance." Mark jabs.

I'm done talking about this, so I punch back. "Hey, how's your shoulder?"

Mark clears his throat. "It's feeling good. I'm ready to get the season going."

"It's completely healed and pain-free?" I try to clarify. "If not, you need to take it easy so you don't end up like me."

"It's good, man," he insists, with just a hint of bite.

We discuss the upcoming season before we hang up, but I remain on the couch scrolling through pictures of Maggie until I land on one of her beside Danny Z.

It must have been taken at a show opening. Danny's arm is wrapped tightly around her, holding her close. Her hand rests on his chest, eyes bright, and a blinding smile. It's definitely more than a friendly pose, and I'm surprised to find I don't particularly care for it, especially his fingers pressing against a sliver of her bare stomach.

I toss my phone on the couch, trying to get the picture of Mr. Dancing Machine's fingers on Maggie's skin out of my head. I'm just marrying her, I remind myself. That's all this will be. Just Paperwork.

But, I'm suddenly in a piss-poor mood and feel like punching something.

I need to sweat it out, so I head back to the garage and grab some weights. I turn on music and get to work, trying to clear my mind.

I push hard, just as I've always done, when I'm agitated. I have to remain unattached and unaffected.

But these annoying feelings, disturbing my usual calm, quiet state, can take a hike straight to hell.

There's just the little thing that by the end of the week, the little spitfire will be my wife.

Chapter 11

MAGGIE

"You're sure you want to do this? We can leave right now and figure something else out." Cole squats in front of me, and he looks so much like Dad that it almost brings tears to my eyes.

This isn't how I'd pictured it. Throughout my life, I've always envisioned my wedding day as one of the happiest days of my life. It was supposed to be my dad walking me down the aisle toward a man who'd look at me like I was his whole world.

I have neither of those things today, and I feel like some part of me is breaking. I'd accepted long ago that my dreams of being a prima ballerina were over, and it was a difficult loss. It took me a long time to accept my dancing career was on a different trajectory than I'd imagined. But I've found fulfillment in teaching and working with students.

But this, this is different. Saying vows, promising my life to a man, one whom I'm supposed to love, honor, and cherish, forsaking all others. This isn't how it's supposed to be.

Shane stands with the kids, Coach Cavanaugh, and Clara. I see a man who I believe will hold up his end of this deal. But for me, this is a sacrifice that's so much bigger than walking away from my dream of being a professional ballerina.

I want friendship, companionship, and undying love. I want my dad here to give him "the talk" about never hurting me and to hug me and give me away to a man he trusts will love me beyond. I want my mom to smooth my dress, kiss my cheek, and light a fire under everyone's asses to make sure this day is perfect.

But there's none of it. No parents. No church. No . . . love. This is it. This is how it will be, and the four kids standing in the hall are worth it.

I offer Cole a small smile. "I'm good."

"You sure?" He searches for confirmation.

I place a hand on his shoulder and give it a gentle squeeze. "Yeah."

"Hey, lady. It's about time. Let's get you ready." Simone grabs my hand and pulls me to my feet. My stomach rolls into a knot, and as much as I want to run, I won't. "All set?" Her perfectly shaped eyebrows tip in, and I ignore her concern as Carmen joins us.

"You look beautiful." Carmen wraps an arm around me.

I glance at Shane again, and his gaze meets mine. He looks so handsome in a charcoal gray suit, crisp white shirt, and lavender tie, which makes his eyes appear more mossy green.

"I need a minute with Shane." I'm already in motion.

"Ok. We'll round up the kids." I hear Carmen say softly.

I move swiftly to Shane's side, not missing his furrowed brow as I pull him toward a short, dark hallway that houses the janitorial closet. I face him, and his eyebrows are so close together they almost form a unibrow.

"Are you ok?" His large hand lands on my shoulder, and I have no idea why he isn't completely freaked out by what we are about to do. "Tell me what's wrong."

I can only stare at him as if somehow I'll be able to make sense of why he's agreed to this and why he's so calm. "How can you be so sure? We're about to go in there and commit our lives to one another. Like, we have to promise forever, just you and me. No one else."

My stomach pinches tight again as a fresh wave of panic swirls through me. "You never wanted to get married, but don't you think someday a woman might come along who makes you change your mind? I mean, there are millions and millions of women out there. After this, you'll be stuck with me, and maybe it won't be forever, but . . . Don't you want the chance to find that person you absolutely cannot live without? The one who makes you smile just thinking about her. The one who would throw down in a heartbeat if someone messes with any part of you."

I try to inhale, but my windpipe narrows to the diameter of a straw. "My parents had that, so I know it exists." My voice cracks. *Shit.* "I'm sorry. I'm completely freaking out. This . . . This is just not how I envisioned—"

"Hey." Shane's large hand wraps around mine, and he waits for me to look at him. "It's all going to be ok. Like you said, it's just you and me. We get to decide how this goes. Nobody else."

I see the solidity of him. The strength, I have no doubt, got him through some really tough times. Times, I'm sure I couldn't even begin to understand. His courage seeps into me as he stares into my eyes.

Despite my sweaty palm, his big, warm hand holds mine a little tighter.

"We're in this together. Ok? You don't have to do this by yourself anymore." His eyes stay on mine, and I have no idea where this giant sensitive man has come from, but I believe him.

I take a slow, deep breath. "Ok. You and me. We got this."

I think I almost see a smirk before he lets go of my hand, and the belt around my chest loosens.

"Guys, you're almost up." Carmen's voice startles me from around the corner.

Shane moves, but I tug him back. "Wait. Kiss me."

"What?"

"Kiss me. Just do it quick. We can't go in there and have pictures snapped of us kissing, looking all awkward and weird like we've never actually kissed before . . . which we haven't. It can't look like that." My nerves dissipate further with his blank stare. "Come on."

I move into him, and now he looks like the one needing a pep talk. I laugh. Like really laugh, where my stomach starts to hurt in a good way, and his frown returns.

"Why do you all of a sudden look nervous?" I smile, feeling so much better than I did a minute ago. "It won't be that bad, really. I brushed my teeth and everything this morning."

His eyes are set on my mouth, unmoving, that deep crease between his brows more visible than I've ever seen it.

"Oh, good grief." I grab his lapels, hauling myself up because even in heels, I have to push to my tiptoes to gently press my lips against his. They're warm and soft, and I feel the slight scruff of his face on mine, which I find I like a lot more than I should.

Shane's hand slides to my lower back. His fingertips press into me, holding me there for just a second before I pull back, but not quite letting him go. His frown is gone, but his eyes flick between mine and show something I've not seen before. It's the first time in this whole thing I've seen something that might look just a little bit like . . . fear.

"Just you and me, right?" I ask, letting myself fall back to my heels.

"Right," he whispers.

"All right then, Grizz. Let's do this." I tug on his arm, so we can find the kids and say, 'I do.'

Chapter 12

SHANE

I unlock my office door, tossing my clipboard on my desk, and it clatters. Kicking one of my players off the field was not what I had planned for practice today. I realize dealing with a loud-mouth teammate looking for a fight is way less complicated than handling a disrespectful, highly talented player with a giant chip on his shoulder.

I grab my keys more forcefully than necessary, still simmering with frustration, and stretch my tight jaw. I have one last load to pick up at my rental before heading to Maggie's, which will give my irritation time to settle down.

After our morning at the courthouse, I moved most of my things while she took the kids to school and then came to campus to teach.

Our drive-thru ceremony was brief and to the point. I was ready. It was game time.

Everything was fine until Maggie pulled me into that damn hallway and peeled away my calm resolve in one swift tug. She stood there in her light blue dress, vibrating with nerves. I didn't understand why until she let loose. It wasn't difficult to remind her that I was in this with her until she demanded I kiss her. Then, her beautiful complex ass laughed. She freaking laughed at me.

She bent at the waist and wheezed as if my hesitation was the funniest thing she'd ever seen. I was prepared to kiss her once we were pronounced man and wife. A quick peck and life would go on. There was no need to sweat it.

I was not prepared for her to demand I kiss her in the dark, isolated hallway. I needed witnesses. An audience. Protection.

But when those honest blue eyes stared up at me, a tiny spark of fire ignited as she waited, and suddenly, I was terrified to know what it was like to kiss her. To feel her body, her lips, against mine. When I couldn't react, she hoisted herself up and took charge.

I stood there, frozen in place, letting her press her lips to mine sweetly and gently like we'd done it a thousand times. Instead of focusing on the feel of her soft lips, how amazing she smelled, or the fact that I wanted to hold her there just a little longer, I forced myself to remain calm, stiff . . . placid.

Our kiss in front of our witnesses was just as brief and innocent, but it felt far less intimate than the one we'd shared only minutes before.

After slipping the sapphire ring on her slender finger and vowing to love her until death do us part, something shifted in that space where my heart should be, and suddenly, kissing her seemed like it should be the least of my worries.

I shove my spreadsheets into a folder and restart my computer as Cole appears in my doorway.

"Hey, coach."

I've been anticipating this conversation, but now isn't the best time. My jaw clenches again, bracing for his interrogation and threats. "What's up?"

"Sorry about what happened out there. I don't know Nick well, but I can talk to him if that'd help."

"I appreciate it, but I'll handle it once he cools off." *And I cool off.*

He peers down at his tennis shoes, which only confirms he didn't come by to talk about Nick.

"I just wanted to thank you for what you're doing."

Of all things, I wasn't expecting him to thank me, so I shut my trap, waiting for what might come next.

He leans against the door frame. "I'm not sure what's in it for you or why you're doing this, but . . . just don't hurt them. Maggie's been doing this alone for a long time, and with me leaving next year, I'm glad she'll have someone. I worry about her. She's given up everything and has survived some tough times, so be good to her."

I want to ask what he means by that, but I refrain. For now.

"When the news of my dad's death hits, it's going to be more than Cliff and Joan coming after them. Please . . . look out for them."

"I will," I say, meaning it.

Cole looks at me, really looks at me, and I see the man he's becoming. "I believe you."

Something about those three words is like a punch to the chest.

I made a commitment today, one I intend to uphold, but for the first time, I realize that this is so much bigger than just myself.

It's a strange feeling. I have people counting on me. Five people who need me after spending my life completely alone. I have no idea how to do it, but I'll do what I've always done, try really hard, and hope I can fumble my way through and not screw it all up.

I park my truck in the garage as instructed and open the door to a three-ring circus.

Liv races through the kitchen, twirling in a glittery princess dress with something red smeared across her mouth. Dirty dishes are piled in the sink while Maggie is hunched over the island beside Garrett, building some kind of contraption with toothpicks and marshmallows.

Teddy slides in wearing a gi and swinging his arms into a karate chop. "Hi-yah!"

The toothpick structure crumbles and crashes to the floor. Maggie groans and puts her head in her hands. After a moment, her head pops up like she's recovered.

"Oh hey. There's spaghetti on the stove if you want some. I have to run Teddy to karate, and then we'll be back. Make yourself at home." She spreads her arms wide, her lips curling upward with an apologetic smile.

She turns to Garrett, resting her hands on his shoulders. "Bud, we'll get this to work. Let's take Teddy, and on the way, we'll see if we can figure out what we're doing wrong. Ok?"

Garrett nods, his shoulders slumped with frustration.

"Liv, we gotta go! Get your shoes on. Any shoes, princess," Maggie hollers as she tries to quickly clean up the sticky mess.

I set my keys down, and survey the kitchen again. "I can take Teddy if you tell me where to go."

Maggie stands with a handful of marshmallows and tiny sticks. "Are you sure? I have to pick him up. They won't let him leave with anyone but Cole or me."

"Yeah. Then you can help Garrett with . . . whatever that is." I point to the sticky mess cupped in her hands.

She rubs her neck with one hand. "Wait. Do you know anything about building a bridge?" She looks around to make sure Garrett isn't in the room. "I'm about to lose my ever-loving mind. I was never good at this kind of stuff, and he's so discouraged."

I majored in architectural design, but no one knows that. "You go, and I'll see what I can do if he can give me instruction."

"He can explain it much better than I can." Maggie rubs a hand over her face. "Ok. Hank should be home soon, and he'll find the food. Are you sure about this?" Her brow scrunches, and she bites her lip.

"Yes. Go." I nod towards the door. "Oh, and you should make sure I'm on the list to pick the kids up and whatever else there is."

Maggie stares at me for a long second before she nods, grabs her purse, and heads to the garage.

Garrett returns to the now silent room and me.

I point to the pile of toothpicks. "Come on, partner. Tell me what you're trying to do here."

We both sit down at the island, and he grabs a piece of paper, pushing his glasses up his nose.

"We're supposed to build a bridge with just toothpicks and marshmallows. It's for the science club. They'll measure to see whose can hold the most weight. It's due Monday, but I don't want to wait, especially seeing that we can't even get one to hold together."

I take the paper from him, reading the rules and requirements. "How often do you have these kinds of assignments?"

"Once a month. Usually, I can do most of it myself. Maggie tries to help, but . . . she's not very good at it," he says quietly like he doesn't want to offend her even though she's not here.

"Ok, well, let's get to work and see what we can do." I find my glasses and then hold out my fist.

He bumps it with a small smile.

An hour later, I take another bite of spaghetti as we sit back, examining our standing structure that holds the weight of four Hot Wheels.

"What do you think?" I ask.

"Do you think it would hold more if we put more reinforcements underneath?" His tone is much brighter than when we started.

"Let the marshmallows dry out and harden, then see if you can add more cars."

"Ok. I'll wait until tomorrow." Garrett takes the cookie sheet holding our bridge to his room, and I hear the garage door open. Seconds later, Teddy and Liv race through the door with Maggie trailing behind.

I rinse my dish and put it in the dishwasher, where I placed the sink full once Garrett got going on his bridge.

"How'd it go?" Maggie asks from behind me. I glance at her over my shoulder, realizing that in a matter of minutes, I'll have to try to sleep next to her.

I clear my throat, drying my hands, and turning toward her. "Good. We have a standing structure that I think he's happy with. He's a smart kid."

She stands perfectly still, staring at me. "Um . . . what are those?" she points to my face.

I know she's referring to my glasses, but there's no way I'm giving in. "What?"

"Um, those things on your face."

"Glasses."

"Good grief," she mumbles under her breath.

"What? I wear glasses." I have no idea what her deal is.

She shakes her head, setting down her purse and keys. "Anyway, if you were able to get something to stand, he's not the only smart one . . . Clark Kent." She turns to get a glass of water before spinning back. "Do you have to step into a phone booth to put those on?"

I roll my eyes and pull my glasses off.

She laughs. "Is Hank home?"

"Yeah. He grabbed food and went to his room. I hope that's ok."

She sighs, leaning against the counter. "Yeah. I'm cutting him a little slack. His first game is tomorrow. Some of the guys on the team have been giving him a hard time because he's starting, and they're not. Plus, he gets nervous before games even though he'll outrun and out-score all of them."

"What time is his game?" I'm curious to see what this kid can do.

"Two o'clock."

"I can meet you there after practice," I say, like this isn't completely foreign territory to me. I've gone from spending my nights alone to science club experiments and soccer games.

"Ok." She takes a sip of water. "How's practice going?"

"I kicked one of my best players off the field today. He can't keep his mouth shut and has a massive chip on his shoulder."

"Sounds fun. I made a girl cry once. Guess I was pushing a little too hard." She smiles softly. "I have a feeling you'll do just fine in this new gig."

Silence lingers between us, and she pushes away from the counter.

"I've got to get them through showers, and then I'm going to bed. I know this is weird, but just do whatever you normally do."

Weird? This is unprecedented.

"I'm going to work out." I hope to wear myself the hell out, so I fall into bed like a dead man.

"Ok." Her eyes roam over the kitchen from the doorway. "Hey, thanks for helping Garrett and cleaning up the mess."

She leaves, and I stand there like a dumbass in an unknown environment. I can't even think about going to bed. Sharing a bed with her will be . . . different. Mainly her tiny, very feminine body lying next to mine. I've tried not to think about all the ways in which this could be challenging, but it's imminent, and I need to get my shit together.

I shove my earbuds in and descend the stairs, trying desperately to ignore thoughts about Maggie and me. In bed. Together.

I push hard for an hour, then stop in the kitchen to refill my water bottle. The house is quiet, and I just need to get this first night over with. I need to grow a pair and sleep next to my wife.

I've slept with women before, not a lot of women, and maybe not all night, but it's no big deal. Just like Maggie said on our one and only date, we're both adults, and we're going to sleep in the same bed.

No touching. She'll be on her side, and I'll be on mine.

The problem is sleeping with Maggie feels . . . different. It's different in a way I've not experienced before, like we should've had way more dates and kissing before I'm allowed in her bed.

I walk down the hall to find the door open. Maggie is propped up in bed, scrolling her phone with the quiet whispers of *SportsCenter* in the background. Her oversized T-shirt falls off her shoulder, her hair is pulled back, and she looks tranquil and relaxed. *Shit.*

I inhale through my nose, slowly readying myself. Her clean vanilla scent mixed with mint fills the air, and it's calming. I force my feet forward to my designated dresser and pull out a pair of shorts and a T-shirt.

"Did I make enough room for all of your stuff?" Her question is casual, like we've known each other for years.

"Yeah. Thanks."

"You don't need to thank me. It's weird seeing all your things in the bathroom. I'm sorry I didn't get a chance to clean it." She puts her phone down. "Just so you know. I'm kind of a slob. I'll try to do better, but I think this is the first time in my life I haven't had dirty clothes and piles everywhere."

"It'll be fine." I try to convince myself of just that as I head into the bathroom to shower.

Fifteen minutes later, I crack the door to find Maggie in the same spot in her massive bed. *Dammit. Why isn't she sleeping?*

She pats the empty side of the bed. "Come on, big guy. Once you lie down on this baby, you'll never want to sleep anywhere else."

How is she so calm? She's as cool as a cucumber, while my nerves eat away at my insides like Jaws having a snack.

As a kid, I had a lot of first nights in new beds. Playing football meant traveling to different cities and staying in hotel rooms. Nothing about sleeping in a new place is foreign to me, but this is not the same. This is sharing a room and a bed with a beautiful woman who, today, became my wife. This shit is going to take just a bit of time to get used to.

I sit next to her and stretch out my legs and neck, turning my attention to the TV. "You always watch this at night?" I wonder if she turned it on for me.

She shrugs. "I find it relaxing, but you can change it. I'm trying to figure out what to get Liv for her birthday. It's in a few weeks, and she doesn't need any more princesses."

"When's her birthday?"

"September nineteenth. I checked the schedule. I don't think you'll be away that weekend. We usually have a small party with a few friends. If you're not here, Shaney, it'll break her heart."

She bumps my shoulder as if we're buds, and this isn't incredibly awkward. I have no idea how she's acting like we do this every night.

"I'm pretty sure those big blue eyes don't get told no often."

Maggie laughs. "She's cute, sweet, and the baby. We don't have a chance, and she knows it. I have no doubt she'll be quite the firecracker when she gets a little older."

I exhale, crossing one ankle over the other, as my tense muscles begin to relax. "I bet your dad thought the same thing about you," I say, not thinking, and immediately wish I hadn't.

Shit. Maggie hasn't said much about her dad, but I know she still has to be grieving.

After a long pause and my body freezing back up, she speaks, and I don't miss her change in subject.

"Do you think this is what it felt like to be a ship bride?"

"A what?" I hear just a hint of uneasiness in her voice, and it settles some of my edgy nerves.

"You know, the English women who walked off a ship and were instantly married. They spent all that time on the ships in awful conditions, then went straight to some strange man's home and bed. Maybe, in our case, you're the ship husband." She laughs.

I think again about all the nights I found myself in a strange new bed. I'm surprised this one feels the most comforting and inviting and, for the first time, less lonely.

"I bet those women didn't find themselves lying in a big mess of fluff."

Maggie smiles. "It's the best, right?"

"Eh. It's ok."

She swats my arm, and somehow she's put me at ease about this whole thing.

"You better now, Grizz?"

I glance at her.

"You looked like you might puke there for a second." She giggles, and I bump her side, making her laugh more.

As much as I don't want it to, it warms my cold, tense insides.

"You're like a little firefly. You flit around, then something strikes, and you light up with all that sass."

"Well, this would be no fun at all if I were boring. No way are we going to be one of those awful coexisting couples." She pats my arms. "Don't worry. It'll be my pleasure to keep you on your toes."

Shit. I'm already aware she knows exactly how to do that.

Chapter 13

MAGGIE

Did something just hit me in the forehead?

"Ow. What?" I whine.

"Maggie. What is all that?" I hear a muffled, gruff voice, but ignore it.

"Stop." I snuggle in closer to the warm, large body that smells like a dreamy walk in the woods.

The body shifts, and it shoots me awake.

"Maggie. Please make whatever it is stop," Shane's low, growly voice demands.

I sit up straight. Thanks to the blackout shades, I can't see his face, and he can't see mine. I reach over, smacking each alarm clock and my phone to turn them off.

The room falls silent, and I flop back on the bed in complete mortification.

"Maggie." Shane's sleepy morning voice breaks through the blackness, making me want to smile.

"Yeah?" I pray he didn't notice my body tucked fully next to his. I pull the covers over my face as if he can see my embarrassment, and hope I didn't put my legs or arms over him.

"That can't happen again."

"Ok." My face lights on fire. "I'm sorry."

"Only one alarm. I will push you out of bed. I don't know how many just went off, but I'm sure the space station heard all that."

I breathe with relief that maybe he didn't notice my little intrusion into his space *and* person. "I should've told you I sleep like the dead. It takes a lot to wake me up."

"Clearly." I sense amusement in his tone, and I like it.

I groan, sitting up. Warm. He's so warm, which will make getting up even harder, and it was pure torture before. I sit for a minute, willing myself not to look in his direction even though I can't see him.

A vision of him standing in the kitchen with those glasses flashes in front of me. Holy moly, people. How can a gorgeous man slip on a pair of horn-rimmed glasses and suddenly turn even hotter? He seriously looked like a larger, less pretty boy version of Superman.

I rub my face. I have to get up and quit thinking about my new, super sexy husband.

I throw a hand over my mouth before laughing hysterically. *Am I dreaming? Is this real? Someone needs to smack me. How did this become my life?*

"Maggie, do I need to literally push you?" Shane's gruff voice breaks through my insanity.

I climb down, trying to feel my way through the darkness. My toe meets the leg of the bed. "Ow. Shit." I stumble forward into the bathroom door, hitting my head on the frame. "Shit. Owwww."

"Are you ok?" Shane sounds closer like he's sitting up.

"No," I grumble. "All my piles are gone, and now I'm walking blind."

I hear his low chuckle, and I glare, rubbing my head although he can't see it. "It's not funny," I mumble, closing the bathroom door.

I shower quickly, realizing I didn't bring clothes with me.

Great. Just great.

I wrap the towel around me and open the door to a bright room. Shane is sitting on the edge of the bed, pulling a shirt over his head. I stand attempting to pretend I didn't just see all the fabulous muscles now hidden under the soft white fabric that I'm pretty sure I felt up while sleeping. *Dammit.*

Shane stares back, and his eyes trace down my bare legs before moving back up.

Ok, then.

I grab panties and a bra from my dresser before darting into the closet and closing the door. I'm not bashful about my body. I wear leotards and tights, but something about Shane seeing me like this feels vulnerable.

I quickly throw on jeans and a shirt, knowing I need a hot cup of coffee and a dose of confidence to face Shane and all his manliness.

I exit the closet, happy to find he's left the room. After drying my hair and putting on a hint of makeup, I drag myself to the coffee pot.

Shane sits at the island with his phone in his hand and a scowl on his face. He sets his phone down as I turn around with a steaming cup of coffee.

"What's up today?" he asks.

"Teddy and I need to get a gift for a birthday party, and I'm dropping him off before Hank's game this afternoon. Then grocery pick up and home for dinner." I cross the kitchen to grab the list from the refrigerator and hand it to him. "Anything you want from the store, just add it, and I'll order it."

He looks at the two-page list, probably wondering if it's possible we go through this much food in a week.

"You don't have to buy my groceries."

"There's no reason for us both to go to the store. If you don't mind eating whatever we're having, write down whatever else you want."

He looks at me with those intense eyes. "Ok. I can drop Hank off on my way to practice if that helps. I should be done in time to make it to his game."

"Great." I hold a finger up. "Oh, hold on."

In the laundry room, I find the bag that holds the jerseys I had made for Hank's game and return to the kitchen.

"Here. I got you a jersey just in case you want to wear it. It's a soccer jersey, so it can't be too unbearable to wear someone else's name and number." I smile at him. "Don't feel obligated. We go all out when it comes to cheering each other on."

"Thanks." He looks at the blue jersey with the number five and 'Matthews' written across the back. "I need to call my agent today and tell him about us."

Us. That's going to take some getting used to.

"Ok. I should call my dad's agent and give him a heads-up. Maybe they should coordinate. I'm certain when news of us getting married hits the stream, questions about my dad are going to fly."

"Sure. If you give me his number, I'll pass it on. I have no doubt Rob will have the press poised and ready for pictures and an interview after the home opener next weekend. Will you be able to be there?"

"Of course." *Did he think we wouldn't be there?*

I take a sip of coffee and hear my ring clink against the mug, which reminds me I didn't think to get Shane a ring.

"I'm sorry I didn't get you a ring," I blurt out the thing that's on my mind. "Honestly, I didn't think about it, but I'll get one and—"

"It's fine."

I search his face. *Is it fine?*

Before I can ask, Liv stumbles into the kitchen, still half asleep, her hair a mess, and her bunny clutched to her chest. She makes a beeline for Shane and pushes her way up into his lap, curling into his large chest.

I almost burst out laughing at Shane, looking like a deer in headlights.

"We Matthews aren't morning people, well, besides Teddy. Though I'm not convinced he ever sleeps." I watch as he leans back in the chair to help Liv get comfortable, then begin my morning tasks.

"Are you all snugglers?" The big man mumbles it under his breath, knowing I'll hear him.

Crap! He caught me. But then, I realize the giant shit is playing with me. He should know by now that I'll definitely play this game.

I whip around to look at him. He sits there with his phone in one hand and his other arm supporting Liv, as nonchalant as ever.

Because I am who I am and can't help it, I lean over, resting my elbows on the island with my coffee between my hands. "I have a distinct feeling that you, Shane Carter, are a closet cuddler. It goes right along with that grizzly bear personality. All big, tough, and broody on the outside. But sweet and gentle and snuggly on the inside."

He groans, and a grin creeps across my face.

I get to work pulling things from the fridge and cabinets to marinate chicken for dinner, knowing we'll likely end up with Cole and Hank's friends for dinner.

We made it through our first day and night as man and wife. Things are just getting started. I turn around to see Shane wrap one of his big arms around Liv to ensure she's secure on his lap as he returns to his phone. I have no doubt the man I married will be full of surprises. I just hope only the good kind.

I pull into the high school parking lot after a stop at Target and dropping Teddy off at the birthday party. Shane's "It's fine" comment this morning about a ring has stuck with me. I'm not sure if it was the way he said it, like there was a slight hint of disappointment, or if I'm reading too much into it. Or maybe it's just my guilt that I didn't think to get him one in the first place.

I take a deep breath and push it out. I won't be making this into something it's not. Been there, done that, and walked away with a shattered heart. I have no intention of going there again, and I have a feeling it'd be really easy to fall for Shane. All that gruff swagger and mysteriousness. His calm, quiet confidence. The softness I know lies underneath. The man seriously seems to have no clue what we ladies see, and why does that have to make him all the more appealing?

I think about his big, warm body and how good he smells. The way he looked at me in my towel.

Stop. Just stop it.

I have no doubt our lives are about to blow up after the news about our nuptials and my dad's death hits the media. I need to be focused on getting the kids through that and be on my game for the phone calls I'm certain are coming. Not daydreaming about my husband.

As I reach for my bag, the sunlight catches my ring. I stare at the beautiful, ornate sapphire surrounded by tiny diamonds. I'm not sure how Shane picked it, but it's absolutely gorgeous and completely perfect.

I, for one, am happy to wear it today as I gather my things and head to the soccer field. Hank's assistant coach hasn't quite gotten the hint that I'm not interested, despite my repeated rejections. He's arrogant, has a bit of a slimeball aura about him, and isn't interested in anything other than a good time.

Now, I don't have to make excuses. Hopefully, with a flash of the ring, he'll move on.

I grunt, lifting my large bag filled with drinks and snacks for Liv and Garrett, and climb out of the car.

"Guys, grab your stuff." I unbuckle Liv, and she hops down as Garrett comes around to our side, both dressed in matching blue jerseys.

I scan the parking lot for Shane's truck and Cole's car but see neither. I text both.

> ME to COLE: Meet you in the bleachers. You better have your blue on. Hank's all nerves, so get your butt here.

> ME to SHANE: If you make it, look for us in the bleachers. We'll be the long line of #5s.

I slide my phone into my back pocket and start toward the field as the players warm up. Before climbing up the bleachers full of home team parents and friends, I stop to search for Hank, wanting to be sure he knows that we're here. Even though he pretends to be indifferent, I know we help calm his nerves.

I spot him across the field, stretching, and I feel a sudden dose of my own nerves. Each time the kids, even Cole, take the field or have an event, my body prickles with excitement and pride. It was the same all those years ago with my dad.

Our dad instilled in us a drive to give our all for the things we love, and that doesn't stop where the field lines end. Thinking of him and how much he's missing makes my eyes sting with tears.

Hank looks in our direction, and I swallow my emotions. I pump my fist in the air three times as my dad always did after a win. Then turn to show my jersey with our name and his number, which I know he'll roll his eyes at but secretly love.

I turn to the kids. "Let's find seats and get settled, then I'll see what's at the concession stand."

We find an open row a few down from the top as Cole climbs toward us.

"Hey. Did Hank see our jerseys?" He plops down next to me.

"Yeah. His glare told me he loves them."

I notice some of the parents tuning into our conversation. I'm used to not being loved in every setting, and it's fine. Being the child of Tim Matthews doesn't always make things easy or friendly, but I hate how these parents look down on Hank. He's incredibly talented, and maybe part of it's genetics. More than anything, it's his desire and drive.

These people will never get that. They only see what they want to see, which just so happens to be the name on the back of his jersey.

"I'm going to check out the concessions." I stand, ignoring the stares and whispers. "You want anything?"

"We want popcorn." Liv jumps up as Cole pulls her onto his lap, tickling her.

"Just a water," Cole answers.

I zig-zag through people and make my way down the sideline, but before I get too far, I hear someone call my name. I turn to see Assistant Coach Get-a-Clue jogging over.

I keep inching my way closer to the concession stand because, one: I don't really want to talk to him. And two: I don't need to add fuel to the other parents' fire.

"Maggie," he calls, gaining on me.

I stop, turning slowly and hoping he needs something other than attempting to flirt and suggest we go out again.

"Hi."

He stands closer than I'm comfortable with, so I step back.

"Hank is looking really good this year. Whatever he did this summer worked."

I nod. "Yeah. He had a great team this summer and has been training."

"I told him I'd be glad to help him after practice or on weekends if he wants." He smiles, but it's smug. *Ewww.*

"Well, that's nice of you, but Hank's got a pretty good thing going. I actually don't think he needs *more* training. He puts a lot of pressure on himself as it is."

He nods like he understands, but I catch a glimmer of irritation. "You know some of the parents aren't happy he's starting this season."

Oh boy, here it comes.

I stiffen. Hank doesn't need this joker to help him, and he needs to get the hell out of my space.

I push my hair behind my ear, hoping he catches a glimpse of my ring. "Yes. I've heard, but he's earned that starting spot. He works hard and has continuously demonstrated his ability. I don't think anyone can dispute that."

"Well, they want us to bench him until the first quarter. They think the seniors should start."

I scoff. "I'm sure they do."

He wraps his hand around my elbow. "Look, I have to get over there. Let's have dinner, and we can discuss it. I'd hate to see him lose his position."

I stare at him and his audacity, keeping my fist at my side so I don't punch the smugass look off his face.

If I need to talk to anyone about Hank, it'll be the coach, *not* his assistant, and it won't be over dinner.

I plant my feet, knowing I don't want to cause a scene, but this jerk just hit every wrong button in my playbook, and he's about to find out where he can shove his suggestion.

Chapter 14

SHANE

I'm stuck in traffic and tired of listening to Rob drone on about the positive press that will come from me marrying The Rocket's daughter.

For the last five minutes, I've tuned him out because, outside of explaining the high-level details of how Maggie and I met and our 'whirlwind romance,' it's just none of his business.

I'm done telling him the only thing he needs to know is that we're married and starting our life together. I told him about Tim and gave him his agent's number. Trusting him to use discretion, I'll allow them to work out the timing and details of releasing a statement.

"Look, Rob, I have somewhere I need to be. Please keep this simple and call me if you hit any snags. Maggie doesn't need anyone calling her, and Tim's death needs to remain private as long as possible."

"I got it. I'll be in touch. Enjoy your new wife." He lets out a low whistle. "I never thought I'd hear myself say those words to you. Take care, buddy."

I disconnect the call, my frustration building at the backed-up cars.

Practice went well. We fine-tuned some things, and surprisingly, my conversation with Nick, the-giant-chip-on-his-shoulder, went better than expected. We have an understanding, and he may even let me help him. But it's the little chat I had with Hank this morning that's tempting me to plow over these cars.

He was quiet. Based on what Maggie said, he gets nervous before games, which we have in common. I was content to let him have his silence, but as we pulled into the parking lot of his school, he didn't immediately get out. Instead, he asked me if I was coming to his game. When I said I was planning on it, he seemed relieved. He told me his assistant coach was constantly hitting on Maggie and had approached him about her.

My anger was instant that a coach would put a player in that position, let alone a kid. I've seen that kind of manipulation happen at the higher levels, but even asking Hank about Maggie crosses a line in my book.

Then there's the matter of this guy hitting on Maggie. Given she's married to me, she's not interested.

As cars finally start moving, I refuse to analyze why the idea of someone, anyone, cozying up to Maggie makes me pissy. Instead, I remember what it felt like to wake up this morning with her body tucked against mine. Even in complete darkness, I knew her face was pressed against my chest, her leg wrapped around me. Admitting I didn't mind it won't help when it comes to sharing space with Maggie, nor is examining this feeling of needing to be where she is right now.

After another long ten minutes, I pull into the school parking lot, throw the jersey over my T-shirt, and head toward the field. I round the corner of the stands, and my eye catches on a blue jersey, the same as mine, further down the sideline. It's the little firefly that only hours ago stood before me wrapped in a towel, and I liked what I saw just a little too much.

Walking toward her, I notice her stiff stance and the hand wrapped around her elbow. The hairs on my neck bristle, and for the first time since she called me one, I feel like a bear on the prowl.

I make it within three feet of her to hear her say, "You're not seriously suggesting what I think you are?"

I step up behind her, making my presence known to whom I assume is the assistant coach. His gelled hair, school polo, and prickish look make me want to punch him in the face, and that's before I find out exactly what he said.

"Hey." I slide my hand around Maggie's waist, pulling her away from his grasp.

His eyes tip up to mine and grow wide as Maggie rests against me.

"You're . . . Shane Carter," the douche says, stuttering just slightly.

"Yeah, I am, and I'd like to know exactly what you were suggesting to my wife."

Maggie's head snaps up to look at me, and I feel her body tense for the briefest second before her attention moves back to the dick.

He takes a step back, his eyes flicking from me to Maggie and back again. He takes another step back. "I was just telling her how great Hank is looking this season."

"That so." I glare, letting him know I don't believe one dirty, rotten word. "Well, that definitely has nothing to do with you, so why don't you go make yourself somewhat useful and get your other players ready for the game, coach."

Maggie's small hand slips into mine, and my temper calms with the warmth. I'm not one to throw punches, but I don't like men who think they can push women or kids around.

"Hank starts as long as he's earned his place, which is what Coach Miller has told him. If that changes, I'll discuss it with him," Maggie clarifies before he turns and walks away.

She twists to look up at me. "Well, that was handy timing. I'm pretty sure if you growled he would've crapped his pants."

I grunt, and she grins, pulling me by the hand further away from the stands and into the concession line.

"I have to get popcorn for the kids. What do you want, big guy? My treat for scaring off that numbnut."

"What did he say to you? I didn't like his hand around your arm or his face or the fact that he looks like he shouldn't be responsible for coaching toddlers."

"Well, tell me how you really feel." She laughs. "He offered to help Hank train. When I said more training isn't what he needs, he tried to get me to discuss it over dinner." She rolls her eyes. "When I gave him the big hell no, he tried to nonchalantly threaten Hank's starting position."

"He's a douchebag and should be fired." I tried to keep my temper in check, but why hide it when it's the truth.

"Yep, to both, but for today, we're going to watch Hank own the field and show these other jokers what true hard work and dedication can do." She pays for the snacks, and we walk back toward the bleachers. "Nice jersey. Does it sting a little?"

I look down at the shirt and then at the line of matching shirts in the stands waiting for us. I realize how unnatural this is for me. There wasn't a single time in my career when someone sat in the stands just for me. It's weird to be here, but at the same time, part of me is curious about the experience, just as I'd been when we spent the afternoon together.

We climb over a few people to join Cole and the kids. I slap Cole's hand and squeeze between him and Maggie.

"Nice work running off that little dirtbag." Cole's annoyed tone is quiet as he takes a sip of his water.

I glance at him. "Is there anyone else I should be worried about?" Realizing both Cole and Hank had their eyes on this guy worries me that there might be more.

"Not in this city."

I don't like his answer. "Care to elaborate?" I try to say with less tension than I'm actually feeling at the moment.

"No, just her ex did a number on her, and he likes to play games."

I turn my full attention to him, and Cole must see smoke starting to rise.

"Hold on," he whispers with just a hint of amusement, like anything about this is funny. "She'll never get back together with him. It's not like that. He just likes to pop in every now and then, and it only takes her right back to that time."

My hackles calm, and the relief I feel at his words is concerning, but I decline to investigate why.

Cole jumps to his feet, cups his hands, and hollers "Matthews" as Hank takes the field. The ball goes into play, and I watch him move up and down the field like a man on a mission. I know little about soccer, but it's clear this kid is exceptional.

Hank scores the first goal of the game, and I can't help but stand and yell along with the rest of my row, feeling proud of the young man who has honed his skills. It reminds me of a time when football gave me the escape I needed.

We sit back down, and Maggie bumps my shoulder. "In case I forget, thanks for being here today."

"I'm just sorry I wasn't here earlier so you didn't have to deal with. . . numbnuts."

She bursts out laughing. "Well, now that I have you, I might just keep you around, you big bear."

I meet her beautiful, blue, joy-filled eyes, and an unfamiliar feeling comes over me, almost as if that joy is contagious. She's got me. I think that's exactly what I'm afraid of.

I've never been anyone's anything, but what happens when she doesn't need me anymore?

Chapter 15

MAGGIE

I'm alone in Shane's truck, and I'm tempted to search every nook and cranny to see what I might discover about my new husband. But if he isn't the freaking cleanest man I've ever met. No receipts or empty coffee cups. No gum or wrappers. *What coach doesn't chew gum?* I don't think he even leaves fingerprints behind. He's probably filing for divorce after seeing the interior of my car.

The growly, gentle giant offered to take the kids home after the game, so they didn't have to run errands with me on my way to pick up Teddy.

Um. Ok. Yes, please.

So here I am, driving his big truck and running into a jewelry store. Shane's declaration to the pathetic excuse of a coach made the decision. He laid the 'w' word out there like it was the most natural thing in the world. Wife. He called me his *freaking wife*, and in a way that told that asshole he should cover his balls.

It's just a word, and for us, it's only a title printed on a signed legal document. But it was the first time in so long I felt protected, cared for, and not like I had to deal with every single thing on my own.

After a quick search through the glass cases, I found just what I wanted, and it should be ready in a few days.

I dash to get Teddy, hoping he's not the last child remaining. The kid is wild but fears being left behind. I try to always make sure I'm on time, and as I pull up to the ice rink, I see him standing with the group, waiting for rides. He climbs in the back, hyped up on sugar, and gives me a play-by-play that lasts the entire ride home.

Pulling into the driveway, the garage door is open, and the hood of my Suburban is propped up. I find Shane with Liv on a stool and Garrett by his side, inspecting whatever is under there.

"Um, what are you doing?" I ask, really hoping they didn't break my car.

Shane must hear something in my tone because he straightens, with his growly face on. "Did you realize you're five thousand miles overdue for an oil change?"

Is he mad? I stare at him, trying to determine if he's serious. Do I understand I needed to change my oil, like yesterday? Yes. Does it look like I have time to stop in and get that done any day of the week? No.

"Uh, are you mad?" I want to fully understand what's going on here.

His massive hands move to his hips, and even though I want to be pissed for feeling like I'm getting a lecture from my dad, Shane, in a tight, white T-shirt smeared with grease and looking irritated as hell, is just about the sexiest thing I've ever seen.

Damn him. I want to smile but bite my lip.

"You can't let it go that long without getting it changed. It's hard on the engine. If there's a leak, you could have an issue. You should check it regularly."

I don't want to like his protective nature as much as I do. "Ok. Does an oil change come with this lecture?"

The big man huffs, his broad shoulders lowering just slightly. "Yes. After I saw the sticker, we stopped and picked up some oil. The sludge is draining now."

I look at Garrett, who's studying the dipstick.

"Maggie," Liv says, scrunching her nose. "Shaney just made the car poop oil. It was gross, but he said the new stuff will look like pee."

I raise my eyebrows, and he shrugs. "Well, I'll let you three get back to it while I start dinner."

As I suspected, we have a houseful for dinner, which is fine by me. The more Hank and his friends hang out here, the more I know he's not doing something he shouldn't be.

Since he came in from the garage, Shane's been quiet, like he's retreated to somewhere I can't see. He grilled the chicken while I pulled out extra food to feed all the growing kids, and then we ate in chaos and shifts while the boys remained entrenched in video games.

After cleaning up the dinner mess and starting a load of laundry, I find Shane on the couch.

"Is master fire starter another hidden skill set in addition to mechanic?" I ask.

He turns to look at me.

"I need to get the kids in the shower, but there's wood out back if you want to start a fire in the pit. When I'm done, I'll bring the beer." I don't know what happened, but I hope I can pull him back from wherever he might be.

"Sure."

Ok, then.

Two showers and a bath later, I open the back door to a roaring fire, and my mysterious husband stretched out in a chair. I hand over a beer, and he takes it. I plop down in the seat beside him and look up at the clear sky, enjoying the peaceful night.

Shane also seems content in the silence, and we stay like that for a bit before I break into the quiet night.

"How did practice go today? Did you get things straightened out with Chip?"

"Chip?"

"Yeah, the bad attitude and giant chip on his shoulder."

He takes another pull at his beer before answering. "My guys are looking pretty good. We have some minor things to work on this week, but I think they're ready. I want to see what they've got. Nick and I had a chat. I think we have an understanding, but we'll see. He's got talent. It's up to him what he does with it."

"I'm helping the dance team with their routine, and I know how you feel about girls on the field, but we'll be interrupting one afternoon this week. Good luck keeping your guys focused." I poke the bear to see if he'll come out from where he's hiding.

"Great," he huffs. "You do that often? Help out with the dance team?"

"Sometimes. It's the home opener, so . . . " I shrug. "Although I'm pretty sure the captain doesn't care for my input. She's into all that booty-flapping stuff that looks ridiculous out there on the field. Some of those girls are really good and choreograph way more entertaining and classy routines."

"Is she the tall redhead?"

I side-eye him, curious why he's asking. The girl is drop-dead gorgeous. Tall, with long legs and flawless skin. "Yeeeesss."

"That girl freaks me out. She was at the team party and wouldn't leave my side. She happens to run into me way too often, wanting to chit-chat and dropping hints about where she'll be hanging out."

"Noooo." I don't believe it.

"Yes."

I smile. "Shaney, she's got it bad for you. I bet her walls are covered with your face, and she's planning your wedding and how many kids you'll have."

"You're not helping," he says, unamused. "Girls like that freak me out, not to mention she's too young."

"She's not that much younger than me."

"You're different."

"How?"

"I don't know, you just are. You're mature and don't act all . . . stalkerish."

"Oh my gosh!" My head back. "Shane Carter likes the chase. The hard to get." Laughter burst out of me. "I need to put out a news bulletin for all your female stalker fans."

He pulls the bottle from his lips. "The only news bulletin going out is that I'm now off the market. Hopefully, Big Red will get it."

I bend forward, holding my aching stomach muscles. "If she's truly a stalker, the only thing that's going to do is make her want you more now that she can't have you."

Shane rubs a hand over his face. "You're seriously not helping."

I reach over and pat his shoulder, trying to calm myself. "Don't worry, big guy. I won't let her kidnap you and tie you up in her basement. I'll chase her down and scare her off with my secret whoop-ass powers. Deal?" I hold out my hand, waiting for him to slap it.

Shane turns to me with an intensity in his gaze that wasn't there before. It kills my laughter. Something is happening behind those eyes, and it makes me squirm just a little.

He slaps my waiting hand but holds on to it. "Deal."

After a few long seconds, he lets go while I try to sort through what just happened.

"See, we got this," I say in an attempt to lighten things up again and decide to change the subject. "So, tomorrow morning is church if you'd like to come with us, and then it's sports highlights, movies, and relaxation. I don't want you to feel like you can't have time to yourself."

When he doesn't say anything, I try again.

"Thanks for changing my oil. I know it needed to be done, but finding the time for stuff like that is overwhelming."

"You're welcome." He's retreated again, so I push.

"Where did you learn to do that? Most players I know wouldn't even know how to pop the hood."

Shane takes a breath and rests his bottle on his leg, taking his time like he's trying to determine how to answer the question or if he wants to.

"One of the homes I was placed in, the guy owned a shop. Part of the requirement of being there was earning my keep, so he showed me, and I learned quickly. One of the more useful things I picked up."

I glance at him out of the corner of my eye, sensing the uneasiness that rose with asking a question about his past. He's only shared with me that he grew up moving from one home to the next, and I've not pressed it beyond that, wanting him to share what he's comfortable with. At some point, I hope he'll trust me with more.

"Can I ask you a question? You don't have to answer if you don't want to." I give him an out, and I'm perfectly fine with him taking it.

His eyes meet mine in only the light of the fire. "Does that go both ways?"

"I guess that's only fair." I take a sip of beer, hoping my question doesn't make him retreat further. "Did you know either of your parents?"

He exhales and takes another pull on his beer. "I entered the system when I was five. I have only a vague memory of my mom. I didn't know anything about my dad until after my first season in the pros. I hired someone to help me find him and didn't like what I found."

He doesn't say any more than that, and it's clear he doesn't want to talk about it.

"I know I'm sorry doesn't help," I say, knowing it really doesn't. "Some people just get dealt really shitty parents, relationships, and situations. Hopefully, it makes the good ones all the more special."

That big head turns in my direction again, but he doesn't say a word. I can't tell by his expression what he's thinking. We only stare at each other. Him contemplating something, and me, wanting to know what it is.

I smile, sitting up a little taller in my seat, preparing myself. "Ok, Grizz. I'm ready, but be nice."

He thinks for a minute, turning his beer bottle between his fingers. "What made you leave New York?"

There's just a hint of growl added to his question, which I don't understand, but of course, this is what he'd want to know. The question is simple, but the answer is not. I take a minute to figure out how I want to answer. Really, it's how much I'm willing to give away.

My time in New York was amazing until it wasn't, and then I came home. Those years in that big city are where I grew up. I had to. I went there looking for an escape, and that's exactly what I found until life caught up with me again.

"I'd just gotten a lead role in a ballet, and it was my dream coming true. Before rehearsals even began, I broke my ankle in two places. I was devastated. I hadn't even had the chance to learn the choreography or meet the rest of the cast. I didn't get to set foot on the stage." I bite my lip, deciding to omit the part about my ex's role in the whole thing. It doesn't matter anymore.

I pick at the label on my bottle, feeling a sudden wave of vulnerability and wondering if I'm willing to admit something to him I've not told anyone. If I want friendship, a real friendship with Shane, it takes guts and openness.

I peek at him, solid and steady but closed off. There's a twenty-foot-thick concrete barrier surrounding Shane that I want to take a jackhammer to. So I decide to risk it, hoping he'll let just a bit of that wall down in return. Or I'll just chip away at it, crumbling one minuscule piece at a time.

"When I went to New York, I . . . was struggling. I'd made dance my whole life and thought fulfilling all my dancing dreams would somehow make everything better, and it did . . . until I couldn't dance. I didn't know how long it would take for my ankle to heal, and when it did, if it would ever be the same. I was scared and alone and . . . done."

"When I called my dad, I knew he was declining mentally. I sat for a couple of days feeling sorry for myself, but the truth is, I was lost. I'd been hiding behind dance, a big city, and a dream. When I was forced to slow down, everything I'd been running and hiding from was still there, waiting for me to return."

I stretch in my chair, arching my back, hoping it will help release the tightness in my chest. "It was time for me to come home, and when I got here, there wasn't a chance I was going back. My dad couldn't take care of the kids, and I had things to work through, which included saying goodbye to that dream." I shrug. "It took me a while, but I think sometimes dreams are there for a reason, to get us through until we're strong enough to face the world without them."

There's nothing but silence as I finish my story, and I want to crawl under my chair, feeling naked and raw.

After a minute, Shane speaks, his voice so soft in the darkness. "These kids are really lucky to have you."

I peek at him, seeing the honesty and tenderness behind his words. My heart squeezes inside my chest because I really want him to be right.

Chapter 16

SHANE

I pull out a stool next to Teddy in the middle of the morning rush. The kitchen is silent except for the boys crunching cereal and slurping milk. The cup of coffee waiting for me is a pleasant surprise after battling to get Maggie out of bed this morning—a job that's become a double-edged sword.

I've tried to ignore that I'm attracted to her, but it's becoming increasingly difficult.

I peek at her standing at the counter with her back to me, and thoughts of her warm hands wrapped around my bicep and her face pressed into my shoulder, light that small fire within me all over again. I avert my attention to my phone, needing to get back to a place where barriers and blindfolds exist.

Right. Who the fuck am I kidding?

Today, she's traded the tight black leggings for gray sweatpants rolled at the waist over one of her strappy leotards. How she makes baggy sweatpants look so incredibly sexy, I'll never know. I want to throw one of my T-shirts over her and not let another man see her like this.

"Come on, boys. Get moving. You can't miss the bus today," she says, taking a big sip from her mug.

I grab the mug in front of me and bring it to my lips to take a drink. Instead of the liquid being hot and rich, it's cold and salty and . . . gross enough to make me gag.

I spray whatever the hell it is all over the counter. Teddy immediately erupts into laughter along with Garrett. I even hear Hank snicker. Maggie doesn't turn to look at me, but I see her shoulders shaking.

I glare at Teddy, and he grins. "What did you do?"

He hops off the stool, unable to contain his amusement. "It's soy sauce."

I stand, towering over him, then pick him up by the armpits to hold him out in front of me. "This means war, you little prankster."

"Yes, sir. I'll look forward to it, sir." He salutes, and despite my attempt to keep a straight face to show my complete irritation, I feel the corner of my mouth tip up.

I release him, and he runs from the room laughing. I settle back on my stool as Maggie holds her nice warm coffee, smirking.

"What? Don't think you're off the hook. I thought we were on the same team."

She puts a fresh cup of coffee in front of me. "It's his joy, and I'm not about to burst that bubble." She smiles. "He'll be waiting, you know? For you to retaliate."

"Hmmm."

"I'm looking forward to seeing what you come up with, Grizz."

Liv stumbles in, climbs onto my lap, and snuggles against my chest. I have no idea what this little girl sees in me. Never in a million years will I admit how much I like our little morning ritual, but I do.

Going into this, I knew I wanted to help, but I didn't expect to like spending time with each of these kids.

Garrett's nerdy side matches the one I keep hidden from the world. Most people just assume I'm a big, dumb football player. Teddy and his mischievousness are a glimpse of happiness and joy I've not known. I'm getting to do all the things I would've never dreamed of as a boy, and the way Maggie allows it and encourages it makes me want to take part even more. Even Hank and I seem to understand each other's quiet presence. And well, Liv, she had me wrapped around her little finger from day one.

It's Maggie, and whatever is forming between us, that's unnerving. After Hank's game yesterday, it all suddenly started to feel real. First, I told that jackass she was my wife. I said it. Out loud. I claimed her as mine, but she's not. We're contractually bound together . . . for now, and that's it.

Then, when I realized how long she'd gone without an oil change, I was pissed. Then I was pissed that I was pissed. I *do not* want to care about these things, but I found myself hunched under her hood, changing the oil, because I couldn't stand the thought of her stranded on the side of the road.

It's Maggie. She's the one who worries me. Keeping my distance is becoming more challenging by the day, and no part of me wants to acknowledge or even be aware of it. I want to be a man walking in this unconsciously. I need amnesia, but only when it comes to Maggie.

I don't want to remember how good she smells or what she looks like first thing in the morning, especially wrapped in a towel. I don't want to hear her laugh or tease me with all that fire and sass. I want to forget what her blue eyes look like when I know something more is happening behind them that has to do with me.

I want to wake up and have all of these feelings go somewhere other than pressing down on me. I have no clue what I'm supposed to do with them other than run as fast as I can. And that's not turning out so well with a bum knee.

I was fine, retreating and keeping my distance. I held fast until we sat around the fire, getting cozy with our pasts. When she'd told me about her time in New York and how she'd lost herself, I could hear the devastation and the pain she'd gone through. I know there's more to that story, and maybe with time, she'll tell me the rest.

But it was the moment in front of the fire when she held out her hand and declared she'd open a can of whoop-ass for me that I felt a force pull me under. I wanted to kiss her so badly, right then and there.

Since our courthouse peck, I've only mildly wondered what it would be like to kiss her for real. But at that moment, the wonder became a desire. I wanted to kiss her and know exactly what a real, deep, desperate kiss with Maggie felt like.

This woman has a way of infiltrating all my closed-off places. She takes all my calm security and agitates the hell out of it. It's making it hard to be around her because I don't know when or how she'll chip away another piece of my walls that were built and fortified long ago. I'm like an iceberg. Maggie is the sun getting way too close, melting one layer at a time.

"Bye, Shane." I hear my name, and I snap to.

The front door clicks closed, and Maggie returns to the kitchen.

"Hey, beauty. Want to get dressed before Gwen gets here?" she asks Liv, who has yet to move since she climbed into my lap.

Liv burrows in further like she's trying to hide. "No, Shaney is warm."

I want to smile because Maggie unknowingly said something similar when I tried to wake her this morning.

"Gwen will be here any minute," Maggie says as the front door opens and closes again. "Speak of an angel."

The older woman strolls in, looking like the grandmother I never had. The other morning when I met Gwen for the first time, she moved right to me and hugged me like I imagined she would one of her own children. It was warm and tight and only slightly uncomfortable.

"Well, good morning." She smiles brightly, moving to hug Maggie, and then turns to me. "Prince Charming."

"I've never been accused of being charming," I say, and she laughs.

"Well, sweetheart, let me be the first." She winks. "I see you've captured a princess again this morning."

Liv peeks out between my arms and giggles.

Gwen turns to Maggie. "Ok, love. What do you need today?"

"I have everything laid out for dinner. Would you mind getting it started this afternoon? I have to help the dance team, so I'll be home a bit later today."

"You got it. I thought Liv and I would make cookies too."

"Yay," Liv cheers. "Can we make Snickerdoodles?"

"Well, I suppose. Let's get you dressed and let Shane get started on his day. We have lots of playing and reading to do."

Liv hugs me tight for a long second, like a Maggie hug, as if she somehow knows I need it, and then I help her down.

The kitchen is suddenly quiet, and I hear Maggie let out a breath. "Ok. I need to finish getting ready and grab my stuff. I'll see you later when I meet the dance team."

"Ok." I watch her leave the kitchen, knowing I'll see her later on the field where this whole thing began.

Standing on the field today, there's a different kind of anticipation running through me. Maggie didn't tell me when she'd be here, but I want to see her. This woman is slowly dissolving my will to keep my distance, but after this morning, I kind of want to draw her near.

After working out and taking a shower, I went into the kitchen for my keys, and next to them, I found a small black velvet box and a note.

Sorry, this is late, but I wanted to give you the option. For when the rest of the world falls away. Maggie

I opened the box to find a tungsten ring plated with rose gold. I held it in my palm, feeling a tightness in my chest grow as I weighed slipping it on my finger. No matter the reasons, I committed to Maggie. It may not be for love, but I made vows to her that I intend to keep.

For some reason, sliding the ring on my finger makes it feel real. It would be a declaration to the world that I'm tied to another. Do I want that? Do I want to let the world and Maggie know I'm in this with her and only her?

Contemplating this, I rolled the ring between my fingers and saw the engraving. I had my answer.

I got you

She'd engraved the ring with the words I fear and want and need the most. She's said it before that we had this. Together. That she's got me. And as much as it terrifies me, I want her to know I've got her too.

This isn't about love. It doesn't have to be. This is about commitment, and that's something I can do. What no one has ever done for me. I want the world to know that she's mine, and I want her to know that I've got her in whatever way that means right now.

I hear a whistle and rub the ring with my thumb, trying to get used to the feel of it as I approach the fifty-yard line to call my guys in. I give orders about what we're working on today and send them back out. I glance around, looking for Maggie, but instead of her, I see the tall redhead strutting in my direction.

Awww, shit.

She stops next to me, way too close. "Hey, coach. You don't mind if we borrow the end zone for a bit, do you?"

"It's fine," I say, intentionally not looking at her. Beads of sweat form on my brow, remembering Maggie's teasing comments.

"You ready for the big game?" She slides in front of me, trying to meet my eyes, but I'm not playing.

"Getting there." I don't want to converse with her, so I take a big step away and focus on my guys. "Let's do that again!" I holler.

She's clearly not getting the hint, so I move further away, still trying to ignore her.

"Well, the team is celebrating at O'Malley's after the game if you feel like joining." Her fake bashfulness makes me want to laugh.

I push out a breath, ready to tell her to go find someone her own age who's interested, but I feel familiar small arms slide around my waist.

"Hey, babe," Maggie says, in a too-sweet tone, pressing her cheek to my back and squeezing me. "I've been waiting all day to see you."

I'd breathe with relief, but standing here with her pressed against my back makes anything like breathing suddenly difficult.

She slides around to my side, keeping one arm around me. Her chin tilts upward, and a mischievous smile tugs at her lips. I want to know exactly what she's up to.

She sets her eyes on the redhead.

"Oh hey, Cassie." She says it casually, like she didn't see her there. "We're practicing over *there*." She points to be specific. "I'll be there in a minute. I just need a second with my husband."

Cassie, as I now know her, looks between us with her mouth hanging slightly open before redness washes up her neck to her face. She turns and marches away with what might be irritation.

Maggie moves in front of me, and instead of stepping away, she pushes up to her tiptoes, links her arms around me, and nuzzles into my chest. As much as I don't mind it and might even like it to continue, I know my guys will take notice any minute.

"What are you doing?" I try not to sound perturbed, but it's the best I can do with this new level of physical contact and my inability to know how to handle it.

"Making sure she gets the hint. She's pissed. You can bet your good knee that in two-point-two, she'll be looking back over here to confirm you're with me. Given the look on her face, I'm not confident she won't start stalking you. For real. Plus, I've had a crap day, and whether you like it or not, I could use a hug."

"What happened today?" I'm trying to focus on anything but Maggie's body pressing against mine.

"I got a call from my dad's lawyer. He has to contact Cliff. *Clifford*," she says with a snooty tone. "He said he can't wait any longer to read the will, and finding out from the press that Dad passed away will only make things worse."

"What does that mean?"

"It means that avoiding them has come to an end. He and Joan will be here in a matter of days, bringing all their stuck-up, arrogant, two-faced ideas with them. The lawyer said he'd call me after he talked to him. I'm tired of anticipating what they'll try to pull, so we just need to get on with it."

I hear the worry in her voice and wish I could take it away. "I'm sorry."

She squeezes me a little tighter as whistles and hollers are thrown in our direction.

Maggie pulls back and grins, but doesn't let me go. I roll my eyes. Then, without thinking about it, I dip her, wanting to get a rise out of her and rile up the team in the process.

Her eyes widen, and she laughs, which is becoming my favorite sound.

I whisper in her ear as the cheers grow louder. "It'll all be ok. We'll figure it out, or I'll kick his too tight ass."

Maggie squeezes me as I pull her back up, and I hope I've at least done part of my job to make her feel better.

"Get back to work, or we'll do push-ups and sprints until dark!" I yell with a growl.

"I better get over there." Maggie tips her head in the direction of the dance team. "Cassie's going to want to shoot me for more than just stealing her man. I'm about to vote out her booty-shaking routine, so if it turns ugly, come rescue me."

"My money's on you."

"Yeah? I'll see you at home, then."

"I'll find you before I leave and walk you to your car. Otherwise, come find me."

She takes a few steps backward toward the end zone. "Will do, hubby." She smirks, but it's strained, and I don't like it. "I like the ring, Grizz," she hollers as she turns around.

I try to get my head to focus back on the team, but I'm left thinking about Maggie. She's worried. That hug and that look told me so. I have a feeling there's more to the story than she's been willing to share with me. I just have to figure out how to get her to tell me what that is.

I return to my team, walking out on the field and discussing specifics with my players. There are only a few days left until our first game, and things are looking good, but there's always room for improvement. We make some adjustments, talking through details, and then I return to my place on the sidelines.

My eyes find Maggie at the far end of the field, and she's watching them demonstrate something.

Then, I hear her voice, "If you want to walk out here looking like a bunch of amateurs humping the field, I'll leave you to it. But if you want to make the crowd feel alive, then we have work to do."

My little Firefly means business, and with that tone, I know she's far stronger than she realizes.

Two minutes later, a different song comes over the speakers, and I have no doubt she won the battle. I'm also certain that, whatever her history with Cliff, Maggie won't go down without a fight. I just hope she'll let me help.

Chapter 17

MAGGIE

ME: Good luck today. Keep your offensive line tight. Make those kitty cats chase their tails.

COLE: Get ready to be dizzy.

It's been a strange, quiet morning. The boys and Liv are still sleeping, and I'm in the kitchen, knowing chaos will break loose any moment. Shane was more growly than usual when the alarms went off and didn't wait to make sure I actually got out of bed before heading downstairs to work out.

He's nervous. He has that same look of being all in his head that I'd see when the screen focused on him during a game. I have no doubt Shane's coaching ability is just as stellar as his physical talent, but I hope he knows we'll cheer him on regardless of what happens on the field. If nothing else, maybe my little surprise will show him that.

For now, I sit in this eerily quiet kitchen, alone. This never happens, so I submit the grocery order, trying not to think about my conversation with *Uncle* Clifford.

As expected, I received a nasty lecture and a large dose of condescension for not calling him about Dad, which I could handle. But the comments about it proving my immaturity and inability to take care of the kids have my stomach in knots.

This man only gets what he wants, except for not being able to have my dad's life. Now, he just wants the most important things my dad left behind—his children.

My history with them has started to haunt me all over again. I've only spoken to my lawyer about it in minor detail. But given the potential repercussions, he agrees that we leave it tucked away for now. I'd be fine if that part of my past never saw the light of day again. It only makes me committed to walking through fire before I let Cliff and Joan take the kids anywhere.

I'm not one to hold grudges or even allow hatred to fester. It takes too much energy. But Cliff and Joan are the exception. These two people can buy the world, but it's never been enough. I don't care what I have to do. I won't let them get custody of the kids. I'm not perfect and only marginally capable of raising them. But it's a thousand times better than the oppression and abuse they'd suffer in their household.

I've known that it'd be only a matter of time before I'd have to face them, but this week is still too soon. They'll be here on Wednesday to read the will, and I know they'll fill me in on their intention of trying to gain custody.

I put my head in my hands, needing the swirling in my stomach to subside.

Shane's loud footsteps provide a nice distraction as he enters the kitchen, sweat-soaked and gorgeous. Seriously, this man gets hotter every day.

"How was your workout?" I ask, trying to ignore all the veins and muscles.

"Fine."

"You feeling good about the game today?"

He leans his elbows on the island beside me. Even sweaty, he smells fantastic. It's as if his pores ooze a natural manly musk of evergreen and spice.

"Yeah. We'll see."

Even quiet, Shane is more verbal than nervous Shane. I know he's completely in his head, so I take a risk.

"You know when you used to come through the tunnel and walk out on the field?"

He peeks at me from the corner of his eyes like he's afraid of what I might say.

"I could see you were all in here." I tap his temple with my knuckle. "Going through tape all over again, the plays, and everything you know about the opposing offense. Probably thinking through every scenario and how you'd react."

He turns his focus back to the counter. "It never mattered how many games I played; it was always like it was the first time. A bad play, a miss, a hard hit . . . It's never been acceptable to me. Now, I'm relying on these kids to make it happen, and I just have to stand back and watch."

"But this time, when things go awry, you'll share what you learned and get them back on track. You'll teach them so they won't make the same mistake twice. No one, not even you, Grizz, is perfect. All you can do is show them how to recover and do better next time."

When Shane doesn't say anything, I hope he's reflecting on what I said. But then my insecurities kick in, and my sassiness takes over.

"I can do what I do with the kids when they get nervous."

He gives me another unamused side-eye.

"Are you ready for this, big guy?" I waggle my eyebrows. "Lose Yourself" by Eminem starts filling the room, and I start dancing.

Within a few seconds, Teddy and Garrett enter.

"What's going on? Who's got the nerves?" Teddy asks.

I grin at Shane as he stands to his full height. I keep sing-rapping along, and Teddy and Garrett join me, gathering their breakfast. Shane tries hard not to break his stone face, but I can see it's doing the trick.

Hank walks in wearing shorts and a look of complete annoyance. "Seriously, who's got a problem this early?"

That makes Shane chuckle, and people, I've done it. The big man is out of his head and standing here in the kitchen with us.

The kids and I pull into the stadium an hour early to be sure we don't miss Shane and Cole running onto the field. Shane left this morning just as quietly as he always does, only this time, he looked a little green.

I have to assume that, given how he grew up, moving from foster home to foster home, he doesn't know anything other than handling things on his own. I want to show him he's not alone anymore. I wanted the ring to prove that, but I also know it takes more than just saying it. It takes repetition and breaking old habits and expectations.

My quiet morning turned into complete chaos, trying to get out the door to drop Hank off for an away game. Then, there were internet errors in submitting my pick-up order and a full-on meltdown about not being able to wear a princess dress to the game.

Somehow, we made it to our seats in the first row, directly on the fifty-yard line, with snacks and no spills. Garrett, Teddy, and Liv sit and get comfortable as I scan the field. The sun is high, the sky is blue, and the fall air is just beginning to push in. It's a perfect day for football.

As the announcers' voices fill the stadium, excitement rolls through me with the anticipation of Shane and Cole coming through the tunnel. I'm ready for a good game, but not quite ready for the reporters afterward.

The latest word from Ed, my dad's agent, is that he and Rob have leaked information, and reporters will be poised to ask Shane about the growing rumor that he's married. He said Shane should also be prepared for questions about my dad and to decline to comment, as the official statement will be released this week.

I push all those thoughts aside as the teams are introduced. For today, I'm going to enjoy the game.

I spot Cole and nudge the kids. We stand and give him the official salute, pumping our fists in the air three times. The kids smile and giggle as Cole gives us a goofy face in return before he gets back to business.

I wait, still searching for Shane. Walking out today will be very different for him, and after what he shared this morning, it'll be difficult. I know he wasn't ready for his playing days to be over, and so much of him still yearns to be the one suiting up and running onto the field.

Then I see him walking down the sideline toward us, game face on. His broad shoulders are rigid under his snug team pullover. The man was striking in pads and a helmet, but he might be even more so sporting the Moose logo with headphones around his neck.

As he nears, I stand, cupping my hands around my mouth. "Carter." I see the instant I break through his force field, and his eyes snap to mine.

Liv sees him and waves. "Shaney."

There's just a hint of a smile before his eyes return to mine. I twist, revealing his name and number on his old jersey on my back. His eyes never leave mine, and I can't read them. He just looks at me, frozen in his tracks. It's a long, hard look, and the world around us blurs for just those few seconds. Then, before I'm ready, he places a hand on his chest, giving it a slight rub, and nods ever so slightly.

I have no idea what just happened. I need a replay. A redo. Someone call a referee over to interpret what in the world just went down. It was intense, like the calm before the storm. Eerily quiet but extreme.

I shake myself from it, resolving to revisit it later. The announcer asks, 'Who's ready for some football?' as players move to the center of the field for the coin toss. The ball is punted, and Cole jogs into position. We all go crazy, ready for some action.

My gaze lands on Shane again. His back is to me as he talks and pumps up his players. My heart can't help but be filled with pride. He's strong and kind, taking his career-ending hit and turning it into something amazing, not just for himself but for each of the young men hanging on his every word.

Chapter 18

SHANE

"Defense looked good today. The team is starting off the season right. How does it feel to be on the sidelines instead of leading the league in sacks?"

I hate this part. After a game, the last thing I want to do is speak to a group of reporters. I want peace and quiet to reflect.

Today went well. My guys played like they were in it to win, and they did. Cole was spot on, and even though we have work to do, it felt great to be part of a team again.

I rub my jaw. "I'm uh . . . I'm just happy to be here. We've worked hard preparing for this season. We'll continue to play to the best of our ability and hopefully keep bringing in the wins."

Another reporter pops in.

"Only a few months ago, you were out on the field. Seeing you take on this position was a surprise, but the Moose defense looks better than ever. Is it safe to say you're quickly settling into the coaching role?"

"I'm excited about this opportunity, and I have a lot to learn. Coach Cavanaugh is an exceptional coach, and I'm fortunate to get to work with him. This is an outstanding team with a lot of potential, and I'm looking forward to seeing what we can do this season."

My eyes catch movement in the back, and Maggie squeezes in along the wall. She's still in my jersey and beautiful as ever.

Thousands of fans have called and chanted my name over the years. But her voice hit my ears over the music and the roaring crowd, and it was as if all my nerves melted away. Turning to see her bright smile and wearing my jersey, something shifted inside me that could have registered on the Richter scale.

I've played football since high school and never had someone I know wear my name and number. Maggie has no idea what it means to me.

At every turn, she surprises me. Her gaze meets mine from the back of this suffocatingly small room. She crosses those bright blue eyes and sticks out her tongue as if she knows exactly how much I hate this. A grin follows, that's just for me, and brings a sort of peace over me that's foreign and could be addicting.

Getting back to the raised hands, I point to one, hoping I'm almost done. This room is hot, there are too many people, and I'm starting to sweat.

"There's a rumor you recently married the daughter of the great Tim Matthews. Judging by the ring on your finger, I'm speculating that might be true. Do you care to comment, and if it's true, do you see any conflict with coaching her brother, Cole?"

I knew this was coming. I'd prepared for it, but talking about my private life was always where I drew the line. Today, I can't avoid it.

I find Maggie again, hoping her presence will ground me. "I'm sure you all remember how I feel about addressing personal matters." The room fills with soft laughter. "It's usually off limits. I'll only confirm that Maggie and I did marry. As far as impacting the team in any way, my relationship with her is personal, and my job as a coach is professional. Cole is a player in his own right, has his own coaches working with him, and it will remain that way."

Hands shoot up like fireworks.

"Fans will be sad the perpetual bachelor is off the market. Can you tell us how you two met and whether that was part of your decision to join this team?"

That smart mouth turns into a smirk, and I'd like to force her to come up to answer these questions.

"I thought we were here to talk about the game," I joke, but not really. The room waits quietly for an answer. I shift my weight, trying to decide what I'm comfortable sharing. "Maggie was quick to school me on a few things about football." The room erupts with laughter. "The rest is history. Many factors contributed to my decision to come to Colorado State. When things aligned, it was an opportunity I couldn't refuse."

"Tears will be shed all across the country. Can you give those broken hearts a little more? How did you know Maggie was the one?"

I take a minute to gather my thoughts, aware it will be published everywhere. I search for the truth, knowing there's a couple who wants to rip away everything that matters to Maggie and is beginning to matter to me.

"Maggie shows me every day the kind of person I want to be. She's smart and brave and a fighter. She's the kindest and most self-sacrificing person I've ever met. It really wasn't a decision. If there were someone I'd spend my life with, I wouldn't want to be anyone other than her."

I find Maggie again, and she's studying me like she's deciphering what I just admitted. Distracted and caught up with her, I don't catch the next question.

"I'm sorry. Can you repeat that?"

"There are reports that Tim Matthews has been ill and passed away recently. Can you confirm?"

I take a deep breath. This was the question I was dreading and hoping to avoid. Rob said to decline commenting, but these people are only focused on the death of a legend, having no idea he was so much more than that. He gave my brothers and me, and kids like us, hope when we had none. But I see the man he truly was every day in his children. It's so much greater than football.

I grip the sides of the podium a little tighter. "This is my last question," I announce. I'm ready to hug Maggie for the cameras, but secretly more for myself, and move past this.

"I won't comment, but I'll say that the only reason I'm here today is that, as a boy, I dreamed of becoming just like The Rocket. I mean, what boy didn't? I've been honored to learn that the man off the field was who we should all aspire to be. Thank you."

I wave in thanks, stepping away from the mic as reporters throw out questions and cameras click in unison. I walk straight through them to find Maggie waiting for me.

As if it's the most natural thing, I pull her into my arms and hug her tight.

Her thin arms wrap around my neck, and she nuzzles in the way I'm only beginning to get used to. "You did great. If this coaching thing doesn't work out, you should look into commentating or hosting your own sports show."

I groan, knowing she's teasing me.

"Amazing game, coach," she whispers into my neck. "I knew you were going to kill it."

"Yeah?"

She pulls away and peers up at me. "Uh . . . yeah. No way I'd wear the jersey of some has-been."

My lips turn up despite my protest.

"You've got talent, Shane Carter."

I stare into her eyes, still hearing the clicks of cameras. We're giving them what they want, but I wish this were private. Just me and Maggie. I know this is for show, but it doesn't feel that way. There's a war beginning to break out inside me.

"You're the first to wear it," I admit, and Maggie's head falls to the side just an inch. "No one's ever worn my name and number before."

I see understanding take effect, and she bites her bottom lip, hiding a smile. "Well, I'm glad I get to be the first. Get used to it, Grizz."

My eyes wander to her mouth, and I give in, allowing myself to lean down and press my lips to hers like I've wanted to for days. I release her enough to cup her face, keeping the kiss innocent and under control while trying to ignore the immediate desire to take it much deeper, which would be entirely inappropriate for where we are at the moment.

Her slim fingers slide into the short hairs on my neck, and it takes everything in me not to back her into the wall. Her soft, warm lips press against mine. Once. Twice, holding it just a bit longer.

As if we're done feeding the cameras, I pull back, and Maggie hugs me tightly. I breathe her in, unable to decipher what's happening. Wanting to kiss Maggie was not part of the plan.

"Ready to get out of here?" she asks. "The kids are waiting. We thought we'd go out to eat to celebrate."

"Ok," I say, trying very hard to remember why kissing my wife is a bad idea.

"I knew you'd be calling."

"Man, you could have warned a brother. You sure this isn't legit? Those pics look awfully cozy."

If we were together, I'd punch Mark's smugass. "Glad you're entertained."

I just left the pizza place where we ate dinner, and our phones sat ringing and dinging the entire time. I knew the news would travel fast, but this is ridiculous.

"My big bro, all grown up and married." I hear a fake sniff. "It's enough to bring a tear to my eye."

"Do you have anything valuable to say?" I'm already annoyed with all the attention, and it's only the beginning.

"Ha. Yeah, how about be careful? You're all conceal, don't feel, but she's smokin', and since you married her, I know there's a whole lot more to her than that."

I choose to bypass the opportunity to razz his ass about the fact that he's apparently watched *Frozen*. Even though I have Liv to thank for all of my Disney princess knowledge, I don't have the energy to go there.

"Good game today. I caught some of it. Defense was on point." Thankfully, he's moving on.

"We have some things to tighten up, but it was a good start."

I hear a buzz and see that Maggie is trying to call me.

"Hey, man. Maggie's calling. I gotta go."

"Tell the wife I can't wait to meet her. I'll be out for bye week."

"Great." I hit the button to switch over to Maggie's call. "Hey."

"Where are you?" Her whisper is full of irritation.

"I stopped to get gas. Are you all right?"

She makes a noise in the back of her throat. "Seriously. You need to get your big, muscle-filled butt here ASAP. You know how Hank texted me and asked if Shelby could come over?"

"Yeah."

He messaged her while we were at dinner, told her he was home, and asked if his girlfriend could come over.

"Well, he knows the rules. No girls in his room. And guess what?"

"What?"

"Seriously, Shane. That little shit is in his room. Music is playing, the door is shut, and if you think I'm walking in there alone—"

"I'm not going in there." This is where I draw a hard line.

"Like hell you're not. You deal with these hormone-driven nutballs all day. He's my brother, and I'll never be able to remove the images going through my head right now, let alone witness the real thing. I'd have to burn my eyeballs out with a hot curling iron. Do you want to be married to someone who's blinded by the vision of teenage . . . relations? I can't even say it. Hurry up!"

I really want to laugh, but I'm smart enough to know that won't help things.

"Shane."

"Yeah?"

"I thought you hung up on me. Are you about here? I'm going to go out of my mind. We cannot have any babies being made in the basement. I haven't talked to him about this. I don't know if Cole has. I should've made sure he did. Do you think he has condoms? Are fourteen-year-olds responsible enough to buy condoms?"

"Maggie, calm down. I'm here. I'll be in."

"Thank God."

I park, open the door, and find her in the laundry room, pacing.

"Get down there and stop it." She tries to push me into the kitchen, but I resist.

I did not sign up for this.

I rest my hands on her shoulders. "Hold on. Calm down. Do you even know if Shelby is here?"

Her eyes are large and wild. "I can only suspect. I've not been informed otherwise."

I counter with rationale. "There's no car outside."

"Someone probably dropped her off. Seriously, get down there." Her palms push against my chest. "Do you not remember what it's like to be fourteen and home alone with a big-boobed hottie?"

Actually, I don't because I never had my own room, and I sure as hell wasn't stupid enough to take any girls back to where I was staying. I do have an idea of what I would've done if I could've.

"Ok. I'll go down there, but you're going with me. We'll knock and go from there. First, you've got to chill the hell out. Panicking is never good."

"I'm so glad you can be Mr. Cool and Calm about this. Move it. We're wasting valuable time."

We head down the stairs, where music plays a little too loudly to hear anything, but Maggie presses her ear to the door.

Oh, for real. I roll my eyes and knock. A second later, the music lowers.

"Yeah?" Hank hollers, annoyance filling the entire single syllable.

"Uh. It's Shane." I stammer because this should not be my role.

"Yeah?" Hank hollers again.

Shit. Why the hell am I doing this?

"Uh. We're home. Just checking to see if you want some pizza. We brought leftovers."

Maggie looks at me wide-eyed, like she might puke. I shrug.

"No thanks."

Out of patience, Maggie huffs, taking matters into her own hands and knocks again.

"Hank. Open the door. You know the rules about girls in your room, and so help me if you're in there doing anything other than your nails or braiding each other's hair, I'll—"

The door flies open, and Hank. Is. Pissed. His face is red, his eyes are squinted, and his hands are rounded into fists at his sides.

"Maggie, I know the rules, so get off of it!"

Maggie sticks her head around the door frame and takes a long gaze around the room. "Do I need to look under the bed or in the closet?"

Hank crosses his arms. "Be my guest, Sherlock. She's not here."

"I thought you said she was coming over." Maggie pushes, her hands on her hips.

"Yeah, well, she did, and now she's gone, but she wasn't in my room."

Maggie's entire presence deflates. Her shoulders and her arms hang as she comprehends this information.

"And if I were going to have sex, it definitely wouldn't be here."

Great, Hank. That's really going to help things.

I shoot him a look of warning, telling him to stop talking.

"You better not be having sex with anyone, anywhere. You're too young. It's a big deal, despite what people think and what your friends are doing. And unless you want me to provide you with a sack full of condoms, you better talk to Cole or Shane before you even think about doing anything like having sex. Otherwise, I will talk about it day and night and make you watch videos and read books and—"

"Maggie, stop." Hank runs a hand over his face. "Shelby broke up with me, so if you could just spare the sex talk right now, that'd be great."

Maggie's spine straightens and stiffens. "What? Why'd she break up with you?"

I've only known her for a month or so, but this woman can shift from freak-out mode to poised for battle in the blink of an eye.

Shit. I need to get her away from here because I'm certain Hank has had enough.

"Maggie, does it really matter?" His shoulders sag.

"Yes. It absolutely does. Homecoming is next weekend, and you asked her instead of some nice girl like Sadie."

Hank's head drops back to the ceiling.

I jump in. "Hey, let's give him some space."

Hank meets my eyes, and I see his silent appreciation.

Maggie ignores me and moves forward, wrapping Hank in a crushing hug. "Do I need to kick her ass? Because I will. I don't discriminate by age."

Hank smiles behind her back. "No. You were right. She wasn't with me for my brains."

Maggie doesn't release him. "Damn straight she wasn't." He laughs. "She just made a big mistake, huge. You, Hank Matthews, are a keeper through and through. Don't you ever let anyone tell you differently."

She lets him go and steps back, inspecting him like she needs to be sure he's ok.

I clear my throat. "Sorry, man."

He shrugs. "It's all right."

Even I can see the tender heart underneath the tough exterior. I wonder if that's what Maggie sees when she looks at me, or at least the black hole where a tender heart once was.

"What are you going to do about homecoming?" Maggie asks.

"Maggie," I growl.

"What? I just want to know if I need to call Simone and tell her she's going back to high school. You've seen her. She's supermodel hot, and that chick will strut in there and give that little twat something to think about."

Hank breathes and rolls his eyes, but I know she's made him feel better.

I put my arm around her and slide her away from the door. "Let's go. You need a beer and to chill out."

Hank chuckles, and I widen my eyes at him behind her back. "Have a good night, buddy." I force Maggie up the stairs.

In the kitchen, I pull open the fridge and grab two beers, twisting off the tops before handing her one. "Firefly, you need this."

She doesn't take it. "Firefly?"

I take a swig. "Yeah. When something strikes you, it's like you catch on fire and flutter around like you might explode."

She crosses her arms. "For real? Is that supposed to be flattering? You're saying I'm like a bug."

"And Grizz?"

Her head drops even farther to the side, knowing I made a point. "I need to check on the kids and read Liv a book."

"I'm certain I have a few calls to return. My phone has been ringing nonstop."

Maggie disappears upstairs, and I walk to the bedroom, sitting down on the edge of the bed. I have a bunch of missed calls. This first is from Sean, a few are unknown, and one is from Greg Carter, which will remain unanswered.

I dial Sean, trying to forget the other name listed in my incoming call log.

"Hey, man. You doing all right with this attention?" Sean should've been the one here a few minutes ago to handle Maggie and Hank. He's the stable one. The collected one. The smart one. The one you go to for advice and no-nonsense feedback.

"Yeah. It's a lot. I knew it would be, but it's just starting. Soon, news will hit about Tim."

"I know you hate it, but you looked like the real deal behind the mic. This might be the start of something really great for you. Your guys rocked."

"Thanks. We'll see how the season goes. It's one game at a time."

"How's it going with Maggie? The pics look pretty convincing. I thought Mark was going to lose his mind. He thinks you're smitten."

"He's worse than a schoolgirl. It's fine. She's . . . " If there's anyone I can talk to about this, all the confusing and conflicting feelings, it's Sean. "I meant what I said to the reporters. She's great."

Sean doesn't say anything, and I know he's interpreting my response, but also accepting that I don't want to talk about it.

"Mark's insistent that we come out for bye week. Are you good with that? I'm sure you already have your hands full without adding his dramatics."

"Do I have a choice?"

He laughs. "Probably not."

"Then you better come to keep me from killing him."

"Sounds good. Hang in there." He pauses, then adds, "I'm here when you're ready to talk about it."

"Yeah. Thanks."

I hang up, and a minute later, Maggie walks into the room and flops onto the bed face-first next to me.

"Can we just hide in here for the next week?" Her words are muffled against the quilt. "I thought I was ready for all this, but no thanks."

I wrap my hand around her ankle. Her skin is so soft. "What happened?"

Her head rolls to the side. "You mean besides almost losing my cookies tonight?" She pauses, and I wait. "Just a bunch of people expressing their shock and congratulations. Then there's Clifford's voicemail relaying his disappointment in finding out about our *nuptials* from the media. He's looking forward to discussing it further on Wednesday."

"Even though Cole will be there, I'm going with you. I'll sit in the waiting area, and Cliff can discuss it with me. I'll look forward to it." I'm ready to meet this man and let him know where he can shove his disappointment.

Maggie flips over and sits up next to me. "They're . . . awful. It's embarrassing."

"You don't have anything to be embarrassed about."

She shrinks a little, and I wonder what that's all about. Maggie's not one to shy away from anything.

"I need a shower." She bumps my shoulder. "You did great today. You're going to make some big waves in the coaching arena."

I bump her back. "Thanks for being there."

She closes the bathroom door, and it's my turn to fall onto the bed. My phone buzzes again. I'm ready for the calls to stop and for the one person I'd hoped would never call me again to go back underground. He clearly didn't get the message the last time we talked, but the man better keep his distance from Maggie and the kids if he wants to remain alive.

My body presses into the mattress. My muscles are stiff and tight. I close my eyes, trying to set the weight of it all down. My mind snags on the vision of Maggie in the stands in my jersey, smiling . . . *at me.* That kiss. I shouldn't have, but I wanted to kiss her. I wanted to kiss her and hold her for a lot longer than I did.

This woman is slowly and delicately peeling away my protective layers, but it's got to stop. Nothing good has ever come from giving in to temptation. That's why I don't do it, but each moment, it's getting harder not to. I'm not sure what this means, but it all feels big and overwhelming, and all I know is it scares me a whole lot.

Chapter 19

MAGGIE

This is what I've been dreading. For the past few weeks, it's been a noose slowly tightening around my neck, but the fear has lingered in the background for years.

Facing the couple sitting across the table from Cole and me is suffocating. I'm a fighter, but swallowing my shame and the regrets that return with their despised glares feels like swimming against the current, threatening to drown me, and I can't catch my breath.

It's clear the picture-perfect couple, with their fine clothes and exceptional manners, hasn't changed a bit except for the gray bushes growing out of Cliff's ears.

With the stench of arrogance wafting around their every move, I imagine sticking a hot glob of wax in there and yanking it out. Both ears at the same time. These people are unceasing and unaffected, taking no ownership for their manipulative and destructive ways.

Bile floats in my throat, and I press a hand to my stomach, needing it to recede.

Breathe. Don't give them power.

There was no welcome or catching up for lost time. No pleasantries. There's no facade here, and I'm grateful for it. Anything resembling kindness would've been fake and gross, so I prefer the harsh, coldness of reality.

For the last thirty minutes, I've watched Cliff—tall, skinny, with hard, dark eyes—sit stiff and aloof, only acknowledging the attorney like Cole and I aren't worthy of his presence. On the other hand, Joan, with her meticulously styled blonde hair and makeup, shifts and fidgets like she's got a rod shoved up her butt. Her beady eyes only flick towards us when she can manage to get her nose out of the air long enough.

My chest burns as my lungs shrivel, and I run my clammy hands over my thighs, needing to get out of this small, confining space.

Nothing is surprising in the will. The only reason my ass is still in this chair is that Cole is beside me, and Shane is on the other side of the door, waiting. I don't know if he could see my nerves, but he stuck close to me while we waited for the attorney to call us back and squeezed my knee as if to give me courage before I stood to come in here.

I try to take a deep breath, willing my body to relax as the attorney finally starts shuffling papers back together. My pits are drenched, I need a drink of water, and to never see these two people again.

"Are there any questions?" the attorney asks, tapping the stack of papers on the table to straighten them.

Cliff clears his throat and leans back in his chair, crossing one ankle over his knee while Joan scrunches her nose like she's sniffing out fear. It's what these people thrive on. They had me there once. Not ever again.

I'd like to shove my fingers up her thin nostrils and give a good, hard tug, reminding her and myself I'm not a young, naive girl anymore.

"Tim wasn't mentally sound when this was last modified," the asshole says. "It seems unlikely he'd leave things this way if he understood the ramifications."

"I can assure you these were Tim's wishes. The will was last updated shortly after he was diagnosed with CTE, and he was in complete control of his thoughts and wishes," the attorney clarifies. "That can easily be verified with his doctor's notes from that time."

Joan squirms in her chair again. "Well, he couldn't have possibly left his fortune and young children to these . . . Margaret."

Cole grumbles beside me, and I put my hand on his arm as my heart starts beating wildly again. Reacting to these narcissistic bastards will only make things worse.

I inhale slowly. *Don't let them see your fear.*

"Mr. and Mrs. Matthews, Tim was very clear on where and with whom he desired his children to reside. Maggie has been their assigned guardian for the past two years, and the children will remain in her care. Unless you have any further questions, that about wraps things up." He shoots us a soft smile, clearly ready for Mr. and Mrs. Plastic to get out of his office.

"We're all good." Cole pushes out of his seat, nods to the attorney, and I follow. "Cliff." He calls him because he knows he hates it. "It's been real. I hope the organization appreciates the sizable donation. Stay away from us, and maybe you'll be able to save face." Cole extends his hand for me to exit in front of him.

I don't hesitate. I open the door, and immediately, Shane stands tall and strong. My lungs expand with air at just the sight of him, even though I still feel the evil presence behind us, fully aware this isn't over.

Shane's gaze runs over my face. "Everything ok?"

I don't have time to respond before Mr. Jekyll and Mrs. Hyde move into our space.

"This isn't over," Cliff announces like he has authority. "You can't possibly think you're capable of raising those children. You've barely ever been able to take care of yourself. All that money and four kids. You're in way over your head." He narrows his eyes at me.

Cole bristles, and Shane physically expands while wrapping his hand around mine. I didn't think he could get any larger, but he just did.

"Careful," Shane says, and the warning in his tone is unmistakable. "The kids are exactly where they're supposed to be. With us."

I want to burrow into his massive body and hide.

Cliff adjusts to face him. "We haven't met. I'm Clifford Matthews." He offers his hand. "This is my wife, Joan. We were sorry to have missed the wedding. We didn't even know Margaret was engaged. How long has *this* been going on?"

Of course, it's "this" as if our relationship is inferior.

Shane grunts, completely ignoring him and his hand, turning to look at me. "You ready to go?"

"Yes." I reach for Cole's arm.

"We aren't finished," Cliff demands.

I force my body straight, refusing to cower as I turn to face my uncle. "We are. Dad's wishes were plain and clear. Your issues with him were between the two of you. The kids are happy and healthy, and they belong with me. Find some other way to deal with your bitterness or revenge or whatever it is."

Joan makes a snooty noise that comes from her long, wrinkled neck. It's likely the only place not stuffed with Botox. "How dare you? We were there for you when you needed us. Now, you treat us like this. It just shows how ungrateful and incapable you are."

The knot in my stomach lurches, and I might throw up.

"Enough." Cole jumps in. "You can take it up with the lawyers, but don't think for a second anything will stay hidden, so be careful."

I close my eyes and turn, walking away, unable to handle any more being said. My body flashes hot and cold, and I hold my stomach, swallowing the rising contents back down.

Shane's hand lands on my back, and it feels safe, but the worry of knowing this is far from over, combined with shame as the memories flood my mind, overwhelms me.

I climb into Shane's truck as he and Cole exchange goodbyes.

Cole pops his head in my door, his calm confidence never waning. "It's going to be ok. Let them try. There's nowhere better for the kids to be than with you. Anyone will see that."

I nod, closing my eyes, breathing in through my nose as he backs out and Shane climbs in. I can't look at him. I want to disappear. I have no doubt he has questions, but I can't talk about it. Not right now. Hopefully never. It's painful and more than humiliating. My time with them left scars that just got ripped open wide.

It's not a time I want to relive or try to explain, especially not today. I want my dad back. I miss the safety of his arms and knowing no matter what, he'll be there to help me and rescue me just like he had then. But he's not. He's gone.

"Hey." Shane's low, soft voice startles me over the rumble of the engine. "Are you ok?"

No. Not even a little bit.

I nod, still not able to look at him as my eyes sting with tears and my throat burns with grief and worry. "This is just the beginning."

He pushes out a breath like he's uncomfortable and unsure of what to say. That makes two of us.

"Let them bring it. We've got four kids and the two of us. They've got one dimension, and giant sticks up their asses." He's trying, and I force myself to look at him. He holds out his hand. "I've got a stockpile of whoop-ass of my own. We've got this."

A solid knot lodges itself in my throat as I slide my hand into his. His large, calloused fingers surround mine, and only then do I feel just a little less scared about what lies ahead.

Our ride to campus was silent as I tried to decompress, and Shane gave me the space I needed. He dropped me off at the gym, and luckily, I didn't have a class for another hour. I dashed into the locker room, tore off my clothes, and jumped into a leotard, ready to lose myself in my favorite escape.

Walking into the dark studio, I flip on the lights and pair my phone to the sound equipment, scrolling to one of my favorite songs. I slip on my ballet shoes and stretch, trying to drown out the voices in my head and the thoughts of the battle that's coming.

I face the mirror and take an account. I'm not the weak person I once was or the child whose mother was gone in the blink of an eye. It's been years since I've let these old feelings threaten me, and here in this room, the only person I have to face is myself.

I turn the music loud and get lost in the movement that's so familiar. I imagine it's how a bird feels, spreading its wings wide and soaring. It's the rhythm of my heart, the one that calls to me when I'm spinning out of control and helps me find my way home.

I dance until I'm sweaty and out of breath, and like I've climbed back into my skin. With only minutes to spare before students arrive, I pull out my phone to check my messages, which I've ignored all morning. Scrolling through, I see another text from my ex.

Danny and I haven't spoken since I left New York. He called and messaged me for weeks afterward, but slowly got the hint that I wouldn't be returning either. Beyond that, it was a random text here or there.

It's been a while, but I wasn't surprised by his message of congratulations on my marriage. The following texts expressed his shock that I married a football player, which included how we needed to catch up, and that he missed dancing together. It started to piss me off all over again. The man was always relentless when he wanted something, but not so careful once he had it.

This time, he's insistent that I call. He has an "opportunity" that's too good to refuse. My curiosity is piqued, but not enough to forget the past.

Dancing with Danny was the time of my life. His skill and ability are unmatched. I discovered a whole new way of dancing with him. Dating Danny was great until it wasn't, and I came home with a damaged ankle and a severed heart.

I don't know if I want to crack any part of that old door open again, let alone with Danny. No part of me is interested in reconnecting with him, now or ever. That ship not only sailed, it sank, but a small piece of me is curious about what this opportunity might be.

I stand as students file in, my mind drifting back to Danny's message, and I can't help but wonder what it would feel like to dance at that level again. I'm not even sure if I could do it. I'm not in the shape I once was, and given the stiffness in my ankle after thirty minutes, I have serious doubts about it holding up under intense training.

All of that, and I still can't help but think about what it would be like to be on stage again. The music. The lights. The energy. Doing what my mother told me I was born to do. One more time.

ME: What opportunity?

DANNY: Hey. You and me. The big stage. One night only.

ME: Why me? You've got your pick of the litter.

DANNY: You know why. You're the best.

ME: Not anymore.

DANNY: Lies.

DANNY: I'm still so sorry. Don't let the past keep you from this. It's a chance to give you back what I took. You're amazing, Maggie. Everyone should get to see you dance.

ME: Thank you, but my life is full. I don't have time, and even if I did, I'm not what I used to be. Good luck. I know you'll kill it.

DANNY: I'm not giving up.

Chapter 20

SHANE

I hear the garage door go up, and I'm a lion waiting in the tall grass for its prey to make its way into the clearing. In this case, it's a blue-eyed, one-dimpled little boy who's about to get a taste of his own nasty medicine.

"Shaney, can we have a soda every night? Maggie never lets us have it." Liv is propped up on the counter beside me while Garrett finishes his homework on the other side, sipping a small cup of Coke that I split between them.

"Probably not. This is a special night."

The door opens, and I hear Teddy telling Maggie about some kid getting kicked in the nose and it gushing blood. He enters the kitchen with his usual gusto. Maggie follows closely behind, looking more relaxed than when I left her at the gym this morning.

"What's up, party people?" Teddy sets his blue belt on the counter and takes off the top of his gi, his scrawny chest slightly muscular.

"Shaney is letting us have Coke," Liv announces.

Maggie cocks an eyebrow.

I hold up my hands in defense. "I only had a small bottle, and they're splitting it."

Maggie gives me a teasing glare and turns to put her travel mug in the sink.

"Hey, why don't I get any?" Teddy pouts.

"There's a small amount left if you want some," I gesture toward the fridge.

He jumps up, running to the refrigerator and grabs it from the door.

Garrett puts his pencil down, his eyes flick to mine for the briefest glance while I focus on my phone.

Teddy takes a big gulp. "Oh yuck!" He coughs and sticks his tongue out.

Garrett and Liv giggle.

"What is that?" He wipes his mouth with the back of his hand.

"Old car oil," I answer with a straight face.

"Great. I'm going to die." He starts melting to the floor and grabbing his neck. "Shane, what did you poison me with?"

His dramatics are entertaining, and I can't help but smile. "Super dark, stale, completely awful coffee. Think twice, Daniel Son, before you mess with other people's stuff."

"You got me. That's awful," he laughs, rolling on the floor.

Maggie smiles and looks at Teddy. "All right, tough guy. You smell like stinky feet. Hit the showers and wash everything twice."

Teddy groans and picks himself up off the kitchen floor, but before he disappears, he stops. "That was a good one, Shane." He grins, slaps me on the shoulder, then runs up the stairs.

Maggie starts talking, and we all shush her. "What?!"

I put my hand up to tell her to wait. Then we hear it. One loud *POP*! and Teddy screams like a little girl. He bursts out in laughter and yells, "You guys suck! I think I peed myself!"

I fist-bump Garrett, knowing I got the little punk.

"What was that?" Maggie asks with a huge smile, and I hope I've successfully fulfilled my husbandly duty of making her feel better when she's had a bad day.

"Balloons. We taped them behind the door with some nails so they'd pop as soon as he pushed it open."

"You guys." She continues to laugh. "That was a good one, especially with the coffee diversion. You know he's totally going to up his game now."

"He can bring it." I mean it. I've seen enough to know that this is Teddy's joy. His playful teasing. He's a good kid.

"Did you eat?" Maggie asks me.

"Did you?"

Maggie looks out for everyone and puts herself last. I've learned there are times when Maggie either doesn't eat or just settles for the scraps of whatever the kids have left because she runs out of time or energy. In any case, I don't like it.

"She didn't," Garrett speaks up quietly, keeping his eyes focused on his homework.

I'm getting to know each of these kids. They're unique in their own ways.

The more time I spend with Garrett, the more I understand him. He's calm, studious, and extremely protective. He speaks up when it's important, just like now when he's looking out for Maggie.

"I will. I just haven't had time yet," Maggie defends.

Garrett closes his book. "I'm done. I'm going to shower after Teddy and hope there's not a layer of bacteria left behind."

"Can I have a bath in your tub tonight?" Liv asks.

"Sure," Maggie says.

"With bubbles?"

"Can you keep them in the tub this time?"

"Yes. I'll be very careful." Liv uses my shoulder and leg to climb down from the counter. "Let me get Ariel. She needs a bath, too."

I hold my arm out, preventing Maggie from following her. "How about you tell me what you want, and I'll make your dinner?"

"You don't have to do that. I'll get something once the kids are in bed." She tries to push past me again.

"You can tell me what you want, or I'll make something. Your choice."

"Well, you're bossy tonight." Her lips curve into a smirk.

"Yep." I wait. She doesn't give me anything. "You know you don't have to do everything."

She shrugs. "I'm not used to having help."

"Well, I'm here, so let me help." I see how tired she is. I want to ask how she's feeling about this morning, but I don't want to bring it up right now. "I know it's not good timing when I'll be away many of the upcoming weekends, but I can help when I'm here."

"Ok." Her eyes shift to the floor.

"Have the calls slowed down any?" My phone has been ringing nonstop, and Rob has been breathing down my neck about more interviews since news of Tim's death broke two days ago.

She weighs her head side-to-side. "Ed's trying to keep them off my back as much as possible, but some are breaking through. It's mostly kind messages and condolences." She takes a breath. "I did get a call from the principal at the boys' school wanting to talk."

"Yeah?"

"He wants to discuss how this might be impacting them." She rolls her eyes. "I'll stop by in the morning and see what this is about. Surely, Mr. Pascal has seen the other news."

Something about how she said the last part pricks my grizzly instincts. "What other news?"

She looks at me like I'm dumb. "That we're married."

I sit back slowly, keeping the bear tamed. "Wait a minute. Has this dude asked you out?"

Maggie's slender shoulders move up and down like this is no big deal. "Uh, yeah. He's a single dad, seems to find reasons to call me about the boys, and suggests we get together."

"How many times has this happened?" I keep my tone calm and cool, but I feel like roaring. How many more are there?

One side of her face scrunches. "I don't know. It doesn't matter. I'll go tomorrow, flash my ring around, mention you, and he'll get the hint. He's not like Hank's coach."

"I'll go with you."

"Shane, it's fine. Besides, you can't be with me whenever some guy tries to be nice and see if I'm interested. Just like I won't be with you at all these games, where basically naked women with long legs and self-tanned skin are shoving their number into your pocket."

She sounds huffy. *Is she worried about that?* I sense a bit of jealousy, and I like it. I allow one side of my mouth to perk up.

"What?" She crosses her arms over her chest, and her blue eyes turn a shade darker.

"Firefly, are you worried?"

"About what?"

I'm going to make her squirm. "About women cornering me and slipping their number in my pocket."

"Oh, my goodness, get over yourself."

I think it's possible I see a hint of a blush. *This might be what happiness feels like.* I laugh, and her eyes form slits, hiding those beautiful blue irises.

"If you're not too busy taking names and numbers, don't forget Hank has homecoming this weekend, and Liv's party is Sunday."

My head tips back with a laugh at her ridiculousness. Her eyes grow wide, and her nose flares. She tries to push past me again, but I throw my arm out, catching her by the waist. She stills, her arms cross over her chest tightly.

"Did Hank find a date?" I wonder if the kid most like me took a leap or shied away.

Her upper body relaxes and shifts to the side. "Actually, he asked Sadie. Of course, he had to clarify repeatedly that they're only friends. I hope he doesn't break her heart. She's way too sweet, and he doesn't even see it."

Somehow, I feel like Hank and I are the same in this as well. The difference is that I see Maggie and all her beauty and goodness. I just have no idea what to do about it, so it's best to keep things locked down tight.

Teddy comes flying into the room in his pajamas, and I release Maggie.

"Shane, that was awesome." He steps up on the footrest of my stool and hugs me around the neck. "Good night, and watch out, sucka."

Before I know what to think, he's gone.

Maggie smiles. "I need to see what's happened to Liv and throw her in the bath." She turns back in the doorway. Her gaze falls to the floor, and then drifts back to me. "I'm not very good at that, you know . . . letting people help me."

I stare at her, seeing the vulnerability of her admission.

Her lips push to the side. "Peanut butter and jelly, an apple, and Doritos. Light on the jelly."

She leaves me with her simple order.

Damn. I have no idea what to do about any of this. I'm way out of my element here. I need a playbook, a manual, a damn spreadsheet. Something to help me figure out what in the world I'm supposed to do.

Chapter 21

SHANE

Before the game.

MAGGIE: Good luck today. I've got the game and your jersey on. You've got this. Don't forget to smile for the cameras:)

After the game.

MAGGIE: Picture attached: Hank and Sadie in their homecoming attire.

ME: Did you stuff his pockets with condoms?

MAGGIE: Haha. You're so funny.
MAGGIE: Good game. Cole was on fire. What's up with 38?

ME: 38 is a hotshot. He's going to find out what the bench feels like.

MAGGIE: What time will you be home?

ME: Google says 10:37. What time is Hank supposed to be home?

MAGGIE: Are you worried?

ME: More about you than him.

MAGGIE: Then, hurry up so I don't have to sit here by myself thinking about all of the things he could be doing. Drinking, smoking pot, sex, fights, meth, crack.

ME: Don't forget STDs, oxy, heroin, fentanyl.

MAGGIE: You're so helpful. Lord, help me when it's Liv's turn.

ME: I can't think about that.

MAGGIE: SEE!!!!

ME: I thought you said Sadie was a sweet girl.

MAGGIE: SHE'S IN LOVE WITH HANK.

ME: So

MAGGIE: ***eye roll emoji***

MAGGIE: When a teenage girl is IN LOVE with a teenage boy, she'll do anything to get his attention and go along with *things* to be cool, hoping he will finally see her.

ME: Is there a former teenage boy whose ass I need to kick?

MAGGIE: No. I was dancing, remember.

ME: Go to bed. Hank is a good kid.

MAGGIE: Keep your phone on. If he's hauled down to the clink, he'll call you.

I got home last night to find Maggie sitting in bed with a package of Double Stuf Oreos, watching *SportsCenter*. It only took about five minutes after I lay down in bed for her to try to covertly inch herself closer to me, burrow into my side, and fall asleep.

Now, I stand here watching her laugh with her friends amidst pink and purple streamers and balloons, not listening to the dude next to me drone on about insurance. I'm having a difficult time trying not to think about how I settled her. I was aware of every millimeter she scooted closer. But I kept my mouth shut because what she'll never know is the moment she fell asleep, I put my arm around her and pulled her closer.

I've gotten used to sleeping beside her. Now, when I'm in a hotel room alone, it feels weird. I miss her talking to me and cracking jokes, her softness, and the smell of vanilla and lavender.

We won the game, and my guys played great, but it was harder to be away from all of this than I would've ever imagined. It wasn't that I didn't enjoy being on the field coaching or being part of the game. I did. In fact, I'm finding it more rewarding than I could've expected.

I just haven't ever had anyone other than myself to think about. For so long, I believed human interaction was overrated. I didn't need it or care to let anyone close enough for it to matter. I've never had anyone to come home to, but when Maggie asked me what time I'd be home, it struck me. Home. My home was now with Maggie and these kids.

I knew I was giving up my quiet, simple life when I married Maggie. I hadn't realized it was too quiet and too simple. Before, it didn't matter if I was home or not. Now, I have someone waiting for me. Maggie was waiting and wanted me here.

"Do you have comprehensive coverage on your truck?" the guy next to me asks, interrupting my thoughts.

"Sorry, I need to check on something." I step away, not even trying to hide my annoyance, and make a beeline for the laundry room.

Maggie must have seen me, because two seconds later, she comes in and shuts the door.

"What are you doing?" Her beautiful face scrunches into a frown.

"That guy is a prick. If I stood there listening to him talk about insurance for one more second, I think I might rip my eardrums out in case I ever see him again."

Maggie's face relaxes, and she bursts out laughing, putting a hand over her mouth to cover the noise. "You . . . are being dramatic." She wheezes and leans over, laughing. "He is kind of pricky."

Her bright smile and laughter make everything lighter, like sunshine after a storm. She has no idea how beautiful she is.

"Maggie, I cannot talk to him. Not ever. I'll punch him in the face to put us all out of our misery."

She braces her hands on my biceps, laughing again and stifling her giggles with my chest. I think about putting my arms around her and pulling her closer, but I stop myself. More physical contact won't help anything.

"Carmen and I can't stand him either. I'm pretty sure John steers clear for the same reason. We have no idea why Simone is still with him."

"Don't make me go back out there."

Her face tips up, still bright and joyful. Those blue eyes I missed in the stands yesterday twinkle.

I run a hand over my face. "Where's Teddy? I'll pay him to shoot a Nerf round at him."

Maggie starts laughing again, and I want her to keep doing it. "Are birthday parties not your thing, big guy? Let's go sing "Happy Birthday" and let Liv blow out her candles. Then we'll shove cake at these people and kick them out so we can watch Mark drop dimes. But stay with me. I got you. I won't let that dipstick anywhere near you, Grizz."

She grabs my hand and tugs me back into the kitchen.

I don't need her to protect me, but I'll go along with her dramatics to hold her hand a little longer. Her small hand inside mine is all I'll allow, but when she intertwines our fingers, a jolt of alarm zips up my spine and down my limbs. My pores explode, and my skin is instantly on fire, but cool at the same time.

Maggie's other hand wraps around my forearm, her body sliding close, and I freeze. I know it's innocent, and she doesn't mean anything by it, but somehow it feels too . . . intimate. I don't want to give her the wrong idea or let her think I'm offering something I'm incapable of.

I drop her hand and step away, needing space and air to calm the hell down. Thankfully, Maggie doesn't seem to notice. The last thing I want is to confuse or hurt her.

"Who's ready for some cake?" she asks.

"Me," Liv shouts from her perch on Cole's lap, where she adjusts the tiara on his head.

Hank is beside him with a matching tiara, cocked to the side. It's a nice distraction, but I can't laugh after she placed a gold crown on my head a couple of nights ago, along with three necklaces. I drew the line when it came to makeup.

Carmen lifts the cake from the counter while Maggie grabs plates, forks, and the lighter.

Maggie glances at me over her shoulder. "Stick with your man," she winks.

I want to stick with her as long as she'll let me, but that's just it. Eventually, whatever this is will fade. She'll disappear.

I grab a cold water bottle from the refrigerator, taking a second to pull myself together. I want to slam the door on my head. Maybe leave it in there, and see if I can find my commonsense lying around somewhere because I'm afraid it's freaking gone.

I won't mix things up with Maggie. She's my wife. That's it.

I stay put in the corner, watching her move to the end of the table that looks like it was glitter-bombed.

Birthday parties aren't something I've ever experienced. It's a bit overwhelming, but the smile on Liv's face, illuminated by the light of the five candles and surrounded by the people who love her most, tells me how important it is. At five, I was being shuffled from one foster home to another, hoping I didn't end up with someone who'd hurt me.

The group sings, and Liv makes a wish as she takes an exaggerated inhale and blows the candles out with the biggest smile on her innocent little face.

Carmen cuts the cake, and Simone serves slices as the room fills with chatter.

"Next, we'll be eating cake at your wedding," Maggie says to Carmen.

"I know. Shane, dust your suit off and shine your shoes. Don't think Maggie won't pull you onto the dance floor."

Maggie's only mentioned the wedding in passing. I didn't know I was expected to go.

"I don't dance," I say, as my agitation simmers underneath my skin.

Simone laughs. "Well, with Danny trying to get her back to New York, you'd better change that."

Maggie's eyes hit mine from across the room. DannyZ? Mr. Hippity-Hop? Her ex?

"What does Danny want?" Cole jumps right on that, his irritation evident.

I listen as the space between my ears fills with a bit more pressure.

"Nothing," Maggie says quickly. "He's producing a show and wants me to dance with him. I said no."

Cole sets his water bottle on the table with a little too much force, and tiny droplets jump out of the top. "Of course he does. His timing is uncanny."

"Cole," Maggie warns as if asking him to drop it, but I want to know exactly what's going on.

Simone cringes. "Sorry."

John asks Cole about the team, and everyone moves on, but I'm still hung up on Danny, this show, and why Maggie hasn't said anything.

This is why I remain distant and detached. Relationships with people are always complicated and highly disappointing. When you don't have expectations or get emotionally involved, they're a breeze. I want to kick my own ass for letting this information about Danny sting.

Thirty minutes later, Maggie shuts the door behind Simone and the prick. I glance at her from my spot on the couch. I'm tired, irritated, and ready to watch football.

She flops down on the couch next to me, her attention on the screen where Mark is warming up. I watch closely, looking for soreness or weakness. I don't notice anything beyond the possible stiffness Maggie pointed out weeks ago.

She yawns. "Do you know what the boys are doing?"

"They challenged Cole to some racing game. Liv is playing with her new toys in her room."

I've been waiting to ask about the wedding and Danny. Danny isn't any of my business, and I'm not even sure why I care, except I remember Cole saying there wasn't anyone *here* I needed to worry about. Then, there was his reaction tonight. Neither sits well with me. If anyone is messing with Maggie, I want to know about it. I shouldn't. I know it. I should keep my nose out of it and mind my own fucking business, but dammit, I can't.

"So, when's the wedding?" I dive in, not even attempting to make this smooth.

Maggie straightens a little, likely sensing the bite in my tone. "Two weeks. You have a game that day, but I was hoping you'd go with me. I'm in the wedding, so I have to be there early, but maybe you could meet me there." There's an abnormal shyness in her tone, which dissolves some of the protective layers I'm piling back on.

Damn her.

"I'm not dancing." I draw a line.

She bites her bottom lip. "We'll see about that. I have a feeling you can move, Grizz."

I groan, and she smiles as I shove right into the next topic without giving myself time to second-guess it. "What's the deal with Mr. Dancing Machine messaging you?"

She shifts slightly, and I see her smirk out of the corner of my eye, which is not what I was expecting. "You know who Danny is?"

I don't respond. No way am I admitting I spent an hour looking at pictures and videos of them dancing. I'm not sure the dude ever buttons his shirt, if he's even wearing one.

She tugs on the hem of her shirt, which I'm learning is one of her tells. She's uncomfortable, and it only confirms my suspicion that something about this guy stinks.

My grip on the remote tightens, waiting for her to offer something.

"He messaged me about a show he's producing and wants me to dance with him."

I hold in a grunt. "What'd you tell him?"

"I told him no."

"Why?"

One side of her face scrunches up. "Uh, because I have responsibilities."

"What if we could figure something out?" I push, wanting the real reason because that sounds like a load of shit.

"Shane, I can't. My days of dancing at that level are over."

"Why? When is the show? What would you have to do to prepare?"

Throughout the afternoon, my mind has twisted around and around like a rubber band about to be looped over one too many times. I want to know what's really going on and what in the hell Danny has to do with it.

"Shane. I can't. I don't have the time." She tugs on her shirt again, her eyes focused on the material. "I don't know if my ankle would hold up under intense training. Plus . . . "

She won't look at me. I want to know what she was going to say. "Plus, what?" I focus on her face, waiting.

Her chest rises as she inhales a deep breath. "It's a long story, and it doesn't matter."

I wait for her to meet my eyes. "I think it matters a lot."

"Danny and I—" She starts, but Liv runs into the room sniffling and climbs into my lap, linking her arms around my neck and burying her face.

Every sense is on high alert. I have no idea what to do with anyone crying, let alone a little girl—my favorite one. I was about to fly to New York and kick Danny's ass, but someone else was just added to the list because whoever made Liv cry is about to get torn apart.

"Hey." Maggie scoots over and tries to brush Liv's hair out of her face. "What's wrong?"

Liv only squeezes my neck tighter, so I place my hand on her back.

"Liv, what happened?" Maggie tries again.

The dampness of her tears trickles down my neck, her little fingers digging in, and I hold her a little tighter.

"Liv," I try. "What's wrong?"

"My mama didn't come." Her voice is small and muffled.

My eyes dart to Maggie's, which are wide like she has no idea what's going on either.

"What do you mean, sweetie?" Maggie asks.

Her little voice wobbles. "I blew out my candles and wished my mama would come to my party, but she didn't."

I run my hand over her hair and continue to hold her tight. This part of the birthday experience I can relate to. Not that I have any idea how to make it better.

Maggie blows out a breath and rubs her back, her fingertips brushing mine. "You know what my mama said about wishes? She said they're like prayers. Sometimes we ask God for things, and He answers our prayers. But sometimes He decides it's not the right time or He has something even better planned."

She pauses, but when Liv doesn't move, she continues. "Beauty, it's the same with wishes. Sometimes, our wishes come true, and sometimes . . . maybe it's just not the right wish. Your mama couldn't be here today, but look how many people *were*. All the people you invited, who watched you blow out your candles. They were all wishes that came true, and every one of them loves you so much."

Liv raises her head and wipes her face, her little lip still quivering. "Do you think she will ever come?"

"I don't know, sweetheart." Maggie rests against me to look at Liv and pushes the damp strands of hair away from her face. "But you have me, Shane and Cole and the boys. We all have each other, and it's the best."

Liv's tiny hands loosen on my neck. "Will you always come to my birthday parties, Shaney?"

I don't even hesitate. "You bet. I wouldn't miss it. It was the best birthday party I've ever been to."

She smiles. "Really?"

"Really."

"I'm glad you're a part of our family now," she says, placing her hands on my scruffy cheeks.

Every ounce of my piss-poor attitude evaporates along with her tears.

"Maggie says families are like wolves. The pack sticks together. So, I guess you're stuck with us."

I smile, but my chest feels like it might burst with hope. The kind of hope I shouldn't let surface, let alone expand. "That sounds good to me."

She hugs me again, her sweet smile returning.

"How about a bath with extra bubbles tonight?" Maggie asks.

"Yeah. Can I bring my new toy in?"

"Sure. Go get it."

Liv hugs me once more and hops down. Thank goodness she's feeling better.

"I thought I was going to have to murder someone." I roll my neck, needing to get my own emotions back under lockdown.

"Sad tears are the worst." Maggie shifts away from me, her warmth and scent gone. "When someone hurts these kids, I want to rip their head off, and right now, I want to call Monica and tell her what a selfish piece of shit she is."

"Do I get a turn?"

Maggie snorts, getting up as Liv returns with toys.

"We aren't done with that other conversation," I warn.

She glances at me over her shoulder but doesn't respond, following Liv down the hall.

I rest my head on the couch, watching Mark call a play with Liv's tears still fresh on my shirt. It's been a long time since I've revisited my birthdays, and I really don't want to think about them now. If it was celebrated at all, it was with people I didn't want to be with.

So many times, I'd wished for my mom or dad to walk in the door and take me back, but they never did. If I'd understood anything about God and prayer, I would have been on my knees day and night. I share in Liv's tears and heartache, wanting something so badly that's likely never coming true.

Cole drops onto the couch. "What's the score?"

"Seven to nothing, New York."

"Are Mark and Sean still coming out for bye week?"

"Yeah." Mark will bring his large ego with him, and Sean will try to read too much into all of this.

"The guys will lose their minds if they come to practice."

I roll my eyes. "Mark's a giant diva, so level your expectations."

Cole laughs. "Where's Maggie?"

"Helping Liv with a bath."

He slumps into the couch. "I bet all of this is more than you imagined." He pauses. "Thanks for being here. The kids love you. Teddy told me about your pranks, and Garrett showed me his science projects. I laughed so hard I couldn't breathe when Hank told me about Maggie thinking he had a girl in his room." He laughs again and then sobers. "I wish I could be around more, but it's nice to know you're here. I'm glad they have you now."

I'm not sure what to say. "They're great kids."

"Do me a favor and keep an eye on Maggie? She's tough, but the stuff with Cliff and Joan will hit her hard, and now with Danny texting her. . ."

I wondered about Danny, but if Cole doesn't like him, that tells me enough.

Since he brought him up, I won't waste an opportunity. "What about Danny?"

"He's just a piece of work."

"Do I need to kick his ass?" I'm in the mood to punch something.

"Only if I get to help." His tone is serious compared to moments ago. "Look, they're her stories to tell. I just worry about her. She's got a lot to deal with and doesn't need anyone messing with her head."

This doesn't make me feel better, but I drop it because he's right. It should be up to Maggie. I want to know, but I want her to be the one to tell me.

"You're a good brother."

Cole stands. "Yeah, well, I hit the jackpot when it came to siblings, so I'm the lucky one. I gotta study for a test tomorrow. I'll see you at practice."

He slaps my hand and heads out the door. I try to get back to the game and Mark, but all I can think is that I feel pretty lucky to be here at all.

Chapter 22

MAGGIE

I step out of the shower and into the steam-filled bathroom. I'm ready to fall into bed, then make like a sloth and subtly scoot closer to Shane's warm body inch by inch. Seriously, the man's temperature must run ten degrees higher than the average person's. I sleep in a heated cocoon beside him, and it's amazing.

When I pull the door open, Shane is propped up against the headboard, wearing his glasses and holding a book while the game plays low on the TV. My head falls back with an exhausted groan because those glasses only make me want to snuggle him in a completely different way.

"What's the problem?" He studies me over the top of the black rims.

"Nothing," I grumble, falling onto my side of the bed.

"How was Liv?"

"Better. She was asleep before I even made it to page three. Monica sent a card, but I'm not sure I'll give it to her. I worry it'll just confuse her even more." Shane doesn't say anything, so I continue after spreading flat on the bed, like an overdone pancake. "I don't know how to handle any of this stuff."

His chin tips down so he can look at me. "I wish I would've had someone to tell me the things you told her tonight. These kids are really lucky to have you."

I want to laugh, but I'm too tired. I feel so inadequate. "What are you reading?"

Shane's brown-green eyes shoot to the corner. "It's about a guy who walks through the Himalayas."

"I would've never pegged you as a brainiac. Read to me."

"No."

"Come on, pleeeeaaase. I hate reading, but audiobooks I can handle. I bet you have a very sexy reading voice." He doesn't say anything. "Come on, Grizz. Read to me."

He slaps the book shut. "Nice try. Tell me what's up with Danny the Douche and the show."

"Danny the Douche? How do you know he's a douche?" I fold my arms and tuck them behind my head.

"I have good instincts."

I don't want to talk about this. Discussing Danny and everything that led to my leaving New York only dredges up bad feelings and old scars. "Can we not talk about it? I'm not doing the show."

"I won't make you talk about something you don't want to, but you shouldn't give up an opportunity because of him."

I huff and throw an arm over my face, wanting to hide from his astute gaze. Shane can be a real pain in my ass when he wants to be.

"It's not because of him." I'm getting snippy now.

"It's not?" he challenges.

I groan. "It's complicated. I don't want to go back there, and I certainly don't want to dance with him."

"But do you want to dance in the show?" the freakishly big guy next to me asks like he's somehow figured out how to read my mind.

I push a surrendering breath out between my lips, sit up, and prop a pillow behind me. "I don't know. It'd be an incredible opportunity, but Shane, I don't know if I can even do it. My ankle is weak, and it's not the same. Dancing is one thing, but pointe is another."

"Pointe?"

"Yeah, you know, pointe shoes, where ballerinas dance on their toes. If I'm going to dance, that's the only way, and he knows it."

Shane's dark brows come together. "He's a hip-hop dancer."

"Yeah, but you should see what happens when you mix that with something incredibly conservative and classic like ballet. It's contradictory. Exotic. Captivating. Alluring."

"Never mind. You definitely shouldn't do it."

I swat his arm. "This show will be a huge undertaking and grueling. He doesn't accept anything but perfection."

"And that's why he wants you." The way he says it, so calm and casual, awakens my nerves.

I shake my head. "I can't dance like that anymore. He doesn't understand that."

"What if you could? Would you do it?"

I roll it around in my head for a moment. "I don't know. There are too many things that just wouldn't work."

Shane's quiet before he speaks. "If there were even a chance I could run back out onto the field, I wouldn't think twice to give it everything I've got to at least try."

Well, crap. He just has to go and get all tender and vulnerable. Now I'm going to get into all the things I didn't want to. He knows exactly how to push me until I give.

"But there's more to it than that. It's not only my ankle and the kids and the fact that he's on the other side of the country."

"What is it then?"

I pull the hem of my tank down and put my hands in my lap. "It's opening a door I closed and locked. If you crack it open, you have no idea what you might find. Danny is one thing, which is enough, but then you add in . . . "

I peek at him and all the tenderness he tries so hard to hide, waiting patiently to understand.

"What if I find out I'll never dance like I used to? I put it behind me, and I'm ok with it. I love teaching, and I don't know . . . " I shrug. "I'd like to open my own studio someday. But trying to get back to what I used to be and finding out I can't . . . I don't know if I can go through the heartbreak all over again."

His bicep rests against my shoulder, and it's comforting and steadying. "One thing at a time, Firefly. Danny shouldn't be a factor." He says it so matter-of-factly, as if it's that easy.

I hug my knees to my chest. I didn't want to talk about this, but here I am. "Danny and I dated, or at least that's what I thought we were doing. I was young, naive, and infatuated. He was a bit older, good-looking, and I'd never seen someone dance with his uninhibited rawness before. We became friends. He was my best friend. He taught me a whole other side to dancing, and it made me better. It was amazing, combining our styles. I thought, like any young, dumb girl, that he was it. That *I* was it for him. I was blinded by love or fascination or whatever."

I shake my head, remembering. "When I got the lead in the ballet, I couldn't believe I'd actually done it." I glance over at Shane, his gaze set on me. "I went to his apartment to tell him. I had wanted to surprise him, but I found him in bed with a woman. Another dancer we were friends with. He was my best friend. It was humiliating. I couldn't understand and just stood there, staring, wondering what I'd done wrong. I didn't think about what I was doing. Everything I thought I knew just blew up in my face in a second."

I'm pretty sure I hear Shane grunt, but I keep going.

"I freaked out and took off, tripped down the stairs, and broke my ankle in two places. I didn't even feel the pain until I hobbled out and hailed a cab, realizing I needed to get to the ER. Then I had to carry myself in and tell the producers I couldn't dance in the ballet when they'd taken a chance on me. It took me a long time to get over it. I lost my best friend and my dream in one night. I was so embarrassed. I'd lost everything over a big, fat lie I let myself believe."

I wipe my palms on my bare thighs. "I've moved on. I know now I was meant to come back here. I wouldn't have given up my spot in the show by choice, and I would've missed out on time with my dad. Who knows what would've happened with the kids? I don't want to go back there or dance with him again. I'm different. It could never be the same, and I don't want it to."

Shane bumps my arm with his. "You shouldn't give him the power to keep you from doing this. He doesn't deserve that kind of weight over your decision. If you want it, you do it on your terms this time. You call the shots."

I rest my head on his shoulder, exhaustion taking over. "My life is here, though. I can't just pick up and fly to New York every other day."

"When you want something, you figure out how to make it work. Make him bring his douchey ass here, then I'll kick it all the way back to New York."

Sitting here next to Shane, it somehow seems possible. "I don't know, Grizz."

"I know you can do it. You can put the hurt aside and show the world what you've got. It's what we do. We play through the pain and hurt because we can't not play, never knowing when it will be our last time."

I grab his arm, tugging it to me, and squeeze. I know how much he misses playing. "I'll think about it. Will you come in all Grizzly-like and intimidate the shit out of him?"

"If I find myself in the same vicinity as him, he'll understand exactly what's up," Shane growls.

I laugh, having no doubt he means it, and I definitely wouldn't mind seeing it. We sit together quietly, while I rest against him.

"Will you read to me now? Please."

He huffs, and I know he rolled his eyes. I scoot down to lie on my side while he opens the book.

"One chapter. That's it."

"Deal."

I move an inch closer to him as he starts to read. His rough voice is just as soothing as his strength and warmth. I think about what he said about not giving Danny or that awful situation power, but mostly, it's his confidence in my ability that makes me want to try. His faith that somehow, I could figure it all out and dance one more time.

Chapter 23

MAGGIE

"What is that?"

There's a buzzing sound, but why isn't he doing anything about it?

Shane groans. Not his usual growly groan. It's weak and pathetic.

I'm tucked tight next to him, but when my hand grazes his arm, he's hot and clammy. I sit up and search for whatever is buzzing. It's not my phone. I crawl over Shane, resting my body across his to reach for his, and he whimpers.

I shut his alarm off, noticing the time. *Crap*. It's late.

I roll back to my side and pat around. My hand glides up his neck to his ear, and then his hair.

"What are you doing?" he whines.

Shane just whined like a little boy. I stifle a laugh.

"Trying to find your forehead. You feel hot."

"I feel awful. Everything hurts. Please stop touching me," he grumbles.

I shift to get out of bed, but his big hand reaches out and grabs my arm. "Don't go."

I freeze. Seeing Shane like this, even though I can't *really* see him, is a whole different ball game. I'm not sure what's happening, but I kind of like needy Shane.

"I have to get the kids up and ready for school. It's late, but we need to take your temperature."

He lets go of me, and I climb off the bed to get the thermometer from the bathroom. I use the light to guide my way and swipe it across his forehead.

"I'll be back with Tylenol and some water."

He grunts, and I take that as an "ok."

I hear the boys upstairs as I pull the basket of meds from above the fridge and find what I need before returning to the bedroom. I get Shane to sit up long enough to swallow the pills and drink some water, and then he's back down for the count.

I leave him be while I feed the kids and get them on the bus. By some miracle, Gwen arrives early and helps Liv get ready for preschool so I can check on Shane and make it to class on time.

In our room, I retake his temperature, and he stirs, slightly opening his eyes. His fever is down.

"I'm freezing. Come back and lie next to me," he slurs.

Oh man, snuggling this guy is becoming my jam, and now I wouldn't even have to hide it. It's open season, but I have to teach a stupid class.

"I have to get to the gym." I try really hard not to sound disappointed. "I'll check on you when I get back. I set an alarm on your phone for when it's time for more Ibuprofen, so make sure you take it."

I brush his forehead with my fingers, and he grabs it. "Don't go."

I laugh. "This is my bed. I'll be back."

He looks so pitiful and unhindered. I can't imagine what it was like for him growing up and being sick, likely not having anyone to care for him. It makes me want to crawl back into bed with him even more.

"I'll be back," I promise again, and he lets go of my hand.

I fly around the room, changing and trying to get out the door on time. I take one last look at him before I step out, and he's sleeping peacefully.

After finding someone to cover my last class, I return to find Shane mostly naked, except for his boxer briefs, lying on his stomach, with the duvet and top sheet carelessly tossed on the floor. I take a second to peruse his sculpted back. No blemishes. No tattoos. Just beautiful skin over So. Many. Muscles. He probably has more muscles in his back than I have in my entire body.

He coughs, breaking the spell, so I move to the side of the bed to feel his forehead. I run my fingers through his short, dark hair, and he moans.

"You came back." His deep voice sounds even lower, and I don't miss the surprise in his tone like he didn't believe I would.

"I found a sub so I could come back and check on you."

He turns his head to the side, and I feel his forehead with the back of my hand. He's cooler than this morning.

"You have practice. Are you going to be able to make it, or do you want me to call CC?" I ask, leaving my hand on his head.

"How long do I have?"

I check my phone. "A couple of hours."

He rolls over, revealing his bare chest.

"Good Lord." I press my lips together, having meant to keep that to myself.

"What? What's wrong?" Shane growls.

"Nothing," I choke, trying not to laugh with hysteria.

Shane's body is chiseled from head to toe. It's ridiculous, and I have to sleep next to him every night, knowing exactly what's underneath all that soft cotton.

"I have an hour for you to pretend you're not snuggling me then." He says it like he's doing me a favor, but there's no way I'm cuddling his almost naked body.

I want to. Oh, I really want to, but it's way too tempting, and then you add on his apparent sickly neediness, and we have a recipe for disaster.

Shane wants simple. Platonic. Unhindered. I kind of want to mix things up and see what happens, *but* not when Shane is clearly out of his mind.

"How about you sleep a little longer? I'll make you something to eat and wake you up in a little bit."

"No. Stay here. Talk to me." He says it so quietly, like he's embarrassed to ask.

How in the world could I say no?

I take a breath, feeling like I'm crossing my own line in the sand. A line that once I toe over, feelings will start to take shape that I know will be one-sided.

Shane has an impenetrable, cinder block wall he's built around himself. But sick Shane seems to be peeking over it, and succumbing to a teensy bit of vulnerability. Whether it's due to the fever or not, I like it. I like it a lot, but I know it won't last.

So, I climb up on the bed and sit beside him. He flings his big arm over my legs and pulls me closer, burying his face in my thigh. I run my fingers through his hair, feeling him relax. I don't talk, hoping he'll go back to sleep.

I'm pretty sure Shane's brain goes a hundred miles a minute All. The. Time. Looking at him now, his features soft and gentle, I can't help but see the little boy who had no one. I let my fingers drift through his hair, hoping to soothe him in a way I'd guess he's never been comforted before.

I want to hold him and let him know he's safe because a big part of me thinks he's never felt that way. Hopefully, asking me to stay and me sitting here is a beginning for him.

After a while, surrounded by his warmth, I rest my head against the headboard and snooze, waking when he rolls over. I check the time and see that if he's going to make it to practice, he needs to get up soon.

I scoot off the bed and in the bathroom to run water into the big tub. I hear rustling and turn around to see Shane sitting up, rubbing his face.

"What are you doing?" He coughs, and it sounds awful.

"Running you a bath. Get your big butt in here and soak in some bath salts. It'll help open things up and get you through practice."

He groans and looks around. "A bath? What?"

"Don't ask questions. Get in here. You kind of smell."

"At one point, I thought I was burning alive."

"Well, yeah. You destroyed the bed. While you're gone, I'll wash everything. Hurry up. I have soup in the kitchen. I'll get you some and a Gatorade to take with you."

I let the steaming hot bath run as the room fills with the scent of eucalyptus and spearmint. I collect the duvet and sheets as Shane stands, stretching.

"Maggie." His soft tone causes me to stop.

"Yeah?"

"Thanks . . . for staying."

I smirk. "Will you take care of me when I'm sick?"

He stares at me for a few long seconds. His intense gaze causes my skin to prickle with heat.

"I'm probably not very good at it, but I'll try." He's so serious, but there's a hint of insecurity.

Ugh. I'm so confused about what is going on here. I don't need confusion. I need straightforward. Too many things are happening right now, and Shane and I need uncomplicated. Easy. Simple. Friendship.

I finish stripping the bed as he closes the bathroom door.

Friends. We're going to be friends. So, it doesn't matter how many muscles he has, or how sexy he looks in his glasses, or how I could listen to him read to me for hours about some trek across mountains. I will not think about how confident and strong he is, or how underneath the tough exterior resides a sweet and gentle and generous man. All these things will make an excellent . . . friend.

Now, I just need to get my mind and body to quit playing tug of war because I can see myself falling hard for someone who has no desire or intention to ever fall back.

Chapter 24

SHANE

I wake up in my hotel room groggy and coughing. We flew in last night, and even though I'm feeling better, I'm still not one hundred percent. I miss Maggie's small body curled against mine. The king-size beds I've been used to since I could afford one no longer feel the same if she's not in it.

I have a vague recollection of the morning I woke up sick, and I've replayed those memories over and over in my mind, not wanting to let them slip away. I remember asking Maggie to stay with me, and at one time, I would have been ashamed of my weakness. But I can't be embarrassed about something I want to do all over again.

A stronger man wouldn't have let his guard down. He wouldn't have craved the presence of his wife, but I did. I caved. I wanted Maggie next to me. I wanted to hear her voice and be surrounded by her scent and touch. I wanted her comfort and only hers.

So, I allowed myself to indulge in Maggie. Then, after taking my temperature and making sure I was ok, she hurried about and stripped right in front of me, likely thinking I was asleep. She stood there taking off and throwing on clothes so quickly that I barely saw a thing. What I know is I want to see more, and not just of Maggie's bare skin.

Oh, I want to see a lot more skin, but also all the things that make up the insides of Maggie Matthews—Carter. Maggie Carter. The one who signed the paperwork, putting her name next to mine. I want to know her like I've never cared to know another person.

I know I shouldn't, but I want more than the feel of Maggie's hand on my forehead. I want her to run her fingers through my hair every night because it's natural and comfortable. I want her to talk to me and tell me everything like she told me about Danny and what happened in New York. I want her to dance again—to prove to herself she can and not give up over some guy who shouldn't have had her in the first place. I want her to know she's that good because I have no doubt.

I want all of this, but I can't have it. I won't be selfish, not with her. Having her means I'll eventually hurt her. How long would it take her to see I have nothing to offer? That I'm empty inside. Maybe she already does.

I run a hand over my face and sit up, pulling my phone from the nightstand. I have three missed calls from Greg.

He's continued to call. I know what he wants, and I'm not paying. I see a missed call from Maggie, and my empty stomach stirs with worry.

I tap her name.

"Hello," she whispers.

"Hey. I'm sorry. I just saw you called. Everything ok?"

"No." I hear her pull the phone away to cough. "Grizz, I need you to get your big booty back here. I want you to lie your overly heated body beside mine and read to me. I'm so cold," she whines. "Liv's sick too, but she's not a hot box like you are." She coughs again.

I feel awful I'm not there, but I can't help my smile, and I'm so glad she can't see.

"Maggie, I'm sorry. I wish I could be there."

She sniffs.

If she's crying, I won't be able to stand it.

"Do you really? I'd probably cough all over you, and I'm sure I smell."

"Yes." Never in my life have I wanted to care for someone, and I don't know how to do it, but I don't want to be here. I want to be there.

"Well, that makes me feel a little better." She pauses.

I'm ok just listening to her breathe, and I realize I have a big problem that I need to get a handle on fast. *Shit.*

She sniffs again. "Good luck today. I'll be watching."

"I'll be there as soon as I can."

"Ok."

"Try to sleep."

She laughs. "Yeah, right. Liv keeps kicking me."

We say goodbye, and I'm ready to be on the plane headed back home. Instead, I have a game to focus on and guys counting on me to help them get one step closer to the championship.

I climb out of bed and shower, allowing myself to think about Maggie for a few more minutes. I need to go home with my head in check, where I ignore whatever these feelings might be, and any growing desires are squashed and forgotten. Maggie is becoming way too important, and beware of danger signs are popping up everywhere. The problem is, with Maggie, I kind of want to ignore them.

The wheels hit the tarmac, and I power on my phone, checking for missed calls from Maggie. I have another one from Greg, who left a voicemail.

I grab my bag and quickly make my way to my truck, listening to the message from my dear old dad on my way home. It's exactly what I expected, but his mention of contacting Maggie if he doesn't get what he wants sets me on fire. He won't be contacting Maggie about anything. Ever. I'll make sure of that.

I pull into the garage and enter a dark house, except for the flicker of the TV from the living room. Maggie is curled up on the couch with Liv, and the boys are spread out on the floor with blankets piled on top of them.

I crouch in front of Maggie and just look at her. She has the blanket tucked under her chin, her mouth is open, and her hair is falling out of her short ponytail. Somehow, I still find her to be the most beautiful woman I've ever seen. This little firefly is becoming very hard to resist.

After the win today, I relaxed on the flight back, reminding myself of all the reasons why letting myself want Maggie is impossible. There's really only one. I don't have what she needs or deserves. Looking at her, I know I'll have to tattoo that reminder on my brain.

I push a loose strand of hair out of her face. She shifts and stretches before opening her eyes.

"Hey. You're home. Good game today."

"Yeah. Do you want me to carry the boys to bed?"

She sniffs, and her nose is full of snot. "No. They're sick, too. We're all camping out here tonight, so I can give them more medicine when they need it, and I know they're ok. I have alarms set for each of them."

"Do you need me to get you anything?"

"No." She sits up a little surveying the kids. "I think we're set for now. I'm glad you're home."

Me too.

I stand. "I'll be back." I head to our room, use the restroom, and change into joggers and a T-shirt before returning. "Move over."

"Shane, you should just go to bed and rest. You're still getting over this."

"Move over."

She huffs but moves so I can sit. Leaning back, I open the footstool, and Maggie rests her head on my thigh.

"Tell me about the game," she whispers.

I tell her about the hotshot not cooling his jets after our last go round, and in a matter of minutes, she's back asleep. I look at the kids and back down at Maggie before resting my head against the couch, realizing how happy I am to be home. A huge part of me is scared of how attached I'm becoming to this family. It's like a dream, and at any moment, I'm going to wake up and find out they'll never be mine.

Chapter 25

MAGGIE

Each sewn-on tiny gold reflector shimmers in the afternoon light pouring in through the window of our dressing room. My reflection stares back at me in the full-length antique mirror, and I tug at the neck of the scratchy sequined material.

I hate dresses like this. It's not this gown in particular. It's gorgeous—a fitted maxi with a high neck and cap sleeves, leading to a low-cut back that dips close to my behind. The sparkly gold is exquisitely elegant and makes Simone look like a goddess, but my short stature doesn't do it justice.

I wish, like Liv, I could feel like a princess. But it's suffocating and I want to crawl out of my skin. There was a time when I wore a beautiful dress, and I felt mature and pretty, but it was a turning point. A moment in time when I was no longer innocent. One second, a little girl holding my mom's hand, thinking the world was good and kind. And in the next, darkness enveloped me, as I encountered the ugliness and harshness of life.

I pull at the neck again and check my phone. I've been expecting a text from Shane telling me he's here, but I've received nothing. Something about knowing he's here will help me breathe easier. His calm, strong presence grounds me, and I need that today.

It's like we've settled into a rhythm these past few weeks. Since getting over the flu, something changed between Shane and me. We've become friends who live and sleep together. I've shared personal things with him, and he's been supportive and caring. For the first time in so long, I don't feel so alone, and I hope Shane feels the same.

"Hey." Simone stands beside me, fixing her long, dark curls. "You ok? You're fidgety."

"Yeah. I'm fine. I'm just . . . excited," I lie, looking over at Carmen with her mom, blinking back tears so her mascara doesn't run. She's the spitting image of a blushing bride, and I have to look away as a sharp pain sears through me at the moment I'll never have.

I need to get a grip. Watching her walk down the aisle with her dad will be a knife in a freshly scabbed wound. This isn't how I want to feel today. I want to be full of joy for one of my very best friends, and I am. I'm so happy for her and John. They'll have an amazing life together, and I'm grateful I get to be a part of it. Selfishly, though, I can't help but grieve all the things I'll never have.

I check my phone again. Still nothing from Shane, but I have a voicemail from my lawyer, and given that it's Saturday, it's not good news.

I close my eyes and take another deep breath as someone peeks their head in the door.

"About five minutes, ladies."

I put my arm around Carmen, willing myself to let go of lost dreams and things I cannot control. "I don't think I've ever seen a more beautiful bride."

She squeezes me. "You ok?"

A lump forms in my throat, but I quickly swallow it down. There's no room for tears today, and Carmen deserves my full attention.

I force a smile. "Weddings are an emotional roller coaster."

"Tell me about it. I don't think I've cried this much since they announced *Gilmore Girls* was ending. John is going to freak when he sees what a mess I am."

We laugh and gather our bouquets.

"Nah. You'll have to hand him your hankie when he sees you. Trust me."

"Come on, girls," Simone says in her best diva voice. "It's showtime."

I made it through the ceremony with only two tears and one bout of searching each face, hoping it was Shane's. I took slow, calming breaths through every step of Carmen's saunter down the aisle and all through their vows, and I freaking made it.

I slide my arm through Carmen's brother's, ready for the party and one step closer to getting out of this dress.

I'm still waiting for Shane, and that voicemail hangs over my head like a guillotine.

As the bride and groom greet their guests, I slip away to the dressing room to check my phone.

SHANE: I'm not going to make it. Bad game. Sorry. I'll see you at home.

Tears prick my eyes all over again, but this time, I let them hang on the edge. I wanted him here. I wanted his steadiness and banter. I wanted him to take my mind off all the heavy and put it back on easy and fun for a little while.

My fingers hover over the letters to type back something like I understand, but right now, I don't. I don't understand. He told me he'd be here, and even though he's had a rough day, he's not the only one.

I get he knows nothing about what I've been through or how I'm feeling, but he told me he'd come. I was counting on him. I needed him to be here.

I close the text box and pace for a minute, gearing myself up for what is likely in the voicemail. I don't want to listen to it, but just like facing today and this dress and all of the grief swirling inside me, ignoring it won't change a thing.

I stop in front of the window where the last light of the day creeps below the horizon. I hit play, put the phone to my ear, and close my eyes. I didn't think it could be worse than Cliff and Joan suing for custody of the kids, but it is. It's worse.

My stomach falls to the floor and bounces right back up, with nothing but the taste of bile. I set my phone on the window ledge where I rest my arms, trying to pull in a breath, but my lungs won't expand.

"Hey, there you are." Simone enters, but I can't turn around or put on the brave face I've been wearing all day. Not right now. "Hey, you ok? What's wrong?" She's closer now, and her hand falls on my shoulder.

"I heard from my lawyer. They're suing me for custody," I choke out. "But . . . they only want Liv." My voice breaks, and I try to suck it all back behind my quivering lip.

I can't even think about it. It's only further proof of how awful these people are. How could any judge not see it based on this?

Simone wraps me in a hug. "What can I do?"

I shake my head and hold onto her. I'm mad. Angry. Sick.

"How could they do this?" I ask, knowing there's no answer.

"I don't know, honey."

I pull away, needing to hold it together. "Not a word to Carmen. Not today."

"Will you be ok the rest of the night? Where's Shane?" she asks as if somehow she knows I need him.

"I'm going to make myself be ok. This is Carmen's day, and I won't bring my drama to it. Shane's not coming, so can I ride with you?"

Simone frowns in annoyance, but I know it's not at me. Being the awesome friend she is, she doesn't say anything. "Of course."

I gather my things and throw them in my bag, including my phone. I hope with the big toss, I can set it all aside for the night.

I wanted Shane here before, but I wish he were here to tell me we'll figure this out together. It suddenly feels like I'm back to facing it all alone.

Maybe I'm being ridiculously emotional or immature, but I thought something was growing between us—a friendship or maybe even something more. Regardless, friends don't leave you hanging, and Shane ghosted me today, all because he had a bad game.

None of that matters, though. My focus has to be on Liv and figuring out what I need to do to keep her safe and with me. I know what will likely be required. It involves digging out the remains tucked away in a large envelope, which I had hoped would never see the light of day again.

For Liv, I'll do absolutely anything. No matter what. But tonight, I have to join the party and pretend everything is fine. Just fine.

Chapter 26

SHANE

"Do not call me again. You aren't getting one more dime, not a single penny. If you threaten my wife in any way, I'll have your picture plastered on every screen across America and let the entire world know just what kind of man you are. I imagine you don't want any more attention from law enforcement than you already have. Do we understand each other?"

Greg's creepy low chuckle sends my temper through the roof. "Be careful, son. I never pretended to be anything other than what I am. You're nothing but a guy who came from a drug dealer and a strung-out prostitute. Just think about what your fancy world would think about that, not to mention your new bride. I'm certain you've left those little details out for a reason. At least no one can say she married you for your money, but you certainly snagged a ripe piece of fruit. A loaded one at that."

I clench my jaw so hard I'm surprised I don't crack a molar. "Your past has nothing to do with me. It never did, and it never will. Your sperm donation is the only thing that connects us. How you make your living only reflects on you. Don't ever call me again, and make sure you never even speak of my wife."

I hang up, not giving him a chance to spout any more venom. This lowlife doesn't affect me, but there's no way in hell I'll ever let him pull Maggie into his messed-up way of life.

I step out of my truck and head into the house to relieve Gwen and let her get home before it gets too late. That phone call, combined with my best player getting ejected for being a hothead, has me wanting to punch something.

I find Gwen cleaning up the kitchen.

"I wasn't expecting to see you this early," she says, turning from the sink.

"I skipped out on the wedding. I had to deal with a player after the game, which took longer than I expected."

Gwen's hands fall to her hips, and she gives me a look I don't understand. "Maggie's there by herself, then?"

"Yeah, I messaged her. I thought I'd just come home and let you get going before it gets too late."

Her head tilts to the side thoughtfully, in what I assume is a motherly way of examining me. "Are you doing all right? It was a heck of a game today."

"That kid is trying my every nerve."

Gwen pats my arm. "You'll handle it just fine. The kids are all in bed, and there are leftovers in the fridge, plus some cookies in the container." She points to the counter by the stove, grabbing her purse. "Take it easy and make sure you take good care of my Maggie. Today was probably a hard day for her."

She gives me another gentle pat and heads for the front door while I try to make sense of what she said about Maggie.

I run a hand over my face, needing a shower and a beer. Twenty minutes later, I'm resting on the couch when my phone vibrates. After what Gwen said, I hope it's Maggie. I haven't heard anything from her, not that I expected to. It's Sean.

"Hey, what's up, bro?"

He chuckles. "After that game, I think I should be asking you."

"I almost laid that kid out. He's so damn talented and willing just to throw it all away."

"Let me guess. You're in a bad mood and nursing a beer."

It's annoying he knows that.

"What do you want?"

"I'm trying to book tickets to come see your grumpy ass, but now I'm having second thoughts. Maybe I'll take myself to the beach for a few days. I could use a dose of cocktails and bikinis."

"Whatever suits you," I grumble.

"Why's it so quiet there? Where are the kids and Maggie?"

"The kids are in bed, and Maggie's at a wedding." I'm trying really hard to keep my irritation under control.

"Maggie's at a wedding, and you're not. How'd you get out of that?"

"I texted her and told her I wouldn't make it. I was in no mood to play nice this evening."

Sean makes some kind of disbelieving noise. "And she was fine with that?"

"Yeah. I haven't heard from her. She's busy."

Sean lets out a long, soft whistle. "Let me know how that turns out."

I rub my temples. First, Gwen. Now, Sean. "What does that mean?" I'm losing the patience I don't have.

"Uh . . . I'm pretty sure there hasn't been a woman in my life who'd be ok with me ghosting her, let alone at a wedding."

"I didn't ghost her. I sent her a text and told her I had a shit day." Well, I kind of explained, but I definitely wasn't going to mention Greg's phone calls.

"Sure, brother. I'll try to match my flight time with Mark's, so you only have to make one trip to the airport." He's quiet for a second. "Good luck tonight. I hope it all works out for you."

I groan, tossing my phone on the couch, unable to handle his condescending tone while my nerves stand on edge. I in no way intended to ghost Maggie. They're her friends, so I assumed not showing wouldn't be a big deal, but she had asked me to go with her.

Shit. I'm sure it's fine. She would've texted me if it weren't fine, right?

I sip my beer that's no longer cold, trying not to stew, when I hear a key in the front door. Maggie steps inside in a long, gold sparkling gown, followed by a man with whom she turns to give a hug to thank him for bringing her home.

Awe fuck.

First, I'm an idiot. Plain and simple. No excuses. Second, I don't like any part of the hug that just happened, and it's my own damn fault. And third, she looks incredible in that dress. It'd bring any man to his knees, and I let her spend the evening alone in a room full of them.

I stay still as she closes the door and steps out of her heels, only making the briefest of eye contact before turning away.

Shit. Shit. Shit!

I'm in trouble. Big trouble in so many more ways than one.

She ignores me, heading toward the hallway that leads to our room.

"Hey." I test the waters.

"Hey." She doesn't break her stride.

Because I'm a fool, and there's no changing it, my following words don't do me any favors. "Who was that?"

She stops dead in her tracks, and I'm pretty sure if it had the power, her gaze would slice me in two. "Carmen's brother." She says it so softly, and that softness has me worried. "I'm going to bed."

"Wait." I stop her. "What's wrong?" I have a feeling Sean was right, but I need confirmation. She doesn't say anything. "I'm sorry I didn't make it to the wedding. The game . . . " I know it will sound lame, so I shut my mouth.

Her eyes shift to the floor and then back up at me. "It's fine." She starts moving again.

"Maggie." I push.

"It's fine, Shane. I'm tired, and I just want to go to bed."

She disappears, and all I know for sure is it's not fine. I curse, turning off the TV, and with Gwen and Sean's voices running through my head, I follow her down the hall to have it out.

I want her to tell me why she's upset. Just yell at me and get it over with. I know I screwed up.

I find her standing in the middle of our bedroom, facing the doorway like she expected me. It hits me all over again how stunningly beautiful she is, but the look on her face is a fast punch to my gut.

"Shane, not tonight." She says it like a warning.

"I just want to know what's going on. I said I was sorry."

"Yes, I heard you."

"Ok. Then we're good?"

Please say yes because I have no freaking clue how to deal with a woman I actually care about being mad at me.

"Yep. We're all good." I heard that 'p' pop, and I know we're anything but good.

I rub my face. "Maggie."

"Shane, seriously. It's been a long day, and I'm not interested in talking to you right now."

"I want to know what's wrong."

"Stop. Please." She pulls on the neck of her dress and turns to open the closet door, looking like she's going to take it off.

"What are you doing?" My hands jut out to stop her like a little kid about to see something he shouldn't.

"Taking off this dress. One more second, and I'm going to hyperventilate. Turn around or don't. I don't care. I'm sure you've seen bigger and better anyway."

She starts clawing at the fabric like she's panicking, trying to find the zipper among the sequins.

I step forward, laying my hands on her shoulders. "Hold on." I find the zipper and tug it down, wishing I were doing this a whole other way.

She holds the dress up, and I turn around.

I hear the long exhale of relief as the material hits the floor. There's some shuffling, and when it fades, I turn around to see her crouched on the floor in one of my t-shirts, which looks almost as amazing as the dress.

Shit. I'm pretty sure I shouldn't be focusing on that right now.

"What's wrong?" I ask again. "Tell me, please."

She stands and turns to face me. "Stop pushing." I hear her voice crack. "It's been a long day. I'm so tired. I thought . . . "

"You thought what?" I feel like we might finally be getting somewhere.

Her chin drops, and she shakes her head. "It doesn't matter."

"I don't understand. It matters. I had an issue to deal with after the game today, which took a while. I wasn't in a good frame of mind, and then—"

She holds up her hand. "Shane, it's over."

"Clearly, it's not. I want to understand, and for you to tell me what the problem is."

That fire ignites in her eyes. "Fine. I just want to go to bed and let this be, but since you won't, fine. Today was hard for me. Seeing Carmen with her parents. Her mom fixing her hair and helping into her dress. Her dad walking her down the aisle. It was hard. I'll never have that. Any of it."

"And the dress . . . " She kicks at the pool of material lying on the floor. "I hate it. Every moment was like walking around with fire ants all over my body. I honestly would've rather been naked in front of all those people. Wearing dresses . . . "

She pauses, tears welling in her eyes, and I hate myself. "All I can think about is blood. Everywhere. The smell. The sound. Watching my mom die all over again."

Her chest expands, and her throat bobs as she swallows her tears. "All day, I tried to focus on Carmen and John, but I couldn't. All I could do was miss them and everything that will never be. Reliving the most horrific and terrifying moment of my life over and over again."

She stands tall like she's reloading, and I deserve it. I close my eyes, disgusted with myself that I wasn't there. I had no idea.

"I was waiting for you. You told me you would come. I kept checking my phone, thinking you'd be there, and then—" She pauses, her voice breaking into a whisper. "I wanted you to be there."

I step closer, wanting to wrap her in my arms. "I'm sorry. I didn't know. I probably should have, but I didn't."

When she doesn't move away, I pull her to me. She falls against my chest and I wrap my arms around her, holding her tightly. We stand that way only for a second before she pushes me away.

"Stop. I'm fine. I know where we stand now." She steps away.

I'm confused. I have no idea where we stand. "What do you want?"

"What do I want?" She scoffs and shakes her head, letting it fall forward. "I want to take a long, hot shower, scrub my skin until it feels like mine again, and then go to bed."

I step away, seeing her exhaustion and how hard she's trying to be ok. But this conversation isn't finished.

She heads into the bathroom, leaving me to loathe myself. She wanted me there, and I wasn't. She was waiting for me, and I didn't show. The worst part is that she didn't just want anyone there. She wanted me. Maggie wanted me, and I let her down.

I sit on the edge of the bed, trying to absorb all she just let loose. A lot is happening here, and I'm sitting in the dark. She may not want me beside her tonight, but I'm not going anywhere.

I screwed up. I don't know how to fix this, but I will. All I have to do is figure out how to show her it won't happen again.

Chapter 27

MAGGIE

I stand with my head bowed, eyes closed, swaying to the music, hoping it will speak to me. Lift me. Give me something to go on.

I didn't sleep well, even with Shane beside me. Memories and worries flooded my mind and dreams.

Once, I woke to Shane's large hands cradling my face, and without saying a word, he wrapped me up and held me while I cried myself back asleep. It took a while, and as much as I didn't want to need his comfort, I did. Having him there in my time of need felt strange, but there he was. Big and strong and quiet. We didn't speak. He just held me.

But today is another day, and I pray that somehow everything will be ok. I have to lay the memories and grief down so I can focus on doing whatever is necessary to keep Liv with me. I need strength and direction. I won't be weak. I won't let Cliff or Joan intimidate me or use me ever again. I'll fight this time, even if that means reopening old wounds.

I feel Shane's massive presence beside me and survey him out of the corner of my eye. I was hard on him, and that wasn't fair. He didn't know about my mom and couldn't have anticipated how yesterday would hit me.

I wanted him there, but as something more than what we are. This was an arrangement, nothing more.

My phone vibrates in my pocket, and I can't help but look at it, waiting for more bad news.

DANNY: What can I do to change your mind?

I shove my phone in my pocket as Shane stares down at me.

At a different time, dancing with Danny in a show like this would have been a no-brainer. Even now, if I'm honest with myself, I want to dance like that again, or at least try to.

If it were one of the kids, I'd tell them to give it everything they've got. If my dad were here, he'd tell me that if we're lucky, we get to decide when the game is over, not letting anyone or anything dictate that for us.

Shane's words come back to mind. I shouldn't let Danny or our history have the power to keep me from fulfilling a dream.

My mom would hold my face just as she did before every recital.

"Maggie, we step onto the stage to show the world what's in our hearts. It's how dancers communicate. So tell them, whatever that is. Hold nothing back. Show the world who you are."

I'm not sure who I am as a dancer or what I'm made of anymore, but I think it might be time I find out. It'll require stepping onto the stage one more time and showing the world, but mostly myself, exactly what I was made for.

I raise my head, feeling like I have a chance. A chance to make a change. No longer a victim but a fighter. I'll fight for Liv, for my family, for myself, and . . . I'll fight for Shane. I want the friendship we were building to continue to grow because, regardless of how and why, he's become more important to me than I ever could have imagined.

Chapter 28

SHANE

ME: You were right. What now?

SEAN: APOLOGIZE!!!! You dummy. Grovel.

ME: Already did that. It wasn't enough. She's quiet.

SEAN: I'd prefer a root canal to the silent treatment.

ME: It's worse. She's different with me now.
ME: She was counting on me, and I wasn't there.

SEAN: You're an idiot.

ME: Thanks. So helpful. I should've texted Mark.

SEAN: Go ahead. He'll tell you to kiss and make up. In the bedroom.

ME: That's why I texted you, dummy.

SEAN: I feel so honored, dumbass. Show her differently. Tell her and then show her you're still there. A little wooing wouldn't hurt.

ME: Wooing???

SEAN: ***Face palm emoji***
SEAN: How are you married?
SEAN: Take her on a date. Buy her flowers. Do the things that show her she matters.

ME: I don't think she wants to be wooed. That's not Maggie.

SEAN: Yeah, right, shithead. All women want to be wooed. It's just how?

ME: We don't have that kind of relationship.

SEAN: Keep telling yourself that, bro.
SEAN: Ticket purchased. See you in a few weeks, and I'll see for myself.

I toss my phone down, trying to figure out what in the world I'm supposed to do. I'm not made for this. There seriously needs to be a freaking manual on what to do when we screw it all up.

This weirdness between Maggie and me is no good. All I want is for things to go back to the way they were. I want my Maggie back, except is she mine?

It sure felt like when I held her through the night. She'd been tossing and turning and whimpering in her sleep when I scooped her up and held her against my chest while she cried.

I want to know what's going on inside her. Yesterday shook something loose within her that's been hidden, and now it's haunting her. I can see it. I want to make it better, but I can't if I don't understand who these ghosts are or where exactly they're coming from.

I've wanted to talk to her, but I have no idea what to say. In church this morning, she stood with her eyes closed, head down, and barely made eye contact.

Now, I'm sitting on the patio because one more second of this might send me over the edge.

The door clicks shut, and Cole settles into a chair beside me.

"What's up with Maggie? She's been super quiet, and I just saw her shoving some flashy gold thing in the trash before hauling it outside."

"I didn't make it to Carmen's wedding yesterday," I say, not really wanting to talk about it.

"She was there by herself?" Cole's alarmed tone makes me want to punch myself in the face.

Why does everyone have this reaction like I should've known something?

"Let me guess," he says. "That was the dress."

I don't look at him because I can't stand to have one more person tell me how big of a jerk I am. Taking my silence as confirmation, he lets out a breath as he rests his arms on his knees.

"I didn't know," I try to defend my sorry ass. "I still don't, at least about the issue with dresses. I should've probably guessed she'd have a hard day, but . . . I'm not used to trying to analyze someone else's emotional response to things."

Cole looks at me like I have two heads. "Dude, you better get used to it. You're married . . . to my sister."

I groan. "Now, you sound like Sean. Yet, neither of you is married, and you don't even have a girlfriend. This shit is hard and frustrating as hell. Understanding a woman is like trying to read a different freaking language blind."

Cole laughs. "Exactly, that's why I don't have one." He pauses. "Maggie's tough. You know that, and she'll be the last one to yell for help even if she's drowning. She's been like that her whole life. Sometimes, it's gotten her into trouble."

What the hell does that mean?

I want to ask, but just like with Danny, Cole will respect Maggie's choice to open up in her own time if she wants to.

"I don't know how to make it better." I slump down in my chair, crossing my arms over myself. I'm irritated as hell that I don't know what's going on, and I can't fix anything without having a freaking clue.

"Give her time. I don't know how this works with you two, but she finally has someone. My guess is that you not showing yesterday made her second-guess whether or not she really does. Just remind her that even though you didn't show, you're still here."

Huh. That was similar to what Sean said. Maybe it wasn't such bad advice. I just have to figure out how to do it.

Silence lingers while I ponder this bit of young wisdom.

"So," Coles says. "When are Mark and Sean coming?"

"Shit." I rub my face. "I haven't told Maggie they're coming in a few weeks."

Cole laughs. "This just keeps getting better."

I tip my head back, staring up at the blue sky, wanting to punch something. The door clicks shut again. This time it's Maggie.

"Here's your chance," Cole chuckles.

"Chance for what?" Maggie asks him, evidently still pretending I don't exist.

I clear my throat. "I forgot to mention Mark and Sean are coming to visit."

She sits in a chair across from me. It would've made me feel better if she'd sat next to me, but no, we're still keeping our distance, and I hate it. Every single inch of it.

"Ok. Hank can bunk with Garrett and Teddy, and they can have the basement."

I frown. "They can stay at a hotel. Mark's kind of a big girl about things."

"Uh. No. They're your brothers. They're staying here." She says it like it's final, and today, I'm not arguing. "I need to talk to you guys about something." She inhales and tugs at her shirt, which makes my already frazzled nerves tremble. "I had a voicemail from my lawyer. Cliff and Joan are suing for custody."

Cole scoffs. "Those sons of a—"

"When?" I ask, really hoping the answer isn't what I think it is.

"When what?" Maggie's forehead creases, and her eyebrows tip inward.

"When did they leave the voicemail?"

She pinches the hem of her shirt between her fingers, and I know.

FUCK!!!!!

"Yesterday."

"Maggie," I breathe, and she holds up her hand.

"It's worse," she says quietly, but glances at Cole, whose jaw is clenched tight. "They only want Liv."

Cole jumps up. "I'll kill them. Maggie, there's no way. You've got—"

"Cole." Maggie stands. "Calm down."

The door opens, and Hank steps out, gazing at the three of us. "Everything all right?"

"Yep," Maggie answers quickly, sounding completely normal.

Hank frowns like he knows a load of crap when he sees one. "I'm going for a run. The boys are playing games in the basement, and Liv is watching *Moana*."

Maggie nods, and he leaves, but not without giving us all another glance.

"Maggie, there's no way this can happen. You know this," Cole hisses.

"I know." Her calmness concerns me.

"I don't understand." I'm missing something, but they both just look at me. "Why only Liv?"

"Because they're demented scum of the earth. They want Liv because she's young and a girl, and they think they can turn her into some freaking southern debutante thing, passing her around like she's some prize to be won." He takes a breath. "Maggie, you've got to stop this."

"I know," she says again. "I need to talk with Ben and see what our options are."

"Options?" Cole huffs. "There's only one option. You need to tell them."

"Cole," Maggie warns, and I don't miss that something passes between them.

He runs a hand over his face.

"Listen, I'll call Ben tomorrow and see what he says. I will do *anything* to keep her with us. But I need to know where we're at right now. Ok?"

Cole nods. "Ok."

She shifts in her seat. "I also wanted to tell you both I've decided to take Danny up on his offer if he'll agree to rehearse here. It's the only way it'll work."

Cole shakes his head. "Maggie, this is not the time to have him worming his way into your head again."

"He won't worm his way anywhere." I jump in without thinking about it.

Maggie's eyes dart to mine, and it's possible I see the slightest hint of a smile.

The tightness in my chest eases a little. "I think you should definitely do this."

Cole looks at me like I've lost my mind. I have. I most certainly have, but I want this for her.

"Thanks," Maggie says. "I haven't told him yet. It may not even work. He'll have to make a lot of concessions, and he likes things his way."

"Do you really think it's the best time for this?" Cole places his hands on his hips. The young, calm, cool, and collected man looks like he's about to lose his shit.

"I think it's the perfect time." Maggie's eyes meet mine. "I'm in the mood to kick a little ass."

I see the fierce flicker of determination in her eyes. There she is—my little Firefly.

Cole throws his head back and groans. "I need a minute. I don't know how you can be so calm about this."

"I'm not," she says. "I freaked out. Panicked. Cried." She glances at me, and I understand the tears that soaked my T-shirt. "All I can do right now is continue to show these kids what it means to stand up and fight.

Part of that is fighting for what we want. You two do it on the field. I'm going to do it on stage." She pauses. "Then I'll do it in the courtroom if I have to."

Cole blows out a breath. "If Danny even—"

"I've got it." I cut him off. "I'm sure Mr. Hip Hop wants to continue to have full use of his legs."

"I've gotta go," he waves a hand. "This is . . . a lot."

Maggie hugs him, and he slaps my hand before heading inside. She turns to face me.

"Why didn't you tell me?" I ask.

She fiddles with her shirt. "I couldn't."

I actually understand that. I step toward her, and without thinking about it, I wrap her in a hug. "I'm proud of you."

She hugs me tightly, resting her head against my chest.

All my tension and agitation disintegrates. "This ass you're going to kick, you're not doing it alone."

"Yeah?"

"Yeah."

Chapter 29

MAGGIE

ME: I have conditions.

DANNY: Name it.

ME: This is about dance only, or I'm out.

DANNY: Done.

ME: We rehearse on my turf. I only have to be in NY a few days before the show.

DANNY: Hmmm. How does that work with the rest of the dancers?

ME: You're smart. You figure it out.

ME: We choreograph together online, and you work with a backup until I get there. I'll be ready.

DANNY: That might work, but it'll be tricky.

ME: My ankle may not hold.

DANNY: Let's do it. I'll see when I can make it out so we can get started. Time is ticking.

ME: Works for me.

DANNY: I don't deserve to dance with you again, but I'm really glad I get the chance. You're going to tear up the stage.

ME: We'll see. It's been a long time.

DANNY: Maggie, you've never known how good you are. Now, we'll show the world.

I'm on a hunt to find the Easter egg that is Shane's office. It's the first time I've been in the bowels of the practice facility, but it's like a maze with no signage.

I turn a corner, hearing voices as I inch along, searching for the big grizzly bear.

His support and confidence yesterday meant the world to me. When his massive arms slid around me, the ones I'd missed the day before, they were like a warm, cozy blanket, and I felt like I could actually do this.

A few guys walk toward me in the dingy hall lit by the glow of fluorescent lights. I pass what resembles tiny offices, and I think I might be getting close.

Tucked back in the corner of the building, I find the big guy. His giant frame is squeezed behind a desk that appears made for an elf, and he's wearing those freaking glasses.

"Hey," I say, pulling his attention from his computer.

"Hey." His expression barely changes, but I still know I surprised him. He pulls off his glasses and sets them on his miniature desk.

I look around the tiny, sparse space. "How do you fit in here? You could be like a jack-in-the-box. Fling the door open, and the bear pops out."

"You're ridiculous," he says, trying not to smile.

"*This* is ridiculous." I wave my hand around the small space.

"I try to be in her as little as possible. It's claustrophobic."

"Really." I'm small and feel like I'm stepping into a Polly Pocket world. I hold up a bag. "I brought you lunch. It's just a bagel and cream cheese, but it's something." I pull a bottle of water out of my bag and set it on his desk.

"Thanks. What are you doing here?" He looks in the bag.

"Oh, I just thought it was finally time to check out your digs, but I'm sorely disappointed, Grizz. This is like a teeny tiny holding cell."

An unamused gaze hits me from under his thick, dark eyelashes.

I rest against the wall directly in front of him because there's nowhere else to go.

"The current pain in my ass is supposed to be here in a few minutes, although I expect him to be late."

"Nice to know that's not my title today," I sigh. "So, Chippy. What are you going to do with him?"

Shane rests back in his chair. "I don't know. He's got potential, but he won't be going anywhere if he can't control his temper and attitude. I can't have him thrown out again for unsportsmanlike conduct. No one will even look at him if he doesn't keep his cool." He pauses. "I think he's a good kid, just misguided."

"Huh. Well, you're probably the perfect person to knock some sense into him." I smile.

Shane rubs his face. "I have no idea what to do. I've already talked to him twice and threatened to bench him. It's like talking to a wall."

"Then kick his ass to the curb or at least make him think you have."

Shane takes a bite of his bagel. "Did you eat?"

"Yes, before my last class." I push my nose in the air. "Now, I came by to tell you that I texted Danny. He's willing to work with me and drag himself here to practice. We'll work online the rest of the time, but I'll have to be there a few days before the show to rehearse with the group and get a handle on the stage and music."

"When is he coming?"

"Probably in a couple of weeks. He might be here when Mark and Sean get in, but it'll just be for a day or two."

Shane grumbles, "Good. I'll make sure we run into him."

"Grizz."

"Firefly."

I inhale and hold it, steadying myself for the other reason I came by. "I also talked to Ben this morning. He's not overly concerned. He's contacting Cliff's lawyer to see what their basis is for the suit other than trying to steal someone who isn't theirs." My heart beats faster, and my palms start to sweat just thinking about it.

"They have an excellent lawyer, but so do I. Ben is the best there is. He thinks it might be a good idea to get a social worker involved to preemptively prove their claims are irrelevant and unfounded, but I don't want to get the kids worked up if we don't have to. He said that being married will help my case immensely. It's not just me with four kids anymore."

"So, we can't do anything right now?"

There's something, but I don't want to go there unless I have to, and that includes telling Shane. I may be able to shield the kids from Cliff and Joan, but I'm not sure if I can protect them from this, so it's a last resort.

The last thing I want to do is add on more painful family stuff that shouldn't ever affect them. The people who know are limited to those present at the time. My dad, Cole, and Monica. Simone and Carmen know a little, but far from the entirety.

Discussing this with Shane is like giving away a piece of myself to him. It's dark and complex, and reserved for those I trust most.

I force my gaze to his. I don't know what Shane and I are. We're friends, maybe a bit more than friends. At least, it feels that way. I've brought him into my life, our lives, and I've trusted him with the most important things in this world to me. I know I can tell him. I just didn't want to be forced into it.

I suck in another breath, needing courage and not to be suffocated by my anxiety. "There's . . . something that could help, maybe even make this go away, but—"

"Knock. Knock."

I jump, nearly out of my skin, at CC's loud, gravelly voice beside me.

Where in the hell did the spry old man come from?

"Maggie, my girl." He throws his arm around me, squeezing. "Clara and I miss you guys. You need to bring those kids over for dinner soon. Clara needs someone to fuss over."

"Yes, we need to do that." I force a smile, momentarily saved from spilling my guts. Maybe time will make me brave.

"Bring this big lug with you, will ya?" He points at Shane. "He's as quiet as a church mouse unless some knucklehead gets out of line. I need to get to know him better."

I laugh because it's true.

"Anyway, I'm glad you're both here," he continues. "The annual benefit is coming up. Shane, you'll be the belle of the ball. Folks are expecting autographs and pictures, so dust off your charm. Cole and some of the team will be attending."

CC turns to me. "Formal attire, as you know, and there's no getting out of it, so don't even try."

Shane stifles a groan, and I smile.

"We'll be there. We wouldn't miss it. Plus," I point to Shane. "This guy owes me a dance."

Shane rolls his eyes and tips his head back like he's in pain.

CC chuckles. "Hey, fella, you better be on that dance floor. Plenty of men will be looking to fill her dance card, and you might never get her back."

Shane's brown-green eyes hold mine with an intensity that causes my skin to tingle with a burning sensation.

"Darlin, you better save a dance for me. I may be old, but I can still keep up with you."

I smile, stomping out the flames that ignited. "You got it."

"Now, it's a fundraiser, so get to signing things." He points at Shane. "And you figure out free dance lessons or some fancy thing so that we can raise some real cash this year."

"We'll do it," I say.

"All right. I'll let you get back to it. Come over anytime. In fact, bring the kids, and you two can have a date night." He taps the doorjamb with his knuckle twice and disappears into the dim hall.

I smile at Shane.

"What?"

"I don't care how bad of a day it is; you're not getting out of this one."

He rolls his eyes. "The rule still applies. One dance."

"Just remember, the more you dance, the less you have to talk. Plus, I happen to be a very good dancer, so you might want to stick with me."

He glares, but I can see he likes my logic. I hope he likes the idea of being stuck with me, too. Being close to Shane just might help me survive another flesh-eating gown.

I hear a shuffle in the hallway and twist to find a tall, broad, disgruntled-looking young guy beside me. Clearly, someone screwed him three times over. I haven't seen him with his helmet off, but I assume he's number thirty-eight and the pain in Shane's completely muscled behind.

"Hey, Chip," I say, and Shane tries not to spit his water. He's kind of successful.

"It's Nick."

Ohhhhh, the attitude is thick.

"Huh? The chip on your shoulder says otherwise. Coach, here, wasn't quite sure how to get through to you that your behavior sucks. I suggested you might need to understand that if you want to play in the big leagues, you need an attitude adjustment. Or, you know, just piss away your talent and opportunities because you can't get your head out of your ass." I shrug.

The little punk laughs. "Yeah. I bet you and your brother know a lot about opportunities. Must be nice to have everything handed to you."

Shane shifts with what might be a slight growl.

I shoot him a look. "Listen, think whatever you want about Cole and me and every other overprivileged SOB out there, but this guy, as big of a pain in the ass as he may be, has worked tooth and nail for every single thing he has. He earned it, and I can tell you it wasn't with a big mouth and sour grapes attitude. If you're smart, you'll listen, do exactly what he says, and cut the Polly Pissy Pants crap off. He's trying to help your sorry butt."

I glance at Shane and then back at Nick. "Otherwise, just kiss away your future opportunities. No sweat off his back. Reality is there are a million others out there just like you, only some of them will make it because they'd rather focus on playing hard than talking shit and throwing fists. Your choice."

Shane's mouth curves upward into what might be a . . .

Is he smiling? Smirking maybe? I'm. Not. Sure.

"All right. I have class, so I'll let you two chit-chat. I'll see you later," I say to Shane as I lift my bag. "Oh, and Chip, if you find your head somewhere down there," I gesture to his behind. "We're having Thanksgiving next week since you're playing during the real deal. You should come. It's chaos, but then you can meet the rest of us overprivileged, opportunistic Matthews. We'd love to have you. Catch a ride with Cole, but that unbecoming, piss-poor attitude stays at home."

I leave, but not without peeking at Shane over my shoulder through the miniature window, and I think I might just see a real, genuine smile. It's like sighting a rare and endangered species in the wild, and I made that happen. I pump my fist three times in the air. Score!

Chapter 30

SHANE

I have a lot to decipher about what's happened in this rabbit hole over the last twenty minutes. But right now, I'm trying to get over the straight-up talking-to Maggie gave this kid. She said exactly what needed to be said in the most unattached way. By the look on Nick's face, he doesn't know what to make of it either.

Why is her handling these kids so damn sexy?

She's like this cool, smooth force that starts as a spark, and then you watch as she comes to life and turns into a full-on blaze. Every day, I'm finding it harder and harder to keep my distance from my own wife.

I'm beginning to want to close the divide and find out what it feels like to kiss her until she's limp in my arms. To feel her body beneath my hands and understand her in all the ways only a husband would.

"She's your wife?" Nick's annoyed voice tears me from my thoughts.

"Yep. I'm damn lucky." I meet his dull eyes.

"I bet it's interesting living with her."

"You have no idea. She's right about everything she said, and whether you want to believe it or not, she knows a hell of a lot about football. Kid, you've got a real chance, but not the way you're playing."

He rubs his jaw, slumping against the wall.

"If you're ready to kiss the game goodbye, you're doing a perfect job of attaining that. But if you want to see what's beyond this campus, then you've got to quit the pity party, close your mouth, and think of this as a business because that is exactly what it is. The question is, what brand are you selling? Currently, you're not offering anything that anyone is willing to buy. No matter how good you are and how good you might actually be, you're too expensive. Too risky. No one wants a loose cannon."

He rolls his eyes and lets out a breath. "I get tired of having to work for every single thing while these guys get handed cars, sweet deals, sponsorships. I have to fight for everything."

"You think I haven't been there. I haven't had one thing handed to me my entire life. Even this job, I worked for it. Not in a coaching capacity, but I spent my time on the field year after year, and when I wasn't playing, I was training. I was in conference rooms working with my team and management. I would've gotten nowhere if I held every hard and bad thing I've been through against them."

He shakes his head.

I'm tired of messing around, and it's time to be frank like Maggie had. "Do you want to go beyond this facility and program?"

After a minute, he answers. "Yeah."

"Are you sure, because that sounded half-assed to me?"

"Yes. I want this."

"Then quit making it so hard. Play because you love it, not because you're trying to prove something or get people to notice. They'll notice, but you want them to see your talent and what you have to offer them. Show them. Show me what you've got."

He gives me the slightest lazy nod, and I know that's all I'll get. It's up to him now.

He pushes away from the wall but stops. "Do you think she meant what she said about Thanksgiving?"

"Which part?" I ask, making him say it.

He huffs. "The part about coming to dinner." He pauses. "I don't. . . have anywhere else to be."

"She meant it. You should come only if you can handle noise, pranks, and playing princesses."

He scoffs. "Yeah, I bet Cole plays princesses all the time."

"Cole," I say matter-of-factly. "Is the prettiest princess of them all, and he'd be an excellent person to have your back this season and in the future. Not everybody is who you think they are. Give them a chance to prove you wrong."

There might be something in that bit of advice I might also need to chew on.

He nods and leaves while I rest back, curious if this conversation will actually change anything. Hope. I have hope. He's young and has a lot to learn, but maybe he'll give himself a chance.

I try to finish some computer work in the short time I have left, but my mind keeps rolling back to my conversation with Maggie.

She's dancing with Danny The Flip-flop.

I groan and run my hand over my head. I don't know this guy, but I don't like him. At all. He hurt Maggie, and I want to rip his head off. I can't do that if she needs to dance with him, but I will make sure he and I have a clear understanding—she's mine.

I remember we didn't get to finish our conversation about what her lawyer advised. Maggie was about to tell me something when Coach interrupted. She was fidgeting with the hem of her shirt and seemed to shrink before me, so I think it was important and not necessarily something she wanted to share.

I shuffle the few papers on my desk and shut down my computer. I need to get focused and out to the field so I can go home and try really hard to keep my hands to myself and off my wife.

I walk into the scent of garlic and the sound of rap music. I drop my keys and phone on the counter. Hank is at the stove, dumping a large box of pasta into a steaming pot. Teddy and Garrett are at the island doing homework, and Liv is playing with one of her dolls.

"Who knew you were Chef Boyardee?"

Hank rolls his eyes. "Yeah, right. Maggie said if I burn the pasta, I'm cooking dinner for the next two weeks."

"So, you're watching the pot boil?"

Hank scoffs. "Absolutely."

I'm just about to ask where she is when I hear her scream from down the hall. It's a blood-curdling scream that has me running. I push through the bedroom door like I'm ready to take a hit. The screaming hasn't stopped as I throw open the bathroom door, and Maggie launches herself at me, still screaming.

I spin around with her clinging to me like a spider monkey and see. . . nothing. I try to scan her for wounds or blood, but I quickly realize she's plastered to me, practically naked. At some point in my state of panic, my hands found their way to her thighs, holding her legs wrapped around me tightly. In the mirror, I see she has on some very tiny shorts and nothing else, but she's covered because she's glued herself to me.

"Get it! Get it!" she yells.

"Get what?" I try to search with my limited mobility, but see nothing.

Her face is tucked into my neck, and I have no idea what she's talking about. Given there's no immediate danger, I'm perfectly happy to stay just like this for as long as she wants to.

"Down there," she points towards the floor. The feel of her breath on my neck makes it difficult to think straight.

"What?" I attempt to focus on the matter at hand, rather than the woman whose skin is so soft that it feels like silk.

"The mouse! It's somewhere in here! It came flying out of the cabinet. Shane, if it even goes into our bedroom, we'll be moving. Tonight."

It takes me a second to shake all of the thoughts I should not be having. I peek over her shoulder toward the floor. Lying next to the tub, I see a tiny, fluffy, fake, gray mouse. Part of me wants to say nothing because holding Maggie almost naked and pressed against me is everything I want and will never let myself have—if she would ever let me have her. But her death grip on my neck and the simple fact that we can't stay like this forever has me opening my big, fat mouth when I really, really don't want to.

I know who did this. I know she'll kill him, but I have to admit it's pretty damn funny, and I'm getting serious benefits from this little prank. I channel a little Teddy.

"Maggie."

"What?! Do you see it?!" Her legs squeeze tighter.

"Yes."

"Well, get it!"

"I can't. You're cutting off my circulation. For being so small, you've got some kind of superhuman strength."

She pulls her head away slightly. "Oh, sorry."

"It's ok, but you should know it's not a mouse."

"It's not?" She pulls away from me a little further, meeting my eyes like she's still afraid.

Those beautiful blue eyes cause my voice to catch in my throat. I shake my head. "It's not?"

She hesitantly peers down between us, and it's like she realizes she's naked from the waist up. I can't help my slight smile.

"It's a rat."

Her eyes grow wide, and her legs tighten around me again as she screams. "Get me out of here!" She starts clawing for the door as if she's going to pull me out.

I laugh.

"This is not funny!" she screams, her arms searching for something to grab onto. "Get me out of here, and then get it! Why are you just standing here?"

I let one hand slide up her bare spine, and if it doesn't feel amazing. "Maggie."

"Get moving! Shane, I'm serious. If you don't get me out of here and get that thing—"

"Maggie," I try again.

"What?!"

"It's fake. It's not real."

She stops. The silence grows loud as she stares into my eyes. "No." Her tone is low in disbelief.

"Yes." I step closer to the counter to grab a towel and set her down.

"Noooooo," she repeats slowly.

I smile. "Yes, it's fake."

I place her on the counter, handing her a towel to cover herself. She puts it over the front of her, peers down at the floor like she doesn't quite believe me, and then exhales a long, slow breath. "I'm going to freaking kill him."

I laugh.

"This is not funny! I about peed myself and had a heart attack all at the same time." She tucks the towel underneath her arms, fists my shirt, and pulls me closer to rest her head against me. "I'm pretty sure I saw my life flash before my eyes."

"Maggie, you can't be scared of a little mouse."

"There was nothing little about that."

I bring my hands to her head, pulling her face away to see her. "Are you ok now?" I can't help my smirk.

"I don't know." Her eyes spear mine and her lips push out into slight pout. "The only reason he will remain living is because he made you laugh. You should do that more often."

"Yeah?" I stare her. Her eyes. Her mouth. That sassy mouth I want to kiss, and possibly never stop.

"Definitely. It's a really nice sound."

I stoop down, bringing my forehead to hers. I know I shouldn't cross this line, but I've never wanted to trip across one so badly. The consequences are sky-high, but at the moment, I want to convince myself that everything will be fine. That taking this step isn't me being a selfish bastard when she deserves someone who can give her everything.

But she's not pulling back. I close my eyes, feeling her nose press into my cheek as her hands fist my shirt, and then the softest brush of her lips along my jaw. Those lips I want to tackle and taste and permanently mark as mine and mine only.

She whispers my name, and the urge to capture her mouth is too great.

"Maggie." A small voice breaks through my fog.

I quickly pull away as Maggie sits, looking as dazed and confused as I feel.

"Maggie." I hear Liv again through the door. "Are you ok? Teddy's worried you're really mad."

She clears her throat. "Yeah. I'm ok. Tell him he's on bathroom duty for a month."

"Ok. Dinner is done. Are you coming?"

"Yeah. I'll be there in a few minutes." Her gaze creeps up to meet mine. The spell is broken, but she looks like she, too, is wondering what would've happened. "Thank you for rescuing me."

I should be thanking Teddy. "Anytime."

I leave her to shower, but everything in me wants to stay and get right back to what we were about to do.

I close the door behind me and take a long, deep breath, scrubbing a hand over my face. I have to get a grip. Going there with Maggie will only end up leaving her hurt and disappointed. I'll do anything to prevent that.

I wish I could be everything she needs and deserves, the man she's envisioned sharing her life with, but I'm not. I've known that for a long time. You can't give someone something you've never had.

I wasn't made for love and partnership. I spent too many years alone, never knowing that feeling or experiencing that kind of connection to be anything worthwhile for someone else.

Being alone is all I know. It's all I'll ever be. This is it.

I shake my head. I can't let this happen again. I can't let Maggie think I have something more to offer her when I don't.

I will do anything to help her. I will protect her and these kids, which includes guarding her from me.

Chapter 31

MAGGIE

Shane's large calloused hand runs across my face, brushing the hair away. I lie perfectly still. Maybe I'm dreaming. I've likely manifested his touch.

After that almost kiss during the mouse incident, things have gotten real, at least for me. The longer I go without kissing Shane, really kissing him, and understanding every single detail of what it's like, the more frustrated I get.

Do I know it's likely not a good idea? Yes. Do I understand that, as far as Shane is concerned, kissing will just be kissing? Yes. Do I want more than that? Another big fat *yes.*

So, I don't move, not even a flinch, taking anything I can get as his fingers move tenderly across my face. I want to lean into them. I want to move closer, find his lips, and let my hands roam over the muscle underneath the thin layer of cotton. I want to take my time and finally know the depths of Shane that I know exist, but remain completely closed off.

I barely withhold a moan, catching it before it's released.

"Maggie. Hey." Shane's hand disappears from my face and wraps around my shoulder. "Maggie."

I whine, rolling over, wanting him to go back to doing exactly what he was doing and so much more. I'd even take him sitting up and reading to me like he has been on the nights he's been home, rather than getting up.

"What? I don't want to get up. There are too many things to do." I roll onto my back and stare at the ceiling. A stream of light filters through a crack in the curtains.

Shane stretches his arms in the air. His forearms, rippled with veins are masterpieces, all on their own. *Ugh. Good night.*

I put a hand on my forehead. I seriously have to get this under control and fast. We are married. That's it.

"Are you ready for today, big guy? I hope we have enough food. I put ten on Hank bringing friends home with him when they get back from the game."

"You think he will? Isn't the girl next door coming over? He said she's been helping him with some soccer flip thing."

"Sadie?"

"Yeah."

Shane's growly morning voice is sexy as hell and is not helping me want to stay on my side of the bed.

"He's like so many and will only see her after it's way too late. Besides, I invited her dad."

Shane's big head rolls in my direction. "Her dad?"

"Yeah. He's single, good-looking, and totally helped me out of a bind a time or two."

He grunts. "Great."

I peek at him from underneath my arm. "Grizz."

"What?"

I snicker.

In the dim light, I can make out his broody, scruffy face, which makes me want to tease him even more. I pull the sheet over my mouth to hide my smile as I roll onto my side to see him better. He pretends to ignore me.

"You know I'm married, right? I can ask the hot dad next door for early Thanksgiving when my husband is here. My younger, much stronger, totally nerdy by nature, big bear of a husband." I try to say it with a straight face, but I'm unsuccessful.

He groans, but I sense the smile behind it.

"I did, however, ask him in hopes that Simone might be interested because he's nice and way more interesting than the prick she just broke up with. After Carmen's wedding, she finally saw the light."

"Great. You're matchmaking now?"

I scoff. "No, just getting two people in the same room together. You and I will sit back and see what happens. The man has eyes. Simone is gorgeous, and she needs to stay away from losers."

Shane yawns. "I'm not watching anything but the game."

I roll onto my stomach and prop myself up on my elbows. "Shane, you'll be watching every bit of the shit show that is going to go down today, including the soap opera of Simone and Todd."

"Todd? He sounds just as boring as the last guy. Let me guess. Is he an accountant?"

I shove him, but he doesn't move an inch.

"Look. Just put on your happy pants today. I don't profess to know how to cook a Thanksgiving meal, but somehow, we always manage to eat something. It will be lively and eventful. There will be shenanigans of the best kind, and I will drag your butt through every bit of it. I have no idea what your Thanksgivings have been like, but saddle up and get ready for the ride."

He sits up and looks down at me. "Firefly, you're ridiculous."

I grin. "I've never pretended to be anything else. Now, get dressed so you can help me figure out what to do with that giant turkey before one of us has to run Hank to school."

"Maybe you should call Todd, the hot dad from next door. I bet he'd be happy to run right over and help."

I whack him with my pillow. "Jealousy is not becoming."

"I'm not jealous," he claims, meeting my eyes. "I know exactly where you sleep at night."

Oh really. The room suddenly feels a thousand degrees hotter and so much smaller. So many thoughts zip through my mind at lightning speed that have nothing to do with sleeping.

I force my gaze away. "I'm going to take a quick shower. Then, will you please help me with the turkey?"

"Fine." His voice is low and tight, and I'd give just about anything to know exactly what he's thinking.

"You want me to put my hand where?"

"Just reach in and see if there's anything?" I say, trying not to gag.

The smell, the slime, and now this invasive task of searching for the giblets. Who freaking knew preparing a turkey was like dissecting a cadaver?

Shane steps away. "Nope. Not happening. Just throw it away, and we'll order pizza."

I push my hair out of my face with my shoulder. "Come on, Grizz. Just do it. Then we can stuff it and put it in the oven."

"No. I'm done. I'm not shoving my hand anywhere or stuffing anything."

I groan.

"Where's our medical professional? Get him in here. He'll be down with all this." Shane moves to the sink to wash his hands.

I try to act cool. *Be cool. Don't smile or gawk. Be totally cool.*

He has no idea he just called Garrett *ours*. It's the first time he's ever personally claimed one of the kids, and I'm pretty sure I have hearts blooming from my chest. I want to hug him, kiss him, and keep him forever.

I breathe slowly. *Be cool. Don't scare the bear.*

"Go get him then, you big chicken."

"Funny, you're not willing to stick your hands in there either."

Just the thought makes me gag a little. Shane sees and smirks. "Stop it. It's not funny. My gag reflex is strong."

He leans close to my ear. "Just think, Firefly, you'll be gobbling up that turkey in a matter of hours."

"Shane, unless you want me to pick this giant dead-feather-plucked-friend and throw it at you, go get Garrett."

He grumbles, leaving the kitchen. After a minute, Garrett comes in, ready to assist. Five minutes later, he's shoving the last bits of stuffing into the bird and then washing his hands like a surgeon.

"That was cool. I wonder how they get all the stuff out of the inside," he says, drying off his hands while I shove it in the oven.

"Garrett, just keep those thoughts and ideas to yourself. I'm going to stretch and do some exercises before I have to make the rest of the food. Warn Teddy that he's required to help, too."

"Do you think that's a good idea? We have people coming. He might lace it with something."

"Well, we better keep both eyes on him then."

Garrett grins, passing Shane and Hank on the way out of the kitchen.

"I'll run Hank to school," Shane says.

"Ok." I point at Hank. "Kick some serious butt today. I want names and numbers and stats. We'll be at your final game next week, so don't even think about trying out that new flip throw-in until then. Got it?"

"Yeah, yeah," he says, unaffected as I hug him.

"We'll see you for dinner. Bring your appetite."

"Don't expect turkey," Shane mumbles as they head for the garage.

"Hey. It's going to be the best damn turkey you ever tasted," I yell after them.

I wipe the counter down and find Liv in her room, trying to fit Barbie in a pretend bathtub. Since agreeing to do the show, she's become my stretching partner.

"Hey, beauty. I'm going down to stretch. Want to come?"

She hops up. "Ok. Let me find my shiny leotard." She dresses in a pink and silver leo, and we head downstairs to get to work.

I turn on the instrumental tracks for *Beauty and the Beast*, Liv's favorite, and pull the ballet barre away from the wall where there's just enough room to the side of the weight bench. It's the same one I used when I started—the one my mom and I used to share.

Liv and I stretch, then work through combinations. I've been working in my pointe shoes during class to increase my flexibility and strengthen my ankle. I need to get to where I can focus on endurance and stamina, but soreness and swelling are complicating factors. I'm trying to ease into it, but running out of time.

The show will highlight the diversity of the dance world, but Danny and I will be combining hip-hop with pointe like we've experimented with in the past. It will be the headlining portion of the performance, although we'll each have a solo. I'm determined to choreograph a classic ballet routine set to contemporary music to fit the show.

I'm excited to get to work. What Danny has planned will be epic. Adding my spin and flair will bring it to a whole new level. One I hope will leave the dance world and audience with an appreciation for both the classic and the contemporary.

As I move, I hear my mom's voice calling out combinations and picture her standing in front of me, demonstrating. I hear her gentle voice counting and reciting. It feels so familiar and yet so far away.

I watch Liv attempting to follow my movement, and it's a mirror image of how I was with my mom. She was a purist when it came to ballet. She was demanding and exceptional, and I wish she were here to help me. I wish she could see how Danny and I combine the contradictory styles to make magic.

Lost in memories and thoughts, I clutch my chest at the massive figure standing behind us, watching. Liv notices I've stopped and runs to Shane while my heart attempts to find its normal rhythm again.

"Shaney, will you do ballet with us? We're strengthening our core and working on combinations."

Shane scoops her up like she weighs nothing. His bulging arms are on full display with his cut-off T-shirt.

Somebody help me.

Could he be just a little less manly and gruff and . . . powerful?

His eyes rake over me as if he's memorizing each detail. My skin prickles with heat and I shiver.

Liv puts her hands on his scruffy cheeks to get his attention. "Shaney, come do ballet with us. I'll show you."

What the hell was that? And all the touching this morning?

I'm not complaining, but What. Is. Going. On?

"How about you do weights with me?" Shane says, shifting his eyes from me.

She giggles. "I can't lift weights. I'm too small. Hank says they'll fall on me and squash me like a bug."

"How about this?" He flips her legs over his arm, holds her horizontally, then lowers her and pulls her back up in a bicep curl. "You can help me."

She giggles as she goes up and down. He's so good with these kids, and I don't think he even realizes it. I'll be damned if it doesn't make him all the more appealing, and he doesn't need the extra help.

After a few reps, he releases her, setting her on the ground, and she bounds out of the room, off to her next great idea.

Shane steps closer to me. "You ok? You were somewhere else when I came in."

"Yeah." I look down and flex my ankle out of habit. "Sometimes I still hear my mom like she was standing here. Something about slowing things down and getting back to the basics. She's really loud right now." I shake my head, turning down the memories.

He studies me. "How's your ankle?"

"It's ok. Sore after class sometimes, but ok so far. I'm trying to be careful. I know it'll get a workout when Danny's here."

Shane grunts, making me smile. "Ok if I work out?"

"Yeah, I'm almost done. I have stuff to do in the kitchen."

I stretch as he fiddles with his earbuds and phone. There's no way I'm staying while he works out. Nopity nope. My mind is already too liberal with thoughts of Shane, and it doesn't need any more material to work with.

"Hey." I stop in the doorway before heading out. "I forgot to tell you. We play bingo each Thanksgiving. It's tradition, so don't overexert yourself. You'll need your strength to push those markers around."

"Bingo?" He questions, like it's offensive.

I set my hands on my hips. "Grizz, are you new? This isn't just any old bingo. You're about to be enlightened on the fascinating world of what I like to call Hostage and Negotiation."

He gazes at me from under his thick eyelashes. "Sounds riveting."

I push my lips to one side. "You've no idea. Just wait, big guy. I'm pretty certain you'll be very invested."

"Firefly, what makes you think you have anything I want?"

Oh boy.

That look a few minutes ago told me a lot about what he wants.

Did he just declare war? I think he did.

Hot flashes of our almost kiss, the soft touches this morning, and the intense perusal he just took, pierce my mind like three giant darts hitting their target. This joker thinks I don't know exactly what he wants. It's the same thing I want.

The difference is, I will not break. My will and resolve not to get hurt are far stronger than any amount of intoxicating manly smell, gentle caress, or downright sexy swagger that exudes from him like water from a geyser.

I glare at him. "Well, I guess we'll just see about that."

I'm tucked in the kitchen with Simone and Gwen, shuffling things in and out of the oven while the guys are outside with the kids. The house is quiet except for our subtle conversation.

Simone tosses hot rolls into a basket. "Who's the new kid with Cole?"

"Nick. He's one of Shane's guys. He's a transfer and finding his way. I like to call him Chip. He needs a little love."

Gwen peeks out the kitchen window. "When he walked through here, he looked like a deer in the headlights."

"We are a lot. Not everyone can handle us, so we'll see if he survives."

Simone bumps my hip with hers, although it's more like my ribs because her legs are so freaking long. "Honey, those pants on you are hot. If I'm rejoining the dating scene, I need a pair."

I laugh. "You could wear joggers, and men would fall at your feet."

Gwen turns to us. "Maggie, those pants and your booty would make any man weep."

My mouth falls open, and Simone gasps.

"Miss Gwen."

I look down at the fake leather leggings I've paired with a cream-colored ballet wrap top that hits just above the high waistline. I'm no supermodel, but these leggings fit like a glove, and I know it. They are a weapon in disguise, and Shane declared war earlier.

"Gwenie!" I say, astonished. "You have been hiding a sassy side. Who knew? Please let her out to play more often."

She raises her eyebrows. "Ladies, I was once young and cute, too. Don't think I don't know what's going on here. If you're trying to kill that big hunk of a man out there, those will do it."

I'm stunned speechless.

"For real," Simone adds. "You should be careful. He might swallow his tongue, which will be a real disappointment when you finally quit trying to fight it and make out with your *husband*. Sheesh, I wouldn't have lasted a day, let alone all this time. I'm getting flustered just thinking about all that pent-up angst." She fans herself.

I glare at her. We didn't need to be spilling my almost make-out with Shane.

"There will be no making out. We're just . . . friends. It's complicated."

Gwen spins around, her hands on her hips, giving me that motherly look. "There's nothing complicated about it. I've seen the two of you. You're married, and don't you think it's about time you both let yourselves see what this can really be?"

I sigh. "It's not that simple. We have an arrangement and can't mix things up with . . . sex. Plus, I want more than that."

"Who says it's not more than that?" Gwen asks as if I'm missing something. "Don't forget I'm around both of you, coming and going, and my eyes aren't what they used to be, but I can see he cares. Quite a lot."

"He's still so closed off." This is *not* the conversation I was expecting to have today. "Sure, the attraction is raging, at least on my end, but I need more than that. I don't want to let things go too far, only to find out I don't really know him. I want him to want to share things with me. I want to know who he is inside and what he's thinking."

Simone raises her eyebrows at me. "And you've shared things with him?"

I huff and drop my head to the side, knowing I've only given him bits and pieces but none of the big stuff.

"Maybe you need to lead by example," she says, as if it's that easy. "Seriously, those pants might just have him spilling his deepest, darkest secrets."

"See!" I squeal. "That was my dirty little plan. The good ole look but can't touch. Drive him crazy until he breaks."

Gwen scoffs. "Sweetheart, he's at least as stubborn as you are. At this rate, I'm scared what might combust if the tension gets any thicker. Shane is cool as a cucumber, and you've all but set that man's peace on fire."

I laugh. "My dad always said my mama was like a firecracker. You just never knew when she might go off. I can't help it. I come by it naturally."

As we laugh, the back door opens, and Shane steps in. The kitchen is suddenly silent, and he stops in his tracks. Those thick, dark eyebrows pull together, the crease appearing between them like he's aware we were talking about him. Then, his eyes find me, and he stares long enough to make everyone uncomfortable.

"What are those?" he asks, and it almost sounds like a growl.

I play dumb, trying hard to ignore the snickering in the corner where Gwen and Simone have gathered. I want to burn holes into their backs with my laser eyes.

"I'll set the table," Simone announces.

"I'll round the kids up and get their hands washed," Gwen adds, leaving me alone with Shane's scowl.

I glance at him and then back at my task. "What are you talking about?"

"Those." He impatiently tries to clarify the subject, but I'm not accepting it.

I stop and huff like I'm put out. "Grizz, you're going to have to be more specific."

He moves beside me, stopping so close that I feel the heat radiate from his body. I return to my task, completely ignoring him, his intoxicating scent, and the fact that I'd like to grin up at his highly irritated state.

He speaks, and it's so low and soft that my stomach quivers. "There's no way those boys are coming in here with you wearing *those*."

I glance down at my pants and then back up at him. "First of all, I'll wear whatever I want. Secondly, they're leggings, which I wear all the time. And thirdly, those boys won't be looking at me. I'm like a mom. They're gawking at pretty young things like Sadie and, well, Simone because she's an exception to the rule."

"No," he says like he's decided.

I want to laugh, but I hold it in. "Shane, I'm not changing. No one cares what I have on."

"There's a whole group of adolescent boys and Nick, who I can tell you will care very much that you have *those* on."

I roll my eyes. "Shane, are you telling me that when you went to your functions with some hot young model on your arm, you dictated what they wore?"

"No."

"That's what I thought. The funny thing is, they probably would've worn anything you asked them to. Not me. I'm not changing."

He stares at me, and I see something brewing behind his completely annoyed eyes. He bends at the knees and grabs me, throwing me over his shoulder and carrying me back toward our bedroom.

"Shane," I warn as Simone laughs.

When he doesn't listen, I pound my fist on his butt, but his buns of steel likely don't feel it.

In the bedroom, he sets me down, blocking the doorway with this giant frame as if I might try to escape.

"Change," he demands.

I can't hold it in any longer. The ridiculousness of it all makes me laugh. "I'm not changing. I love these pants."

"Oh yes, you are," he says, clearly not thinking any part of this is funny.

"Why? Why do I need to change?" I smile and put my hands on my hips, waiting for him to admit it.

His eyes flick between mine, and he lets out a tight, exhausted breath. "Because."

I step closer, getting all up in his space this time. "Because why?" I peer up at him.

His voice is low and rough. "Because if you wear those pants one minute longer, you'll be in for something that I'm not sure either of us is ready for."

Well, shit.

I swallow. It's me taking a breath this time, seeing the honesty in his eyes. He's right. I *so* want to be ready for what my body wants, but he's putting me first, and I'm so grateful.

Why does that have to make me want to give in so much more?

I step back and try to lighten the mood. "You said earlier, I don't have anything you want. This seems like quite a change." I smirk.

He grumbles and runs a hand over his face. "Firefly, you're making this very difficult." He actually looks in pain, so I give him a break, just this once.

"Fine. I'll change, but I love these pants. So, just to be clear, I will wear them. Next time, I'll make sure you aren't around."

He groans, and I laugh.

"Get out there and cut the turkey while I find some not-so-tempting pants."

He grunts, leaving me to change.

I want to know Shane. That needs to be the next step, and maybe Simone is right. If I want him to open up, I might need to be the one to lead the way. Plus, Gwen is dead on in her observations. If this tension goes on much longer, one of us might internally combust, and it's likely to be me.

This man. I'm afraid he might be the best and the worst thing that's ever happened to me.

Chapter 32

SHANE

She's going to kill me. Maybe it's better that way. She'll put me out of my misery. First, that damn strappy leotard and baggy sweatpants rolled down at the waist, and then . . . The pants. Tight black leather things that should only be taken off one way. By me.

How much can one man handle in a day?

If she comes out of that room in anything other than a garbage bag, I'm taking her back in there, and round two is going to look a whole lot different. This woman is testing my patience and my will, and she's about to find out that I've hit my limit.

In the kitchen, Nick is meticulously cutting the turkey into thin slices with Liv at his side. The little girl is a sucker for lost souls.

"I should've known you were Martha Stewart underneath all that animosity."

"He's got mad skills with that knife," Gwen says in her grandmotherly way, peering over his shoulder.

I see just a hint of a smile at the compliment, or maybe it's her attempt at talking like a teenager.

"Any other hidden talents I should know about?"

"I worked at a deli in high school. That's all," Nick says shyly.

The back door opens, and Cole and the boys come barreling in, along with Hank and his friends. Sadie and her dad, a tall, thin man with dark, graying hair, follow behind. We talked about football, and he seems like a nice enough guy, but I'm even happier now that Maggie isn't wearing those pants.

I watch as he wanders over to Simone, and I want to roll my eyes because Maggie called this. I stop myself just as she reenters the kitchen carrying a box.

This outfit is only marginally better. To anyone else, she's wearing regular clothes. Her normal leggings and a sweatshirt that just so happens to be my favorite hoodie. She's swimming in it, but I'll be damned if it isn't almost as sexy as the pants. Almost.

She meets my eyes, and her perfect lips offer me a gentle smile. "Better?" she mouths.

I shake my head as she nears. "That's my favorite sweatshirt."

"Really? I had no idea."

I know she has every idea.

"Get ready for bingo. Maybe you'll get this back." She winks.

What she doesn't realize is that I don't want it back. She can wear it every damn day.

She approaches the island lined with food, where Nick continues to work with the precision of a surgeon. "Nice work, Chip. See, I knew you belonged here." She pats him on the shoulder. "All right, everyone, grab a plate, fill up, and let's eat."

Maggie sets the box in the corner and fusses around while the room fills with teenagers piling their plates with food. Gwen helps serve, ensuring everyone gets a little of everything, and before long, they're spread out around the house eating.

I follow Maggie through the food line, and she bumps my elbow.

"Do you see where Simone is sitting?" she whispers.

I glance around, and she's at the far end of the table beside Todd.

"And have you noticed that Sadie is chatting up Chip and Cole? I think she's maybe found a new crush."

"Yeah, well, Hank seems oblivious."

She scoffs. "He is, but Cole and Chip are innocent threats. Just wait until the real deal comes along. He'll be all bent out of shape."

Maggie checks on Teddy, Garrett, and Liv as we hunt for a place to sit. I find a spot on the end couch where Hank and his friends, along with Sadie, Cole, and Nick, have landed.

A second later, Maggie squeezes in next to me. "Eat up, boys, and then it's time for bingo."

There's a collective groan, but Cole speaks up.

"What's in that box, Maggie? What do you have that's not yours?"

"Yeah," Hank adds. "I'm going to start pilfering your stuff and holding it hostage."

Maggie chews and swallows before responding. "You'd actually have to pick something up for that to happen. You know how the game works. Don't leave your stuff around after I've asked you to put it away, and bingo will disappear. The magic is that you guys never know what's in there."

"So, you make them play bingo to get their stuff back?" I ask.

She slumps next to me. "Grizz, you seriously underestimate me. No, whoever wins gets to pick from the box, and then the bartering and negotiation begin. Trust me. Each year, the box is a little lighter because these slobs realize they need to be more attentive about putting their stuff away."

"Don't even try that. You're a thief," Cole injects. "I don't even live here, and I have stuff that appears in the box."

Maggie talks with her mouth full. "Cole, you leave your stuff here all the time. I give you one week to pick it up, and then . . . " She shrugs innocently. "We have enough mess around here without adding your junk to it."

Teddy peeks around the corner. "Is it bingo time? I can't wait to see what's in there." He rubs his hands together.

We finish eating, and the plates are tossed in the trash while Gwen and Simone pull out dessert. The rest of the group crams into the living room for bingo. I take seat on the couch again, and Maggie drops the box beside me.

"What do you have in there that's mine?" I ask, trying to determine if my wife is really a thief in disguise.

She leans close to my ear. "You're lucky. You're actually pretty tidy. Although I could toss the pants in there." She presses a finger to her chin in contemplation.

This woman is evil. Plain and simple. I want those pants because I'll burn them and make her watch, knowing no man will see her in them. Ever.

"All right, people." Maggie sits on the floor between my legs. "Let's see who gets the first peek in the box."

And so, the game begins. I help Liv with her card until she leaves me to wiggle her way into the space beside her new BFF, Nick, while the boys play two or three cards at a time. Maggie calls out a letter and the number while squares are marked.

Five minutes in, we hear, "Bingo!"

Hank and Simone both have bingo and get first dibs on whatever is in Maggie's secret box.

"Ha." Hank pulls out a pair of AirPods and holds them up.

"No way, man." Cole's voice rises. "Hand them over. Those are mine."

Hank grins and returns to his spot on the floor. "Rules are rules, bruh. Me winny, me keepy."

"We'll just see about that after this thievery is over," Cole warns.

Simone returns to her seat with a five-dollar bill. "Someone's awfully careless with their money."

"Hey. That's mine," Teddy whines.

"Yeah, right," Garrett chides. "You never have any money."

"Ok, boys. Clear your cards for round two," Maggie directs.

Soon, laughter fills the room as Gwen pulls out an unreturned library book that Garrett is determined to get back to collect his fee. Sadie takes a Barbie doll, which she immediately hands off to Liv, causing the room to erupt in protests for showing favoritism. She only grins, not giving a single shit what all these boys say.

Nick is next in the box, grabbing a can of Pringles that shoots out a spring snake along with tiny spiders that have Simone crawling into Todd's lap.

Teddy rolls on the floor laughing as Nick flicks the spiders off his head. "Dude, I wondered where that went. I had it set out for Maggie."

Nick tosses spiders back at him, which only makes the group laugh harder.

"Teddy, there is something wrong with you." Simone shivers.

Garrett finally has a turn and, after digging around, pulls out a small white envelope. "Hmmm. What's in here?"

Hank jumps up. "I'll take that."

"This is where it gets interesting," Maggie says, wrapping her arms around my legs and squeezing.

"Oh no, you little punk." Cole jumps up. "That's mine. Garrett, you and me. Tickets to the next Marvel movie and all the snacks you want."

"Garrett, if you want to sleep at night, you bring that right over here. These AirPods are yours. Think of all the amazing medical podcasts you can listen to in peace," Hank counters.

"What's in there?" Teddy asks, and no one answers.

Liv's sweet voice chimes in. "Garrett, I'll give you my Belle doll."

The room goes quiet for just a second as Garrett tips his head to the side, thinking, but then Todd enters the bidding.

"My brother is a surgeon. I bet he'd be happy to give you a tour and let you interview him."

The entire room turns to look at him. Both Cole and Hank are speechless.

"Sold," Garrett exclaims, handing over the envelope.

Todd holds up the envelope, inspecting it.

"Wait," Hank jumps up. "I'll shovel your driveway for the entire winter."

"You suck," Cole says, but then looks to Todd. "You can be my date to this year's benefit. Think of the networking opportunities."

Todd laughs. "That's tempting."

"Ha," Cole says.

"Free haircuts for a year," Simone barters.

"Deal." Todd hands the envelope to her, and she waves it in the air.

Maggie pinches my calves like she knows she called this.

Simone beams. "All right, suckers. What do you have for me?"

And so it goes as I watch this family be a family with traditions, laughter, and teasing. Everything I dreamed of as a child but never had. Everything, as a man, I've never allowed myself to find.

My chest aches right in the center, but a ring of warm hope surrounds and eases it. I've been welcomed here, but the fear of it all disappearing remains.

Maggie leans against my leg, but I'd like to pull her into my lap and hug her for allowing me in. She's given me a chance to see and feel what this is really like.

The envelope gets passed from Simone to Gwen to Sadie to Nick, where Cole negotiates a ride to church and Sunday dinners, which buys him the envelope.

"One of those tickets is mine," Hank demands. "I won those."

"Well, you should've kept better track of them." Cole grins, ripping open the envelope that contains four ski lift tickets. "You give me my AirPods, and you'll have a better chance of going."

"I want to go." Teddy jumps up. "You've got to take me. I'm cute and will help you with the ladies."

We all laugh.

"I don't need help with ladies." Cole throws the crumpled-up envelope at him. "If I did, I'd take Liv."

"Yeah. Take me," Liv says as Cole scoops her up. "I was getting pretty good last year."

The bantering and bargaining continue, filling the room with joy and laughter as these kids claim and negotiate exchanges over gum, lucky socks, fake poop, and all kinds of other useless shit.

Maggie tips her head back and looks at me with a bright smile like she's the one who won the game. "You should've played. You might've had a chance to get your sweatshirt back. I guess you'll just have to wait until next year."

Next year. I really like the sound of that.

Chapter 33

MAGGIE

I tiptoe down the stairs and switch the lights off in the kitchen. Our Thanksgiving was a success on all levels, including completely wearing the kids out. I grab a bottle of water and carry it to the bedroom, where I find Shane propped up in bed reading. I'm not sure I'll ever get used to seeing his big body in my bed.

I climb in next to him. "I'm pretty sure they were all asleep the second they lay down."

He sets his book on his lap. "They all had fun today."

I bump his shoulder. "How about you?"

"Yeah. I had fun. Even bingo was fun."

"Ha! See. Don't knock what you haven't tried."

"Where'd you come up with that?"

I sigh, thinking back to my conversation with Gwen and Simone. If I want to know Shane and everything he keeps locked up, then I have to take a risk. I have to be willing to be vulnerable and share things with him. I have to be brave and show him I'm safe and trustworthy.

I know he's been hurt badly. I want him to know that won't happen with me.

I draw my knees to my chest and shore myself up to be brave. "Actually, my mom started it. She got tired of asking Cole and me to pick up our stuff and did the same thing. She collected it, saved it, and then we had to win it back. The funny thing was my dad usually ended up with the most stuff in the box."

"Yeah?"

"Yeah. It was pretty good stuff, too. Money, gear, his favorite hat. It's more fun with all the kids, but she was tricky. I'm pretty sure she stuck stuff in just to get a rise out of us. It was like getting new toys all over again. We only played for a few years. Then she was gone, and we never played again."

"I'm sorry." His tone is soft and gentle, and I want to lean into him. "She sounds like a fun mom."

I smile as memories flash through my mind. "She really was. In the studio, she was tough, but at home, she was a little spitfire. Lit my dad up all the time, but I think he loved every second of it."

We're quiet for a second, then he asks the question I've been waiting for.

"What happened?"

I rest my head on his shoulder, not wanting to go back there, but I will for him and for a chance at whatever we might be. If I want more of Shane, the man he keeps tucked away, I have to allow him more of me, too.

"I was eight. We were all dressed up. Like the full-on glittery, puffy dress every eight-year-old girl dreams of. She took me to the Nutcracker for the first time. It was the real deal, a professional production that came to town. I was so excited. I counted down the days. It was my first ballet, and I already knew I wanted to dance for the rest of my life. My dad was supposed to go with us, but didn't get home in time."

I inhale as every muscle in my body constricts, returning to that night. It's been years since I've talked about it, and I've never talked about it in detail, even with my therapists. Talking never helped. Nothing could ever make it better.

"We watched the show, and I was in awe. On the edge of my seat the entire time. From that moment on, I knew it was all I'd dream about, someday being the Sugar Plum Fairy. We stepped into the cold night air, hand in hand. I can still hear her laughter and see her smile and dance as we pretended to recreate the ballet on our walk back to the parking deck."

I close my eyes, squeezing them together, remembering. "I can still feel the sting of the frigid air on my face and the squish of the slush under my shoes from the snow that had fallen while we were inside."

I start to shake, and Shane slips his arm around me and pulls me closer to him. "One minute, she was there, and the next, gone. Just like that. A car lost control and came up onto the sidewalk."

A single warm tear rolls down my cheek. "I've relived that moment a million times, trying to understand how it missed me. One second, she was beside me, right there, holding my hand, smiling and laughing, and the next . . . " Another tear slips from my eye. "I knelt on the sidewalk, my knees frozen in the snow, holding her cold, lifeless hand, begging her to stay with me while I watched her slip away. She didn't come back."

More tears drip down my face as my throat swells with grief. Shane's large hand holds me to his chest, keeping me there until I can speak again.

I swipe the tears away with my fingers. "It was the most horrific moment of my life. Everything I thought I knew changed in a second."

Shane's calloused hand trails up and down my arm gently.

"In New York, I had to walk as close to the buildings as possible, almost pressed against them. Danny used to make fun of me, as if I had some kind of phobia. I never told him. And as you know, fancy dresses, the fabric, the feel, and even the swoosh of the material take me right back there."

"Maggie, I'm so sorry," Shane whispers against my hair.

"I struggled for a long time after that. Made some choices . . . " I start, but I don't want to go there. Not tonight. This was already a lot for me to divulge. "I'm not sure my dad ever got over not being there."

"I don't think I'd ever be able to forgive myself either." His voice is soft and soothing.

I pull away slightly to wipe my face before tipping my chin up to look at him. "You know, it's strange. Sometimes, I look at the kids and my life now and think about how none of this would be if she and I hadn't been on that sidewalk at that exact moment that night. I mean, I miss her so much and want her back so badly. I'd give anything, but I don't know. It's like I see now that even the bad stuff plays a part in getting us where we're supposed to be. It's so difficult to make sense of it all, but eventually, it feels like everything might be all right." I shake my head. "I don't know if that makes any sense." I laugh a little, wiping my nose.

His warm, safe body next to mine is comforting, and I realize letting him in isn't as terrifying as I thought. Shane is as solid as they come, and he proves his stability and trustworthiness every second.

"It makes sense to me," he offers quietly.

"Yeah?"

"Yeah."

I put my head back on his shoulder, and I like that he lets me leave it there. "Hey, Grizz."

"Yeah." His voice is back to low and rough, like he's processing it all.

"Thanks for being here. I don't think I've told you. All of this . . . I know it's a lot, but it's nice having you here."

He doesn't say anything, but I know he heard me.

I smile at him. "Will you read a chapter to me?"

After a second, he responds. "Sure."

I stay where I'm at, leaning on him as he opens the book and begins to read. This man. I already know he's one of the good ones. I've known it for a while. I just hope he knows it. How much he deserves to be happy, and how sometimes all the bad stuff can bring you to where you're supposed to be. I just can't help but want that place for him to be me.

Chapter 34

SHANE

"No cussing. No hitting on women. No acting like total idiots. Do we understand each other?"

"What about that bozo? The assistant coach. Can we pull him aside and kick his ass for good measure?" Mark asks from the passenger seat.

"No, there'll be no fighting. This is a high school game, and you will act like mature adults. Now, put your hats on and sunglasses. We don't need to draw a crowd."

"Yes, Dad." Sean pulls his stocking cap down over his short blond hair. "Why didn't we get Matthews jerseys? We're family, after all. If this kid is as good as you say he is, I want one."

"You just wait and see. He does this flip throw-in thing. It's freaking insane."

Mark pats my shoulder. "Look at you being the proud papa. Who would've ever guessed it?"

I glare at him as we pull into the school parking lot for the last game of the season, where we're meeting Maggie and the kids. I just picked up these two shitheads from the airport and came directly here. Maggie insisted we could skip the game, but there was no way. I want to make sure Hank's assistant coach doesn't pull anything. He's steered clear since the first game, and Hank said he hasn't approached him again. More than anything, I want to see the kid play and be here to support him.

We climb out of my truck and make our way to the bleachers, already filled with families. I spot my group of matching blue jerseys as Maggie and Liv smile and wave.

Since our early Thanksgiving, things have been busy. I had an away game on Thanksgiving Day, and got back just in time for Mark and Sean to arrive. I've not been too busy to think about Maggie. A lot. Probably way more than I should.

When she told me about her mom, the only thing I could think of was how I wanted to make it better. I wanted to take away all her pain and hurt and carry it for her. I understand how that kind of trauma never goes away. It's something you learn to live with. You carry it with you, living and breathing in the background of everything you do.

I feel even worse for not going to Carmen's wedding, now fully understanding everything she was going through that day. Having her share that with me meant a lot. It felt like a step in her trusting me with more than the day-to-day stuff. She shared her heartbreak, something she hadn't told many people. I don't take that lightly.

It makes me want to trust her in return, but where would I even begin? Opening the door to my past brings the possibility that she might look at me or treat me differently. I don't want to be pitied. I don't want to be fixed or mended, and I don't want a single thing to change how Maggie is with me. I couldn't stand it, so the past will stay where it is.

We climb through the crowd as people watch the three of us with interest.

Maggie stands and slides over to make room. "Hey, guys. I'm glad you made it."

Mark pushes me out of the way to grab her and hug her tightly, holding on extra long, knowing it'll irritate me. "Are you ready to dump this big dummy and run away with me?"

"Mark," I growl. "Sit your butt down and get off my wife."

Maggie laughs as we sit, the boys and Cole in the row below us.

Sean reaches across to shake her hand. "Please ignore him. He has no manners. It's nice to finally meet you."

"Oh, I have excellent manners." Mark grins, and if we weren't here, I'd smack his pretty face.

They introduce themselves to Cole and bump fists with the boys as I lean closer to Maggie. "It's still not too late for me to drop them off at a hotel."

"Not a chance, Grizz." She smiles. "Hey, I got a text from Danny. He's catching a flight tonight and will be here in the morning, so I need to be at the studio after lunch. Can you guys hang out with the kids for a while?"

Great. Danny.

I knew this was coming, but that doesn't mean I want Maggie to spend time with him. At least I have Mark and Sean to distract me from wondering what is happening and counting the minutes until she comes home.

It's not that I don't trust Maggie. I do. I don't trust him. I don't want him messing with her head or any part of her.

As if she can read my thoughts, she bumps my shoulder. "It'll be fine. Ok?"

I nod.

"Shaney." Liv climbs over Maggie to sit on my leg, and I hear Mark snort at the nickname.

She eyes the two guys, leaning into me. "Are they your friends?"

"Yes. They're kind of like my brothers."

She studies them for a long time, probably assessing their need for love. When she's done, she shifts toward them. "I'm Alivia. I have lots of brothers, too. Hank is going to kick some serious butt today."

They laugh, and before long, she's sitting between them, talking their ears off and interrogating them on everything from their relationship status to their favorite Disney princess.

Fifteen minutes into the game, Hank scores, and we're all on our feet yelling. Mark and Sean high-five as some of the parents turn as if they're taking offense to our cheering.

"Hey, Matthews. Keep it down. This is a team sport," a balding man yells from down in front.

"I don't see much team action happening out there," Cole shouts back calmly.

The jackass runs his mouth further. "Maybe if your boy would settle down, someone else could have a chance."

The ball is kicked out of bounds, and Hank picks it up. "Watch," Maggie says, half standing and ignoring the asshole in front of us.

We all watch as Hank picks up the ball and takes a few steps back before running into a forward flip, launching the ball long and far.

We roar.

"That was awesome," Sean says.

The loudmouth below pops up. "Seriously, this isn't the NFL. They're just a bunch of kids. You need to tell that little show off to put a cap on it."

I stand along with Mark, Sean, and Cole.

"You four sit down," Maggie scolds, and we follow directions.

The guy laughs.

The four of us are one more comment from wiping the smug look off his face.

"You all think your name will carry you through life. In the meantime, these kids suffer while you skate on by. It's ridiculous." He waves his hand and sits down.

Maggie's posture goes rigid, and she slowly stands.

Oh, shit.

The look on her face is one I've seen before. I turn to Mark and Sean, unable to prevent my smile.

"Hey, pinhead," Maggie calls, and he turns around to look. "Yeah, you."

"Maggie," I say quietly, but of course, she ignores me.

"Maybe if you'd get your head out of your butt, you'd see that the only reason you're even sitting here is because *our* little show-off has carried this team on his shoulders the entire season. When you want to talk about hard work, dedication, and skill, someone might actually listen. Until then, close your yap and be grateful he brought the team this far, and your kid is getting to add this achievement to his applications."

The people around us snicker as she sits down.

Mark whistles softly. "Maggie, remind me to have you in my cheering section."

"Don't encourage her," I say, even though there's no way I'd let Maggie be in anyone's cheering section but mine.

Hank scores two more goals, but the asswipe down front keeps his mouth shut.

At home, we order pizza while Mark and Sean play video games with the boys, and Liv easily convinces them to let her paint their nails. During baths, I build a fire in the pit, and we relax while Maggie helps the kids get ready for bed.

"This is a little different than our last time together." Sean's messy red fingernails reflect the light of the fire as he brings his beer up to his lips.

"You think?" For me, everything is different.

"Maggie's great," Mark says, tossing his beer label into the fire. "She's gorgeous, and I bet she has you running in circles." He points to his head, but he has no idea.

She's been the best surprise of my life.

"The kids are great, too, and you're a natural. Who would've ever thought?" he teases.

"They're all great." It's all I can come up with or am willing to admit out loud.

"So, when are you going to finally admit this is more than an arrangement?" Sean takes another pull at his beer, staring at me over the end of his bottle.

I stare back. "There's nothing to tell. Maggie's great. She's pretty much perfect, but I wasn't made for this."

He looks up at the sky. "Looks to me like you might've been made for exactly this. You seem to fit right in, and you and Maggie seem tight."

"Don't read into things." I need to change the subject.

We listen to the crackle of the fire in the cold night air, and then Mark adds his two cents.

"Don't be an idiot. Make sure you don't let a good thing slip through your fingers because you're too busy denying what might be right in front of your face."

The pressure is mounting in my chest with this serious relationship talk, and I need a release valve. "Are we talking about me, or are you reminiscing about Lex?"

Mark scoffs. "You know I pissed that away long ago. I was an idiot. Now, she's getting married."

Lex was Mark's first and only long-term girlfriend, his only love, whom he's never been able to get over. Even though he pretends to be the playboy, his heart still wholly belongs to her, and I'm afraid it always will.

"I'm sorry, man," I say, knowing that bit of news hurts.

"Yeah, well. Make sure you learn from my mistake."

The patio door opens and closes, and Maggie appears with a beer. There are no empty chairs, and without hesitation, she sits on my thigh with her legs in between mine as if it's the most natural thing in the world. I have no doubt both of these morons notice, but because they value their lives, they don't say a word.

"Alright, boys. I want all the goods." She grins. "He's really quiet when it comes to the two of you, so let's hear it."

Mark and Sean laugh and tell her how we met, but keep it light. Given what the three of us have been through, we respect each other's boundaries and privacy.

Maggie laughs at their embellished stories and tells some of her own from our first days living together.

I pull her closer, letting my hand rest on her hip. Before I know it, she's curled against me, and it's nice. Feeling close to her is becoming more than a desire. It's something I need. The feeling of her next to me. The quiet closeness between us. It's innocent, calming, and safe, something I don't want to lose.

I think about what Sean and Mark said, about this being more than an arrangement, and me fitting into this family. Over these past months, I've felt more at home with Maggie and the kids than anywhere in my life, but it could all change in a moment. If Maggie's lawyer gets Cliff and Joan to drop their case, what then? What happens when she doesn't need me anymore and realizes I have nothing more to offer her?

The pressure from earlier returns, and I try to push the thoughts aside. Focusing on the what-ifs won't help anything.

Maggie's voice breaks into my thoughts. "I have to be at the studio around lunch tomorrow. Do you guys think you can handle the kids for a bit? Then I thought I'd meet you for dinner if Cole or Gwen can watch the kids."

"Sure. How about I drop you off?"

Maggie looks at me with those bright blue eyes. "Grizz, it'll be fine. If not, the three of you can come and let him know how it is."

"What's going on? Who do we need to rough up?" Mark's ready with a mischievous look in his eye.

"No one," Maggie says.

"Mr. Hip-Hop. Maggie's working with him on a show that's happening in New York about a month from now."

"You're dancing with Danny Z?" Sean asks, and Maggie turns to me with a smirk, realizing I've talked to them about Danny.

"Yes, and it's no big deal."

"It's a huge deal," I say.

Mark pulls out his phone. "When is it? I'm getting a VIP ticket so I can see you before and after, and get the best seat. I can't believe I didn't know this. I hope I don't have a game." He scrolls his phone. "Wait, you guys should stay with me."

Maggie's eyes drag back to mine. We haven't talked about the logistics.

"It's ok." She jumps in. "I'll get a hotel room close to the venue. It's likely I'll barely even see the room until the show is over. We'll have tons of rehearsal and kinks to smooth out."

"So, you're rehearsing here and then just flying out for the show?" Sean asks.

"Yeah. It's the only way I could do it."

Sean nods. "He must have really wanted you."

His wheels are turning, and I shoot him a glare to tell him to knock it off.

Maggie shrugs. "We used to dance together, but I hurt my ankle a while back, so tomorrow will be a good test to see if it will even hold up."

I hear doubt creep into her voice. "You'll be fine."

"Well, I'll leave you guys to it. I'm going to bed." She stands. "I'll see you all in the morning. Oh, and make sure you watch your back. Teddy is our resident prankster. If you're under this roof, you're fair game."

Her eyes meet mine for the briefest moment before she disappears inside, and the only thing I want to do is follow her. I want to leave these boys to their beers and go read to my wife about a man walking the Nile. We've moved on from the Himalayas, and this has become my favorite time of the day. There alone in the quiet of our room, where she gives me shit and begs me to read to her. I pretend to hate it, but secretly, I love that she listens and then makes me stop so we can talk about the insanity of this guy's experiences.

But there isn't a chance in hell I'm getting out of this chair, knowing I'm about to get an earful from these two. My ass stays planted, waiting. Then it begins.

Mark goes first. “She’s dancing with Danny Z, huh? And you’re good with that?”

They don’t know Maggie or how much she needs to do this. How much she deserves to have this one thing.

“She’s going to be great,” I say. “This is huge for her.”

Sean leans forward, resting his hands on his knees. “You know you’re awfully cool about this for a guy who’s way more wrapped up in her than you’ll ever admit. I wouldn’t want my girl anywhere near Danny Z or any other guy.”

“Maggie and Danny are over. This is strictly business,” I say, knowing it’s true but still disliking any part of her being near him.

I don’t like him, but more than anything, I don’t like how he disrespected and hurt Maggie.

“Just be careful, Shane. I know how hard it is to let someone in. Don’t be so set on protecting yourself that you push her away and miss out on what could be,” Sean warns softly.

I’m not missing anything. I see exactly what’s in front of me. The problem is that what I can offer Maggie is nothing compared to everything she should have. And I want her to have it all.

The question is, will I be able to give her up so someday she can have it?

Chapter 35

MAGGIE

I lay in the middle of the hard studio floor, and I'm unsure if I'll be able to move tomorrow. My ankle hurts pretty damn bad, but so does everything else.

"You all right, down there?" Danny asks from his perch against the wall.

This guy is pretty much the same guy I danced with years ago. I just view him in a whole different light.

He's all chiseled, lean muscles. His light brown hair is held back with a band, and he has enough charm to win over a prude. It's all the same.

"I don't know. I might have to tell Shane I'll be sleeping here tonight." He laughs. "I knew I was out of shape, but this is depressing."

We've been dancing for the last four hours, and I'm done. The only thing keeping me from saying I'm not doing the show is that it will be amazing.

Danny came prepared, already having choreographed most of our dances, but I put my spin on them. It's reminded me of what a good team we make.

Danny stands over me, holding out his hand. "Come on. Lying still will only make it worse. You've got to keep moving before your muscles lock up."

I let him help me up and check my phone. It's getting late, and I'm supposed to meet the guys for dinner. Shane was nervous about me working with Danny today, but I tried again this morning to reassure him that everything would be okay.

I didn't know what to expect from Shane last night when I plopped down on his lap. There wasn't anywhere to sit, and we sleep together every night. It seemed like the natural thing to do, but as I sat there I wasn't sure.

I was surprised not only when he didn't seem to mind but tucked me closer to him. His large hand wrapped around my hip was definitely giving me more than friends vibes. But ever since our almost kiss in the bathroom and his confession at Thanksgiving, we've both been pretty careful not to cross any lines.

Last night, I took a risk to see what would happen. But pushing for something that's purely physical will only get me hurt.

Pulling my phone from my bag, I see I have a few missed calls from an unknown number and a text from Shane.

SHANE: When will you get here?

ME: Are those big boys picking on you?

SHANE: No, there's a bachelorette party that won't leave us alone.

ME: Get up and move. Go somewhere else.

SHANE: We're waiting for you.

ME: I'm tired. I smell. And I'm not sure I can move more than an inch a minute.

SHANE: I don't care. Get your ass here.

ME: Fine, but I warned you. You may have to carry me.

SHANE: Hurry up before I lose my shit.

I limp over to shut down the sound equipment. "I have to go. I'm meeting Shane and his brothers for dinner."

"It sounds like you're happy," Danny says softly as if he's surprised, and I kind of want to punch him.

"I am," I tell him bluntly, feeling like I need to remind him of our agreement.

"I'm glad. You deserve to be. You've taken on a lot, and I'm glad you've found someone to share it with. Especially if he makes you happy."

"Thanks." I'm done talking about Shane and me or anything else personal with him. "Let's go. If I'm going to make it through dinner, I have to keep moving."

Twenty minutes later, we pull into the parking lot of the bar where Shane and the guys are. Yes, 'we.' Danny convinced me to let him tag along rather than dropping him off at this hotel, and I decided he'd be a good distraction for the bachelorettes.

I hobble in with Danny following close behind, really hoping bringing him wasn't a terrible idea.

Shane, Mark, and Sean aren't hard to spot at the bar, and he wasn't exaggerating when he said they were surrounded.

A group of women wearing skin-tight dresses no bigger than cloth napkins are swarming like moths to three flames.

Do I wish I was in something other than a leotard and tights with sweatpants over them? Hell, yes. Even more, I'd like not to smell like I just ran a marathon.

Whatever, I'm married, and Shane is stuck with me. At least for now.

I limp toward them, feeling like every muscle in my body tears a little more each time I move. I push through the cloud of perfume and glitter, ignoring the pouts, huffs, and whines. At least these ladies' scent is strong enough to cover me.

"Excuse me." A girl in a tiny black dress with her boobs pushed up to her chin turns to look at me.

She's probably my age and standing all up in Shane's space, trying to steal his attention, but only getting his giant shoulder.

I point to him. "Sorry, this one's mine."

She gives me a once-over, clearly unimpressed by what she sees.

Shane doesn't wait for her to move as he slides his arms around my waist, pulling me between his legs and forcing her to shift out of the way.

That helps her get the message, and she moves along.

"You weren't kidding." I lean closer, resting my hands on his neck.

"If I have to listen to one more giggle or squeal, my head might explode."

"Maggie!" Sean and Mark erupt beside me.

I smile. "Looks like they're having a good time."

We turn at the sudden gasps and cheers as the ladies notice Danny.

"What's he doing here?" Shane growls.

"Easy, Grizz. He makes a nice decoy." I grin.

Shane holds me a little tighter. "How's your ankle?"

I glance down at my UGGed foot. "Really sore and a little swollen. I need to ice it as soon as we get home."

"Let's get away from here and find a table so you can put it up." Shane stands, using his big body to create room for us to get out of the cluster. "These losers can do whatever they want."

Shane sees my struggle and, without hesitation, scoops me up like I weigh nothing. "Seriously, I can walk."

"Doesn't look like it to me. Plus, you need to keep the weight off of it."

He finds a table in the back and sets me down. I take a seat on a stool, and he disappears.

Mark, Sean, and Danny appear a second later, having escaped the single ladies' club. They all take seats, joking about the numbers they just scored, which they toss into the middle of the table.

"What? All that attention and no winners?" I ask.

I'm quickly learning Mark isn't the playboy he'd like everyone to believe he is, and Sean is a lot more like Shane than I'd imagined. Just a softer version.

"I learned my lesson a long time ago," Danny says.

"What lesson was that?" Shane reappears with a bag of ice in his hand. He sits beside me, grabbing my foot and resting it on his leg. He pulls my boot off and settles the ice around my ankle.

The table is silent as Shane's gaze returns to Danny, waiting for an answer.

Danny meets his stare, sitting a little taller. "Not to mess around with people's feelings. I have a girlfriend, and she wouldn't appreciate me holding on to another girl's number."

"Good. Make sure you don't mess with my wife's, or I'll break your legs." Shane's no-nonsense threat is clear, and Mark and Sean try to hide smiles while my entire body ignites with fire and need.

This no-kissing-Shane thing is for the birds.

I want to find a dark corner in this joint and make out with this big hunk who just laid down the law on my behalf.

This table is full of good-looking men, but Shane and all his gruffness are by far the sexiest of them all, and for now, he's mine.

Why in the hell am I not taking advantage of all of the benefits of that?

Danny raises an eyebrow. "I have no intention of doing anything to make that necessary."

"Well, I'm glad we got that little detail out of the way," Mark says, breaking the ice.

I can't stop staring at Shane, and I don't care. He's supported me, helped me, and defended me. Now, he's carried me, got me ice, and said he'd break another man's legs for me.

What am I doing? Why am I so afraid of him not caring or being able to open up? I'm not sure anymore, or maybe I'm just clouded by lust for my husband.

I force my eyes from him, knowing it's starting to get weird, but I want to leave this minute and figure this out. I want to know what he and I can be if we let ourselves. He's making me want to risk it all.

If I let myself fall and let him have my heart, can I trust him not to break it and then take it with him when he moves on? Or is it possible that he and I can be everything I imagine we can be?

Chapter 36

SHANE

Maggie is staring at me, and I'd give my good knee to know what she's thinking.

Is she mad about what I said to Danny? If so, I don't care.

This dipwad needs to know exactly what will happen if he messes with her in any way.

Mark starts telling a story, and she pulls her gaze away. I can tell her ankle hurts, and she's trying to tough it out, but I'm pretty sure physical pain is not what's on her mind. I'm ready to get out of here so she can tell me how her day was and maybe whatever is brewing inside that pretty head.

A waitress appears to take our order, and I hope she makes this quick. I want to go home and listen to anything Maggie is willing to share.

"You should have heard him. He screamed like a little girl for about a minute." Sean laughs.

"Hey, I'd like to see you wake up to a giant snake hanging over your head, and see how you react," Mark defends.

"At least it wasn't a mouse," Maggie says, her eyes flicking to mine. "You're lucky he doesn't have a phone yet. He would've blasted that all over the web. I gave you fair warning, but now he's waiting for you to retaliate."

Mark grins. "Oh, don't worry. I'm planning my revenge."

They move on to football and this season's stats, then switch to critiquing the Moose defense.

"After what you've done with these guys already this season, it's only a matter of time before other schools hit you up," Mark says.

"We'll see how the rest of the season plays out." Thinking about the future creates chaos in my head that I can't handle, so I avoid it. I haven't even considered what that would mean to my situation with Maggie, and I don't want to think about it. "I'm learning a lot here, and it doesn't get better than working with Cavanaugh. He's tough but a genius."

Sean nods. "Yeah, I wish he'd been my coach in college. Things might've looked a lot different for me coming out of the gate."

The waitress brings our food, and Maggie picks at her plate. I don't know if she's just that tired or if there's more going on.

Danny discusses the show and what he and Maggie have been working on. "Don't let her fool you. She's the best there is. When she started at Juilliard, she was so quiet. Wouldn't talk to anybody. I saw this skinny little thing walk into class one day. She looked like she might break. We all wondered what in the world she was doing there."

Danny smiles. "Then, one night, I caught her sneaking into the studio to practice. It was like watching someone come back to life. I'd never seen anyone dance with that kind of rawness."

"You shouldn't have been watching. That was private," Maggie says, her eyes on her plate, and there's something in her tone I'm not familiar with.

Danny laughs as if it's a joke, but she doesn't think it's funny. "Yeah, well, it only took her a month or two to set the whole place on fire. There wasn't a guy there who didn't want to dance with her, and the girls never wanted to be in the same class. We all thought she only got in because her dad made a phone call. I mean, you looked anorexic and strung out when you showed up. You definitely didn't look like you belonged there."

Maggie drops her fork as Danny moves on to graduating and starting his own studio. Mark and Sean chime in about the people he's worked with, but Maggie is somewhere else, and I don't like it.

I put my arm around the back of her chair, leaning close to her. "Are you ok? Want to get out of here?"

She only nods.

"It's been fun, but we're going home," I announce. I toss my keys to Sean. "You can either follow us or hang out here."

I stand and help Maggie to her feet after removing the ice and putting her boot back on. I reach to pick her up again, but she insists she can walk, and I don't push her.

In the parking lot, I lift her into the passenger seat and climb in beside her. We drive in silence as she stares out the window, and all I know is this is not the same woman who found me at the bar tonight. I don't know what happened or where she went, but I'm going to find out.

Chapter 37

MAGGIE

Shane pulls my car into the garage, and all I want is to sit in a hot bath until I'm perfectly pruned. I don't want to think anymore today. Besides my entire body feeling like it's burning from within every time I move, my brain is functioning on overdrive. Too many neurons are firing, and there's not enough energy for it to do any good.

Shane hops out, and before I can move, he's opening my door and leaning in. I ease myself to the side, ready to climb out, but he blocks me.

I blow out a breath, knowing I don't have the strength for this.

He leans in even closer, his big body hovering as he rests his hands on the seat so we're eye to eye. His hazel eyes are soft and tender under the bill of his hat, and they make me want to crawl into his arms and hide there forever, where it's safe and warm.

"Tell me what happened." His gentle demand sparks conflict within me.

I look at him in all his goodness and sincerity. Where would I even begin? I feel like I walked into the restaurant tonight as one person and walked out as another. It's not true. It's all me. I'm just a lot more confused. Add to it a bunch of shame and embarrassment with a little layer of anger tossed in, and my complete exhaustion isn't helping.

"What do you mean?" I know exactly what he wants to know, but I don't want to tell him.

One dark eyebrow raises slightly, those earnest eyes focused on nothing but me. "Something happened between the bar and the table. I want to know what it was?"

He stares into me. Not at me. It's like he's looking so far inside he might just be able to see my soul, and it makes me want to curl into a ball. I'm not sure I want him to see that much.

But here I am, being held prisoner in my own car by this man who's causing a butt load of feelings, emotions, and hormones. He's turned everything upside down, and I have no idea what to do about it.

Do I want to tell him that at the moment? No. Do I want to kiss him and hope we can skip the rest of this conversation, maybe figure it out later? Definitely, yes. Will it help anything? Probably not, but it'd likely feel really good and be a wonderful distraction.

Dammit!

I wish I could just hand him my heart and ask him to hold it for safekeeping.

The thing I know about Shane is he would. He'd hold it with tender care. The problem is, how will I get it back when all of this falls apart? When he's ready to move on to whatever is next for him.

"Maggie." The way he says my name so patiently makes me want to grab onto him and hold on for dear life.

I tug the bottom of my coat down, trying to chase the endless list of things running circles in my mind, making it really hard to think straight or even at all.

Let's see, what can I say?

How about I'm possibly, very likely, almost surely falling for you, big guy? I could say that. Or wait. What happens when you get the call that Sean was talking about? The one that has you taking off to coach at another school. Hmmm. No. Oh. Perhaps I should discuss with him what Danny said and the misery I carry because I was young and naive and just wanted to feel something. Maybe we could talk about that and how, any minute, I'll have to hand over that load of humiliation to the attorneys, potentially spilling the most private and embarrassing details of my life. Nope. Definitely not going there right now.

I take a breath, feeling like I'm being swallowed whole by my emotional baggage, and force myself to meet his searching eyes. "Can we just go with I'm exhausted? Can that be enough for now?"

"No." Shane doesn't move an inch.

Someone help me. Why does he have to smell so freaking good and look at me like that?

"Grizz," I say, trying to keep myself calm.

"Maggie. Tell me."

"How about a hug instead? That will help."

He shakes his head. "No. I'll hug you after. Extra long if you want."

Oh hell. Oxygen can no longer make it through my windpipe, and my lungs are on fire. Tears spring forth, and I yell at them with hysterical warning to retreat.

Shane cups my cheek with his hand.

Oh shit. What am I supposed to do with this?

I close my eyes and allow myself just one second to savor his touch while I muster the courage to pull forth gut-wrenching honesty. "I don't want to tell you," I whisper. "I don't want to talk about any of this now or maybe ever. Can you understand that?"

When he doesn't respond, I drag my eyes back up to his. They flick between mine. I know he understands. Probably better than anyone, but even then, he surprises me.

He releases my cheek, pulls me to him, and hugs the absolute shit out of me. He stands there hunched over, halfway inside the car, hugging me like I've never been hugged before. I'm completely engulfed by him, and it's warm and safe and the only place I want to be. I want to stay here with him forever, and this realization is what has a single tear rolling down my cheek.

I allow just the one and then decide to hug him back, thanking him for understanding and caring enough not to push. I want Shane. I want all of him. Every single bit. I have freaking gone and fallen in love with him.

Poop. Crap. Baaaallllls. Shit… Shit. Shit. Shit. Shit. Shit. Shit!

Chapter 38

MAGGIE

"Mark, that was awesome." Teddy slaps Mark's hand. "I seriously thought I peed myself."

Mark grins, and Sean laughs as Teddy grabs his lunchbox.

"You be good, you little gangster." Mark pats his head. "And it's your job to make your bed when you get home."

"Yeah, yeah," Teddy says, and then he and Garrett bump fists with the two big guys on their way out the door.

"Hey," I holler. "Where's my hug?"

"Later, bruh," Teddy yells, throwing me a peace sign as Garrett runs back to hug me.

"See you later and keep him out of trouble." I squeeze him before he runs after Teddy.

The door closes, and I'm left in the kitchen with three big dudes and my little Liv, who's tucked into Shane like she might hide there for the rest of the day.

Me too, girl. Me too. Move over and let me in there.

I have a meeting with my attorney this morning. Shane offered to go with me, but I encouraged him to stay and drop Mark and Sean off at the airport. I'd rather handle this part on my own and then determine what needs to happen next.

"Mags, you be sure to hit me up the minute you touch down. I don't care if I have to drag you off the stage. You're having dinner with me." Mark shovels the last of his breakfast into his mouth.

I smile.

"I'll do my best to make it, but I'm not sure my schedule will allow it," Sean says, sipping his coffee.

"It's ok, really. Guys, it's not that big of a deal."

Mark scoffs. "Whatever. I'm not missing it. Plus, Danny's already sent my backstage pass. Somebody has to keep this idiot in line while Danny's got his hands all over you."

Shane groans and rolls his eyes, which makes me laugh. I don't know if Shane is considering coming to the show, but I really want him to be there. Given he hasn't said he's not, I hope it means he's coming.

"All right, boys. I have to go. Guard this princess with your lives until Gwen gets here and kicks you all out."

Mark slides off his stool to give me a big hug. "Be patient with him," he whispers. "He's kind of slow when it comes to things that really matter." I smile, and then louder, he says, "Are you sure you're not fed up with this lug yet? I'm sure the kids would love New York."

"Mark," Shane warns with a teasing tone.

I laugh, and Liv's head pops out from between Shane's arms.

"Can I come with you to New York? I've never been there."

"You can come visit me anytime you want." He winks.

Sean hugs me next. "Thanks for putting up with us and finally getting Shane to relax a bit."

My eyes meet Shane's over Sean's shoulder.

"Good luck with everything. I'm sure it'll be all over the internet, so even if I don't make it to the show, I'll be sure to watch it."

"Thanks," I say, gathering my things. Shane eyes me, likely to make sure I haven't changed my mind about him coming with me. "I'll talk to you a little later. Ok?" I try to reassure him.

He nods. "Will you call me when you're done?"

"Sure." I hurry out to get on with it.

My drive wasn't nearly long enough to calm my agitation and nerves. I pull into the parking lot, and my sweaty palms glide over the steering wheel as my skin prickles with chills. I park and grab my coffee, hoping it'll give my hands something to do while I face what I know is coming.

I take a deep breath, wishing I'd let Shane come with me, but this would only blindside him, which I have no intention of doing. I'll do whatever it takes to keep Liv safe and with us. That's the only thing that matters. So, if I have to suffer and bleed, that's what I'll do. All I can hope is that Shane and the boys will understand and that no part of this ever touches them.

The woven seam of my steering wheel bites into my fingers as I grip it, forcing slow, deep breaths while my heart pounds to the rhythm of fear. The lump in my throat is obstructing my airway, and no matter how hard I try, I can't swallow it down as bile rises.

I crack the windows, letting the cold air drift in.

I knew this was coming. I fall back against my seat and squeeze my eyes shut tight, needing the burn to ease.

My phone vibrates, and I grab it from the passenger seat, expecting it to be Shane, but it's the same unknown number that keeps calling.

I hit ignore and toss it on the seat. It immediately starts buzzing again. I'm sick of it. I cannot handle one more thing.

"Hello." I choke out.

"Is this Maggie Carter?" a deep, raspy male voice asks.

I shift in my seat, startled by the question. Not many people call me Maggie Carter.

"Yes."

"Well, it's nice you finally answered. I was beginning to wonder if you were avoiding me."

"Who is this?" I'm not sure what it is, but the man's voice makes my skin crawl, which doesn't help my current state.

He chuckles, and it's full of vengeance. "Sweetheart, we're family now. It's a real shame Shane hasn't introduced us. Although I've seen the pictures, I'm not sure I blame him."

Gross.

My best guess is this is his sperm donor, but I don't have time to deal with one more creepy asshole. "What do you want?"

"Hey now, no need to get your panties in a wad. Like I told Shane, it's time we get to know each other. I'm sure we'd manage to find some common ground."

"I have a feeling there's no such thing as common ground with you. I'll be sure to let Shane know you've called."

He sucks air through his teeth. "I can imagine why Shane married you. All that feistiness. At least you've got more going for you than money."

"Do yourself a favor, and don't call me again," I say with as much force as I can. My hands tremble, having had enough of every single thing.

"Honey, we'll just see about that. We wouldn't want your squeaky-clean husband to have to start answering questions about where he really comes from."

All anxiety turns to rage with that threat. "And blackmail is considered a felony," I bite back. "I'll jump out on a limb here and assume you aren't looking for any legal trouble. Just in case, though, I'll have my friends at the FBI do a little digging around. Don't be surprised if they come knocking just as a precaution."

Threatening Shane is a hell no. I'm pissed. This man should just try me. "Now, stay away from Shane, and don't ever call me again, or things will get much worse for you than a visit from the Feds."

As he begins to cuss me out, I add, "Oh, one more thing. Don't be stupid enough to think I'm bluffing. I have far more connections than you could ever imagine."

I hang up and want to throw my phone out the window and run it over. How the hell did that loser get my phone number, and why wouldn't Shane tell me he was threatening him?

I rest my head on the steering wheel, needing to get every cell of my body back under control. I inhale and exhale, reminding myself that Shane and I don't even really know each other. But here I sit, knowing I have to tell him about what happened with Cliff and Joan. Shane doesn't have a reason to tell me anything. He made it clear from the beginning that he was only helping me. He didn't want a relationship. He doesn't owe me a damn thing.

I clench my jaw, wanting to scream or hit something. Everything is spinning out of control, and I have no idea how to hold it together. I want to shut down and close myself off, but I can't. I want to be pissed at Shane and go back to when I didn't care. I don't want to have to give him the most personal and ugly pieces of myself. I want to keep them safe and hidden, but I'm forced to give him more, knowing I'll never get anything in return.

I told him I'd call him, but I can't. I hit the voice command, calling Cole instead.

"Hey, Mags. How did it go?"

"As well as I expected. Ben wants me to hand over the packet." I can't hide the quiver in my voice.

He's quiet for a moment. "It'll be ok. I know you don't want to do this, but they wouldn't ask for it if it weren't necessary."

"I know." Everyone has a breaking point, and I'm very close to hitting mine. "I have to tell Shane."

"Maggie."

"I know. I should've told him, but Cole, it's torture . . . saying it out loud." Even Cole and I haven't discussed this in detail, nor has he seen the pictures and documents.

"Maggie, no one will feel anything other than disgust. For them, not you."

I snort. "Yeah, if they believe me."

"No one who matters would ever think you did anything wrong, and anyone else . . . who gives a shit what they think? Shane cares about you. He knows you. Maggie, you have to tell him."

"What about the boys?" I sniff as the dam begins to crumble. "How will I explain this to them?"

"If it comes to that, we'll do it together, but hopefully, this will be enough to get them to drop it. I don't know how it couldn't be."

"It's my word against theirs." I try to keep the tears from falling, but the ache in my throat is overwhelming. I have to be in class in fifteen minutes, and I can't be a mess.

Cole sighs. "Yes, but they rely on their reputation and status. This could destroy them. I hope it does. What they did to you is unforgivable."

I swipe at my face, shoving it all down and pulling myself together.

"Want me to come over later and talk to Shane with you?"

One corner of my mouth tugs up. "No, but you are the best brother for offering. Just pray this is enough. Liv can't go with them."

"I know it may not seem like it, but it's all going to be ok."

"You think so?" I ask because, at the moment, nothing feels like it will be ok.

"Yeah. I don't know how anyone could look at how you provide for the kids, you and Shane, and think there is any place better in the world."

Tears well my eyes again and I blink them away. "Thanks. I'll let you know how it all goes."

"I'm here if you need me."

I sniff. "I love you."

"Love you too, Mags."

Chapter 39

SHANE

I've waited all morning for Maggie to call and tell me what her lawyer said, but she hasn't. I have to head into a meeting, and I'd rather be doing anything else. I don't want to sit in a room attempting to listen as my frustration continues to build.

A dull ache grows at the base of my skull and down through my neck as I take my seat, and my entire body seizes with tension.

I want to know what the hell is going on and what her attorney advised. The thought of fighting for Liv is like a fist to my stomach. I can't imagine her being separated from Maggie and the boys. It's all Liv knows, and she already struggles to understand why her mom abandoned her. This suit can't go forward, but given that Maggie didn't call me like she said she would, my stomach twists with dread.

Things have been off with Maggie the last few days. Really, since Danny showed up. When I tried to get her to open up, she asked me to drop it. How could I not? I could see her struggle and hear the pain in her admission that she didn't want to tell me. I understood.

I have a mile-long list of things I don't want to talk about or discuss. Ever. Watching her try to be ok when I know she's not has something festering inside me. She allowed me to be a part of all of this. I'm part of their lives, and she's keeping things from me that matter.

I want to know what they are, and I want to help. I don't want to be left out in the cold. Does she not trust me? Have I not shown her I'm in this?

I check my phone again as Coach Cavanaugh enters the conference room. No message. If this meeting weren't important, I'd drive to the gym and wait for her class to be over. Instead, I sit with my knee bouncing, my head pounding, and my level of patience very close to hitting its limit.

The meeting runs long, and I hustle to practice, only stopping in my office to grab my spreadsheets. On the field, I don't have to hide my boiling temper. Nick rolls his eyes after I tell him his sloppy attempt isn't good enough.

Halfway through practice, my phone vibrates in my pocket. I yank it out, wanting it to be Maggie so I can ignore her.

My stomach hits the turf, seeing it's Garrett and Teddy's school.

My frustration is replaced with a sudden uneasiness as I press the green button. "Hello."

"Mr. Carter. This is the nurse at Franklin Academy. I wasn't able to reach Mrs. Carter. Garrett has had an anaphylactic allergy attack, and he's being transported to Mercy Hospital as we speak."

The wind is knocked out of me, and a burning ignites in my chest, but my feet force me into action.

"He administered the EpiPen right away, and Principal Johnson is riding with him in the ambulance."

"Ok. I'm on my way. Thank you." I hang up and start running, yelling to Coach Cavanaugh that I have an emergency.

I dial Maggie as I run to my truck, but it goes to voicemail. I leave her a frantic message even though I know she already has one from the school.

In my truck, I floor it out of the parking lot as my heart and mind race with thoughts of Garrett and what he's going through. I try to remind myself that the nurse said he administered the EpiPen. Maggie told me that's what I needed to do if he started to have an attack.

I suck in a breath and try to call Maggie again. She doesn't answer.

Fuck!

I've been scared in my life, but I'm not sure I've ever been this scared. I hit a red light, and my fist slams into the steering wheel. Pain shoots through my knuckles up to my elbow.

Come on. Come on.

I pull into a parking space in the emergency entrance as blood pulses through my veins. I jog to the entrance, where I meet the security guard who appears to recognize me. His eyes widen, but I ignore him, giving him Garrett's name. It takes him a second before he starts typing.

"Are you family?" he asks.

"I should be on his emergency contact list."

"Shane Carter, right?" the man asks.

"Yes."

"He's in room four." He pushes a button and points as the automatic doors open.

I search the ceiling for the number four, swallowing the vomit threatening to force itself upward. My throat swells with relief when I see my buddy resting comfortably in the bed. He looks so small and pale, but just being able to lay my eyes on him almost brings me to my knees.

I step into the small, sterile room, and Garrett tries to smile.

"Hey, partner. You doing ok?"

He nods, and the thumping of my heart begins to lessen.

A middle-aged man, whom I assume is the principal, stands from a chair he pulled close to the bed.

"He's a brave young man. I'm Craig Johnson, the principal." He holds out his hand, and I shake it.

"Shane Carter. Thanks so much for riding with him."

"No problem at all. We tried to get in touch with Maggie, but I'm glad we could get you."

I nod, my gaze returning to Garrett. "She'll be here as soon as she can."

"Sure," Craig says. "The nurse will be in a few minutes. She can fill you in on what to expect. I have to get back to school." He pats Garrett's shoulder. "Rest up, kiddo. You did a great job today."

Garrett nods shyly. "Can you make sure Teddy is ok?"

"Of course," his principal answers and steps out.

I rest my hand on Garrett's leg. "You're one tough kid, you know that?"

He clears his throat, and his voice sounds breathy. "I knew better than to eat something from someone without checking the ingredients. I'm sorry."

I signal for him to move over and sit beside him on the bed, putting my arm around him. "It's ok. We all make mistakes. Sounds like you knew exactly what to do, and you did it. That takes balls, man."

He smiles, resting his head on my chest. It's a punch to the throat as it hits me that these kids have carved their way into my life. They're more important than I ever could've imagined.

"Where's Maggie?" His voice is soft and small.

I wish I knew.

"She'll be here soon. Should we see what's on that tiny TV while we wait?" I ask, not knowing how to make him feel better.

We flip channels, searching for a medical show, when the nurse returns to check his vitals and informs us that they plan to monitor him for a bit longer.

Just as I pick up my phone to try Maggie again, she bursts through the curtain, looking white as a ghost and out of breath.

She sweeps Garrett into her arms. "I'm so sorry. My phone was on silent." She pulls back to look at him, holding his face in her hands. "Are you ok?"

"Yeah. I did just like we practiced. I knew better than to eat something when I didn't know exactly what was in it. I'm sorry." His voice cracks.

"Oh, baby. You did so good. I'm so proud of you." She hugs him again and meets my eyes, looking like she might literally fall apart. "The nurse said you stayed calm and did exactly what you were supposed to. Do you have any idea how brave you are? You're going to be the best doctor someday."

"You think so," he squeaks out.

Maggie laughs, but it's weak. "Are you kidding me? Not many kids could handle that as well as you did. You're so smart and know how to stay calm under pressure."

After a bit, she releases him and turns her attention to me. She doesn't say anything, but I see so much. Her struggle to be brave at the moment, and whatever it is she's trying to carry alone.

She pushes Garrett's short hair to the side with her fingers. "Why don't you rest until we can break you out of this joint. Ok?"

He smiles and nods. I stand, giving him some space, as Maggie comes around to my side and launches herself into my arms. She hugs me so tight, and it's what I've needed all day—to know that she hasn't left me yet.

"I'm so sorry." Her voice cracks, and the anger and frustration I felt earlier dissipate. "I know I was supposed to call you, and then I left the damn thing on silent. I'm sorry."

She releases me, but her hands slide into mine. Her blue eyes fill with tears again as she peers up at me. "Thank you for being here."

I glance at Garrett. "Scared the absolute shit out of me."

She inhales. "Yeah. Tell me about it." She studies our joined hands. "I need to talk to you about this morning and some other stuff."

"Ok." I want her to tell me right now, but it has to wait.

Her forehead falls to my chest, and it feels like she's coming back to me. Or maybe this is her inviting me in for the first time. I'm not sure, but I want her to let me in. All the way. I'm surprised how much I want that.

I place my finger under her chin, tipping her face up. "You ok?"

She closes her eyes and lets out a breath. When she opens them, those deep blue eyes pierce something deep inside me. "Is it ok if I'm not?"

"Yes. I want to help." I don't just want to help. I want to make it better, but I have no freaking clue how to do that. I've never been that for someone—the person who makes things better.

"I know," she whispers, her voice shaky.

I pull her close again, giving her the hug I know she needs. It's what I need, to feel her close to me. These damn hugs have gotten to me, and now I need them.

Her arms slide up my back, and I breathe her in. The scent of vanilla and lavender that I've missed. Her softness and strength. The way she holds on to me like she won't let go.

"Shit!" she whispers. "Teddy. He's probably completely freaked out. One of us needs to go get him."

"What?"

"He has a fear of being left behind. I'm sure he's heard about Garrett. He's probably losing his mind thinking the worst and worried we won't remember him."

I squeeze her shoulders. "I'll go get him and then call you to see if I should bring him here or meet you at home."

"Ok." Maggie nods. "Thank you."

"Stop thanking me." I pull my keys from my pocket.

She hugs me one more time, and I step out, hurrying to make sure my other little guy knows he's safe and not forgotten.

Chapter 40

MAGGIE

"What's that?" Shane stands at the end of the bed, running a towel over his head.

His shirt clings to his damp body, revealing his enormous strength and stability. I need all that security to transcend the space and straight into me.

The large, manila envelope that's been hidden in the depths of my closet for the last ten years lies on the bed. It might as well weigh a thousand pounds, given the magnitude of emotions swirling within me.

I've been dreading this for weeks. I've prayed I'd never have to open it again.

"I need to tell you about what's in here." I take a steady breath, trying to calm the impending anxiety attack. "And then, I need to show you."

I don't want to look at him, but I force myself to.

His brow wrinkles as he hangs the towel over the door and then sits beside me.

We haven't talked much over the past few days. Mark and Sean were here, and I used them as an excuse to keep my distance. More than that, though, I'm scared. I'm afraid of how much I care about this large wanna-be grump. This quiet, hardened by life man who is gentle and sweet and so tender-hearted under that tough exterior.

Finding him in the ER, propped up beside Garrett, only solidified it all for me. I care about him so much. I've fallen in love with him, but I'm scared he doesn't or won't love me back.

I'm terrified to show him what's inside this envelope. I don't want to see his reaction or know what he thinks. I can't handle his disbelief or his possible doubt in me.

I don't want to relive this, but mostly, I don't want the kids or anyone else to be affected by it. I don't want to see the pictures or read the documents, let alone let the world see them. But I will if there's even the slightest possibility that it will prevent Cliff and Joan from taking this any further. If it protects Liv, I'll suffer any consequences. I'll relive it all. I made it through once. I can do it again.

I sit taller, knowing I just need to get this over with. I shove my hands under my thighs to stop them from shaking.

"I have to hand this over to the attorney, but before I do, I need to tell you about it. First, though, you should know I'd like to burn it all and never let anyone see the contents."

I take another slow breath as every muscle in my body begins to vibrate, and my heart pumps harder. "There's a chance that what's in here will prevent Cliff and Joan from taking things further, but it's a gamble. I hope it'll be enough. If it's not, this could get ugly and become the latest news story. How far it will spread, I have no idea."

Shane sits quietly, and I turn to steal a glance at him. His scruffy jaw is set, and his eyes are filled with apprehension.

I squeeze my eyes shut tight, forcing myself forward. "I'll do whatever I need to keep Liv. Anything. I hoped being married would be enough, but Ben says Cliff and Joan are determined to pursue this and will use part of this information against me, but they don't know I have this."

I pick up the envelope, watching it wobble as I hand it to him. He takes it but just holds it before setting it down.

"Maggie." He waits for me to look at him. "Take a breath."

I try to inhale, but it's like breathing through a cocktail straw.

"Tell me what's in there." It's a gentle demand.

"I don't want to," I say, willing my voice to hold strong.

He grabs my hand, intertwining our fingers. "Tell me."

His closeness and touch loosen the muscles in my throat just enough to suck in a deep breath and I attempt to muster bravery when I feel nothing but shame.

This is it—the worst of me. I handed it to him on a large, yellow envelope platter. Allowing someone else access to this is like handing over the keys to the kingdom. It's the single thing that will shred my soul into a thousand pieces with the most subtle mention.

I'm giving it to him, the whole damn thing. Something I've never allowed anyone before, not even my dad, because we never really talked about it. Telling Shane might be the most terrifying thing I've ever done. Saying it out loud to the man, I only want to see the best of me. I'm forced to give him the very, very worst.

The contents of my half-eaten dinner rise in my throat as I shove myself forward and off the cliff.

"When my mom died . . . " I try to focus on his firm grip on my hand. "Being there, seeing it happen, and watching her take her last breath . . . I started to shut down. For a while, I tried to go on like nothing had changed, even though everything had. She was gone. Dad was traveling all the time. I kept dancing, but she wasn't there. She was supposed to be there, you know?"

He adjusts his hold on my sweaty palm but doesn't let go.

I stare at the security and safety of our linked hands, hoping after I tell him this, he'll still be here.

"The older I got, the angrier I became. I wanted something, anything, to feel normal. I wanted a dad who worked a regular job and was home every night. I wanted to dance without feeling guilty each time I slipped my ballet shoes on. I wondered every day why I was still here and she wasn't. I wanted to go to bed and not watch her die all over again every single night. I hadn't slept for years, and I was so tired."

I rest my head on his shoulder, our hands still linked. He hasn't let go yet.

"I spent a few years in therapy, but I got tired of them telling me that grief takes time. Time wasn't making anything better. Talking didn't help. Nothing did, so I just . . . stopped. I quit talking, quit trying at school, quit dancing. I stopped living. All I could do was lie in bed wanting her back, and when I tried to accept it was never going to happen, I only wanted to disappear."

I clear my throat, needing the large, painful lump to lessen. "The summer before I got into Juilliard, Cliff and Joan invited me to stay with them. My dad agreed, even though they didn't have the best relationship. He thought the change might be good for me, and by that point, I needed something different. Anything. I couldn't live pretending everything was fine when life was moving on without me. So, I went."

"At first, they were nice. They didn't have any children and treated me like I was their own. I went shopping with Joan and attended big fancy parties. They'd introduce me to their friends and their kids, encouraging me to get to know them. I dressed the part and played along well enough."

"I went from one world where I didn't feel like I could go on to another that had me flitting around like a made-up princess. But it was different, and I didn't have to pretend. I still didn't talk unless I had to and wasn't interested in making friends with the spoiled rich kids, but it was all a decent distraction. Then, I heard Cliff on the phone with my dad, telling him something was wrong with me and how he hadn't gotten me the help I needed. I didn't care. I was away from everything that constantly reminded me of all that was missing."

I peek at Shane from the corner of my eye, and he's staring at our joined hands, listening.

"Eventually, Joan wanted me to do the southern debutante thing like all their friends' daughters had. The ballgowns, the coming out, date one of their chosen guys. The more she and Cliff pushed, the more I started to feel the walls closing in all over again. I felt like I was suffocating from the inside out. The dresses alone were torture. I couldn't do it."

"That kind of thing still exists?" Shane's voice is low yet soft.

I nod. "Yeah. It's weird, but in their circle, it's what girls do. I refused, and their disappointment was clear. They wanted me to be something they'd never have otherwise. It was important to them. As time passed, I began to feel different. Lighter. It was like the pain and grief suddenly didn't feel so heavy. Instead, I didn't feel anything. I started talking to one of their friends' sons, who had been paying attention to me. He was older, cute, and seemed to cut through the crap that so many others existed on. He pushed me out of my comfort zone, and I went along."

Sweat pools in my armpits as a chill rolls through me. "I spent weeks walking around, floating on a cloud. I didn't know what was happening, but it was a relief to feel nothing. I quit eating. When I was hungry, I liked the ache. It was something I *could* feel. Talking became secondary again, except to Jared, but he wasn't really interested in talking either."

I can feel Shane's gaze on me now, and I want to hide. I close my eyes, unable to look at him.

"But one night, I lay in bed feeling light, like I could drift away. I was literally numb, and it scared me. All that time, the pain, the hurt, the nightmares, and then just . . . nothing."

I inhale and blow it out. "Cliff and Joan threw a huge Fourth of July party. I found Jared and stole a drink from the bar. I remember looking at it and wondering what it would feel like, wanting a buzz or . . . something. I drank it, then another, and pulled him inside."

"Maggie," Shane says so quietly, like he knows where this is going.

His body goes rigid beside me, and I hold my hand up to stop him.

"I knew what I was doing. Well, I thought I did. I was young and dumb and so not ok. I thought it would break through the numbness. I took him to my room, and . . . I'd not done that before. It wasn't what it should have been. He wasn't . . . gentle."

The sting of humiliation ricochets through my entire body, lighting a fire along its path, and suddenly, I need space.

I drop his hand and scoot away from him, my heart beating too fast. Of all people, this is not what I want Shane to think about when he looks at me. The thought stirs my stomach.

I force the bile in my throat down and push myself to continue. "I lay there afterward, staring at the ceiling. My world was spinning, and he went to sleep, likely drunk. Sometime after, Joan came in and found us. She freaked out, saying she should have known I'd get myself into trouble. Jared left, and she locked me in the room. It was the first time I'd cried in years. All I wanted was my dad. I wanted him to come get me and take me home.

"I don't know how long I was in there before she brought me food, but I was too sore and weak and severely hungover to eat anything. I hadn't even showered, but she left the door unlocked, and I crawled to find a phone. I called my dad, crying. It was like I fell asleep, and then he was there."

"I remember him scooping me up, carrying me out, yelling. I'd never heard him like that, and it scared me. He took me straight to the hospital. That's what's in there." I point a shaky finger at the envelope. "The report and pictures. I'd lost a lot of weight, which I didn't have to lose. I had bruises, and . . . They found narcotics in my system."

"What?" Shane's voice is so low it's almost a growl.

All the tears I've held back pool in my eyes, quickly spilling over. "I never took anything. I promise."

"Maggie. They drugged you? Those pieces of . . . " He clenches his fists and then releases them.

A cool rush of shock rolls over me that he doesn't assume I'd been using. "Yes. I'm not sure how. Maybe it's in my food or drinks. I'm not sure why they did it, other than to get me to submit and follow their lead, so they could mold me into what they wanted. They could brainwash me to fit their ideals. I'd be the daughter they never had. I think maybe in some sick way they thought they could use the fact that I was Tim Matthews's daughter to gain connections and status."

I shake my head, panic filling what's left of my mental capacity. "I don't know, but Shane, all this is my word against theirs. I don't have any proof. All I have are these pictures and the report to show what happened while I was in their care. My dad pulled everything together. He wanted to press charges, but I begged him not to. I only wanted it to be over. I was so ashamed and embarrassed."

Shane grabs my face and holds it in his hands, forcing me to meet his intense gaze. "You have nothing to be ashamed of. Do you hear me?" His eyes are dark and so fierce. More tears escape and roll down my cheeks. He swipes them away with his thumbs.

"You were just a kid, and they took advantage of you." His jaw flexes. "You were grieving, and they used that. They hurt you. They drugged you. Maggie, you didn't do anything wrong, but try to keep living when you didn't want to."

My body lets go, and I fall into sobs. I was trying to keep my head above the water when all I wanted was to drown. To be with my mom again.

Shane pulls me into his lap, and I let go of years of pain and suffering. I cry for the girl trying so hard to fight a battle she wasn't sure she could win, and the woman who's worn an invisible tattoo of guilt, punishing herself for not being smarter, better, or more capable.

"They aren't going to get anywhere near Liv or you ever again." Shane's bossy tone is turned on. "You understand me. Never."

My chin drifts down to my chest again. "Shane, what's in that envelope is awful. I don't want you to see me like that." My voice cracks, and the fear I've locked up finally breaks free from the compartment I've shoved it in for so long. "I don't want to see myself like that. How will I explain this to the boys?"

"You're not going to have to. I don't care what we have to do. We'll figure something out." He sounds so sure. I want to believe him, but I've tried everything.

"I'm giving it to my attorney. They'll threaten to make it public and find the source of the drugs. My dad hired someone to dig around. They're going to contact Cliff's attorney and hope he'll let this go to save face. I want this all to be over."

"Maggie, I'm so sorry." He says it like it pains him. He puts his arm around me and pulls me to his chest. I rest my head against him, feeling safer than I've ever felt.

After allowing my body to calm and relax, I tell him the rest. "When I got home, and the drugs were finally out of my system, I dove into dancing again. It was like a wake-up call. I knew my mom would never want me to give up. She'd have wanted me to keep going, so I went for it. All in and somehow made it into Juilliard."

"What Danny said the other day at lunch about looking like I was strung-out, hurt. He has no idea, but it's humiliating, and I'm so ashamed I didn't realize what was happening, and then Jared . . . I wish I could take it all back."

Shane leans, tipping my wet chin up. "Maggie, you have nothing to be ashamed of. What they did . . . it's inexcusable. It's indefensible. I don't care how Jared got into your room or why. He had no right to take advantage. Maggie, he hurt you."

The warm, salty taste of more tears hit my quivering lips. "I'm sorry I didn't tell you before. I really thought getting married would be enough, but maybe that wasn't fair, and I should've told you so that—"

"Stop. Don't. Don't apologize for this. Ever."

"I want this to be enough. I want to know that Liv isn't going anywhere."

"She's not," Shane says like it's final. "She's staying right here with us."

Us. That sounds really nice. I want to ask how long there'll be an us. I don't want this to end, but one way or another, it will. How long will he stay when it's over?

I can't ask. Not right now. I don't want the answer. For now, I only want to sit here with his arms around me and try to believe these pictures and documents will be worth the pain. That in the end, something good will come of it.

Chapter 41

SHANE

I step into my hotel room, knowing it will be a while before I sleep. I quickly change to find the gym, hoping it will help clear my head.

Tomorrow is the big game that will determine whether or not we advance to the playoffs. I have tape to watch, but all I can think about is Maggie dropping off the documents in the morning. I hate that I'm not there to go with her.

I didn't look inside the envelope. She said she didn't want me to see her that way, and I wanted to respect that. I didn't need to see the pictures to know how bad it was. I also didn't want to see them because I'm not sure I'd ever be able to erase them from my memory once I did.

The fact that she feels ashamed or responsible for any part of if makes me want to finish what her dad started, showing her she was just a kid who was taken advantage of when she was most vulnerable. I can't stand it. Just the thought makes me want to tear them apart, limb by limb. I'd also like to find Jared and remove his head from his body. However, none of that will help Maggie, and I'd never want to make this harder on her. She trusted me with her most private and sacred experiences and feelings. I won't make her regret it. Ever.

My room door clicks shut behind me, and I walk the short distance to the gym. Before leaving today, Liv skipped into the room and jumped up on the bed while I packed, telling me every detail of her morning at preschool. When I sat beside her, she crawled onto my lap and asked when I'd be back, making it harder to leave.

She relies on stability and routine, counting on the people in her life to be there when they say they'll be there. Even at five, she's hesitant to trust that I won't leave her, and even with reassurance that I'd be back, she was reluctant to let me go.

I can't bring myself to think about Cliff and Joan taking this custody case to court. Liv's pure innocence and sensitive little heart wouldn't withstand it. The thought makes me sick, and I need to sweat it out before it consumes me. She doesn't just count on Maggie to keep her safe. She's counting on me, and I'll do anything.

An hour later, sweat-soaked and a little less tense, I head back to my room. Checking my phone, I see I have a missed call from Rob, and I dial him back.

"Hey, buddy. Are you ready for the big game tomorrow?" Rob's chipper voice booms through the phone, and I suspect he didn't just call me to wish me luck.

"Getting there." I pull out my tablet to review the remaining tape I downloaded.

"Well, I'm glad your energy and enthusiasm are spot on, as always. Anyway, do you have a moment to discuss an opportunity? The sooner I get back to them, the better."

"Not sure I want to talk about future opportunities right before an important game."

I don't have the bandwidth to process one more thing, but Rob will push forward no matter what I say. He's not one to let any possible positive opportunity slip by. It's one of the reasons he's my agent and why I've gotten this far. So, even though I don't want to talk right now, I'll at least hear him out.

"Yeah, I got it, but listen. This might be worth the distraction. I got a call from Ohio State. They've seen what you've done this season, not to mention your history there. Their head coach is off contract after this season. This is huge, Shane, and I need to get back to them. They want to fly you out in the next few weeks."

I groan, knowing he's right. This is big and not something I should easily piss away. "When?"

"Soon, they're hoping before the holidays. They'll work around playoffs."

Shit. "I can't. Maggie has a show in New York."

Rob sighs. "Shane, we can't be picky here. They're approaching you. If we don't hop on this, it won't take them long to look elsewhere."

"The timing is horrible. Our season isn't over and Maggie has to be in New York"

"It's just a day or two, and then you'll be back. Shane, you don't want to miss out on this."

I know he's right. Even if it turns out to be nothing, not talking to them would be a big mistake if I want to keep coaching, but I can't miss Maggie's show.

"Find out how flexible they are and let me know." I can't miss being in New York. "Rob, I'm not saying yes to this. It's just a conversation. I've learned a lot here, but I still have a long way to go. I'm not sure I'm ready to take on a whole team, and biting off more than I can chew would be costly."

Rob sighs. "I hear you, but they like what they've seen and know what you're capable of. It's a good match. You don't get that every day."

"Yeah. I know."

"Ok. I'll see what I can find out, but we'll have to react fast."

"Right." I don't need one more thing to think about. "This stays on the down-low. I don't need anyone sniffing this out."

"Got it. Good luck tomorrow," Rob says, hanging up.

I toss my phone and sit on the edge of the bed. I was not expecting this, especially before the season is even over. This is not what I need right now, and not something I want to mention to Maggie until I figure out what to do. Apparently, I'll have to figure it out pretty quickly.

I shower and grab my tablet, trying to force myself into game mode. I need to focus on the team we're facing tomorrow, but too many things are messing with my head.

I dial Maggie.

"Hey." Just hearing her voice calms me.

"Hey."

"Hi." She laughs, and the sound makes me smile, which she'll never see. "Sooooo, what are you doing?"

"Trying to watch the tape for the game tomorrow."

"Yeah?"

"Yeah. What are you doing?" I just want to hear her talk.

"Hmmmm. Let's see. Just got the kids in bed. I'm not sure Teddy did anything at school today but mess around, so we had a heavy load to work through after dinner. Liv is responsible for snacks at preschool tomorrow, so we had to scrounge around for something that would feed twelve. Applesauce pouches for the win. I'm watching *SportsCenter* in the middle of our amazing bed." She pauses, and I don't miss that she called it *our* bed, and that's where I want to be. "How was your flight?"

"Fine. They're pumped up. I hope they can sustain it through the game."

"How about you? Are you pumped?"

"Trying to get there. What time is Danny getting in tomorrow?"

This is his last trip out before the show, and just one more reason I wish I were home.

"Around lunch. Gwen is going to stay late until I get home. He has to be back the following afternoon, so we've got a lot to get through. Grizz?"

"Yeah?"

"You ok?"

Somehow, Maggie has developed this way of seeing through me that I'm not totally comfortable with. I don't know how to answer. I feel like there are a bunch of missiles in the air, and I'm not sure where any of them will land or when they might explode.

"Yeah. It's just quiet here."

She laughs again. "You should enjoy it while you have it. When this show is over, and Cliff and Joan take a hike to somewhere hot and eternal, I'm going to find a beach somewhere and plop my butt on it for about a week, listening to nothing but waves."

Thoughts of Maggie in a bikini on the beach fill my mind. It's better than any reprieve I could've imagined. "Sounds nice."

"Grizz, are you a beach guy? You strike me as an isolated log cabin in the woods with minimal invasions from the outside world kind of guy."

I'm beginning to see I'm a whatever includes Maggie in the fewest clothes possible kind of guy. "Sean, Mark, and I used to head to Florida every year when the season was over for a few weeks."

"Huh. I guess I can see that. Fun in the sun and all those beach bunnies. I get it."

She doesn't get it at all. There was a time when I didn't make the best choices. I was young, dumb, and trying to fill a gaping hole with momentary fun. It didn't take me long to learn that nothing good came from my stupidity, and that was not how I wanted to live my life or the man I wanted to be. Sure, there were women everywhere, but that wasn't my deal.

"I was in it for the heat, rest, and rejuvenation to let my body heal."

"Well, if you read to me while I lie in the sun, I might let you come along."

I see what she's done here. I've seen her do it with the kids. She's completely distracted me, and it's totally worked. I do feel better. "Maggie?"

"Yeah."

"Thanks."

"For what?" I know she's smiling.

"You know. Don't get a big head."

"Me? Never. Want me to call you in the morning and turn on a little Eminem?"

I want to say yes. Call me. I want to tell her that I wish she was here or that I was there, but for some reason, I can't let myself.

"All right, Firefly. Go to sleep and make sure you set all one hundred alarms."

"Haha. I wouldn't mind so much missing out on tomorrow morning."

I don't want her to take those documents in the morning, but I know she has to. When I don't say anything, she speaks softly.

"Shane."

She doesn't call me by my name very often, but when she does, a current of heat rolls over me from my head to my toes. "Yeah?"

"Good luck tomorrow. I'll watch as much as I can from my phone, but I'll be at the studio. You should be really proud of what you've done and how hard you've worked. Win or lose, you're making a name for yourself."

I want to tell her about the call from Ohio State, but I won't add that to her plate right now. I'm not sure if I even want it or if I'm ready for it, and I need to figure that out before I stir up one more thing in her life.

"Thanks. I'll see you tomorrow night."

"Goodnight."

I watch tape for an hour and then turn out the lights, feeling better than I did two hours ago.

Marrying Maggie has changed so many things in my life for the better. All of the things I thought I didn't want exist now. Or maybe it was just that I didn't believe I could have them.

Going to Ohio State would change everything. It may be an opportunity I can't refuse. But choosing between Maggie and the kids and my future in football, seems like an impossible decision.

So, I push it all aside to focus on the game with a little bit of lying on the beach with Maggie mixed in, hoping it will get me through the night.

Chapter 42

MAGGIE

I'm numb. Everything feels so bad, I can't feel anything at all. My body. My brain. My spirit. All three have taken a massive hit and I need to be peeled off the floor, like a cartoon character flattened by a steamroller.

I've lain for the past thirty minutes flat on my back in the middle of the bed, praying. I heard Shane come in, but he went straight into the bathroom without much more than a hello.

The Moose won the game today, and a couple of guys dumped a giant cooler of Gatorade on him, which I'm sure made for a comfy flight home.

I spent the day in the studio with Danny, working out the kinks in our pas de deux, which was the distraction I needed after dropping the packet off with my lawyer.

After handing it to the receptionist, I sat in my car, thinking about Shane and how he'd just sat with me while I told him. I trusted him, and he didn't disappoint. He didn't try to make it better or tell me it wasn't my fault. He just sat with me, held me, and let me tell my story. He helped me see, maybe for the first time, that I was just a girl. I was a girl whose trust had been violated and her weakness exploited.

It's the start of me forgiving myself for something I should never have taken responsibility for. The problem is that when you carry the shame for half your life, reversing the damage doesn't come overnight. It's a process, but handing over that envelope today marks the beginning. It's a step in letting go.

Ben called this afternoon and said he'd be in touch after communicating with Cliff's attorney. He hopes that after the documents and pictures are reviewed, as well as our willingness to reopen the investigation into how the drugs were obtained, they'll drop everything. Now I wait, praying it will be enough and Liv will stay with us.

I adjust the ice on my ankle with my opposite foot. It feels like it's broken all over again, and I'm not sure I can do this.

I've had ice on it since I got home and out of a hot bath. I threw on one of Shane's T-shirts and crawled onto the bed, but it hurts so bad I don't know if I'll be able to walk tomorrow. I take some deep breaths, trying to swallow all my worries, when I feel the bed sink beside me.

I open my eyes to Shane's rippled back.

Great. Juuuuussssst great.

I cannot process one more thing, let alone half-naked Shane. I'm freaking in love with him. I was terrified out of my mind to tell him about Cliff and Joan. I'd never told anybody, not the whole story, but his belief in me, his support, and the fact that he's still here make my heart ache. It's so full of love for him, and I have no idea what to do about it. I care about him so much, and it just soared to a whole new level. It's all too much.

I whimper, and his gaze snaps in my direction.

"Hey, sorry. I thought you were sleeping."

"Noooo," I whine. "I can't move. Everything hurts so bad, even my hair, and I can't turn my brain off."

He rests against the headboard, stretching out his legs, and then reaches over to push a strand of hair out of my face.

"I'm not sure I can do this," I admit quietly.

He leans forward, and his big hand lifts the ice off my ankle. His fingers run over it, making me flinch, and then he adjusts the bag around it again.

When he settles next to me, he's lying down. "How did this morning go?"

"Fine. We just have to wait and see if it works. Ben's going to threaten to reopen the investigation into where the drugs came from and who obtained them. He hopes that will scare them into dropping the matter. They're so manipulative. I'm worried it won't make a difference, especially if they covered their tracks."

Shane nods and squeezes my arm.

I can't think about it anymore and need to change the subject. "Awesome game today. Your guys killed it, and Cole made it look easy. I texted him, and he's out of his mind."

"They were a bit much on the ride back. They dumped the cooler on me, and I was about to lose my shit on the plane. It smelled, and everything stuck to me."

I laugh. "But you did it. You're headed to the playoffs."

He releases a breath. "Yeah. How was Danny?"

I delicately roll onto my side and face him. "Being Danny. A little high-strung. He says some of the dancers aren't cutting it. I'm wondering if I'm one of them." I pause, and his hand brushes mine, but he doesn't pull it away. It's warm. I missed lying next to him and his body heat, but mostly how safe I feel tucked into him, like nothing can get to me there.

"You can do this," he says, grabbing my hand and holding it. "You're so strong. The strongest person I know."

"I don't know." I'm really not sure that I can make this happen. My throat burns. "My spirit wants to believe it, but my body and my brain aren't cooperating."

He rolls onto his side, so we're face-to-face. He's so beautiful, and he has no idea. His dark hair and those ever-changing brown-green eyes. His strong jaw covered in day-old scruff, and all that seriousness.

My eyes sting with uncertainty.

I'm so glad he's home, and I can't hold it in. "I missed you," I whisper.

His eyes roam over my face for a long while, and then one large hand cups my cheek. I close my eyes, leaning into his touch. I want so many things, and one of them is Shane. I want him, but I want all of him, not just the scraps he's willing to throw me.

My eyes drift open, and he's moving closer, his eyes never leaving mine. I can't move a muscle even if I want to. They're so sore, but also because I'm afraid if I do, I'll spook him and he'll stop.

Is this a bad idea? Maybe, but I want so badly for him to take me somewhere else for a while. Somewhere I've wanted to go for quite some time now.

His hand pushes into my hair, and his face is a quarter of an inch from mine. I can't breathe. I can't think. The only thing I can do is lie here and soak up every feeling, every touch, every movement, because I know that after, nothing will be the same.

His lips press against my forehead. Once, twice, so so gently, moving over my temple and then my cheek. His warm breath hovers over my lips like he's waiting for me to decide.

This is a huge risk, but if there's any risk worth taking, it's this one, with this man.

I run my finger along his stubbled jaw, hooking it around his chin to pull him to me. My lips press against his, and I'm no longer numb. My entire body ignites with desire and need.

Shane's hand slides behind my back and pulls me closer, his mouth moving gently, slowly over mine. I bite his bottom lip lightly, teasingly, and I swear I hear him growl. My lips turn up in a smile, but it only lasts a second as his mouth crushes against mine. He slants his head, and our tongues meet, seeking more.

How long have I wanted to know what this would feel like? And it's so much better than I ever imagined.

It feels like a dream. I'm Alice finally waking from the topsy-turvy Wonderland. This is it. He's it. I'm safe and sound with Shane.

His hand slides up my thigh and rests on my hip, gripping it while mine slips around his back, gliding over each defined muscle. Our kisses deepen and linger as our hands roam and explore, slowly discovering what's been hovering around us for so long.

We break apart, needing air, and Shane's lips make their way down my neck. His scent surrounds me, and his massive, warm hands feel so good over my sore body. I want this, but I want more than just Shane's body. He means too much to me.

Shane makes his way back up to my mouth, and what started out slow and patient quickly turns to intense need.

"Shane," I whisper against his lips.

He pulls back slightly, his chest moving in and out against mine. I press my forehead to his cheek, needing him to pull back but not wanting him to pull away. I cradle his face with my hands, keeping him close.

"Shane," I whisper again, kissing his cheek and needing him to understand, but I don't have the words.

"I know," he whispers as if he understands. He presses a soft kiss to my lips and rolls onto his back, putting distance between us that leaves me feeling cold and confused.

I don't want to go back, but I'm not ready to jump that far forward without more. I want it all. I love Shane, but for us to be intimate, I need to be loved in return. It's the only way.

This is so much more than an act of passion to me. It's the two of us coming together. No longer separate, but one. That doesn't leave any room for questions of love and devotion or wondering if he'll ever let me see what's under the surface. I need him to trust me enough to let me see everything he keeps hidden.

I ease in a slow breath and let it out, wishing I didn't feel so suddenly alone. I try to roll over, but before I can, Shane's strong arms come around me, tugging me close once again, only this time he settles me beside him. I rest my head on his chest as he holds me tightly, one hand spread across my back and the other linked with mine across his stomach.

I nuzzle into his neck, needing to feel close to him and trying really hard to just let this thing between us unfold naturally. I want to know what he's thinking and feeling, but I also know he probably needs time to process what just happened. I decide to savor the moment and see what tomorrow brings. Today has enough worries of its own.

Lying next to him, my body and mind relax for the first time today. That's how I fall asleep. Tucked into Shane, safe and warm, and the absolute only place I ever want to be.

Chapter 43

SHANE

So, I guess we're just going to pretend nothing happened. I'm not sure if I'm relieved or thoroughly annoyed, but either way, now that I've tasted Maggie's lips, there's no going back.

I watch her limp around the kitchen, acting like it's just another ordinary day, but there's nothing ordinary about it.

Walking in last night and seeing her lying in my T-shirt was just the tip of the iceberg. Everything that followed only made it all the more difficult to control myself. Just holding her last night took every ounce of willpower I had and then some.

The moment she said my name, I knew. I knew what she was asking of me, demanding, and she had every right. I just don't know how or if I can give her what she wants and deserves.

Teddy's spoon clangs against the floor as Liv stumbles into the kitchen and crawls up on my lap.

"You're home," she says sleepily, curling up between my arms.

"So, do we get to go to Miami if you make it to the championship?" Teddy asks with a mouthful.

"You guys have school, so unfortunately, probably not," Maggie answers.

"But that's not fair. We have to be there," Garrett protests. "Shane and Cole need us in the stands."

Maggie's eyes flick to mine and then skirt away. "One game at a time. Right now, you need to hurry so you don't miss the bus."

They hustle out of the kitchen and up the stairs to brush their teeth as Hank breezes through, grabbing a Pop-Tart.

"I'm getting a ride with Sadie after school. Then we're working on a presentation."

"I expect a text if things change, Hank," Maggie warns, and he's gone. "Liv, you ready for some breakfast?"

I sit, waiting for her to tease me or make some smart-mouth comment, but no. There's none of that this morning, and I hate it. I want to see that little flicker in her eye, her smirk, and the feistiness that lives inside her.

I want to get her off her ankle, set her on the counter, and pick up where we left off last night. Until Gwen gets here, I'll have to settle for being patient. Then, I'll find out what we're going to do about it because ignoring it or trying to forget isn't an option.

My phone buzzes.

GREG CARTER: Tell your wife it was nice chatting, but she'll regret it if she sends anyone else sniffing around. I don't make idle threats.

I glance at Maggie, and her back is to me. My stomach hits the floor.

Did she talk to him? When?

The thought of him getting anywhere near her or even calling her sends anger surging through me.

The front door opens, and Gwen strolls in, but I'm having trouble thinking about anything other than Greg talking to Maggie.

Why didn't she tell me?

"I have to get going so I have time to snail my way into the gym," Maggie says, gathering her things.

"Good game this weekend," Gwen says, pulling me from my thoughts. "Congrats on the win."

"Thanks," I say, needing to catch Maggie before she's out the door.

"Come on, Liv. Let's get you dressed and ready for the day." Gwen holds out her hand, waiting for Liv to take it. "We've got lots to do."

Liv hugs me and climbs down.

I slide off my stool and follow Maggie into the laundry room. She spins around, and I catch her by the elbows to prevent her from falling over.

"Grizz! Make a little noise, will you?"

I lift her, setting her on top of the dryer. I lean down, bracing my hands on the cold metal and caging her in.

"Ok. Hello. What are you doing? I need to get going." She studies my face.

"Not yet." I lean in closer, getting us eye to eye. "We need to talk about a couple of things."

She huffs. "Fine, but make it quick."

"First, I just got a text from Greg that said you and he had a nice chat. Want to tell me exactly what that's about?"

"No."

"Maggie," I growl.

She rolls her eyes. "I kept getting calls from an unknown number, and in a fit of rage, I answered. Your sperm donor's a real charmer."

How is it that in every situation and circumstance, she takes my inner turmoil and turns it on end?

"Did he threaten you?" I need to know where Greg and I stand.

Her eyebrows tip inward. "I think he more so threatened you, but I had Simone's brother send someone to pay him a little visit or at least make him think they were seeking him out. He works for the FBI. What did his text say?"

"The FBI? You had someone from the FBI check him out?"

She shrugs. "Yeah, I didn't like his tone or attempt at trying to scare me into getting you to do something for him."

"And you didn't think you should mention this to me?" I ask, not wanting her to take matters into her own hands, especially when it comes to someone like Greg.

"Shane, somehow, he got my number. The two of you obviously discussed me, and *you* didn't seem to think it was important enough to mention it."

I drop my head. "He's not a good person. I didn't want him to have any contact with you, and I don't want you to talk to him ever again."

"I was waiting for you to tell me about him. I'm not going to pry things out of you." Her tone is soft but adamant.

"Will you please tell me if he contacts you again?"

She sighs. "Yes. Will you tell me if there is something I should know, especially if it involves me or the kids?"

"Yes, of course. He would like not to have any more visits from the Feds."

"Ok. Done, as long as he stays away from us. That includes you." She pushes a finger into my chest. "Are we good here because I have to go?" She scoots forward a little like she's going to hop down, but I wrap my hands around her hips to stop her.

"Not quite."

She meets my eyes, waiting.

"Are we just going to pretend that last night didn't happen because I'm not that good of an actor?"

She closes her eyes. "I'm not trying to act like anything. I don't know how to navigate this."

"Navigate what?" I grunt.

"You and me? Our . . . attraction."

My annoyance rises at her downplay of what's happening. "Attraction?"

"Yeah." Her frustration is building as well. "I'm not sure what we're doing here. I want to kiss you. No. . . " She shakes her head. "I want to do a whole lot more than kiss you, but that can't happen."

I fall forward and rest my head on her shoulder. "Firefly, you kill me."

"What? I'm just keeping it real. We both know I wasn't the only one interested in more."

"Fine. I don't think I can go back to not kissing you," I blurt, surprising myself at the admission.

"Fine. Then kiss me goodbye because I really have to go."

I drag my head up to meet her eyes to see if she's serious. "You want me to kiss you?"

"Shane, are you new?" She smiles, linking her arms around my neck.

I'm not going to argue. I cup her face with my hands and dive in, kissing her like I've wanted to since I woke her up this morning. My hands move into her loose hair as she scoots forward, linking her arms around my neck and pulling me closer. Her body presses into me, and her soft, sweet lips over mine like we've done this a thousand times. I kiss her back with all the desire and need that's been driving me crazy.

When I feel her relax in my arms, I pull back, letting her catch her breath. She rests her head against my shoulder, holding on to me.

"We have to take this really slow," she whispers.

"I know." I place a kiss just below her ear. "We will."

"Grizz?"

"Yeah."

"As much as I'd like to do this a while longer, I really have to go. I'm probably going to be late for class."

I pull away just enough to see her face. She smiles, and I could fall right back in.

She fists my shirt and tugs me close, kissing me one more time.

I help her down, and she gathers her things.

"Be careful with your ankle today. Keep it iced between classes."

"I will."

"I'll see you later."

"Yes. Later," she smirks, closing the door.

I have no idea what to do with this woman. I never know what to expect. Her confidence. Her openness. Her trust in me. I want to live up to it all. I want whatever is growing between us to work. I'm finding I want it more than I've ever wanted anything before.

Slow. She wants to take it slow, and the reality is that's what I need as well. I don't want to hurt Maggie. I can't. I'd never be able to forgive myself. Maybe if we take it a day at a time, somewhere along the way, I can figure out how to do this. To understand if this is all I have, will it ever be enough?

After practice, I step into my tiny office and find a text message from Rob.

ROB: I need an answer. We're out of time. You in or out?

I've held him off as long as I can, and I'm still no closer to understanding what I want. I dial Sean, knowing he'll shoot me straight.

"Hey, man. What's up?" Sean says as I take a seat behind my desk.

"How's your ribs?" He bruised a couple in the last game and is benched, which he's not handling well.

"Sucks. I hate sitting out. It's given me too much time to think, and I'm not sure I like what I'm finding."

"Like what?"

He's quiet for a moment. "Did you ever find yourself lost in all of this? Like you're not sure what's real and what really matters anymore?"

I clear my throat. This doesn't sound like him. Of the three of us, Sean is the most perceptive. He's smart, easygoing, and rolls with whatever life deals him.

"I had to face that when I shattered my knee. Everything came crashing down all at once. All I'd worked for. The only thing that mattered was just . . . over."

Sean sighs. "But that's just it. When the dream is over, what's left? You know? The game. Your friends. The people who only like you for your name. The status and fame. It can all just disappear, and if that's the only thing that matters or that you really have, where does that leave you?"

"You all right? Do I need to be worried?"

Sean laughs. "No, I have too much time on my hands."

"Yeah, well, maybe I can give you something to think about. Ohio State is interested. Their head coach is retiring."

"Huh. I can't say I'm surprised after the season you're having. What are you thinking? What does Maggie think?"

I blow out a breath. "I don't know. I haven't told her." I pause. "She has a lot on her plate, and I don't want to add more if I'm not interested."

"Are you protecting her or yourself?" His bluntness is why I called him. "This is a huge opportunity. Don't you think you owe it to her to be able to weigh in on it? Unless you're still pretending she doesn't matter."

I groan. "It's . . . complicated."

He laughs. "It didn't look all that complicated to me. You care about her. From what I saw, that wasn't one-sided. If you want this to work, to last, then you've got to start acting like it. As scary as it may be, you've got to let her know that she matters."

I rub a hand over my face.

"Letting her in might be a good place to start." His voice is soft.

"It's not that simple," I shoot back defensively.

"Shane, it actually is. You have to fight for what you want. You did that in every game. Whether you realize it or not, you've done that with this coaching gig. It's the same thing in life and relationships."

I scoff. "Is that what you're doing?"

"It's not what I've been doing, but that's just it. I've suddenly realized I'm surrounded by a shit load of superficiality, and when you strip all that away, what's left? It's overwhelming. You work so hard to be something great, and then realize maybe you were working for the wrong things."

He exhales. "Don't lose something really great, something real, because you're afraid. At some point, you have to decide if the risk of losing her is greater than the fear of letting yourself fall in love."

I take a deep breath, trying to let his words sink in. Even though I don't want to hear them, this is why I called him. "That sounds easier said than done."

"Bro, no shit." Sean laughs, and it makes me worry about him less.

"I don't know how to do this." I feel defeated.

"Do what?"

"Be even remotely close to what Maggie deserves. I never wanted this for myself. I never thought I'd care this much."

Sean sighs. "I'd venture that you avoided the idea of a wife and family because the thought of losing something so great was too much. It wasn't that you weren't capable of it."

I have to let that all sink in a moment. Even though I want it to help, it doesn't.

"What about Ohio State?" I focus on something I can actually control.

"See what they have to say and what they're offering, then decide if you're ready. But, Shane, you need to know what you'll be sacrificing if you move on this." He pauses. "I don't want to look back and have regrets. I know you don't either. Look at Mark. Sometimes those regrets are so big you never get over them."

I wanted this to help, but I'm not sure it did. "Thanks, man. Don't climb down the pit too far. I don't have time to dig your sorry ass out."

He laughs, and I lean back in my chair, trying to make sense of it all.

Knowing what you want is one thing. Being able to have it is a whole other ball game, especially when those two things might be worlds apart.

ME: I need exact dates and times. No commitments, just a conversation.

ROB: You got it. This is too big to pass up.

Chapter 44

MAGGIE

"Ok. How about this one?" I step out of the dressing room for what seems like the hundredth time.

"Nope." Simone waves her finger, sending me back in while Carmen continues perusing the racks. "You aren't attending this benefit looking like you stepped out of the Walmart clearance section."

"I like the material, and the color complements my skin tone." I unzip the dress and reach for the next one.

"We did not come here to let you leave with something like that. Shane will thank us." Carmen chimes in.

I pull on the next dress and turn, examining it at different angles in the mirror. "Ok. This might be a winner," I say, stepping out.

I hear a collective gasp and smile.

"He's going to send us thank you notes." Simone steps closer to inspect. "Yep. I think you might be right. You look amazing. How does it feel?"

I run my hands down the soft, slinky material. It feels good. Not confining or suffocating, which are requirements. "Do you think it's too short?" I inch the hem down a little further.

"With your toned legs and behind, it's perfect. Shane better watch himself. You'll make eyes pop out of heads." Simone sits satisfied.

I laugh. "Thank God. I'm done. I never want to try on clothes ever again." I return to the dressing room, ready to leave this place and never return.

"Sooooo," Simone starts. "You haven't said much about Mr. Carter tonight."

I close my eyes, reliving our recent kisses, and my body temperature rises a few degrees. I'm not sure I'd know what to say even if I wanted to.

"He's been busy getting ready for the playoffs, and I've been rehearsing."

Carmen snorts. "Really, that's all you're going to give us. I see that glow. You can't hide that from us."

I step out of the dressing room with the dress over my arm. "Listen, nothing has changed. I like Shane. A lot. He's so different from what I first thought, and if anything more is going to happen between us, it's going to take time. He keeps his thoughts and feelings on lockdown, and I won't pry." I shrug, moving towards the register. "It's up to him how far this goes."

Neither of them move, so I stop. "What?"

Simone crosses her arms. "Honey, I know there's more to this than you liking him a lot. He either needs to poop or get off the pot. He can only play mysterious and guarded for so long. It's getting really old."

Shane isn't playing mysterious, but he is guarded, and from the little bit I know about his childhood, how can I blame him? I want him to let me in, but I know that takes time, and I can be patient.

"There's only so much I can do about it. He'll either let me in or he won't."

"We just don't want to see you get hurt," Carmen says, coming closer. "He seems like a really good guy, but he clearly doesn't know what to do with you."

Oh, if they only knew. Shane knows exactly what to do with me, but I'm beginning to think he doesn't know what to do with himself. He tries to remain detached and uninvolved where he feels safe and no one can hurt him.

"He's not had it easy, and I knew going into this that he had no intention of getting married or even having a serious relationship. My feelings are my own, and I care about him. No matter what happens or doesn't happen, he'll be a part of my life."

Simone clears her throat. "So, if he doesn't offer anything more, you're fine with that?"

She knows I'm not, and it's my turn to cross my arms. "No. I'm not crossing any lines until I understand where we are or aren't headed. Given the circumstances, I'm not in any rush. Trust takes time, and right now, my focus is Liv, so I'm just taking it one day at a time." My stomach squeezes tight thinking about it all, and waiting for the fallout has been torturous.

Carmen puts her arm around me. "Ok. I just want you to be so happy, and I think Shane makes you really happy."

I couldn't prevent my smile if I tried. "He's been nothing but honest and good. I just want *him* to be happy."

"Awwwweee," Simone whines. "You've gone and fallen for that big, solemn hunk. I knew it!"

I roll my eyes as Carmen laughs. "He may be spilling his guts after he sees you in that dress. Girl, you're going to set his eyeballs on fire."

I toss my purse and keys on the counter, finding Shane and the kids in the living room watching a movie.

"Shaney said we could have a movie night." Liv is snuggled up next to him, munching on popcorn.

The boys are on the floor. Garrett's nose is in a book, and Teddy is pretending to blow up his transformers.

"Looks like you have things under control, so I'm just going to . . . " I step away, but Shane grabs me and pulls me onto his lap.

"If you think for one second that you're leaving me here with these little punks, you've lost your mind."

His arms squeeze me tightly, and I turn to smile at him. "Bad night?"

He makes a snorting sound. "I ordered pizza, and they fought about toppings. Liv spilled juice all over Garrett's homework, and I thought he was going to internally combust. Teddy laughed, only making it worse, and then when the pizza got here, he refused to eat it because it had one small piece of misplaced onion. Oh, and Liv asked me where babies come from."

I put my hand over my mouth to hide my laughter. I'm not sure Shane has ever said so many words at once.

"What did you tell her?"

"I told her I didn't know and to ask you. Then she asked Garrett."

I laugh harder, and I can't stop, which Shane doesn't find the least bit amusing. His dark brows pull down, and his head tips back toward the ceiling.

"Looks like things are fine now. I'm going to go take a hot bath." I try to wiggle out of his grip.

"Like hell you are. I'm making my first rule in this marriage, which is you're never having a girls' night again. I'm working out to try to regain my sanity before it's permanently gone."

I rest my head on his shoulder, curling into him. Coming home and having him here will never get old. Snuggling into him after a long day might be my favorite thing ever.

I place a soft, secret kiss on his neck. "Come on, Grizz. Was it really that bad? You survived. You're my hero."

"Hero, my ass. I don't know how you do this day in and day out. I was about to lose my shit five minutes after I got home, and Gwen stepped out the door."

"But you didn't, big guy. That takes balls."

He groans, letting me go. "I'm working out. They're all yours. I don't need any more questions about babies or anything else related to female anatomy."

I move to sit up, but he holds me there a second longer. "How did it go? Did you get a dress?"

"I did. I was sold on a garbage bag after dress five, but Simone and Carmen vetoed it."

"Is it . . . ok?" I know he's asking if I can actually stand to wear it.

"Yeah. It's ok. I like it."

He lifts me off of him as he stands. "Good luck, I'm out." He smacks my butt and bolts from the room, leaving me both surprised at the gesture and falling just a little bit harder for the sensitive, soft grizzly bear.

I get the kids in bed, looking forward to a hot shower and my enormous, fluffy cloud of a bed. I grab one of Shane's shirts. I've gotten accustomed to wearing them to bed when he's gone, but I've given up trying to hide it because they're softer than any shirt I've ever owned.

I unhook my bra under my shirt with one hand and push open the bathroom door with the other, running straight into . . .

Good-night!

Shane stands in the steamy bathroom drying off, his shorts hanging low on his hips. Given that he smacked my butt earlier, I'm not even going to pretend I'm not taking in every glorious, damp muscle.

One eyebrow hitches up half an inch, followed by what looks like a slight smirk. I glare at him teasingly, setting his shirt on the counter. I reach up one sleeve, pulling my bra strap down my arm, and then out the other side, trying to go about my business like this is normal. It should be standard routine by now, but there will never be anything normal about mostly naked Shane.

He stares as if I just performed some sort of magic trick. "It's just a bra, buddy." I try to calm the waters that threaten to boil around us.

Shane turns toward me and leans one hip against the counter, crossing his arms over his chest. "Is there some class women go to that teaches you how to do stuff like that?"

I laugh. "Like what? Take my bra off."

"Never mind," he groans, pushing away from the counter.

I step into his path, tipping my head to the side. "Are you seriously going to tell me you've never seen that before?"

"Actually, I haven't."

That sounded a little defensive.

"But you have seen a bra come off before?" I tease, but then kind of regret it when I see the seriousness in his eyes.

He studies me like he's deciding how he wants to answer, which leaves me wondering where this conversation might lead and if he'll give me more than a one-word answer.

After a long pause, he responds. "Yes, but despite what you might think, it wasn't often."

That has me raising my eyebrows. I'm surprised, but hope is floating that he might actually give me something here. Another nugget of information to file away for trying to piece this man together.

I know I need to keep this light. "Huh. Really? You had drop-dead gorgeous women falling at your feet. You're telling me you didn't dabble in that elite pool just a little bit."

His eyes flick between mine. "No."

I squint, trying to understand. "Why? You had the world and women in the palm of your hand."

"Maggie, I'm no saint, but those women only wanted to hook up with my name until they were ready to move on to the next guy."

Ah. There's something in that.

"There had to be at least one or two nice, honest women?"

"Dating isn't my forte."

I cross my arms. "Big guy, I'm married to you, and I don't buy that for one second." I press a finger to my chin. "Although I imagine it would be difficult to sift through all that fool's gold to find a real gem."

"I kept to myself and played the game, not the field." He pushes off the counter, closing the short distance between us, and rests his hands on my hips. His freshly showered skin is still warm and smells so good. He leans down, speaking softly in my ear. "And you've said before that I've seen bigger and better. Firefly, there's no comparison to what you've got going on."

His hands fall from my hips, and he steps around me. I'm left utterly speechless, with my mouth hanging so far open I might need a snow shovel to help me get it off the floor.

It takes me a minute, but I spin. "Wait, how do you know what I've got going on? I mean, I know the whole fake mouse thing had me in a bit of a revealing state, but I kept my bits hidden."

Shane ignores me, sitting on the bed and scrolling on his phone.

"Grizz?"

He looks at me from underneath his dark eyelashes. "I saw you strip that day I was sick," he says flippantly, like it's no big deal.

My mouth falls open again at his admission. "That . . . You . . . "

He dares to smirk.

"I don't even know what to say right now. I don't know if I should be mad or . . . flattered about what you just said. You suck. You know that?"

Shane laughs, and I can't help but smile. It is the most incredible sound.

"Maggie, get your hot little butt in the shower so I can read to you, and we can get some sleep."

I glare at him. "Is there a class you men take to teach you to say things like that?"

"Like what?" he asks, and I turn my back to him, pull my shirt over my head, and throw it at him before closing the door in his face.

The smug little. . . *Gah! I love him. Crap.*

Chapter 45

SHANE

I tug on my tie, ready to yank it off, and this whole thing hasn't even started yet. The last time I was in a suit was when Maggie and I got married, and the memory stirs something foreign in my belly.

The neck on this shirt feels two sizes too small, and I can only imagine what Maggie feels like in certain dresses.

"Well, don't you look dashing?" Gwen steps into the living room, where I'm waiting for Maggie to finish getting ready. "That tie brings out the green in your eyes."

I glance down at the purple and navy tie Maggie picked out and try to adjust it again to make it more tolerable.

"He looks like a prince," Liv says, hugging my leg. "Can I go with you? I want you to dance with me like Belle and the Beast."

I pick her up, tickling her side. "Are you saying I'm a beast?" I growl as she squirms.

She puts her hands on my face, holding it still. "The beast is really the prince, and he dances with Belle."

I run my hand down her braid. "You can't go this time, but maybe some other time." Even though I hate dancing, I'd dance with Liv because I'll do anything she asks.

She sticks out her bottom lip as I set her down, and then she's off, twirling around the room.

I hear Maggie's heels approaching, and she steps around the corner. I've seen beautiful women, but she's in a league of her own. Her navy blue dress hangs off her shoulders, leaving her collarbone and chest exposed except for a layered, gold necklace. The material hugs her body, cinching her tiny waist and hips with a large ruffle that flows around her thighs.

I can't even speak, and as if she recognizes it, her lips turn up into a shy smile. She runs a hand down her stomach, looking at her gold strappy heels that have to be at least three inches.

"I'm not sure how long I'll last in these, so we should probably get going."

"You look…stunning," I say, unable to find words to do her justice.

Her smile grows wider, and she steps towards me, running her hands over my shoulders and resting them on my chest. "You don't look half bad yourself."

Gwen clears her throat. "Well, Liv and I are going to start dinner. You two have a wonderful time this evening."

They leave the room, and my hands find Maggie's hips, holding her in place. Her short waves fall around her face, resting near her shoulders. Her blue eyes are even more intense with the color of her dress.

"You ok?" I need to be sure.

She nods. "Yeah." She links her arms around my neck. "I'm glad we're doing this together. It makes it easier."

I'm having a tough time thinking about anything right now other than her body underneath my hands. The way she smells. Her eyes and the way they seem to see so much more than I want her to. How much I want to stay here and kiss her for the rest of the night instead of roaming a room filled with strangers.

Like she can read my mind, she runs her thumb over my temple. "It's going to be ok. I got you."

I lean down and kiss her, realizing how much she means to me. The thought of not being here with her at some point is almost more than I can bear, and even though I don't want to, I wonder if she feels that way too.

Her fingers slide through the short hairs at the nape of my neck, and I angle my head, deepening the kiss, wanting everything with her, and it scares me. She releases a soft feminine hum, and I'm ready to carry her back to the bedroom she just exited.

I pull her tighter against me, my fingers digging into her hips.

"Aw, man. Seriously." Hank's voice comes from behind me, and Maggie pulls away.

He needs to go find somewhere else to be. I grunt, and Maggie smiles up at me.

"Go away," I say.

"Nah. I need a ride. Can you guys drop me off on your way?"

"No."

"Sure," Maggie says, pushing up for one last quick kiss before tugging me towards the door.

In the truck, Maggie and Hank discuss what he'll be doing with his friends.

"I thought you were working on a final project with Sadie. Isn't that due soon?"

"She's busy," Hank grumbles.

"What's she doing? This is important, and she's not a slacker."

Hank doesn't say anything at first, and Maggie twists to look at him.

"She's dating one of the football players and hasn't had time to work on it."

"Huh," Maggie says, stopping to smirk at me as she faces forward. "Well, she's brainy, sweet, and super cute. Must be a smart guy. Someday, she's going to be a bombshell. You just wait and see."

"Great," Hank mumbles as we pull into the driveway, and he hops out. "See you guys later."

He closes the door, and Maggie turns in her seat to face me. "See. I told you. Now that she's moved on, he's a sad little puppy."

I roll my eyes, backing out of the driveway. We ride in silence for a while as I try to gear myself up for this dinner.

"You all right over there, Grizz?"

"Yeah. These things are not my deal."

Maggie's fingers grip mine, and she rests our linked hands in her lap. I've never been much of a hand holder, but with Maggie, I want the connection. Her touch is calming and comforting. I'd be happy to hold onto her for a long while. Maybe forever. The realization makes my heart beat just a little faster, and my stomach ripples with waves of possibility.

As we pull into the parking lot and approach the valet, her phone starts ringing. She pulls it from her tiny purse and looks at me, her eyes wide.

"It's Ben. He said he'd call me when he heard from Cliff and Joan's attorney."

"Answer it."

I pull out of the valet line as Maggie looks at her phone for another second before swiping and putting it up to her ear.

"Hi, Ben," she says tentatively, and I see worry take over.

I turn in my seat, watching her nod and listen intently.

"Ok," she finally says. "What now?" She listens again, and I need to know what he's saying. "Ok. Thank you."

Then she hangs up, staring at the phone in her hand.

"What did he say?" My chest pulls tight and gets tighter by the second. I crack a window, needing some air.

Tears settle in her eyes. "They tried to call our bluff, but Ben had someone start digging around. They talked to Jared and threatened him, and he cooperated. I guess that night he tried to come back to see me, and he knew they locked me in my room."

She pauses, glancing at her phone in her lap. "Then Ben spoke with the doctor, who said I should have received medical care much sooner, and he agreed to testify to my condition when my dad brought me in."

A tear trails down her cheek, and she flicks it away before turning to look at me again. "It. . . It was enough. They dropped it."

"What?" I ask, wanting to make sure I understand.

She smiles as another tear falls. "They're dropping the suit. Liv . . . She's staying with us."

I reach across my truck, grab Maggie, and pull her across the console. The strap around my chest bursts free as my heart pounds in relief. I had no idea the weight of it all until it was lifted. That sweet, innocent little girl is staying exactly where she belongs. With us. Me and Maggie. The thought has my own eyes glossing over.

I hug Maggie so tightly. "I'm so proud of you. You did this."

She shakes her head against me. "No, we did this. Thank you. Shane, thank you for helping me."

I pull back, holding her face in my hands. "I'd do it a thousand times over."

"I can't believe it." She closes her eyes as another tear squeezes out. "It's over."

I bring my forehead to hers. I don't want to think about what comes next. All I want to do is be with Maggie and then go home. To the kids. To the life I've grown into and become a part of. I can't bear the thought of that changing.

Maggie tips her chin upward, pressing her lips to mine. Softly, sweetly. I kiss her back, wanting to hold on to this, to her.

She pulls away but still holds me close. "You're making it really hard for me to want to go in there."

"Let's not." I kiss the corner of her mouth, hoping I might convince her.

She smiles, tipping her head back as I trail kisses down her neck.

"Grizz, we have to go in there. It's important."

"So is this." I nip her silky skin.

She laughs and pushes me away. "Come on. Let's go so we can leave early and pick up where we're leaving off."

I groan, trying to regain lucidity so I can make it through this thing and then take my wife home.

We step inside the university event center to flashing cameras. Maggie leads us through the maze of people who've stopped for photographs. We're about to enter the ballroom when we get caught.

"Mr. and Mrs. Carter." A photographer from a news outlet steps in front of us. "Can we get a photo?"

Maggie glances up at me and then back at the photographer. "Sure."

She slides one arm behind me and rests the other on my chest while I crowd her, sliding my hand around her waist and pulling her extra close. She smiles up at me, and maybe this isn't so bad with her by my side.

The ballroom is a sea of white linen tables, people with drinks in hand, and lots of chatter. We wind our way through, saying hi to people we know as we breeze past. Maggie points to Cole, who's standing with Nick and some of the team and their dates. She leads me in that direction, which happens to be across the dance floor.

She glances at me over her shoulder. "Don't even think about trying to renege on your promise."

"One dance," I groan. Although seeing all these people, I might be okay hanging out with her on the dance floor.

"We'll see about that," she winks.

We join the team, and Maggie bumps Cole's elbow. "Hey."

"Hey, Mags." He slaps my hand.

She leans close to him. "I just got a call from Ben." Cole turns to face her. "They've dropped it."

"Really?" Cole says, just a little too loudly, and all the guys turn to look at us.

Maggie nods and grins. Cole grabs her and hugs her while the group around us watches before returning to their conversations.

"You did it. Maggie, this is amazing. I can't even tell you how relieved I am." He releases her.

"I know. I still can't believe it."

"So now what?" Cole looks between the two of us.

I'm not sure what he's asking or, maybe I do, and it's the question I don't want to ask myself or Maggie. My stomach pinches, and my skin warms and tightens.

The overwhelming relief of knowing Liv isn't going anywhere is being replaced by a growing uneasiness about what happens now. Maggie needed my help, but it's over. The hope and possibility I've only recently discovered are crumbling faster by the minute.

Maggie peers up at me and shrugs. "I'm not sure, but right now, I'm not going to think about that." She grabs my hand, squeezes, and then laces our fingers together, giving me the reassurance I didn't know I was hoping for. "Tonight, I'm just going to be happy, and this guy," she tips her head in my direction, "is going to dance."

Cole laughs. "Good luck keeping up with her," he challenges.

He has no idea how hard I'm going to try.

A spoon clinks against a glass, and our attention is brought to the front of the room. We're informed that the silent auction is open and asked to find our table for dinner to be served.

At our table, we're seated with a couple of the other coaches, their wives or girlfriends, and some faculty I've not met before.

"Oh, you're Shane and Maggie Carter. It's so nice to meet you," a middle-aged woman says, scooting closer to us. "We're huge fans. Could you sign this for our son? He'll lose his mind when he finds out we met you."

"Sure." I take the pen and sign the cocktail napkin.

"You're just the cutest couple. I'm pretty sure the whole world was shocked to find out you were together. Tim Matthew's daughter and Shane Carter. Who would've ever thought it?"

Maggie smiles, resting her hand on my leg. "Thank you."

The woman continues to chat but is quickly quieted when Coach Cavanaugh takes the microphone. He welcomes everyone and expresses his hope that we're ready to open our wallets to achieve this year's fundraising goal.

"We have lots of incredible items up for bid. Season tickets, signed footballs, and jerseys, not only from our team, but also from Shane Carter, who has donated some old team gear, along with items from Sean Greyson, Mark Sandberg, and a number of other NFL players. Speaking of Shane, his wife Maggie is donating private dance lessons and two tickets to her upcoming show in New York featuring her and DannyZ. We have lots of local businesses and former alumni who've donated wonderful items, so get to bidding."

The crowd applauds, and Coach continues. "I'm handing the mic over to the head of our organization, who will tell you more about the kids and programs of this past year, but before I do, I'd like to say a few words."

He pauses briefly. "My oldest and dearest friend passed away recently. You all knew him as The Rocket. To me, he was Tim. We played ball together. Stood by each other as we got married. I held his babies and watched him beam with pride. They were his greatest achievement. He was a man who loved as hard as he played the game. He had the biggest, kindest heart I've ever encountered."

I slide my arm around Maggie, and she rests back against me. "Tim founded this organization, and I've been blessed to be a part of it. Coming up in humble means and struggling to make his way through sports, he understood how important they were in helping children develop confidence and relationships and provide a safe place for them outside of school."

"Cole and Maggie are here tonight, and it wouldn't be right for us to continue without remembering this man. So many of us wouldn't be here without him. So, raise your glass. To the man whose legacy will continue to live on through each child who benefits from what he started, and that we hope to carry on."

The guests applaud as Maggie swipes tears away.

I lean close. "He'd be so proud of you and all you're doing."

She nuzzles into my neck, taking a breath. "Thank you. I wish he could have met you. He would've liked you very much."

A warm sensation washes over me at the memory of her dad throwing the football to me. The man who gave me a chance when I was just an angry, lost cause. He believed in me and helped shape me into the man I am.

"Actually, I did meet your dad."

She turns in her seat to face me, her brow scrunched together. "What?"

"This organization helped me attend one of his camps. He gave me a chance in the world and helped me see that if I worked hard, I could make it."

The shock on Maggie's face brings a smile to my own. "Why didn't you tell me?"

"That's not why I . . . " I stop, carefully choosing my words as her eyes flick between mine. "Your dad, this organization, changed my life, but I don't want you to think this is a pity payback. I wanted to help you."

She studies me intently, then throws her arms around me and buries her face in my neck again. "I can't believe you played football with my dad."

Her words are soft and hit me square in the chest because I can't believe I'm sitting here with her.

Dinner is served, and Maggie makes conversation with our table while I try not to dwell on Cole's comment about what comes next. Liv is safe, and that's all that really matters. My mind knows that, but my gut twists with the remaining load of uncertainty.

What if Maggie decides her use for me is up and wants to go on with her life to find someone who can give her everything I can't?

Most of my dinner remains on the plate, but when a band takes the stage, it only takes until song number two before a line starts for Maggie. CC gives me the eye before stealing her away, leaving me to fend for myself at the table.

Instead of trying to make small talk, I order a drink at the bar, keeping my eyes on Maggie as she moves around the dance floor.

Her smile, tight blue dress, and easy laughter make me kick myself a hundred times for not being the one holding her in my arms.

Her eyes meet mine over a man's shoulder, who was introduced as one of Tim's teammates. I see the smile in them and feel the connection the two of us have developed over the past months. A connection I'm not sure I can stand to lose.

The remainder of my drink burns as it slides down my throat before I make my move to steal my wife back and not let her go for the rest of the night.

But what I have to figure out is how I'm going to let her go when she asks me to.

Chapter 46

MAGGIE

Seriously. How long is it going to take for that big gorilla to get over here and keep his promise?

His eyes tell me he wants to, and he's thinking about it, but I know he's nervous.

I'm freaking nervous. These past months have turned into something completely unexpected. Our relationship has evolved from being committed partners, in writing only, to friends, and now to something more. Exactly what the something is, I'm not sure. This is becoming so much more real than I think either of us ever imagined.

I know what I want. It's what I've always wanted, but now I want it with Shane. The question is, does he want that, too? Am I enough? Is what we're building enough that he'll eventually let me in?

Cole's question about what comes next is eating at me. I don't want to think about it. Knowing that marriage and a family are never what Shane wanted, I can't help but pray that somehow, we've changed his mind. Despite his best intentions, I want him to have fallen in love with us. With me. I want him to have fallen in love with me.

I meet his eyes over the shoulder of my current partner and smile. His gaze is intense and determined as he stalks toward me.

"Mind if I steal my wife back?"

I don't miss his fierce tone, and I'd give anything to know what he's thinking.

My partner, my dad's old friend, hugs me and excuses himself as Shane's large hands find my waist and lock behind me. He tugs me close, my body pressing into his.

Feeling a little breathless and full of butterflies, I keep my hands on his chest to help steady myself.

It's just Shane. The man I sleep with. The one who reads to me and sees me at my worst. The one who, quite literally, pushes me out of bed each morning and has unintentionally captured my heart.

"Hi," I say, for lack of anything else. "I was wondering if you were ever going to save me from two left feet."

His arms tighten around my waist just a little more as we begin to sway. I slide my hands around his neck, feeling myself relax.

His ever-changing eyes haven't left mine. "Looked like you were doing just fine to me. Give me a minute. You might want him back."

I push my lips to the side. "Want to know what I think?" I run my fingers through the short hairs on his neck.

He squints his eyes. "With you, I'm not sure."

I grin. Even in these heels, I'm still inches shorter than Shane, so I test my ankle and push up on my toes to get closer. "I'm going to tell you anyway. I watched you on the field when you played. I know exactly what you're capable of, and inside your giant, muscle-filled body is a dancer."

"Wishful thinking, Firefly. This is all you're getting."

I tip my head to the side, searching. The way Shane's holding me tells me he's enjoying this just as much as I am.

"Is it?" I want to know. Is this all we will ever be? I can't force myself to ask the question. "If the next song picks up the beat and I start moving, what are you going to do?"

He locks his arms even tighter, cinching me in. "You aren't going anywhere."

I like that answer.

The music slows, which actually suits me just fine. Being glued to Shane is the only place I want to be. I tuck my face into his neck and breathe him in. He smells so good, and his massive strength fills me with a peace I've never known. I've never felt so protected and loved, but it's the last one I'm left questioning. I don't want this to end, and the thought has me tugging myself up to him a little higher as a burning lump forms in my throat.

I don't want to have to figure out how to go back to life before Shane. I don't want him to tell me that his feelings about marriage and a family haven't changed or that he doesn't, or maybe won't, love me.

One song leads to another, and Shane's lips press against my temple. I return his kiss with one of my own on the edge of his jaw, wanting to find his lips, but I know things would turn inappropriate in a second. It might be my paranoia or my tendency to think a good thing never lasts, but it feels like there's a cloud of desperation surrounding us that's suffocating and terrifying. Like at any moment, this happy bubble will burst.

I meet his eyes, and even though I think they hold all the answers to my questions, I can't let myself believe. What if I'm only seeing what I want to see?

I close my eyes, savoring the feel of him around me for another minute before facing reality. Whatever that will be.

"Want to make the rounds and then get out of here?" I'm ready to get out of these shoes, this dress, and enjoy each moment I have with Shane.

He studies me for a second like he's not ready to let me go. Cradling my face, he kisses me ever so lightly. Then he grabs my hand and leads us off the dance floor.

An hour later, we're still working our way out of the ballroom. We've been stopped by just about everyone. I've been asked a thousand questions about the show and working with Danny. Shane's been signing autographs, posing for pictures, and fielding questions about what he's done with the Moose's defense this season while also listening to unsolicited advice on how things should be in the playoffs.

We've tag-teamed inquiries about how we met, our relationship, and how we make it all work. Through it all, I've held his hand, trying to inch us closer to CC so we can say goodbye and finally go home.

"Excuse me." Cole sneaks up behind me, interrupting our current barrage of questions. "You two trying to make your way out of here?"

"Yeah. My ankle aches, and this one," I nod toward Shane, "has met his word count quota for the next year."

Cole laughs. "We've exceeded the goal already. There's another hour of bidding, and donations are still coming in."

I hug him. "That's amazing."

"You guys deserved to get out of here." He hugs me tight. "Make sure you catch up with me before you head to New York. I'm so sorry I can't be there."

"I know," I say. "Just be ready for the playoffs. Keep your eye on the prize."

I hug him again, he and Shane slap hands, and we're free. I set my crosshairs on CC and make a beeline, determined not to get caught again.

"Maggie, my girl. Did Cole give you the good news?" CC's booming voice surrounds us.

"He did. It's wonderful. Such incredible things are going to happen this next year. You and Clara have done an amazing job. Dad would be so proud."

"I sure miss him," CC says, uncharacteristically soft.

"Me too." I give him a squeeze. "We're heading out."

He hugs me back. "I'm glad you two found me. I've been meaning to find you all night." He lowers his voice again. "I got a call from Ted Kent the other day." Shane's hand drops mine. "Ohio State, huh? You're just going to up and leave this old man after all you've brought this season. If I were ready to give it up, I'd be pushing for you to take my place."

I look at Shane, trying to read through the lines and understand what CC is talking about.

"I didn't realize this was public information," Shane says, and I don't miss the bite in his tone.

CC slaps him on the shoulder. "I've known Ted for years. He just wants to be sure it's as good as it looks. I assured him I'll do everything I can to dissuade you from talking to them. It's a great opportunity, Shane, and you've proven this season you've got a sound future ahead of you on the sidelines."

My chest constricts like someone just knocked the wind out of me. Ohio State is courting Shane. Mark and Sean said people would be calling, so I should have expected this. I just can't believe he didn't tell me.

Ohio State, really?

Shane transferred there, but my dad went to Michigan. I could've been a fan, but hell no. Not now.

"Well, I'll let you two get home," CC says, and I can't speak. "Thanks for being here and for all of your support. Maggie, your tickets are one of our top items."

I try to smile and say goodbye before I turn for the door. I know Shane's following me, but I can't look at him. I don't even know what to think. I'm angry, and I'm hurt. Was he going to tell me or evaluate the offer and then let me know when he was leaving?

I've opened my soul to him. I've given him the deepest, darkest parts of me, and he couldn't even tell me about a stupid job offer. I'm an idiot. I'm mad at myself for yet again letting myself think I actually freaking mattered.

Outside the ballroom, I grab my coat from the rack, not caring whether Shane finds his or not.

"Maggie." He tries as he pushes his arms into his sleeves. "Maggie, I haven't figured out what I'm doing yet. I didn't expect anyone else to know about this."

I turn, shooting him a glance and seeing the worry in his eyes, but I don't care. I don't even know what to say. He didn't expect anyone to know about this, including me. I'm such a fucking idiot.

"Well, that's perfect. You were almost successful. Now, I'm going home, so you can either get the truck or I'll find another way."

I need a minute or a few hours. I'm hot and mad. I can't stand to look at him, but I want to go home.

When he doesn't move, I start walking, his heavy steps following. Eventually, we stop at the valet kiosk.

Pushing out the doors, a gust of cold air hits me, suppressing the blaze that burns within me. Shane struck a match, the fuse was lit, and I'm the bomb waiting to detonate.

I want to be alone. I'm confused and frustrated. I'm pissed, and I just want to understand. What the hell have we been doing?

Shit!

I don't want to face off with this massive man who's just stepped on my heart. I want just a fucking minute to sift through it all and hopefully figure out if I've really been the fool I absolutely feel like I am.

Chapter 47

SHANE

"Would you say something?"

I need her to talk to me. To say something, anything. I know this hurt her. I can see it in her eyes, but that was never my intention. I just wanted to figure out what I wanted first.

The thick, suffocating silence enveloping our ride home was slow torture. It's not like her. Where's the fire that burns within her when something strikes?

This quiet calmness has my heart racing and my pores spewing a cold sweat.

I watch her as she moves around our room, dropping her shoes in the closet before crossing the room to me.

My hope is quickly squashed when she stands with her back to me, pointing to the zipper. "Can you help me, please?"

"No."

"Come on, Shane. You made it clear you didn't want to talk about it with me, so let me know when you get it figured out."

Every single hair on my body stands at attention, singed with frustration. I want to protest, needing her to talk to me, yell at me, anything, but instead, I slowly pull the zipper down, revealing the soft skin of her bare back. I want to press a kiss there and tell her how sorry I am. I want to wrap her in my arms and never let her go.

Ignoring her desire for space, I let my shaky hands fold around her shoulders, not allowing her to escape. "Maggie, I'm sorry. Rob called me last week, told me that Ohio was interested in talking to me, and that's it. I asked him to get more information, specifically dates, but I wanted to figure out what I wanted before I said anything to you."

Her stiff posture relaxes, and a glimmer of hope rises again.

She turns to face me, meeting my eyes. "I know you're sorry. I'm not mad, at least about the opportunity. I just . . . " She lets out a breath, her eyes dropping to the floor. "Look, it's late. I'm tired, and I need a minute to think. I don't want to talk about this or anything right now."

I run a hand through my hair, and if it were long enough, I might actually pull it out. "I want to know what you're thinking."

Maggie takes a step back and closes her eyes, but when she looks back up at me, I think I might see the hint of tears.

FUCK!

The fact that I'm the cause of them is a fist to my stomach.

"Shane, I don't know what I'm thinking." I hear her frustration. "I thought . . . "

She doesn't finish, but I need to know exactly what she was thinking before I lose my mind.

"What? You thought what?" My irritation is coming forth.

"It doesn't matter?"

"The hell it doesn't. I need to know what you were going to say."

"Why? Why does it matter?"

She stares at me, daring me to explain. Her blue eyes are set on mine, and anything I could possibly want to say gets lodged in my swollen throat. It's possible my empty heart might actually beat out of my chest as blood pulses through my ears.

She drops her head, closes her eyes, and takes a deep breath like I've let her down again.

She speaks softly. "I'm going to take a shower. I have to be at the studio early, and you need to be ready for the game."

She disappears behind the bathroom door, and I start ripping at buttons on my shirt, unable to breathe. Finally free of it, I toss it on the floor, trying to understand what just happened. How did I go from thinking I might have a chance to feeling like the best thing that's ever happened to me just slipped through my fingers?

I can't think about that possibility. Somehow, some way, I'm going to make this better. I have to.

The idea of going back to the way things were isn't an option. I don't know what Maggie thought or what she was going to say, but I need to. I need to know what she's thinking and feeling, which is completely unfair when I don't know what I'm feeling. All I know is I have to make this better, and I'm scared shitless of the possibility I won't be able to. I like calm security. Nothing about our situation feels calm or secure, and panic is knocking furiously at my door.

My chest is achingly tight, like a hundred-pound weight has been dropped on it. I try to breathe and release the tension in my body, but inhaling is difficult and ragged. I swallow the vomit chugging up my throat with thoughts of losing Maggie.

I run my clammy, shaky hand through my hair.

Maggie needs a minute, so I'll give her that, but that's it. Just a minute, and then I'm going to make sure she tells me exactly what's going on in that beautiful head of hers. I hope she's ready because when that minute is up, I'm coming for her.

Chapter 48

MAGGIE

It's 6:00 a.m., and I tap the button to FaceTime Danny. Working with him this morning is the last thing I want to do.

I'm so tired. After the benefit last night and finding out that Shane is being considered for the head coaching position at Ohio State, I didn't sleep. I lay there, trying not to touch him, feel his warmth, or think about what it will be like when he's not there anymore.

The longer I lay there, the more certain I was that what I'd told him was true. I'm not mad at him. I'm hurt. I want to be the one he shares his news with, the good and bad. I've bared my soul to him while he remains clamped up tighter than the jaws of life.

He won't let me in to hold him and keep him and never let him go.

Being left as a child broke something inside him. His fears are deeply rooted and have blossomed year after year. He only knows to guard and protect himself from anything and anyone threatening his security. It's his comfort. His safety net. And it's impenetrable.

I'm an idiot. I stupidly let my feelings cloud reality. Shane was honest going into this that he never wanted to marry or have a family. I let myself think he'd see that he has a family now. That he has me. My whole heart. I've given it to him, and I think he's even holding on to it. He just won't let me have his in return.

Even now, he's got it locked down tight where I can't reach it, and I want to. I want to hold his heart and show him I won't break it. I won't let him down or walk away, but how do you show that to someone who won't let you close enough to even try to nudge it loose just the slightest bit? Who won't risk it to give you a chance to prove fear is unwarranted this time?

I want a partner, a best friend, a lover. A man I can build a family of my own with. I want it all, and I want it with Shane, but it will never happen.

I can't live the life I want with only tiny pieces of him. I deserve better than that, and he deserves a life without the pressure of me wanting things he's not offering.

The sting of tears prickle my eyes as the phone rings, and after three rounds of pulsing beats, Danny picks up. I shove my emotions deep down and prepare myself to get to work.

"Two weeks, baby. Are you psyched? This show is going to bring the house down. I watched the last video you sent, and that dance is hot. I've got the team working on it. All we need to finalize is the timing, and you need to send your solo. Then we should be set."

I don't want to think about the show. I want to be at home, curled next to Shane, where I left him. I want him to tell me something, anything, that will give me hope. But instead, here I am. I've committed to this show to prove something to myself, I'm not really sure I care about anymore.

"Ok. Let me show you what I was thinking about our dances." I stand and set my phone where he can see. "I want to throw out the final song and pick something else."

Danny groans. "Why? It was perfect."

"I just don't think it works." I don't have the energy to argue. "I know there's something better, and we need the best."

"Ok. We'll work on that. Show me what you've got."

We worked for the next few hours, giving me a break from my thoughts and heavy feelings. We finalized our dances, knowing we'll have to rehearse like crazy once I'm in New York, but given how well Danny and I work together, we should be able to nail them pretty quickly.

"I'm going to rest my ankle as much as possible, but I'll send you music and video for my solo ASAP," I promise, really hoping I can deliver.

"Sounds good. Maggie, I'm so glad you decided to do this." He grins. "This show is going to create buzz, which will hopefully turn into a demand for more or maybe even a recurring spot."

I won't burst his bubble, but this is it for me. My life is here, and this is where I want to be. Not to mention, my ankle is sore every minute of the day, and I pray it holds up.

"I hope this works out for you, Danny. You know I'll give it my all. I'm going to work on my solo while I have some time left. I'm not loving what I have so far, so I'd better get to it."

"Ok. Good luck. Whatever you come up with will be magic."

Hanging up, my mind is clearer than when I walked in this morning. Like always, I left some of my heart on the dance floor.

My feelings for Shane are messy and unrequited, at least in the way I need and want them to be, but our friendship and commitment to one another remain unchanged.

I need to tell him that. I want him to know that I've got him no matter what. He may not let me in the way I'd hoped, but he's still mine for as long as he'll allow me to be there. I will hang on until my last bit of hope takes flight. Then I'll have to figure out what to do from there.

Love doesn't give up. It doesn't just walk away when it's hard. It stays and fights.

I scroll my phone and my brain, seeking inspiration. I think about all I'm feeling, and as I move from song to song, one hits me, taking on a whole new meaning.

Before I even start moving, it's as if I can feel the music and lyrics in my soul. I tap play, moving to the center of the room. In the four minutes between the first and final note, it's as if everything pours out of me, and tears stream down my face and neck. Tears for my mom and dad. For the kids. For Shane. For me, wanting everything and being scared that this is it. That somehow, I'll have to let Shane go, having given away another piece of my heart I'll never get back.

But maybe that's the risk of falling in love. Giving someone pieces of you because you can't stand not to. So, you jump in and hope, no matter how small that hope might be, that some part of you will matter to them, too. That they will handle your fragile heart with care.

Whether I wanted to or not, or even realized what was happening, Shane has my heart. I can't bear the thought of trying to collect it back.

The song ends, and even though I know there'll be tweaks and lots of practice, I've done it. I've given it everything I've got. I've left nothing hidden or kept anything reserved, but I haven't done that with Shane. I've held things back. My feelings. What I want and the desire to have it all with him.

I inhale and exhale, my chest pumping with adrenaline and squeezing tight with a remnant of hope.

The door to the studio swings open, and in strides the man whom I know, if he had a choice, would never, ever let me down.

Chapter 49

SHANE

I gave her time. About eleven hours, and her time's up. I can't wait any longer. I should be at the stadium, preparing for our first game of the playoffs, but the only thing I can think about is Maggie and how much I've hurt her. I need to understand why.

I woke expecting to find her tucked into me, but all I found was empty space, and I hated it. I needed to feel her, to see her beside me, and know she's still with me. But she wasn't there, and my stomach has been in knots since.

The fact that she got up without me waking her tells me she's pulling away, and I can't have that. I need to see her. To talk to her and understand where she's at and what she's thinking.

As I approach the studio, I hear the music. It's soft and gentle and not what I'd expect from what I know about Danny and this show.

My mind flashes to the dance floor last night. Holding her in my arms, her head against my chest, and feeling like there was no safer place in the world. Now, I feel like the foundation of us, whatever we've built, has shifted, and I'm scared it's irreparable, that she's finally given up on me and is ready to move on.

I stop at the window and watch her dance, my nerves twitching with uncomfortable energy. My tight muscles relax. She's . . . beautiful. Breathtaking. The way she moves is effortless. I've seen her dance, but not like this. I could watch her all day.

I don't know anything about dancing, but Maggie moves like the song was made for her. When she slows and the final notes of the song fade, she leans forward, catching her breath, and I see the damp streaks down her face.

I have to make this right. There's no other choice. I can't go back to a life without Maggie and the kids in it.

I give her a moment before I enter. I'm determined to get her to forgive me and show her that I'm still right here. I'm not going anywhere if she'll have me.

I pull open the door, and Maggie glances up from her crouched position.

"Hey." She swipes at her face.

Her tentativeness tugs the knots in my stomach even tighter. Her fire is still missing, and its absence sends a rush of fear through me. I know it flickers in her belly until someone pours gasoline on it. I want to find it and be the oxygen that sets it ablaze with honesty, passion, and desire.

"Hey." I know I need to say more, but all I can focus on is her eyes, which are red from the tears I've no doubt she doesn't want me to see. "I uh . . . I wanted to talk to you before I have to be at the stadium. I hate what happened last night."

She stands. "It's ok. You should focus on the game. It's important."

Her cool words sting.

"*This* is important." I swallow the coffee I attempted to drink, which is making its way back up. "Maggie, I know I already said it, but I'm sorry. I'm even more sorry about the timing, so I'll call them—"

She holds up her hand. "No. No, you're not. This could be an amazing opportunity, and you aren't going to miss it. I needed a minute to process, and I'm done now."

"They want me out there the same day as your show. I'm not missing it."

I don't know anything about relationships, but this feels a hell of a lot like she's pushing me away, and it's as if alarms start blaring throughout my body. A cool sheen of sweat covers my skin as my chest thumps with the strength of a rubber mallet. I fist my hands and clench my jaw, willing it to stop.

"Yes, you are."

Her calmness is agitating, and that fear of her stepping away from me is growing by the second. My fingers itch to grab her, hold her, and make her promise not to leave me, but I resist the urge.

"This show is not as important as the rest of your career. This is me fulfilling a dream I thought I wanted. It'll be fun and an accomplishment, but it won't change my future."

She's downplaying the importance of this and how big of a deal it really is, but I let it go for now.

Her head falls to the side. "I'm not saying it's not important. It is, but it's not the same as continuing to live out your dream in the way you can. You need to see what these guys have to offer. It could be huge."

I suck in a quick breath. My dry throat aches. "I don't even know if I'm ready for it or if I want it. I thought I'd be signing another contract here for next season."

She forces a small, dull smile. "Exactly. You won't know unless you go talk to them."

I fail at keeping my body relaxed, now poised for battle. "I *don't want* to miss your show. I saw you dancing a minute ago, and Maggie, that was . . . beautiful."

Her eyes drop to her feet, and she flexes her ankle. I know it's hurting. I want to get her ice and stay with her, but I'm running out of time. Understanding where she's at is more important.

"Thank you. Shane, I want this for you if you want it. You're so talented, and after pulling the defense together this season, you're clearly meant for bigger things."

I'm completely failing to get her to see what I want her to see, and I want to ram my head into a wall.

I take a breath, needing to calm my temper. "I don't want this to change things between us."

She inhales a long breath this time, her eyes flicking between mine, searching. "It won't."

"How can you say that? I feel like this has already changed everything." I don't know if she can hear the panic in my voice or see my pulse jumping out of my neck, but in just a second, I'm going to lose my shit.

"Because . . . you're my best friend." Her voice is tender and soft. She shrugs. "There's no changing that. No matter what. I'm not going anywhere."

I grab her and pull her to me, hugging her so tight. It's what I needed to hear. To know she's not given up on me.

My entire body relaxes with relief as I take in her scent and the feel of her body against mine. We remain wrapped together for a minute or two. I'm not willing to let her go.

When I finally do, she takes a step back. "I got you. I hope you know that. I want everything for you. When we made vows, I committed myself to you and *only* you. That hasn't changed."

I stare at her, my stomach hitting the floor with a thud because there's a *but* coming.

"I got a little mixed up." Her gaze drops from mine. "It's my fault. You were honest with me going into this, and I needed your help. I don't want anything to change, Shane, but someday I want everything too."

Acid burns as it rises in my throat, and I'm one second away from sprinting to the trash can. "What does that mean?" I choke out the question.

She looks like she's getting frustrated now. "It means that someday I want to be with someone who will give me all of them. I can't continue to give you all of me and only have you give me fragments in return."

I start to say something, but she cuts me off.

"I'm not mad. I can't even blame you. I know you have reasons for keeping to yourself and being guarded. That's the way you want it or need it to be. And it's really ok. I just don't want to be like that. I want to be with someone who can't stand not sharing everything with me, giving me all of them in return."

I don't know what to say. My mind is spinning along with the room around me. I feel like I need to put my head between my knees, but I fight it.

"But you just said nothing is changing."

"It's not," she huffs. "I'm here . . . with you."

My throat constricts, cutting off my airway, and I can barely whisper my next question. "For how long?"

This is the answer I fear the most. When will Maggie walk away? When will she leave me because she's had enough?

Tears fill her eyes, and I want to punch something.

"I will never leave you, but you may not be able to have all of me. It's . . . It's not fair."

"What's not fair?" I growl.

A tear trails slowly down her cheek, and I can't help but step into her space and push it away with my thumb. I leave my hand there, needing the connection.

She sniffs, and my broken heart shatters. "To ask you for something I don't think you can give me."

I take a tiny step closer, my chest heaving in and out. "What? What do you want from me?" I whisper, knowing I'd do just about anything.

Her watery blue eyes meet mine. "All of you. Every single bit. The good, the bad, your fears, your joys. I want to be the one who gets it all. The one who gets to be the holder of all the things that are you, the ones the rest of the world doesn't get to see."

I don't know what to say, and when I don't say anything, she steps away.

"You need to get going." She wipes her nose with her wrist.

"Maggie." I'm desperate to give her something.

"It's ok." She tries to smile. "Really. I know I'm asking for something you never intended to give away."

Fuck!

Absolutely nothing is ok.

"I don't know what to say. I don't know what to do." My hands shake.

She moves toward me quickly and wraps her arms around me. "I know. I know you don't, and it's ok."

I feel like I've been sucker punched by my own fist a hundred times. I hold her tightly, breathing her in. I want to stay like this, keeping her close, afraid that if I let go, she'll be gone.

"I don't want to leave." My damn throat is consumed by fire.

"Grizz, you have to. The team is waiting for you." She tries to lighten things up, and I want to scream. "Go. You can't be late."

"Will you be there?" I ask to confirm, feeling like I'm about to lose everything.

"Yes."

"You promise?"

She laughs, wiping her face again. "Yes, now go."

I step away, searching her face and her sad smile. "Will you wear my jersey?" I'm back in high school, but I don't care. I need her there wearing my name. I need to know that she's still mine, that I haven't completely lost her yet.

She laughs through a tear. "Yes."

I take another unsteady step back toward the door, not wanting to take my eyes off her, afraid she'll disappear. "I'll see you there."

"Ok."

I stop in the doorway, turning to get one last look at her. My wife.

My eyes sting as my throat swells shut. "I *want* to give you everything. You know that, right?"

Tears form again in her eyes.

Shit! Fuck!

I squeeze my fist so tight my fingers ache.

"I do."

The two words pierce my soul with devastating accuracy.

I leave because I have no choice. I'm already so late. I push out the gym doors with anger coiling around me like a boa constrictor. I'm so angry that I can't just give her what she's asking for. I don't know how.

I want to give Maggie anything she desires. All of me, just like she asked. How to do that? I don't know how to give her something I lost so long ago or maybe never had to begin with.

My heart was ripped out when my mom left me standing there, afraid and alone. She just walked away, taking my five year old heart with her. How can I give Maggie something that is not in my possession?

If I gave her the pieces I have left, would it be enough? All I have is dark, empty space where goodness and love should reside. If I show her my scarred remains, will she still want me?

I jump in my truck and peel out of the parking lot, knowing that if there's anyone I would try to give my whole messed-up self to, it's Maggie. She trusted me and left nothing hidden. She's *my* best friend. The kind I've never known to exist until now.

So that's all I can do, try. I have to try to give her my ugly, damaged remains and hope it will be enough because not trying isn't an option.

I want Maggie. My little firecracker. My fighter. My Firefly. I need her. All of her.

I don't know what to do or say, but I'll fight just like she's shown me. It's what you do when someone matters. You stay, and you fight like hell. So, I'll give it everything I've got, and I might just know where to start.

Chapter 50

MAGGIE

SHANE: Top drawer of the dresser all the way in the back. There's an envelope with a letter inside. Please read it.

ME: Are you sure?

SHANE: Yes

ME: Positive?

SHANE: Maggie

ME: Ok

SHANE: I'll see you here.

ME: Grizz, focus on the game. I'll see you there.

I left the studio not long after Shane walked out the door. I didn't have anything left to give the show today and wanted to make sure I got to the stadium in plenty of time. I've never seen Shane so shaken, and I hate that he's feeling this way today of all days.

A lot is riding on this game, not just for him but for Cole and the entire team. He needs to be focused and be in the zone. If being in the stands, wearing his jersey, gives him comfort, then I'll make sure he sees me as soon as he walks out. I want to be there, and I want to be there for him.

I'm not sure what I expected to come from spilling my heart to him and telling him I needed more, but I hadn't expected him to dive in.

While grabbing something to eat in the kitchen and talking to Gwen about getting the kids ready for the game, my phone buzz. I had to read his text three times to be sure I understood what was happening.

I know this man. He heard me, and he's trying. That says more to me than any words ever could. That tidbit of hope I held onto this morning just ballooned.

He may not be able to say that he loves me or even understand or admit that's what he's doing, but he's trying to give me something, and I'll take it because I love him. That's what love does. It stays, holds tight, and doesn't run when things hit a snag.

That's what he expects. He expects me to leave, to run away, but you don't let something so beautiful and so good go just because it gets hard.

It hurt that he didn't tell me about Ohio State, but it's what happens sometimes. We hurt each other. It's what we do with that hurt that makes all the difference.

After asking Gwen to make the kids lunch, I showered, preparing to do what Shane asked.

I stare at his dresser, unsure of what I'll find inside. Whatever is in the letter is important to Shane, and he's trusting me with it.

It feels big, and my stomach rolls a little with the weight of it.

If I have any shot of protecting his enormous, delicate heart, I need to read it and understand. Then, I will guard his heart with the skills of a Navy SEAL.

I open the drawer, reach into the back, and find the envelope. I perch myself on the edge of the bed, gripping it with care. Taking a deep breath, I open and unfold a single sheet of worn notebook paper.

> *My boy. What can I say? There are so many things, and yet nothing could ever be enough. I know you will always have questions and will probably be angry with me for the rest of your life, but the one thing I know with absolute certainty is that this is the most selfless thing I have ever done.*
>
> *I hope you can believe me someday. I have tried, oh, how I have tried and tried to rid myself of the demons that haunt me. To scour myself clean and make myself worthy of you. A day won't go by that I won't wish I could have been more for you, that I could do the right things to be able to spend my life showing you*

what you mean to me. But here I am, doing the only thing I know to help ensure you have the life you deserve.

You may not believe me, but you are the light of my life. The single bright spot. I won't quit trying. I'm not giving up, but I have to let you go to allow myself a chance, and the only reason is for you.

Having you was the single thing I have done right. You are the only glimpse I have that God really does exist. I'm not worthy of you and certainly didn't earn you, but there you were. The one thing that makes me believe.

It makes me know that giving you a chance in this world is the right thing. A chance I never had.

You may not feel it or understand it, but I love you with all I am. Maybe one day, there will come a time when you are faced with a circumstance or an opportunity, and you will simply know that sacrifice is the only right thing. Doing something for the sake of another because there isn't another choice.

Fly, my sweet boy. Soar to the greatest heights. I will love you until the end of time and beyond. You will always be mine.

Mom

I sit on the bed, trying not to let my tears soak the worn paper. I read it twice, absorbing the words and wondering how Shane feels about them. I want to know everything.

When did he get this? Does he remember her? Is this why he married me?

My mind spins, waiting for understanding to take hold. The pain in this letter is living and real. It's raw, as if blood, sweat, and tears seep from the page, but it doesn't change anything for the little boy. He was still left, abandoned by the one who was supposed to care for him and cherish him always.

I sob for him. I want to hold him and care for him and love him until he doesn't feel alone or unwanted anymore. I want to show him that good and right exist and that even though we live through pain, suffering, and horror, sometimes it makes us who we are, so that we can become who we need to be.

Instantly, I need to see him. I fold the letter and replace it just as I found it. This doesn't change everything for us, and there's so much more, but he's given me this. This one thing, and it's huge.

I love him, and I'll show him what that looks like. I'll hold on to the hope that one day he'll see, even if he can't name it, that he loves me too.

I watch Shane walk down the sideline. He's overcome so much, and I don't even know half of it. He's braver than he'll ever realize, and despite what he thinks, he has an enormous heart inside that massively muscled body. I just need him to see that there's life still pumping through it. He's so full of love, and he's been giving it away, accepting nothing in return.

He stops at the fifty-yard line, scanning the crowd. He doesn't have his game face on, and it worries me.

When he spots us, I wave and smile, tugging on his jersey. I mouth, 'You've got this,' and his shoulders relax.

He nods once before turning his back to me, focusing on his team.

I watch Cole warming up, and he's looking strong. I take my seat, and even though I can't wait to watch this game unfold, I'm even more anxious for it to be over so I can hug my husband and try to set his mind at ease.

Kickoff puts the game in motion, and as Cole takes the field, we chant his name. The game against our rivals is riveting, as expected, and I end up standing with my hands clenched more than I sit. I watch Shane in action, calling to his guys and helping them prevent their opponents from gaining yards.

Three hours later, the clock runs out, and the Colorado Moose are moving on. We stand and scream as the fans go wild. Cole throws his hand in the air, pumping his fist three times just like my dad used to. I've cried so much today, and I feel like I'm going to start all over again.

I search for Shane and spot him in the middle of the field, shaking hands and congratulating his team. As the celebration continues, he weaves his way through the crowd, trying to make his way toward us.

I'm not waiting any longer. I tell Hank to watch the kids, and I climb over the wall, meeting him on the field.

He picks me up and holds me tight.

"I'm so proud of you," I say into his ear amidst the chaos all around us.

"Did you read it?" he asks.

"Yes. Thank you for trusting me." I feel his chest rise and fall against mine with relief.

"Can we talk about it later?"

"We can talk about it whenever you want." I squeeze him as tightly as I can.

"It's a start," he says quietly.

I pull back and cup his scruffy face, wanting to see him underneath his hat. I smile. "Yes, it's a start." I hug him again. "Now, go celebrate with your team."

"Wait for me," he says, and I know he's talking about more than sticking around until he's finished with after-game interviews.

I bring my forehead to his. "Always." I press my lips to his, soft and gentle. When I go to pull back, he chases me, taking the kiss deeper, and I'm happy to reciprocate. I've wanted to be close to him like this for so long, and I think he might finally let me in, even if it's just a little bit.

He keeps it PG, but I'd be just fine if he wanted to try this again later when we're alone.

Pulling away, I see the slightest smile, like he's still a bit unsure. He sets me down for just a second before scooping me up and dumping me back over the wall. Liv jumps into his arms, and he holds her like she's the most precious thing while giving each of the boys a high five and Hank some sort of hand-slapping shake before jogging back to the team.

I watched the interaction and wonder how he doesn't realize what he's doing, what he's been doing all along.

I know he's scared. He's completely terrified. After reading the letter, I understand now that he'd been unwilling to let anyone in out of fear. To allow himself to feel things deeply when, at any moment, they could be taken away or, even worse, walk away. But he's done it. He's taken the big leap, only he crossed one tiny step at a time without even realizing it. I need him to turn around and see how far he's come. He's doing it, and all I need to do is be patient and wait.

I can't help the silly grin on my face. I know we have a hill to climb, but like he said it's a start, and even if I have to lug my big grizzly bear to the top myself, I will because he's worth it.

Chapter 51

SHANE

I step off the podium, needing to find Maggie. The relief I felt when I saw her in the stands was almost more than I could bear. It wasn't that I didn't expect her to be here when she said she would be. I just needed to see her. I needed the confirmation I saw in her blue eyes that she hadn't given up.

These past twenty-four hours have been excruciating. I'm exhausted and feel completely incompetent. Maggie agreed the letter was a start, but what now? She read the only thing I'll ever have from my mother. Hopefully, she understands now how little I have to offer her. I wasn't even enough for my own mother.

She said I only offer her scraps or fragments, but the reality is that's all I have. My life hasn't consisted of happy memories or stability or any sort of example of what it means to be a husband or part of a real family. Unlike football, it doesn't come naturally. My instincts have always been to keep to myself and to remain unaffected and unattached. I've only ever depended on myself.

All of that has changed. Despite my best efforts, I've become attached to Maggie and the kids. As selfish as it may be, I want Maggie to be mine and only mine. I want to be a part of their family and everything they have together, but I'm not sure I'm capable of loving her in all the ways she deserves.

I step out into the hallway and see her leaning against the wall, waiting with the kids.

Liv runs to me. "Shaney!" She jumps into my arms and hugs my neck. "You won! Can we get pizza now?"

"Sure." I hug her, and the tightness in my chest that's been there since last night loosens a little more.

Maggie steps forward, and I set Liv down. She smiles up at me and instantly throws her arms around my neck.

I knew I needed to see her, but I've longed to have her close, where I don't have to let her go for a while. I slide my hand behind her head, unwilling to let her go yet.

"You up for pizza, big guy?" she asks as I close my eyes, finally able to take a full breath and easing the permanent ache in my chest.

This is all I want. I want to go with Maggie and the kids to have pizza and then head home. To our home. The one they welcomed me into.

"Yeah." I pull back, and she brings her hands to my face, searching me. "Thank you for being here."

She smiles. "I'm not going anywhere."

"Are you sure?" I need a promise.

"Yes. Trust me."

She has no idea how much I want to.

She pushes up on her toes and presses her lips to mine for just a second.

"Eww," I hear Teddy whine. "Come on. We're hungry. Save that for later."

Just to mess with him, I kiss her a little harder, feeling her smile under my lips. I look over Maggie's head and see the kids lined up against the wall, snickering, except for Hank, whose head is in his phone. Yes. This is what I want.

"Come on, you little punk," I say, ruffling his hair. "Someday, you'll understand."

"No way. Kissing is gross." Teddy scoffs.

"Think of all those germs and bacteria you just swapped," Garrett adds, laughing.

Hank slaps me on the back. "Good game."

I take Maggie's hand, Liv's in my other, and I walk out of the stadium feeling like maybe, just maybe, everything will be ok.

"Tell me." Maggie slides beside me on the couch. "If you want to."

When we got home from dinner, I built a fire in the fireplace while Maggie ushered the kids through showers and into bed. I've thought about what I want to say, but all I know is to start from the beginning.

She waits patiently, running her fingers over my knuckles.

"I don't remember much about her. She had long, dark, almost black hair. I'd sit on the back of the toilet in our trailer while she put makeup on, telling her I liked her better without it. All the memories I have are snippets, single moments in time. Nothing cohesive."

I inhale slowly and let it out. I hate talking about this and trying to make sense of something I will never fully comprehend.

"She was sick a lot. Couldn't get out of bed. Other times, she'd flip out, and I'd cry while she screamed and yelled. Sometimes we had food and sometimes we didn't. An old lady next door would have me over while my mom 'got better.' I didn't understand then, but men would come in and out all the time. She used to lock me in my room at night. I don't know if it was to keep me in or them out, but it scared me, being trapped in there when I'd wake up."

Maggie slides her fingers through mine, snuggling in closer.

"One day, we went to the convenience store a few blocks from the trailer park, and she walked out alone. I don't know how long I stood there waiting for her to come back and get me, but eventually the cops were called. That letter is all I have."

"Shane." Her voice is so soft, but not a hint of pity.

"I think the authorities tried to locate her but weren't successful. When I was drafted into the NFL and finally had a little money, I hired someone to look for her and my father. All I know is she died of an overdose a few years after leaving me. My investigator was unable to find any additional information about her family or history. Greg, well, you know he's a piece of shit. Dealer and user of all kinds."

I have nothing else to say, and Maggie is quiet, too. I'm thankful she doesn't try to explain it away or make it better.

"I cried when I read the letter." Her gentle words pierce my force field. "You can't fake that kind of heartbreak. I have no doubt she was brokenhearted, desperate, and maybe doing the only thing she could. Maybe it was for you or her or both." She pauses. "The part about sacrificing for the sake of someone else . . . Is that why you married me?"

I try to answer as honestly as I can. "Maybe. At least partly. I hadn't thought about the letter in years until you told me about your situation. From the day I could read them, I've wanted all the words in that letter to be true. I've wanted to believe that her leaving me was out of love. That she really believed it was the only way to save me."

"For years, I could never see how what I was going through would be better than being with her. Maybe it's selfish, but I wanted to test it. To try to understand that kind of sacrifice. When I thought of marrying you, I knew I'd sacrifice a lot, but I also knew I could do it. There wasn't a reason not to. When I saw you all at the team party, I knew I had to help. The thought of the kids being anywhere other than here, with you . . . "

Maggie lays her hand flat over my heart. "You knew what it was like to have everything familiar stripped away."

"I'd never want that for any child, especially when I could see the bond you all have. The love between you and the dependency."

She pushes up, resting her chin on my chest. "Right or wrong, whether those words are trustworthy or not, I'm so glad your mother gave you a chance. She certainly didn't go about it the right way, but I'm guessing that not much in her life had. Look at you, though." She tugs on my shirt and smiles. "Look what you've done with your life. All that you've accomplished and the person you've become."

The tears in her eyes cause a lump to form in my throat.

"Maybe it would've turned out just the same if she hadn't left you, but . . . " She shakes her head. "I don't believe we go through a buttload of pain and suffering for nothing. You miraculously came out the other side. She saved you from the life she was drowning in. One, I imagine, would've taken you right under with her. The sacrifice is real. She could've made that five-year-old little boy hold her hand and watch her drown, and Shane, maybe she wouldn't have let go."

Tears run down Maggie's cheeks, and I wipe them away before she rests her head on my chest again.

What I know for sure is that I wouldn't have ended up with Maggie and the kids and this life I never knew I wanted.

I kiss her forehead as the fire crackles, letting it all ruminate. I want to believe my mom left me because she loved me that much, or at least enough to want more for me. Knowing I'd give anything for these kids, I might finally be able to hold tight to the words she left me with.

Chapter 52

MAGGIE

"So, you've got the kids for the next two nights, and then Gwen will be there in time for you to get to the airport." I frantically dig through my bag, trying to find my lip balm.

Where is it?!

"Maggie, I got it." Shane grabs my hand and keeps hold of it. "Relax. It's all going to be ok."

I look at him, all calm and confident, as he pulls into the departure lane. I want to believe him, but my nerves are on high alert.

I've never left the kids, and this show suddenly feels like a horrible idea. More than anything, I don't want Shane to leave me at the curb without knowing what our relationship will look like when I return.

I crack the window, hoping the fresh air will soothe my queasy stomach.

"I don't know if I can do this." My fingers dig into the edge of the seat as the weight of a thousand elephants presses on my chest.

He takes his eyes off the road for a second, meeting mine. "Yes, you can." His soft tone is reassuring, but it's not enough to make me believe it. "If it's even close to anything like what I've seen through the studio window and what you've shown me on your phone, it's going to be incredible. Maggie, you are incredible."

"How do you know?" I challenge, trying to will my voice and the rest of me to hold strong. "My ankle is a mess, and these next few days will be intense."

"Maggie, breathe." He lifts my hand and presses a kiss to the underside of my wrist, where I'm certain my pulse is thumping. "You know what you're doing."

I inhale through my nose and close my eyes, knowing I want Shane to hold my hand the whole way, reminding me that I can do this. I don't want him to drop me off and leave me.

This past week, something shifted between us, and I finally feel like we are moving in a new direction. One that could be turned upside down with an offer from Ohio State.

I want to grab onto Shane and not let him go anywhere, but I also know he has to do this. He has to see what they say and then decide for himself what he wants. He has to figure out what his future looks like and where the kids and I fall into that. If at all.

He pulls his truck into the unloading zone, and I reluctantly gather my things.

"Anything Garrett eats, make sure there's no trace of peas."

"Maggie, I know."

"And Liv can shower on her own. Just make sure you lay everything out for her beforehand."

"I got it."

He pushes open his door, and I'm not ready to get out yet. I sit there waiting for him to pull me out like he pushes me out of bed in the morning. He opens my door, and I turn to climb out, but he leans in, stopping me.

His finger slides under my chin, tipping it up. "Firefly, you've got this. I'm so sorry I won't be there, but you're going to do this, and you'll be amazing."

I lean my head on his shoulder. "I'm glad you're so confident."

"I've seen what you can do and exactly what you're made of." He kisses my cheek, and his arms wrap around me. "You have no idea how much I want to go with you, but you don't need me."

"Don't say things like that," I whine, hugging him back.

I force myself to let go, shifting to climb out. "Call me if anything happens."

"I will."

"I can't wait to hear what you find out in Ohio." I try to smile, but it's pathetic.

Shane nods. "You'll be the first to know."

"Even before Rob?" I push my nose in the air, faking confidence and sass.

"Even before Rob."

"Ok." I take a step away, trying to pull myself up. Shane stares at me, his almost green eyes intense. "I'll see you in a few days. Good luck." I take another step, and his arms reach out to snatch me back.

"Where are you going?" he growls.

"Uh . . . to catch my flight."

"Wrong answer," he says. "That goodbye sucked."

"Oh yeah, well—"

His mouth consumes mine as his long fingers slide into my hair, holding me so close while he kisses me goodbye. Not the forever kind. It's much more like a don't forget this kind of kiss, and it has my stomach picking itself up off my pelvic floor.

His lips press and pull, soft and slow, but need and desire are alive and real. He kisses me thoroughly before resting his forehead on mine.

"Well, you're right," I say, a little breathless, the skin surrounding my lips burning from his stubble. It's like a branding I'll take with me. "That was much better."

His mouth curves upward into a slight smile, and when they're few and far between, it's my absolute favorite sight. "I'll see you in a few days."

"A few days." I push up on my toes to give him another quick kiss and leave him.

Hope. I have hope, and I have to trust that everything will be just fine. This will all work out exactly how it's supposed to. If Shane and I are meant to be, he'll see it too.

Chapter 53

SHANE

I watch Maggie disappear behind the sliding doors. I want to run after her, buy a ticket, and keep reminding her that she can do this.

She's been to every home game, in the stands wearing my jersey, giving me the encouragement and support I've never had. I want to be that for her, but the opportunity at Ohio State is important.

I hate this. The timing, the conflicting feelings swirling within me, and the fear I saw in Maggie's eyes.

I don't want her to be afraid that she can't do this. I know she can. I can't be in two places at once, and she told me to go. She wants me to see what Ohio has to offer.

I pound my fist on the steering wheel, feeling like I'm letting her down and making a huge mistake.

I dial Mark, needing to ensure he'll be there to pick her up at the airport. At least I know he'll get her to her hotel safely and be sure she eats something before things get crazy in the morning.

"What up, bro?" Mark answers.

"You sure you'll be there pick Maggie up? No flaking out."

"Hi to you, too. Yeah. I'll be there. What crawled up your ass?"

I grunt. "Nothing."

"You sure, because you sound like you've got a problem."

I pull away from the curb. Mark is the last person I should get into this with.

"I don't know how to be in two places at once. Maggie's really nervous."

"Huh." Mark huffs. "Well, you're an idiot."

"What?"

Mark laughs sarcastically. "Man, what's wrong with you? Did your helmet not fit properly? Too many sacks?"

"Excuse me?" I'm not in the mood for his mockery.

"Did you somehow become dumb over the last few months? No. You're just an idiot. A moron. Seriously, man. I'm getting angry now."

"Look, I didn't call for a lecture or a beat down or whatever this is. What's your problem?" My temper is already on edge, and he's pushing it right off the cliff.

Mark takes a breath, which is amusing because he's not one for holding back. "How could you just let her walk away? And not only that, why are you letting her come to New York all by herself? Is this potential job really that important to you? How long do you think she's going to hang in there?"

I bite back. "What do you mean? I'm not letting her go anywhere. Maggie and I talked about it. This is a head coach position. You know it's important, and they wouldn't have sought me out if they weren't serious."

"Come on, Shane. You know that's not what I mean."

"No, I don't know what you're talking about or why you have such a stick up your ass." My voice raises, and after seeing the look on Maggie's face as she walked away, I'm about one second from blowing my lid.

"How can you not see it? Do I really need to spell it out for you?"

I don't have the energy to respond.

"Shane, brother, you are so fucking in love with her, and you can't even see it. You called me to be sure I'll pick her up and be at her show because there's no way you can let her do this completely alone." He pauses. "The thing is. She doesn't want me there. She wants you, and you know you should be there. You're letting this *interview* be one more excuse to hide behind, to keep yourself from admitting that you love her. So, I'll ask again, you big, dumb asswipe. Is this job what you really want? Likely losing the absolute best thing that has ever happened to you."

I pull my truck over, needing to get a grip before I lose my shit right in the middle of a speeding freeway. "I won't lose her. We already talked about it, and we'll figure out how to make it work."

Mark huffs. "Ok. Just like all the other guys who are never with their families. Good luck, man. I'm about to hang up. You might be dumber than I thought. No, you might not lose her. You'll just continue to pull her along, letting her love you because her telling you to go and do this, instead of being with her on one of the biggest nights of her life, tells me exactly how much she loves you. She's willing to forego everything she wants so you can have your cake and eat it too. You know, now that I think about it, you're a real jerk. If you want this job that bad, then cut her loose. Let her have the life she deserves and someone who will actually put her first."

I'm not one to be caught speechless, but I am. I've never heard Mark, the fun-loving playboy, talk like this.

"Good luck with the interview, man," he says. "I'll be at the airport and the show." It's all he says and hangs up.

I crack the window as my chest heaves in and out, and my stomach climbs up my throat. I rest my forehead on the steering wheel, trying not to hyperventilate. Everything Mark said spins rapidly through my mind like a bullet ricocheting from one point to another. I inhale and exhale, trying to get my lungs to expand like there's a freaking mammoth sitting on top of me.

All I can see is Maggie, feel her arms wrapped around me, and the smell of her. I didn't want to let her go, especially with her nerves eating her alive. I want to be with her, now and always. I don't want to be apart, ever. I want to be there. I want to see her dance and for her to know that I'm there, encouraging and supporting her. I want to wear her jersey.

Mark's right. I've been an idiot. A dumbass and a total jerk. I've let my fear keep me from her, but she's given me everything. Patience. Time. Taking the risk for me and waiting for me. Telling me it'll be ok if I take this job, but I know it won't. I won't be ok away from her. I've put walls between us, and I'm the only one who can tear them down to get to her.

I clench my jaw, and for the first time since I was a boy, I taste the salt of tears on my lips. I can't lose her. She's the very best thing that has ever happened to me, and I thought I didn't have anything to give her. I thought my ability to love was lost long ago, along with my heart. But my little Firefly snuck in there, found it, and nabbed it without me even knowing she was digging around. She stole it—the whole damn thing.

Shit! I love her.

I didn't think I had anything to give or that I actually could, but I do. I love her so fucking much.

I don't want to be in Ohio. I don't want to be sitting in my stupid truck right now. I don't want her ever to think again that I've chosen something, anything, over her. She's everything. She's mine, and I love her with all that I am.

"Shit."

I grab my phone and jab Mark's name.

"What?!" he barks.

"You're right."

"Damn straight I am!" Mark sighs. "Man, I'd give anything . . . my career, the money, all of it, to have one more chance with Lex. Don't make the same mistake I did and let the best, most important thing slip away because you're too scared to do something about it. She's chosen you over and over again. What more does she need to do to show you that she's not going anywhere?"

"Nothing. I can't lose her. I won't. Man, I can't live without her."

Mark laughs. "Good, because let me tell you, living without the one person you can't stand to be without is like walking around trying to breathe underwater. It's suffocating, agonizing, and a kind of pain that will never go away. And we know pain, Shane." He takes a breath. "So, what are you going to do about it?"

"Can I stay with you? I've got the kids for a couple of nights, and then I'll catch a flight."

He laughs. "Yes. Get your ass here and finally get your girl."

ME: Are you ok?

MAGGIE: Yeah. Window seat for the win.

ME: You've got this.

MAGGIE: Yeah. We'll see. Don't worry.

ME: I'm not. I know you. You're going to kick ass and take names.

MAGGIE: ***Kicking leg emoji*** ***Donkey emoji***

Chapter 54

MAGGIE

The lights around my mirror are almost blinding as I check my makeup one last time. I take the ice pack off my ankle and wrap it tightly, needing it to hold.

The past three days have been endless. I think I've slept a total of twelve hours since arriving, and I'm exhausted. I'm running on adrenaline, and when this is over, I'm going to crash.

"Maggie, ten minutes," someone calls from the door.

I slip on my gold strappy heels that will be my shoes for the first few routines. My ring catches the light, and thoughts of Shane send a wave of longing through me, missing him and wishing he were here.

We've talked each night, and he's filled me in on everything happening at home, but he left last night for his interview. My already turbulent stomach dips at the thought.

I've pushed thoughts of Ohio from my mind, unable to bear the idea of him leaving or expecting us to maintain a relationship across states. We could do it, but he has to want it. He has to be able to say it, and it has to be more than the paperwork we signed.

My solo tonight will be the hardest. I've poured my soul into it, which would make my mom proud. She always said to hold nothing back and leave nothing unsaid. So, I'm giving it all I've got, especially in the message I want to relay. I wish she were here. My dad, too.

I know video of the show will spread across social media the minute it's over. I only hope I can do it justice.

I take a deep breath and check my phone one last time.

SHANE: Break a leg, Firefly. You've got this, and I got you.

Tears blur the words, and I have to shove them down, or they might not stop. It's the first time he's said it. I want to believe it means what I want it to mean, but I know better than to make assumptions.

I adjust my skirt and head toward the stage. I say a quick prayer that I'll make it through this and that Shane finds the life that will make him happy, whether with me or without.

I find Danny waiting, and he takes my hand and squeezes it. "You ready to kill it?"

I smile. "Ready as I'll ever be."

Chapter 55

SHANE

Mark picked me up at the airport last night, and it's been absolute torture not seeing Maggie. She's worked so hard, and I wasn't about to distract her.

Finally entering the venue, we weave our way through the crowd, trying not to get caught up in requests for photos or autographs, but I can feel the phones and cameras on us as we walk through.

Mark can't go anywhere in the city without being bombarded, and tonight is no exception. Fans are pushing and shoving as they try to get photos.

I'm doing my best to blend in, but having M. Carter written across my back in bright white letters isn't helping.

"Shit, bro. Don't you ever get sick of this?" I groan.

He grins, eating it up. "Nah. Someday, I'll just be some old asshole, and memories are all I'll have to live on."

I roll my eyes, leaving him behind as I press forward with my giant bouquet of flowers, ignoring questions about Maggie. I force a smile and nod but keep moving.

Mark catches up quickly with our VIP passes that will get us into a segregated section near the sound booth.

We slide through the barrier and shake hands with a few technicians who buzz around like worker bees.

"Shane Carter, right? Maggie's husband?" one of the guys says in passing.

"Yeah."

"She's fantastic. On fire. I've never seen anything like it." He slaps me on the shoulder, and before I can respond, he's in a chair behind a soundboard, sliding headphones over his ears.

Mark bumps my shoulder. "You all right? You're being curt and rigid."

My nerves are on edge. My palms are sweaty, and my lunch has settled in my esophagus. I might even be more nervous than before the biggest games of my career. There, I knew what I was doing. Here, I just have to sit, watch, and wait.

"Yeah." I huff out as my temperature climbs to a thousand degrees. All I want is to see Maggie.

The lights dim, and my need to see her intensifies. I may be far away, but I have to know she's ok. Talking to her on the phone hasn't been enough. Only a few more minutes, then my suffering will be over, and in the end, I'll have her in my arms.

The music begins as dancers quickly take to the stage. After a minute or two, Danny appears, and then Maggie. My breath catches in my throat as my stomach flips at just the sight of her. Her brilliant blue eyes sparkle, and her smile kicks my heart into overdrive.

Mark leans over. "I take it all back. Go to Ohio State. I'm stealing her."

I smack him on the back of the head, knowing he's not the only one in this theater with his eyes on Maggie, wishing. At least with Mark, I know it's playful. You can't help but watch her. She's as bright as the sun, and I'd follow her anywhere.

The show flows seamlessly from one dance to another, with performers changing in and out of one routine to another, with Danny and Maggie highlighting most of them. I have to admit that Mr. Hip Hop is quite impressive. His strong and rugged movement, combined with Maggie's grace and fluidity, is mesmerizing. It's electric.

Soon enough, the music slows, the lights fade to almost black, and I know that the show has to be almost over. A familiar song begins. It's soft and haunting, and then the lights flash on.

Maggie stands in the middle of the stage alone, her pointe shoes laced around her ankles with . . . my jersey on.

"Oh, shit," Mark says next to me. "Dude."

My mind stills as she begins to move. I can't think as I watch her twist, jump, and turn. I'm caught in a trance. The song is about being lost and then found. If the jersey didn't do it, the song has. This is for me. She's telling me again that she's got me. She engraved it on my ring and now on my heart. She found me.

My entire life, I've been lost, discarded, thrown away. I was never worth sticking around for, but she stayed and helped me dig my way out. She pulled me out of the dark and brought me into the light, showing me what love is. Real love. The kind that stays.

Tears drip down my cheeks, getting lost in my scruff, as the music winds down. She stops in the middle of the stage, trails of tears streaking her makeup. The crowd erupts, and I'm gone.

I push through the barrier, daring anyone to get in my way. I find the side door that leads backstage, and thankfully, the security guard recognizes me and lets me through.

I ignore the stares as I slip into the wings, making sure to stay out of the way but needing to find Maggie. The audience cheers as the music starts again, and I can only hope I'm in the right spot when she comes off stage.

I lean against the wall, studying the bouquet filled with bluebells that remind me of her eyes, my body tensing with nerves. My heart picks up pace with the anticipation of being able to see her, touch her.

When I glance up, she's there, limping off stage, wiping at the tears still in her eyes. I have just a moment to take her in before she sees me, and nothing else matters. She's everything.

She stops in her tracks, blinking, and then she's limping and running. I drop the flowers and sweep her up. Her legs come around me, and she's crying all over again. I wrap myself around her, holding her, supporting her.

"It's ok. I've got you." I've never been happier in my life, and it's a new feeling. She hugs me so tight I can't breathe, but I will actually die a happy man.

"What are you doing here?" Her voice quivers as she sniffs.

"I had to be here. I'm so proud of you. You did it, and you were. . . "

She sniffs some more. "I can't believe you're here. I wanted you to be here so badly."

"Shhh. I know. I'm sorry."

"Maggie. We need you back out there for the finale," someone yells around us.

Ignoring them, she pulls back, her hands holding my face, just looking at me.

"Maggie." We hear again.

"Just a minute," she snaps, as her legs loosen around my waist. "I don't know if I can walk," she says, holding her tears in.

I set her down gently. "You can. You're almost done." I bend down, tugging and pulling as delicately as possible to unlace her shoes. Slipping one off, her foot is blistered and bloody. I make sure her ankle is still wrapped tight, and she sucks in a breath. I move to the other, and it looks just as bad. She pulls my jersey over her head and hands it to me while someone gives her a skirt to wrap over her black leotard.

"Maggie," we hear again, with more urgency this time.

She grabs my face and kisses me quickly. "Don't you dare move."

I smile as she carefully limps away, peeking at me over her shoulder. "I'm right here," I say, seeing one more tear drip down.

The crowd roars, and I know she's getting the ovation she deserves. In another second, the music turns loud again, and she's back, falling into my arms, and I carry her away.

We make it to the hall, and Maggie directs me to her dressing room.

I close the door, wanting just a second alone with her. I set her down, still supporting her.

"I can't believe you're really here. I've missed you so much. I know that's ridiculous. It's only been a few days, but they've been . . . " She doesn't finish, hugging me again. "Is Mark here?"

"Yeah, I'm sure he's found a few fans to flirt with."

Maggie laughs, not letting go of me. "I'm ready to get out of here. There's a whole thing going on afterward, but I'm starving, need a shower, and want to crawl in bed."

That sounds good to me, especially the crawling in bed part.

Maggie gathers her things, but gasps. "What's that?"

I turn to look at her, ready to help with whatever it is.

"Turn around." She pushes me. "You . . . you wore my name?"

I face her. "I thought it was about time someone did."

"Shane," she whispers, limping toward me when there's a knock at the door.

"I'm looking for the woman of the hour." Mark's obnoxious voice carries through the door.

Maggie smiles, and I roll my eyes, opening the door. He sweeps in and scoops her up. "You were spectacular. There's a line out there a mile long waiting for you. And the two of you have some serious fans after that whole jersey stunt."

Maggie smiles shyly, biting her lip.

"That was the hottest damn thing I have ever seen." Mark lets out a low whistle. "You sure know how to blow up the internet, Mags. Sergeant Solitary, here, just lost his quiet for a while."

Maggie grins, tossing the rest of her stuff in her bag. She slips on a pair of black joggers and a sweatshirt.

"Want to get this over with and then hibernate with me for as long as possible?" she asks me.

That is exactly what I want. "Can I skip the cameras and microphones?"

"Nope. I'm pretty sure I can't walk out of here. Plus, I've seen you. You're really good with the press. You can scowl and give short, quipped answers like you do after games, especially if they try to ask questions about us. Maybe that will get us out of here faster."

"We should just let Mark handle it." I grab her bag and scoop her up.

"Hey, wait." Maggie throws her arm out. "You brought me flowers."

"Yeah."

"We're not leaving here without them. I want to see them."

"I'll buy you more. Let's get this over with."

"Fine. Come on, Grizz."

She links her arms around my neck, and I kiss her softly.

"Come on, you two. The fans are waiting," Mark hollers. "Don't forget, Maggie, I need you in my cheering section tomorrow in case anyone tries to heckle me."

Chapter 56

MAGGIE

After an hour of taking photos, signing T-shirts, and answering questions about headlining a tour with Danny, we finally enter my hotel room. I'm so happy to see the bed, I could cry.

I hop on one foot, ready to flop down, but I know if I do, I won't get back up. Shane's been quiet since we said goodbye to Mark and climbed into the car. I'm not sure what happened in transit, but he's carried whatever it is into the room with us.

I rummage through my suitcase, finding one of his T-shirts and some boy shorts, and hobble to the bathroom. "I need a shower. Will you please order every item on the menu and have it sent up?"

He stares at me. Something is brewing inside him, but I'm kind of out of energy to push it tonight. And if it's about Ohio, I don't want to know. Nothing will burst my bubble. Not tonight. I'm going to ride this high as long as I can.

I stand under the hottest water I can tolerate, remembering seeing Shane standing there when I walked off stage. I couldn't believe my eyes. All I wanted was for him to be there, and there he was. Tall, strong, and handsome as ever. My sore and wobbly legs couldn't carry me fast enough.

I force myself out of the shower and wrap a towel around my hair, needing to ice my ankle if I have any chance of making it to Mark's game tomorrow. I smile at the idea of Shane going with me.

I pull on his T-shirt and brush my hair, excited to eat until I'm stuffed to the max. I open the door, and Shane is pacing along the windows overlooking the city. A bag of ice is on the bed, but I don't see any food.

He turns, his face pale and stoic. I hop toward the bed, and he rushes to help me, settling the ice around my ankle.

"Your feet look terrible. Do you need anything else?"

I smile. "They'll be ok in a few days." I search his face, knowing whatever is happening isn't going to wait. "Hey." I grab his hand. "Are you ok?"

His mouth opens to say something, but nothing comes out. I give him a moment, and there's a knock at the door. Shane bolts to it, throwing it open and hauling back a cart full of food.

I dig in while he watches and paces. I try to ignore him, allowing the time he obviously needs.

I smile as he turns and paces again, seeing the 'M. Carter' on the back of his shirt. If that isn't a declaration, I don't know what is. This man is about to lose his cookies, and part of me wants to laugh, but I hold it in. It's not funny. It only further confirms that I want every part of him.

I don't know what happened with the interview in Ohio, but I know he's here with me. He showed up. He not only showed up, but he stood there waiting, and literally had me just as he said he would.

Now, we have tonight and tomorrow before we head home. That is, if Shane is going with me. The thought that maybe he's not, and that's what he's all worked up about, has me pausing my food binge.

I drop the slice of pizza in the box and glance at Shane, who's apparently been watching me.

Silence. There's nothing but silence, and this won't do. Even though I don't want anything to ruin this night, I have to know what the hell is going on before everything I just shoveled in comes right back out.

Chapter 57

SHANE

My eyes find Maggie again as she licks her fingers and shoves a giant slice of pizza into her mouth like she hasn't eaten in days, which is probably true. I'm like a caged lion pacing with so many things to say and no idea where to start.

I grab the ice bucket like it's a life preserver and step out into the hall to refill it, giving myself a minute to get some balls to say what I want to say.

My stomach is one big knot clenched as tight as a fist, just like I'm leaving the tunnel for a playoff, but this time, it's so much worse, and the stakes so much higher. I'm putting everything on the line. Facing my biggest fear. One I've carried with me my entire life. The thing I thought I'd never have. I'm betting everything on the hope that Maggie will have me just as I am.

I walk back into the room, and she's sitting up, waiting for me.

"What the hell is going on? You look pale. You're pacing. I think you might be sweating. You're freaking me out."

I set the bucket down with a thud and move to the giant windows, giving myself room to spill my guts. "I need to tell you something." The sound of my pulse fills my ears.

She frowns, her spine straightening. "Ok, but can you stand still because you're making me dizzy. Is this about the interview? You haven't told me what happened."

I shake my head while I inhale, filling my lungs with much-needed air. "I didn't go. I realized something, and that's why I'm here." I stop walking, taking a long, slow breath, readying myself to risk my recently revived heart. "I wasn't being fair to you. You were right."

She as still as can be, holding my gaze.

"I thought I could do this with you and . . . keep things the way they'd always been. I thought I'd be fine, that nothing would change. I tried to keep myself from feeling anything. I didn't want to or really didn't think I could. I didn't want to get married. I never thought about having a family of my own. It scared me too much. It still scares the absolute shit out of me."

"Shane—" she starts, but I cut her off, taking a step closer to her.

"You and the kids . . . Cole. You've shown me what a real family is. The love you all share for one another is genuine, contagious, and real. It's lasting. I've never known that . . . until now."

"That's a good thing, right?" she asks tentatively.

I don't respond, but step closer, standing before her where she sits on the bed. "And you. You're the worst. All stealth-like and innocent."

"Uh . . . what?" I see that fire ignite in her eyes that I freaking love.

"You're a thief, Firefly."

She tries to stand despite her ankle, and my hands jut out to grip her hips to steady her. Her nearness, her clean, calming scent that's hers alone, and the feel of her feminine curves under my hands ease my nerves.

I meet her defensive eyes. "You just took it. I didn't even know it was there until it was gone. I've never felt it before. Maybe it was dead. But you stole it without me even realizing it—the whole damn thing. I don't know how or when. Maybe you took it piece by piece. The thing is . . . now there's nothing left without you."

She fists my shirt, pulling herself closer, and I see a hint of a smile. "Shane, can you tell me exactly what it is that I've so maliciously stolen?"

I cup her face and press my lips against her forehead. "My heart. You took it and made it come to life and feel everything I was so afraid of." Tears form in her eyes. "I just . . . really need you to keep doing that, pumping life into it."

Maggie nods as two small tears trail down her cheeks, and I quickly wipe them away. "Ok."

I take a breath, ready to speak the last of it. Words I've never spoken before. "I love you. I love you so much. I didn't think I could, and I do, and I'm scared shitless."

"Are you sure?" she whispers.

I let out a laugh of complete relief and . . . joy, I think. "Yes. I'm sure."

"Like really, really sure? Because there can't be any changing your mind on this, you big bear. Once you tell me you're mine, I'm never, ever letting go. So, you better be sure."

"Maggie, I want everything with you. I want to go home and build that dance studio you've dreamed of, if that's what you want. Maybe I'll keep coaching. Maybe I won't. I don't want to be anywhere else than with you and the kids." A smile, new and invigorating, tugs at my lips. "And not just that, I want to make little Carters of our own. A whole bunch of them. I never want to have an empty house."

Her head falls back with a laugh, and then she throws her arms around me. "Well, slow down there, big guy. That will have to be discussed, but baby, I'm in. All of it."

I let out a breath, feeling free and at home for the first time. "Really?"

"Yes, really. Shane, I've loved you for so long and just been waiting for you to finally accept it. I was so scared that you never would, and I'd somehow have to figure out how to let you go."

"Thank you for not giving up."

"Are you kidding? Never. I got you, and I'm going to keep you always."

I kiss her like I've wanted to, no longer holding back or keeping anything reserved. My mouth moves over hers, the same as before, but so completely different. Maggie holds me tight like she can't get enough, but when she wobbles on one foot, I release her, easing her back onto the bed.

My body hovers over her small frame. "Remember the no sex rule you put into place?" I ask.

She grins. "Oh, I remember."

"Are we finally ready to throw that rule out?"

She laughs. "Yes. Thank God, because if I have to pretend one more night that I'm not snuggling you, I might seriously lose my mind."

"Sweetheart, we're moving way past your horrendous attempts at trying not to lie on top of me." I stare into the only blue eyes I want to see for the rest of my life. "I want you, and we have this night with no kids or distractions."

I lower my head to kiss her, but she pushes against my chest. "Slow your roll, big fella. First of all, as long as I've waited for this, and as much as I want to, it's not happening until we talk about a few things." She bites her bottom lip. "We need to have a little chat about contraception."

I raise one eyebrow. "Are you giving me the sex talk?"

She smiles. "Totally, but it'll be fast because this is about to get real."

I grin and kiss her, talking against her lips. "Please, hurry up."

"I'm not on birth control, so unless you came prepared, then we need to talk about what we want, which may involve you walking to the closest drugstore."

"Maggie, I told you. I'm all in. No takebacks. I'm not going anywhere now or ever, no matter what. And I want a whole football team or a slew of tiny dancers. So, I'm ready to get started on that whenever you are."

She presses the back of her hand to my forehead. "Are you sure you're feeling ok?"

I smile. "Never better in my life."

Her fingers drag along my jaw, and a thumb runs over my lips. "Ok."

"Ok?" I ask, trying to understand what exactly we're agreeing to.

"Yeah. I want nothing more than to create a family with you whenever that happens. Tonight. Tomorrow. Three years from now."

"Yeah?"

"Yeah." She kisses me softly, slowly, and it steals my breath.

I groan, wanting more, and she pulls back, breathless.

"One more thing." Her hands find the hem of my shirt, and she tugs at it, pulling it upward until I do the rest, yanking it over my head. Her eyes meet mine again. "I've only done this once, and you know what that was like."

"What? Maggie—" I shift slightly, but she holds me in place.

She presses a finger to my lips, cutting me off. "I'm only telling you because I want you to know that this means everything to me. *You* mean everything."

"I love you."

She smiles. "I know."

My self-control has been running thin for so long, and now it's run out. I find her mouth, and her lips instantly part as if she's only been waiting. My hand moves up her thigh, over her hip to her waist, slipping under the hem of my shirt.

"Nice shirt," I say against her lips, pulling it up and over her head.

Free from it, she bites her lip. "Don't even pretend that you don't like that I steal your clothes."

My bare flesh meets hers, and she shivers. "Is there anything else of mine that you've so casually helped yourself to?"

She taps a finger against her perfect lips. "Hmmm. I may have, once or twice, used an ounce or two of your soap so that our room and bed would smell like you when you were away."

"I think you might have a problem."

She pulls me closer, and I feel her grin against my cheek. "I have a really big problem. See, there's this guy that has invaded every part of my life, made me fall in love with him, and now, I don't want to be anywhere he's not. I'm a complete addict. I want all of the things that are you."

I taste the skin just below her ear. "You know you didn't have to steal them. You could've just said you wanted my clothes and to smell like me."

"Now, what would be the fun in that? Besides, I'm a thief, and I plan to do a Lot." Kiss. "More." Kiss. "Stealing."

I never imagined this could be my life. I didn't know that feeling like this was even possible.

I pull away and push a strand of hair out of her face, just looking at her.

She smiles and pulls me back down to meet her lips. "You tried every ounce of my perfect and reasonable sanity."

I stop at this ridiculousness. "Perfect? Reasonable?"

"Yes," she says indignantly. "And many times, I thought I might literally go out of my mind." She pauses, sucking in a breath as I trail kisses down her neck. "But you, Shane Carter, are the best desperate decision I ever made."

I tickle the soft skin under her rib cage, and she squirms.

"Maggie, just so you know, I plan to try your patience and test your sanity for the rest of your life."

"Good." She squeezes my neck. "Just remember, two can play at that game."

I groan, and she laughs. I find that spot under her ribs and make her do it again. We can play whatever game she wants. I've already won.

Chapter 58

MAGGIE

"Nooooo."

Shane's whiskers brush against my neck as he tries to kiss me awake. Waking this way is sooooo much better than his big hands pushing me out of bed. Perhaps if I keep protesting, he'll continue.

"Maggie, it's noon," his deep raspy voice breathes into my ear.

"If you keep doing that, I'm going to pretend not to hear you."

His smile presses against my neck as he kisses my shoulder, his hands wrapping around my middle. He flips me on top of him, my eyes snap open, and he laughs.

I rest my head against his chest as his arms slide around me, surrounding me with his warmth.

A second later, I pop up. "Did you say it's noon?"

"Yeah."

I roll off of him, wincing at the pain that shoots up my leg. Shane snatches me right back.

"I promised Mark I'd be at the game. He gave me field passes and seats in the box. I even stopped and bought all of the team gear. We're not missing it, especially now that I can go with my amazingly hot husband and show all those hussies that used to shove their boobs and mostly naked bodies in your face that you're all mine."

Shane groans. "Can't we just stay here, and you can show me I'm all yours?"

His hand runs up my bare spine, and I can't help the moan that escapes. He rolls us over and moves his upper body to hover over me, caging me in.

"Grizz, this is important to Mark."

"He'll understand we have better things to do."

I whimper as he tries to convince me. "He came to my show last night. I don't want to leave him hanging. As much of a showboat as he is, I think he's more sensitive than anyone would ever guess."

Shane's head drops to my pillow like he knows I'm right. "There'll be photographers and press and people everywhere. They're going to ask about us and the playoffs and . . . "

I linger kisses along his jaw, and he turns, stealing my mouth. I bite his bottom lip ever so lightly, and he growls as I grin.

"Grizz, we can't hide out forever. You'll have to get used to all this. Who cares what people ask about us? We don't have to answer anything we don't want to. I still want to keep the kids out of it as much as possible. Wherever Cole ends up next year, we'll try to hit as many games as possible. It's going to be part of our life."

I wrap my arms around his neck. "We've been in this bed since last night. It's noon. We'll go to the game and catch the early flight home tomorrow."

"Do you think you'll be able to handle all that walking?"

I nuzzle into his neck. "Good thing I have this really strong, amazingly sexy man that can carry me." I kiss him again, less lightly.

"It's going to cost you."

"Yeah? How much?"

He grabs my hands and holds them over my head. "Thirty more minutes in this bed and a promise that when the game is over, we'll come straight back here no matter what Mark says or asks us to do."

"You're on," I agree, entirely on board with thirty more minutes.

Shane kisses me just below my ear, and I shiver. "Oh, and you're not wearing his jersey."

"I think I made it perfectly clear last night that there's only one name I'll be wearing."

Shane tackles my mouth and kisses me until I can't even remember my name. Apparently, that was an acceptable answer.

Half an hour later, Shane drags himself out of bed and heads for the shower.

"Hurry up. I'm not going to be late for all the pregame stuff. I want to be on the field so he knows we're there. You have ten minutes, Grizz, or I'm coming in after you."

He stares over his shoulder at me. "Is that a promise?"

I throw an empty water bottle at him and then hear the shower start. I lay, unable to believe all that's happened in the last five months. Never in my wildest dreams did I think I'd be here, but I'm so grateful.

I roll out of bed, standing and testing my ankle. It's swollen and really stiff and so incredibly sore. I try to roll it, and a stabbing pain makes me suck in a breath. It'll be interesting, but if need be, Shane will carry me on his back.

I stumble over to my suitcase and dig around to find what I plan to wear. I lay it out on the bed. A shirt that will go under what looks like an old letterman coat with the team's logo, a stocking cap with the mascot, and my leather leggings. Thankfully, I packed my lace-up boots.

"Firefly." I hear Shane's warning tone behind me, and I can't help the smile that creeps across my face. "Don't even think about wearing those pants."

"Oh, I'm wearing them." I hobble over to him, wrapping my arms around his steamy, bare torso and allowing my fingers to graze his abs on their way around his back. "And if you play your cards right, you'll be the one to take them off this time."

I pull away before he can respond, heading into the bathroom. I look over my shoulder to see him running a hand over his face.

"You're going to kill me."

I laugh, loving him so much I can hardly stand it.

We made it to the stadium in plenty of time to stand on the sidelines, hug Mark, and slowly make our way to the box to watch the game. Shane was stopped at least a dozen times by acquaintances and teammates, who congratulated him on our marriage and on making the playoffs.

Even though it's frigid, we settle into the open-air seating, where it feels like we're a part of the game.

I slide my hand into his. "Do you realize this is only our second date?" He side-eyes me. "The only other time we were out alone was when we met for dinner to discuss getting married?"

He grips my hand to pull me closer to him. "Best damn decision I ever made."

I grin. "You had no idea what you were getting into."

"Nope."

He kisses the top of my head.

"This is fun," I say. "We should do this more often."

He cocks one eyebrow. "What? Date?"

I let my head fall to the side. "Definitely, yes to more dates. Nothing fancy. But it's fun getting to sit with you rather than watching you pace the sidelines. I like having you next to me." Mark throws a forty-yard pass, and the crowd erupts. "What are you thinking about next season?"

"I'd like to stay with the Moose if they'll extend my contract. I'd miss it too much to give it up completely, but I've also thought about opening a training gym or program. I enjoy working at the college level. At that point, they either have it or don't."

I squeeze his arm. "They'd be crazy not to ask you to stay, but I think you can do anything you want. You'd be great working with individuals as well. Maybe you could look into that during the off-season."

"Yeah, Nick asked if I'd help him train and prepare for next season. He could make the draft if he keeps his head on straight."

We fall silent, watching the game, and I'm excited to see what next year brings, knowing Shane isn't going to Ohio.

I hear voices behind us and turn to see Danny descending the stairs.

"Hey, guys. I was hoping I'd see you. Maggie, I didn't catch you before you left. I got tied up with the press."

I try to smile. I wasn't expecting Danny to be here, but I recall Mark mentioning that they had traded passes. His girlfriend, whom I met briefly during rehearsals, sits beside him. I was really enjoying my alone time with Shane, but I'll make the best of it.

"Sorry, I was ready to get out of there. My ankle was done."

"I don't know if you've seen it, but the reviews are raving. I may get a tour out of this. Are you sure you're done? It won't be the same without you."

"Last night was it for me." I rest my hand on Shane's thigh, and his quickly covers mine. "It was a blast, but I'm meant to be at home with the kids and this guy as much as possible with his crazy schedule. Plus, I really like teaching."

Danny sits back and puts his arm around his girlfriend. It's nice to see him and not feel . . . anything anymore. I'm happy for him. He's worked hard to get to where he is, but what happened between us is the past, and I see now that he wasn't my future. Not even close.

Halftime begins, and after a minute, Danny leans toward me. "I don't know if you're aware, but Shane's jersey is also trending as the latest fashion statement."

Shane rolls his eyes. "Great, just what I need. A bunch of teen girls wearing my name and number."

I bump his shoulder. "What're a few more stalkers, Grizz?"

He smirks and bumps my knee with his as Danny stands.

"We're going to get some food."

I want to laugh because I know he's going to see who else he might run into and connect with. It's the name of the game.

"If I don't see you, thank you for everything." He holds out his arms for a hug, and I stand to return it. "If anything comes of this, I'm convinced it's because of you. You were unbelievable. You have such an amazing gift, so don't waste it."

He releases me, and I drop back into my seat. "Thanks. If I ever open a studio, you'll have to stop by and send all the girls into a tizzy. Good luck with everything. If you tour and end up in the Denver area, hit me up."

He nods, and they disappear up the stairs.

Shane turns to look at me. "I didn't have a chance to tell you last night, but you were incredible. I've never seen anything like it. Every rave review is well deserved, Maggie. You blew my mind."

I smile. "Yeah?"

"Yeah. Are you sure you're good with being done if this thing moves forward?"

I rest my head on his shoulder. "Yeah. I'm good. I'm ready to see what's next." I cup his face with my hands. "That was my dream when I didn't have anything else. Now, it's to see what you and I can build together."

I kiss him softly and then slant my head, taking it deeper because, at the moment, I don't care who's around or watching. This is my dream. Sitting here with Shane, talking about our future. The future we're going to figure out together. What I know is, whatever it brings, we've got each other.

Chapter 59

SHANE

I pull my truck into the garage, so happy to be home. I feel like I've been riding a tornado for the last two weeks.

When Maggie and I got home from New York, things picked up at lightning speed. We jumped into Christmas, which was the first time I'd ever celebrated the holiday, complete with a Christmas Eve service and family meal. Given that I have so much to be grateful for this year, the holiday has taken on a new meaning.

Christmas morning started at five a.m. and was filled with joy and laughter beyond anything I've ever experienced. Maggie sitting between my legs and wrapped in my arms while we watched the kids open their gifts was all I could've asked for. Teddy opening the twenty boxes we wrapped inside each other was too good not to rank high on the list, and I know to be on the lookout for his retaliation.

The following day, we surprised the kids and took them to the shelter to pick out a puppy. After stopping at every cage and examining every dog, we walked out with a middle-aged mutt.

Gidget, who looks to be part Australian Shepherd with one blue eye and one brown, is the freaking smartest dog, and Maggie and I have no idea how we got so lucky. No housebreaking, no whining, and she herds the kids around the house. It's like she understands what we say and has made our lives easier, rather than the additional chaos we were expecting.

As a boy, I could only dream of having a dog, and so far, she seems to have taken to me. She's protective of the kids, but when I'm home, she's at my feet. I wonder if I remind her of someone, or if she senses I understand what it feels like to be abandoned.

I grab my bag and close the garage door, stepping inside to find Gidget waiting with her tail wagging. I drop my stuff and reach down to scratch behind her ears.

The house is dark, with the TV lighting the living room. Maggie peers up at me and smiles as I lean down to kiss her. The kids are scattered around the room, watching a movie while the fire crackles in the fireplace.

"Hurry up, shower, and come tell me about the game."

I kiss her again and head to our room to shower. I feel like I've been gone so much with the playoffs in full swing, and missing Maggie has been a constant state.

When I return, she scoots over so I can take my place in the corner. She throws her legs over mine, then adds her blanket on top.

"So, how does it feel to be heading to Miami?" She rests against me as I put my arm around her, bringing her close.

"Really good. Everyone has worked so hard for this, and it's paid off. The next few weeks will be hectic."

"Yeah, but then you'll have a nice break."

"Speaking of that. We should head to a beach after things settle down."

She tips her head back to look at me. "Really? Where?"

"I don't care. Anywhere that involves you and a bikini."

Maggie snorts. "Well, that narrows it down."

I settle into the couch, still unable to truly believe this is my life. Some nights, I still go to bed, worried I'll wake up and realize this has all been a dream.

"You plan it, and I'll drive us to the airport."

She smiles, her hand resting on my chest over my heart. "I can't wait."

The kids giggle at the movie, and Gidget barks from her spot next to Teddy, who slings his arm over her.

"I'm glad you're home," Maggie whispers.

"Me too. I missed you being in the stands. It was a big win, and I wish you could've been there. What do you think about bringing the kids to Miami?"

"They have to be there. I can't see them not being a part of it, and I'm not sure they'll forgive us if we don't take them."

"I want you all there." Win or lose, I can't coach a championship game without having my family in the stands.

Her chin lifts and kisses my jaw. "Well, then it's settled."

When the movie finishes, Maggie ushers the kids to bed while I clean up the snacks and put out the fire.

In bed, I study game tape until she crawls in beside me.

Her cold hands slide over my bare chest. "You and those freaking glasses. Seriously, man."

"You're ridiculous."

Her body presses against mine as she throws one leg over me. "I'm so tired. I don't know what my problem is."

"There's a lot going on." I hit play on my tablet, replaying some of the game footage.

It never ceases to amaze me how much she knows about football and what she sees that I sometimes miss. I love sharing the game with her.

"Yeah, I'm looking forward to you being home more and for things to slow down. Once we get back from Miami, the new semester starts, but my class load will be a little lighter."

Two minutes later, I glance down, and she's sound asleep. These past weeks have worn her out. I've been gone so much, and the kids have been home from school. Life has been crazy.

There was a time, not long ago, when going home meant quiet. Stillness. Solitude. Complete loneliness. Now, it's chaos, and ever-present noise and mess. This is what home is. A real home filled with everything I've never had, and it's only because Maggie didn't give up when she had every reason to.

Chapter 60

MAGGIE

After sprinting through the airport and barely catching our flight, we made it to Miami late last night. Now, I'm sitting in the hotel bathroom on the edge of the tub with my head between my knees, inhaling slow, steady breaths. The muffin I ate thirty minutes ago is threatening to come back up.

We need to leave for the stadium in ten minutes, where we will watch Cole play the last game of his college career. This game will determine if the Colorado Moose are National Champions.

I swipe a cool, damp cloth over the back of my neck again, trying not to freak out about what might appear on the stick sitting on the counter just across from me. I want to look, but I can't. According to the instructions, I have two more minutes, and as impatient as I am, this is not the test to cheat on. So, I wait.

"Come on, Maggie. We need to get going," Hank yells from the other side of the door.

"Keep your panties on. I'll be out in just a minute." I sit up, pinching my jersey and waving it in and out to give my clammy body some air. This one has Matthews across the back. Since this is Cole's final game as a Moose, Shane agreed I should wear his name and number.

The timer on my phone goes off, and I inch myself up to peek at the little strip sitting on the ledge of the counter. I close my eyes, blowing out a breath.

"Maggie, they're going to start the game without us." Teddy pounds on the door.

I swipe the cold cloth over my brow and open the door. The kids are lined up, all in their game gear, looking like they have ants in their pants.

"Ok. Let's do this thing," I say, grabbing my purse.

We walk to the stadium, with the warm winter sun high in the sky. Today, we're sitting in a box with Clara and other families. The kids make a beeline for the food, grabbing plates and piling them high. Garrett inspects the array of fried food carefully, making his selections.

I join the kids in the outdoor seating area, happy to have the fresh air and wanting to see my big bear of a husband. I spot Cole warming up, and Shane on the sidelines talking to some of his players.

The game begins, and things are off to a good start. Cole is taking care of business in the pocket, and I can't help but think how proud our parents would be. He's made it so far, and I have no doubt he'll be high in the draft pick. Selfishly, I'm not ready for him to be far away, but I know he has such an amazing future ahead of him.

At halftime, we lead by three, but as the third quarter starts, things begin to fall apart, and the game clock runs out before we catch up.

The kids and I wind our way through the mass of fans and eventually make it onto the field. We push through people and confetti, and I spot Cole talking with a player on the opposing team. When he's done, we attack, surrounding him with hugs, and he quickly lifts Liv into his arms so she doesn't get swallowed up.

"I'm so stinking proud of you. You played your heart out," I say, hugging him.

He nods. "Yeah. It never feels good to lose, but if we have to, it's not a bad place to do it."

"Mom and Dad would be so proud." I release him. "Get back to your team. You're going to miss these guys. We'll see you at home."

I search for Shane. We weave through people and players until I spot him talking to a reporter. We make our way over to wait. After a minute, he sees us and wraps things up.

The kids tackle him, and the smile on his face is everything. They release him to scoop up confetti and throw it at each other. It's my turn, and he wraps me up, burying his face in my neck.

"I'm so happy to see you. I don't like you all the way up there where I can't see your face."

"Yeah? I kind of miss watching you up close. I find it very sexy." He squeezes me tighter. "I'm so proud of you. Defense kicked ass today. You have to leave here knowing you and your guys gave it their all."

He sets me down and kisses me. "Thanks for being here."

"I wouldn't be anywhere else." I hug him again and then let him go. "Go be with your team."

He kisses me and steps away, but I keep hold of his hand.

"You've got major skills, Shane Carter. I can't wait to see what you've got next season."

His soft smile still does funny things to my heart as I watch him walk toward the locker room. I look around, thinking about all of the stadiums I've been in throughout my life, and there's something about this time that feels a little different.

It's a turning point. Cole is moving on to play at a new level, and Shane is only beginning what I have no doubt will be a promising coaching career.

I find the kids gathered in the middle of the field, the brightest smiles on their faces.

"You guys want to head back to the hotel and swim? Then we can order lots of food and watch a movie." I get cheers from the young ones as Hank throws his arm around my shoulders. "It's going to be you next, you know?" I tip my chin up to look at him. "Leaving me and then playing in a sold-out stadium. You're going to make me fly overseas to see you, though, aren't you?"

"I'll make sure you fly first class," he grins.

"Damn straight you will, you little punk."

I hear the door open, and the garage door goes down. It's late, and I can barely see straight, but there was no way I was going to sleep. The kids and I arrived home this afternoon, but Shane stayed with his team.

He walks in with Gidget on his heels.

"Hey," I say as he drops his bag and kicks off his shoes.

"Hey. I need a shower, but I can't wait to crawl into bed with you."

"Well, hurry up. It's lonely in here."

He takes a quick shower and then flops into bed. "I'm really glad to be home. I'm not sure if it's harder to play and lose or coach and lose. Some part of me feels like I let them all down."

I run my hand through his damp hair, and he closes his eyes. "I'm sorry. It sucks either way."

"They want me back next season."

"I'm not surprised. They'd be idiots not to. What do you want?"

"I think I want to keep coaching and getting better. Find out if I want to be a head coach someday."

"Shane Carter, Head Coach. It has a nice ring to it." He rolls on his side and wraps his arm around my legs. I run my hand over his arm. "How about Shane Carter, Daddy? How do you think that sounds?"

I watch his eyes open very slowly. "What did you say?"

"I want to know what you think about being called daddy?" I can't prevent the corners of my mouth from pulling up.

He sits up a little. "Like ever?"

"Like right now?"

"Right now?"

I watch him try to process this as he shifts to sit next to me.

"Yes. Grizz, there isn't a single thing you do halfway. Apparently, that includes making babies."

In one swift motion, he pulls me onto his lap. "Are you serious?" I nod. "Are you sure?" I nod again. "Like really, really sure?"

I laugh. "Well, those little pee stick things are like 99.9% accurate, so I'm going to say yes."

The biggest smile I've ever seen creeps across his face, but I only see it for a second before he pulls me to his chest.

"I can't believe it. This is the best news of my life. Maggie, you're . . . A baby."

I bury my face in his neck, breathing him in with so much relief at sharing this with him. "I wanted to tell you so badly earlier. I took the test in the hotel yesterday morning and could hardly stand keeping it a secret."

"I love you so much," he says in a whisper.

"I love you too." I rest against him, enjoying the feel of his warmth and security. "Our house will be complete madness."

"Firefly, it's you and me and the only way I ever want it."

Epilogue

SHANE

Six Months Later

I look over at Maggie in her bright red bikini. Her eyes are closed, her hand resting on her protruding belly, and I have never seen a more beautiful sight. I can't even believe there was ever a time when I didn't think I wanted this.

I reach over and spread my hand over her bump, watching her lips curve into a smile. She pulls my hand a little lower, and I feel the bump, bump, bump of my kid's foot. The most incredible thing I will ever experience.

"This kid is definitely yours. I'm pretty sure he's using my bladder to practice kicking field goals." Maggie winces.

"He?"

"Yeah. Today, I'm pretty sure it's a he. Any girl would have to be a little gentler in there."

"Not if she's anything like you," I say, knowing it'll get a rise out of her.

She rolls onto her side, and her belly bumps into my stomach. "Oh, really. What exactly are you trying to say, Grizz?"

I push her hair out of her face. "Firefly, you are nothing if not standing with a match poised to light up anyone's ass who gets out of line. Our little girl in there just might be getting ready to set the world on fire."

She laughs. "What do you want it to be? Boy or girl?"

I feel the baby kick again. "I don't care. I'd be happy if there were two."

She puts her hand over my mouth. "I think the kids and I have officially driven you insane. We just need one healthy baby at a time. Do you know what this little beast is going to do to our lives? Our sleep? Our sanity when she turns sixteen and wants to date the bad boy because all that broodiness is sexy?"

I groan. "If it's a girl, she won't be dating a bad boy. Ever."

Maggie smirks. "Oh, right. Then she'll just sneak out her bedroom window and meet up with him anyway." I roll onto my back, unable to think about this. "Especially when her dad is full of badassness. It's what she'll know and gravitate toward. Liv, too, probably. At least we'll have a little practice with her."

"Maggie," I warn. "This is supposed to be relaxing, and you're making me want to punch something."

She laughs. "What if we have all girls? Like a whole houseful of them, and you have to deal with boys—"

I don't let her finish as I lean over and kiss her until we both forget what she was about to say.

I cup her cheek. "Boys or girls, it'll be the best adventure of my life. And I can't wait to see you lose your shit every time one of them gets into a tussle or goes through a breakup or someone calls them a name—"

Maggie kisses me this time, shutting me up. We cool the kissing as people walk by our cabana, although I'd like to keep going. Her pregnant body is the sexiest thing I've ever laid eyes on.

The next thing I know, I hear her sniffling. There needs to be some type of pregnancy hormone forecasting system that lets males know when things are going to cloud up, or tears are impending, or when the shit is going to hit the fan. This unpredictability is enough to drive a man batshit crazy.

"Hey." I tiptoe my way into whatever the hell is going on this time. "What happened?"

She sniffs again and wipes a tear away. "Nothing," she says, trying not to cry.

"Come on. Tell me." I pull her close to me again.

"It's just . . . I'll probably be the worst mom in the entire world if I can even push your Neanderthal of a child out of down there." Her eyes are big and filled with tears as she looks in the direction of where this kid is supposed to come out. She wipes her nose. "And when we get back, Liv is starting kindergarten in just a few weeks, and she wants *you* to take her. She doesn't even want me to go."

I grab her hand, interlacing our fingers. I'm sad my Liv will be at school all day, and our morning time will be rushed.

"Hank is coming home, and I miss that little shithead like crazy. He'll be driving, and then we'll never see him. Cole is already gone and never calls anymore. Everything is changing."

I want to laugh, but hold it in. I'm not spending what's left of our trip alone. So, I pull her close and hold her.

"A lot is going to change, but it'll be great. We'll do it together."

She buries her face in my neck. "But you'll be gone so much once the season starts, and then it will just be me."

"I'll be gone a night or two for games. Plus, you'll have the whole semester off, and then you can decide if you want to go back, or stay home, or open a studio of your own." I tip her chin up so she'll look at me. "I know this is all scary, and a lot is changing, but it'll be ok."

Her smile returns, and warmth fills my chest.

"Let's go to our room, order food, and see if we can find *SportsCenter*."

"You always know just what I need." She pushes up to kiss me.

"Let's go. Before you make me cry."

She laughs, and I pull her up, walking back toward our room hand in hand.

"You know I'm terrified I'm going to pass out when you give birth, right?" I voice the growing fear as we get closer to Maggie's due date.

Her head swivels in my direction ever so slowly. "Grizz, if you faint while I'm pushing your child out, I will razz your ass until the end of time. If my undercarriage is going to be torn to shreds, you can stay on your feet."

MAGGIE

Three Months After That

I waddle through the stadium with the kids trailing behind me for the first Moose home game of the season. I look like a freaking giant momma duck and her ducklings. I'm wearing Shane's jersey, but this baby is snug.

I make my way slowly through the stands, holding my belly and being extra careful as I walk down the steps.

"Maggie." I hear my name, and Mark jumps up to help me. He takes my hand, leading me to our seats, and Sean wraps me in a hug. These guys have become like two additional brothers.

"I'm so glad you guys are here." I lower my butt into a seat, trying to catch my breath and bracing my belly as it cramps.

"You all right?" Sean asks, sitting in the seat beside me.

"Yeah, these damn Braxton Hicks have been kicking my ass today."

"You said ass," Liv says from her perch on Mark's lap.

"I know. Sorry. I'll put a dollar in the jar when we get home."

"It's two dollars," Teddy chimes in. "You said shit in the car."

I look at him. "Well, you just said it, so now you owe a dollar."

"Man," Teddy whines.

The team jogs onto the field, and Shane follows behind. His eyes find mine and hold as he gets closer to the stands. I hoist myself, wanting a pregame kiss.

What. Is. That?

I look down, and something is trickling down my leg.

Oh, balls.

Shane must see something in my face because when I look up, he's standing on the field in front of me. I can't push my eyes any wider as I try to acknowledge what's happening. I don't move.

What do you do when you pee yourself with baby miracle grow in the middle of a football stadium? No book tells you this.

"Maggie," Shane yells, but it doesn't register. "Maggie," he yells, again snapping me to attention.

Mark and Sean are standing now, both peering down at me.

"I think my water just broke," I announce.

"What?!" Mark says, twisting and turning right and left, as if he needs to move but doesn't know where to go.

Sean grabs my arm and holds onto me. "Are you ok?"

"What's going on?!" Shane yells in a booming voice full of frustration.

I point to the wet stain down my legs. "My water broke."

"Right now?!" he yells.

"Yes!" I try not to sound annoyed, but come on.

Sean, the ever-calm presence, pushes Mark out of the way and tells the kids to stay with him. "I'm getting her out of here," he tells Shane.

"Ok. I'll meet you at the car." He hands off his headphones and clipboard and runs.

I look back, knowing I need him, but he's disappeared.

Twenty minutes and a couple of contractions later, Shane jogs toward us.

Ignoring Sean, he kisses me and grins. "You ready?"

"No." I grab his arms as another contraction takes hold.

"Mark and I have the kids. Keep us posted." Sean slaps Shane on the back as he helps me into the car, leaning in to kiss me again.

Five excruciatingly painful hours later, Shane holds one of my knees to my chest and tells me to push.

"Come on, baby. You can do it." He kisses my clammy forehead.

I lay back, taking a breath, knowing these jokers are going to tell me I have to do it again.

"Maggie, you're so close," my doctor claims. "The head is almost out."

I want to laugh, but hold it in because these people have clearly lost their minds. The only thing I'm close to is my entire lower half being ripped to pieces.

Shane's gaze starts to move toward my lower half. "Shane. Eyes up here, buddy. I can't do this without you."

His wide eyes snap back to mine.

"One more big push, and when I say stop, you need to stop. Ok?" my doctor demands.

"Ok," I whine.

"You can do this," Shane whispers in my ear. "I'm right here."

I grip his hand and bear down, and in a second, I'm told to quit pushing. With another little push, the baby is out and resting on my chest.

"I can't believe it," I whimper, trying to get a good look at our baby through my tears. Shane kneels beside me, one hand on my head and the other on top of mine over our crying baby.

"Congratulations, you two," my doctor says, still working. "You have a son."

I look at Shane. "It's a boy."

His eyes fill with tears as he leans forward and presses his lips to mine. "We have a son."

Shane wraps one large arm over the two of us as we examine our little guy. You think you know what love is, and then someone puts a tiny being on your chest, and it's as if you discover the meaning of love all over again.

Things settle down, I get cleaned up, and before we know it, Sean and Mark are ushering the kids into the room. They stand just inside the door, as if something might jump out and get them.

"So," Mark says. "You're keeping us in suspense. What's the good news?"

Shane and I glance at each other. Our little man is wrapped tightly in a blanket in my arms. "You guys want to meet your nephew?" I ask.

"It's a boy! Yes!" Teddy pumps his fist, and we all laugh.

"What's his name?" Hank is the first to move closer, and the whole group follows.

"Aiden Timothy Carter," Shane says.

"Aiden Carter. It's a strong name," Mark says.

"It means little fire." Shane's eyes meet mine.

"Good work, you two. He's one handsome kid," Sean says, looking over Hank's shoulder and slapping Shane on the back.

"Can I hold him?" Liv's little voice comes from the end of the bed.

"Yes," I say, and Shane helps me scoot over.

"You have to wash your hands." Garrett pops in, helping Liv over to the sink.

"I want to hold him too," Teddy says, waiting in the hand-washing line.

The kids take turns holding Aiden, and then Sean hands him off to Mark.

"Come to your Uncle Mark. I'll teach you how to drive the ladies wild."

Shane groans, and Sean laughs.

"Can you teach me how to get the ladies?" Teddy asks. "At school, Emmie won't give me the time of day."

I bring my hand to my head. "Teddy, you need to worry about your schoolwork. Maybe Emmie's into the studious type."

"Yeah. She talks to me," Garrett waggles his eyebrows.

Teddy grunts, and Hank throws his arm around him. "Come on, Teddy, girls are a real pain in the butt. Let's find the cafeteria and see what snacks they have."

"Can I come too?" Liv asks, hopping off the bed.

Garrett gives Shane and me a hug and then follows.

"We'll let you guys have some peace," Sean announces.

"Thanks for being here." Shane hugs his brothers.

Mark chuckles. "Hey, we just came for the game, but this was so much better. Thanks for making me an uncle."

Shane rolls his eyes. "We did it just for you."

Mark's boyish grin fills his face. "Well, do it again. We need a whole football team."

"Hey," I say. "Ballet might be his calling."

All three of the big guys surrounding me stare, and then their eyes flick to each other.

"Get over here and hug me." I laugh, and they both lean over to hug me before finding the kids.

"Do you think we should warn them not to let Liv and Teddy eat too much sugar?" I ask as Shane sits in a chair beside my bed, holding Aiden.

"Hell no. Those two idiots need to learn for themselves."

I laugh and rest back in bed, feeling exhausted and sore.

I must've dozed off because the room is dark and quiet when I open my eyes again. Shane is still in the chair next to the bed, but now my gorgeously muscular husband is shirtless, and our son is resting in the middle of his broad chest.

"Hey, Daddy. How's it going over there?" I thought I loved Shane before, but there's something about him holding our baby so close and so protectively that has me falling even more deeply in love with him.

"I have no idea how I got here." When he looks at me, a tear runs down his cheek. "I'm the luckiest man alive."

I smile, cementing this vision of my husband and son in my memory. "You got here because you kept going when you had no reason to. Then, against all better judgment and rationale, you married me. You sacrificed everything to help me when I needed it."

Tears roll down my cheeks. "You became my husband, then my very best friend. Shane Carter, you are the best person I know." I reach for his hand. "I love you and didn't think I could love you any more, but today my love for you bloomed even beyond."

He brings my hand to his lips and kisses it. "I love you too, so much." I smile. "I know.

We sit quietly for a moment, and I watch my two guys. "What happened to your shirt?"

"It's called skin-to-skin. The nurse says it's calming and comforting for the baby."

"Really? The nurse told you to take your shirt off."

Shane side-eyes me.

"I'm sorry I missed the show," I tease.

"Firefly." He says it like a warning.

"What?" I say innocently. "Keep it off. I like the view, plus I bet those nurses will be at our beck and call as long as you're in here looking like that." Shane groans.

Ahhhh. This man. I love him so freaking much.

I wink. "Don't worry, babe. I got you."

Keep reading for a sneak peek of book 2 of

Abandoned Brothers Series

Available at: **authorstacywilliams.com**

Chapter 1

ANDIE

"No. No. No, no, no, no, no, noooooo." My forehead presses against the smooth, cool wall. "This can't be happening," I whisper as the emergency lights flick on.

I stay perfectly still, hoping if I don't move, the elevator will. Of course, this would happen to me today. I don't even want to be here and now this. It's a sign. When these steel doors open, I'm going to find Miranda, whoever she is, and kindly explain that I can't do this.

I hear shuffling behind me and spin, remembering the man who slid into the elevator just as the doors were closing.

"Great. Are you going to freak out?" He quickly pulls his phone out of his pocket, clearly annoyed.

I stare at him long enough to see one eyebrow raise a quarter of an inch.

"No. I'm ok," I say quietly, feeling just a bit confined in our dim little box.

He hits a button on his phone and, in the next second, is talking to someone about getting us out of here. I study him, knowing for the next however long we're in here, we'll be comrades, partners in suspended confinement.

His deep voice rapidly explains in detail which elevator we're in, and I realize he's familiar with the stadium. He sounds a little breathy and completely irritated, like whoever is on the other end of the phone is responsible for this.

He's wearing a hoodie, joggers, and a backward cap over close-cut light blond hair. The bagginess of his clothes hides his massive build and likely defined muscles because I'm pretty sure this guy is one of the players for the Tennessee Tigers.

I have no idea who he is or even that he's a player, but I want to smile because I know Josh would be out of his ever-loving mind at this. Of anyone who could've gotten stuck in an elevator with some high-profile professional football player, it's me.

The only thing I know about football is that they play on a field outlined with 100 yards, and there's a weird, oval-shaped ball they fight over. Ok. I know a little more than that, but not enough to care who this guy is.

"Yes. It's just me and one other person," he says into the phone. "You need to hurry up. I don't have time for this. Plus, my partner here isn't looking so comfortable in our tight quarters." His eyes flick to mine, clearly outlined with displeasure and maybe a hint of alarm. "Yeah. Put a rush on it."

He hangs up, and his fingers immediately take over the screen, flying around at the speed of a hummingbird's wings. His light blue eyes, almost translucent in the horrible lighting, sneak a peek at me, but only for a second before returning to his phone.

"It's going to be a little bit, but they're getting someone on it," he informs me casually, but his attention stays on his screen, shifting his weight from one foot to another.

Well, ok then.

I remove my backpack, deciding I might as well make myself comfortable, and take a seat on the floor. I'm tired, thanks to the four hours of sleep I got last night, and now I'm really mad at myself for letting my nerves keep me from eating breakfast on my drive here. At least I was smart and arrived early, giving me time for this little glitch. Although, dangling in thin air isn't going to do my quivering stomach any favors.

The man sits on the floor against the adjacent wall and stretches out his legs as he rolls his neck, irritation roaring from his every move.

"Do you work here?" I know it's likely a stupid question, but I go with it anyway.

A flash of ice blue darts to me out of the corner of his eye like he's surprised I can speak, then moves right back to his phone. "Something like that."

Clearly, he doesn't want to make small talk. *Whatever.* I guess I'm just going to sit here for the next however many minutes or hours, or for the rest of my life, and keep my mouth shut.

"Do *you* work here?" His low, raspy voice comes out of nowhere.

I look up. His head is still down, focused on his screen.

"No. I'm supposed to meet Miranda or her assistant, I think. I guess it's a good thing I'm early."

"Miranda from PR?" His question is quipped.

I wonder why he's even talking to me when he clearly has better things to do.

"Yeah. I guess so. I wasn't supposed to be here until noon, but..." I decide to keep the part about my nerves to myself. "Are you a...player?"

I should feel really dumb because anyone setting foot in this stadium would likely know the answer to this question, but something about him makes me not want to give a crap about what he thinks.

I watch him inhale slowly, waiting for a response. Then what I think is just a glimmer of an arrogant smirk appears like I should be embarrassed.

"You could say that."

"Are you going to be late for warm-up or whatever you do on game days?" I might as well just be out with my ignorance. If we're going to be stuck here, there's no reason we can't be open and honest. Although, something tells me this openness will be totally one-sided.

"I'll be fine. I just hope they don't take too long. You going to be in trouble if you don't find Miranda on time?"

I shrug. "Not much I can do about it if I am."

His crystal blue eyes finally rise from his phone and meet mine, expressionless. "So, if it's not about a job, and you aren't here as a fan, what are you doing here?"

Wow. This guy's a real charmer.

I look down at my freshly painted light pink fingernails because that's the question of the hour. What in the world am I doing here? Every part of me wants to be released from this box on a string and hightail it back where I belong. To the safety of my home, surrounded by the things that are comforting and familiar, and to the one person who still dwells there but doesn't exist anymore.

A lump rises in my throat, and I quickly swallow it down. The last thing I need is a full-on breakdown that's been threatening for the last few days. My best friend, Nora, keeps telling me I have to do this. She all but belted me in my car and tied the accelerator down. She says it's not goodbye, just a place to start. A fork in the road where I have a choice to remain living in the past or see what might lie on the other side.

When I don't answer right away, I feel the burn of his gaze.

"Actually, I'm here to sing the national anthem." I try to sound confident, though I feel anything but.

A noise comes from his throat. "Really?"

Did he just scoff that reply?

His eyes run over me like he's trying to figure out if he should know who I am, and I don't miss his unimpressed conclusion.

I hold back my ass-eating grin. My ripped jeans and wide-neck graphic t-shirt definitely don't scream superstar, but he could be a little less obvious. *Jerk.*

"Yeah, really."

"Are you an artist?" His brows tip inward like he doesn't understand as he tugs at the neck of his hoodie.

"I guess that's debatable. My…someone entered me into a contest. I didn't even know about it until I got an email."

"Huh." He flips his phone over and over in his hands. Flip. Rest. Flip. Rest. Flip. Rest.

It's not that I expected someone of his esteemed caliber to know about the contest, but does he have to be so skeptical? I freaking won.

"So…can you even sing?" His words come out slow and hoarse.

I want to reach out and smack him. Is he socially inept or just a dick?

"I guess we'll find out now, won't we?"

Flip. Rest. Flip. He's focusing on his phone like it's his most prized possession. "So, you don't normally sing…for crowds?"

I smile at his condescending tone. "No. I don't. Although, karaoke on Tuesdays at the bowling alley is usually a packed house."

Flip. Stop. So, so slowly, his eyes pull away from his phone and drag up to study my face, maybe trying to interpret if I'm serious. But then, apparently, I'm not interesting enough for any follow-up questions.

Feeling my snarky side switch to on, I toss a softball back at him. "So, how long have you played for the Tigers, or do you just warm the bench?"

"A couple of seasons," he says, dryly ignoring my sarcasm.

Well, Chatty Cathy is going to have to do better than that. "How's the South treating you? I can see the southern charm has taken full effect." I wait to see what kind of reaction I get from Mr. Social.

"Fine. The weather is nice." His phone rests on his leg, and he pushes his arm out to stretch like we've been sitting here for hours.

Because I can't help myself, I add, "You really should tone down the excitement. We don't want you running out of steam before the big game."

His unamused look makes me want to kick it up a notch higher, but I stop.

This guy seriously has a football stuck up his butt. I hope they find it before game time. *Sheesh.*

I look around the elevator, more than ready to get out of here. "Does this get stuck often?"

He's moved on to some other kind of stretch that involves moving his feet. "If it did, I wouldn't have gotten on."

Good grief, this guy. I should cut him slack. All that arrogance would be a heavy load to carry.

My stomach growls in the quiet, and my jail mate raises his eyebrows, hunger gaining another strike against me.

He reaches for his bag and digs around before tossing an energy bar at me. "You should eat."

"Do I need to worry it's laced with something?" I just can't help myself.

He goes back to his silent…whatever he's doing, and I know I need to eat if I'm going to make it. I pull the wrapper open and take a bite of the peanut butter bar just as my phone starts ringing. I slip it out of the side pocket of my backpack. It's my mom. *Just great.*

I don't want to answer it, not only because talking to her in front of another person, let alone this guy, will be uncomfortable at best, but also if she knew what I was doing today, I'd never hear the end of it. What I know, though, is that if I don't answer it, she'll just keep calling, and I don't need anything else hanging over my head today.

I swallow my bite of the bar, shove my chin to my chest, and swipe to answer. "Hey."

"Andrea, is that any way to greet a caller? The informality is impolite."

"Hello. How's that?" I peek from underneath my eyelashes as my partner in captivity is back to being engrossed in his phone, but I know there's no way to avoid listening to this exchange.

"Andrea, I don't have time for your dramatics. I'm calling you about the benefit. I've yet to receive your response in the mail, and even though you must come, I want to be sure that you aren't trying to slip your way out of this one. You know how important this is. I already have a piece picked out for you."

Only my mother would send a formal invitation in the mail to her only daughter, which is bad enough, but then also expect a proper reply.

"I told you I'd think about it." It's best to keep it short and sweet, but this response will be unacceptable.

"Andrea, you've used one excuse after another for far too long. You can't keep going on like this. It's time to come home and finally get your life together. I'll put you down for the chicken and expect you an hour early."

I close my eyes, inhaling through my nose. I accepted long ago that my parents would never change. Someday, maybe they'll understand that I won't be returning to the only lifestyle or the facade acceptable to them.

"We both know that extra seat won't put you out if I can't make it." I attempt to stay as calm and quiet as possible.

"Andrea, you've been avoiding your place long enough. It's time to put these silly, rebellious antics behind you. Besides, your father and I have decided to make you the focus of this year's event. Please don't embarrass us by not showing. There's no way to find someone to replace you this close to the date."

I clench my jaw. She just had to wiggle the knife in a little further. She seriously should be the one who holds a scalpel for a living. She'll never understand that my silly little choices brought me the greatest joys of my life.

Screw it. I rest back against the wall. "Sorry, I couldn't hear you. Either the connection is bad, or your nose has finally reached a height where the blood isn't flowing properly to your brain. Either way, I'll let you know when I'm good and ready. Until then, I have to go."

I hang up and toss my phone back into my bag, forgetting about the man sitting next to me. My eyes snap to him, and he's looking at me like…something.

"Sounded like a lovely conversation."

"Yeah. This morning has been full of delightful exchanges," I huff. "If you ever want to talk to the devil herself, let me know. I'll give you her number."

He laughs. He actually laughs, his head falling back against his wall. It's low and soft, and I expect the elevator to start free-falling at any moment. One dimple pops in his cheek. Who would've ever guessed there was a dimple hidden in there? I bet no one's ever seen it before. This could be a monumental discovery, and I almost reach for my phone to capture it. *Sports Illustrated* would probably pay millions for the rare glimpse. I resist, feeling sorry for the little concave patch of skin. That cute little dimple never gets show time with all that stiffness.

I smile, and somehow, it loosens the tightness around my chest that could only be caused by my mother.

I survey our space, not wanting to talk anymore about what he just overheard. "I feel like we should be taking stock of our supplies and figuring out what we can use to unscrew the ceiling panel."

As if he's turned into a sloth, his head drags sooooo slowly in my direction like he's back to being bored, and I feel like I should take offense to that, but whatever. Our little moment born of my misery and embarrassment is over.

All I know is they better get us out of here before I have to go to the bathroom. This guy already thinks very little of me. Going number anything in front of him will put us on a whole new level that I'm not at all comfortable with.

"So, do you have family coming later to see your big performance?" my partner asks out of the blue in his same bored, monotonous tone.

I shake my head. "Nope, it's just me today."

His light eyebrows scrunch together, forming a crease between them, and he lets out a long, disapproving breath. "You won a competition to sing the national anthem in a stadium filled with thousands, and no one will be here to see it?"

Why does he have to say it like that? I don't like his patronizing tone or know how to answer this.

I don't want to, but given that we are stuck together, I decide to just put it out there, trying not to sound defensive. "This was a surprise. I didn't know I was entered into the competition, and honestly, I wasn't even going to come, but my best friend replied and said I'd do it. She thinks…" I stop but realize I'll likely never see this man again after we leave this little box on a cable, so I continue. "She thinks it will help me move past some things and be the start of something new."

I shake my head and find him listening intently. "That probably doesn't make any sense to someone like you. The truth is I'm only here singing for one person, so no matter the reason and whether it's just me or thousands are listening, the one that matters will be."

He returns to his normal state of phone-focused silence while his fingers tap on his thigh. One. At. A. Time. Repeat. I'm beginning to think he wasn't really listening, but after a minute, he surprises me.

"You're the only one who gets to decide when it's enough. You know, when it's time to move on and find out what else might be out there waiting."

I'm shocked by this lug's insight and how much it seems like he might understand. "Huh. I'm impressed. It sounds like you might have a soul in there somewhere."

His chest rises with a long inhale and then falls. "Don't read too far into it."

Ok. There we go. I was worried for a second we might become friends through our time stuck together.

"Don't worry. I won't. There's also the little thing of not wanting to embarrass anyone." That earns me a heavy dose of side-eye.

Interestingly, this joker seems to have given me the permission I was looking for. Today can be about whatever I want it to be. Maybe that's why we're stuck here together because it sure wasn't for the good company. I needed to hear that, even if it had to come from a giant egotistical jerk.

This doesn't have to be the end, or it can be the start of something new. Either way, I get to decide.

Acknowledgments

I don't know how to thank all the people who helped and encouraged me to put this book into the world. Thank you doesn't even begin to do justice to how incredibly grateful I am to all of you.

First, thank you to my husband. Seriously, there are no words. You made this happen. You told me I should and could before I believed in myself. You've helped me through this process, and it wouldn't have happened without you. Thanks for choosing me every day.

Ah, my kids. Thank you for showing me what courage is and the kind of person I want to be. I have the best job in the world, spending every day with you. You guys are my life. Your patience, quiet time, and love through the hard days made this possible.

Mom, my number one fan, always. Thanks for being my first reader and for your honest thoughts. You helped me make this into the story it is. And to Roger, thanks for never getting annoyed with my endless football questions and cheering me on each step of the way.

Cait, romance may not be your thing, but you've got an eye for deficiency when it comes to love stories. I love it, and I love you.

Lauren, girl…your years of friendship, unwavering honesty, and feedback mean the absolute world to me. You always have my back, and I've totally got yours. To the moon and back.

Abby, my soul sister, thanks for your eagle eye and the texts and conversations that helped me stay sane and grammatically correct.

Natalie, your friendship, guidance, and encouragement keep me afloat when I want to drown. Thanks for always being here and reminding me to stay true to myself.

Lizzie, thanks for schooling me on all things ballet to ensure I didn't sound like a fraud and for your help and support.

Allison Buehner, my editor, thank you for helping me get this story just right and fine-tuning it to make it really come to life.

Finally, but definitely not the least, to the person who needed this. The one who finds hope in the words of this story. Thank you for being you, for reading, and for believing. Remember, just because we can't always see it or feel it doesn't mean it's not there. Keep your eyes open and your head up. You never know when it might be just around the corner.

About the Author

Stacy Williams lives with her husband and children in Illinois. She writes in five-minute increments between homeschooling and extracurricular activities. She's spent years dreaming about writing love stories that, in a worn and broken world, remind us of what we're truly made for.

Author Page: **authorstacywilliams.com**

@stacywilliams.writes

stacywilliams.writes

www.ingramcontent.com/pod-product-compliance
Lightning Source LLC
LaVergne TN
LVHW100506110826
845146LV00002B/532

* 9 7 9 8 9 8 9 0 4 4 9 1 7 *